GRACE PERIOD

ELISABETH NONAS

Rattling Good Yarns Press
33490 Date Palm Drive 3065
Cathedral City CA 92235
USA
www.rattlinggoodyarns.com

Cover Design: Rattling Good Yarns Press

Library of Congress Control Number: 2023951732
ISBN: 978-1-955826-53-2

First Edition

For Nancy

...laughing and crying
you know it's the same release.

—Joni Mitchell

1

The End and the Beginning

When my thoughts race, I count. Counting is very good for not thinking. Try it: One. Two. Three. Four. Five. Six.

It helps, right? Once I got to three-hundred-thirty-seven. I lost track a few times, may have skipped a few numbers, but it did the trick. Calmed me right down.

Sometimes I count objects. Basically, whatever I see in front of me. Like right now. Eighteen flower arrangements. Ten rows of sixteen seats in a row. Many seats in those rows are filled with people.

I can sometimes think about trivia. Like not too many young girls are named Nancy anymore. Or Eleanor. That's not the same as thinking, or at least the kind of thinking I'm trying to avoid.

"Shall we get started?" Sue puts her hand on my shoulder, gently, like maybe I'm one of the sick animals she treats and she doesn't want to hurt me.

I rise.

It's like I'm watching a movie. I see the grieving widow moving slowly through her spouse's funeral surrounded by friends and community, a podium next to a table filled with photographs and photo albums. So many floral arrangements they pretty much hide the urn. But when I say grieving widow, don't imagine a wailing, weeping, garment-rending type. Stoic is more like it. But not if that implies nobility. I should look up "stoic."

In any case, this movie features me in the lead role. I say that because all eyes in the room gravitate toward me now that everyone is seated. Waiting for something.

Oh. They're waiting for me. I don't know why, but Sue walks me to the podium. Is she worried I'll keel over? How funny would that be. The headline would read: "Old butch collapses at wife's funeral." I look out at the people assembled–our friends, colleagues from the college, even a few of our students—take a deep breath and start to speak. I must say something funny—people laugh. Dab at their eyes through their smiles.

Jordan, very dapper in her bespoke suit and tie, speaks next. She's wearing the tie clip Grace and I gave her for officiating at our wedding.

After Jordan, Diane goes on for quite some time. She's entitled. She introduced me to Grace all those years ago in L.A. She has to fly back tonight, but wanted to be here with us. With me. No more us.

And though I'm watching this movie starring myself, I can't make out anyone's words. There's no sound, and I can't read lips.

Maybe it isn't a movie, but one of those stories you hear of people brought back from the dead: "I floated above everything, saw myself lying on the operating table."

Except I'm not dead. Grace is. And she isn't floating over these proceedings with me. She's…I don't know where she is. Which is probably why my mind keeps drifting away from this event, her funeral. I can't surreptitiously reach for her hand, or slide my foot under the table to find hers. I often had the need to do so, as if I'd lose her if we couldn't have even this slightest contact. After twenty-five years, I still needed that reassurance. As if all that time I knew she'd leave me.

Still, I'm the older one—seventy. She'd just turned sixty. I was supposed to go first. But not yet. Either of us.

"Oh, I might surprise you," Grace would say with a laugh. We didn't know what we were joking about. Not really. Grace hadn't even turned forty the first time she said it. Young, though we didn't think so at the time.

Oliver and Gustavo go up together after Diane. Grace had recruited Gustavo for her department, art history, and had mentored him through his tenure process. Oliver's in English with me, but he teaches lit and I teach writing. Gustavo and Oliver are practically lesbian in their codependence, so both share their memories of Grace.

Once we've covered our lesbian family, origin story, and the scope of Grace's academic reach, I stand at the podium again to thank everyone for coming. I almost thank them even more for going, but would that be inappropriate? Grace was always reminding me that not everyone gets my humor. Debating this with myself causes an awkward silence, so I just say, "Class dismissed," which seems fitting and gets a chuckle.

After that, I'm surrounded. People press toward me, leaning over if I'm seated, patting my shoulder. Hugging me if I'm standing, maybe touching my face gently. Or my hands. Some clearly don't know what to say, so just stand there looking at me and and tearing up.

I am barraged by "remember when's." "I remember when you and Grace took us out for dinner when our dog died. Grace always knew just what to say." "Jeri and I always laugh about the time the four of us were at the conference in Anaheim and ate at that terrible smorgasbord restaurant. Remember?" "Sally found photos of the day we all hiked Watkins Glen. There are some great ones of Grace. I'll email them to you."

I read the concern on their faces, feel the pressure of their touch. But I barely hear them. In truth, my mind is blank. I can't remember a single thing about my life with Grace.

A group of Grace's students huddle together in a corner, crying. Mary, the administrative assistant in Grace's department, brings me a plate of food. She'd given me a big hug when she arrived, a real lesbian full-body hug, not A-frame, and I'd almost lost it. So now I barely make eye contact. Later, Jordan takes the plate away. I don't remember eating anything.

When it's time to leave, Sue and Jordan help me ferry boxes of photos and condolence notes to my car. We go back to see if there's more. Mustn't forget Grace, in her tasteful stainless steel urn. Jordan carries that. I schlep the huge flower arrangement.

When we get to the car, I finally find some words: "I just can't."

Jordan says, "I know, Hannah. I can't even imagine how I'd feel if Janey–."

"That's not what I meant." I shove the arrangement in the general direction of my friends. I don't care who takes it, as long as it isn't me.

Sue grabs it. She'd arranged to donate all the flowers to the hospital. "Are you sure you don't want at least one of them?"

I reach awkwardly around the flowers to hug her instead of answering. Jordan takes that moment to wedge Grace between the boxes in the back of my car. We'd had to fold down the back seat of the Prius to accommodate everything.

"And you're okay to drive?" Jordan asks. "Do you want me to come with you?"

Sue adds, "Or later? Annie and I could come over if you need company."

"I'll be fine," I answer. Whatever fine means. We all know I'm lying.

I manage to extricate myself from the loving attention of my two friends and start the car as soon as I get in and drive away before anyone can change their mind.

I look in the rearview mirror to the backseat. "You okay back there, honey?" I haven't really stopped talking to Grace since she died.

Sun bounces off the urn. Is she winking at me?

I force myself to keep my foot on the accelerator, afraid that if I let up for even a second I'll drift to a stop and stall in the middle of the road. I'm afraid to go home. To pull up our road and onto our driveway and off to the parking area by the barn and turn off the engine. It isn't the empty house that looms. I'm not afraid to be alone out there in what feels like the middle of nowhere to our friends who live in town but had always felt safe to me and Grace. I just don't want to stop. Stopping means this next phase begins in earnest. For real.

Maybe I'll keep going. Drive clear up the lake and to the access road and onto the Thruway. Why not. Stop when I can't drive anymore. Stay in a motel. Wake up the next day and drive some more. Pretend I have to get somewhere. Anything so that I don't have to turn onto our road, into our driveway, get out of the car, walk to the house, enter, and be faced with: Now what?

I've been so occupied with all this—Grace's death, the "arrangements"—since, well, since Grace died, that I haven't had to think about what comes next.

One week ago, Jordan, who happens to be my associate dean, and I are heading toward the faculty lounge to my retirement party. Before I can open the door, Deb, our department assistant, races up to me saying I have to call this number. It turns out to be the hospital. The next thing

I know Jordan is driving me to the hospital and then I'm in a cubicle in the ER looking down at some poor woman who was brought in by the paramedics. I'm not convinced that's really Grace on the gurney.

I mean, I'm standing here looking down at this person who has Grace's coloring, her messy short hair. But this person's eyes are vague and unfocused, even though her face is turned toward me. For a second, anyway, because this person's head is always moving.

I'm holding this person's hand. She's wearing Grace's ring, our wedding ring. So maybe it is Grace. I will pretend it is, just in case this is real, and the person whose hand I'm gripping, whose gaze I'm trying to catch or follow so I can stay in her sight line, is actually Grace. Honestly, it doesn't feel like she's really there. But I talk to her as if she is. "This isn't anything like your show, honey." On *Grey's Anatomy,* her favorite show— "Tease me all you want, but these are my people and I'll watch as long as it's on the air."—the person who had a stroke lies perfectly still, looks like they're asleep, none of this perpetual motion.

The person on the gurney looks at me then. Maybe. So maybe she can hear me. Nothing will shut me up now.

"I was told my wife was in bed three." I smile at that, the word *wife.* "Honey, I'm sorry. I know we'd vowed as part of our vows to never call each other wife. But I had to say that when I came in. It's just so much clearer."

When we were debating whether or not to get married, Grace had said, "Isn't it enough that we've capitulated to the institution of marriage? We don't have to leave our values at the altar. Not that we're even going to be at an actual altar. But the metaphorical altar."

All the years of referring to each other as "partner." We'd had enough of that businesslike term and wouldn't miss it. If we ever needed to use a word, spouse, we agreed, was perfectly specific and accurate. And legal. And no one—however homophobic or homo-ignorant—could misinterpret it.

The institutions in Ithaca, New York, a college town, are outwardly gay-aware, but still, flying through the automatic doors to the hospital, I instinctively went for the word that would give me immediate access, a shortcut to legitimacy, a word someone on any level of the political spectrum would understand: "My wife was brought in in an ambulance. Grace Black." The woman at the desk had directed me here.

I look at the person on the gurney for a response. Just more head lolling. I soldier on.

"I have to confess, honey," I say, trying to look into the person on the gurney's wandering eyes, "I really liked calling you that. Might start using it regularly. But, and this I promise, I'll never refer to you as 'the wife.'"

I figure if anything could get a chuckle or a rise out of her, this would be it.

Nothing from the person on the gurney who wears our wedding ring.

If some part of her recognizes me, clearly some part of me recognizes this stranger whose hand I'm holding, and I am starting to grasp the enormity of our situation.

"Whatever you want, okay? You can let go. Or stay. Plenty of people recover from strokes. If you have to learn to walk again, or talk—up to you. Whatever you need. I'll be there. Your decision."

I speak those words out loud. In my head, I'm pleading: don't go don't go don't go don't go.

Did you see me there? Hear me talking to you? Feel my love grabbing on to you, willing you to stay here for me? Feel me relent, want what was best for you, whatever that meant? Offering this compromise: Stay if you can; I'm here. If you can't, well—whatever you want. I stopped talking then. I'd said my piece.

By then Jordan had called Janey who called Sue who came with Annie, so we all sat together in a lounge area as orderlies moved you from the ER to a room. Janey bought some snacks from a vending machine, and we passed them around. Then Jordan, Janey, and Annie stayed in the room with you while Sue, your second health proxy—"I don't care if she's a vet, doctors understand doctors," you'd said, explaining your choice—came with me into the hall so the doctor could explain our options and someone beside me would be there, someone who could actually pay attention, actually listen and ask questions.

By the time I was allowed back into your room in the ICU, I could tell you weren't there. The person on the gurney, now the person under the covers, wasn't you. Or was some form of you, but what made you you was gone. Your body took up almost no room in the bed, which was dwarfed by all the machines beeping and humming, keeping what the staff referred to as you, but I knew better, alive.

Years earlier, you'd said, "Oh, I'd so totally pull the plug on you. Don't you worry about that."

We'd both laughed. This was years before we were allowed to get married. We were in the lawyer's office drawing up all the papers we needed to give us access to each other in case of emergency. Durable power of attorney for health care. Power of attorney. Health proxy. Wills. Domestic partnership forms. Though we joked around about running off with the other's money, pulling plugs, we took these documents seriously. And once we had them, we never left home without them. We'd heard nightmare stories of gay couples separated in the ER because they weren't "family." I think we still have copies stashed in suitcases, desk drawers, and the safe deposit box.

Back in the ICU, I know it's time. So when the doctor shows up, I make the hardest call of my life.

I needed help with the other hardest calls. While I notified Grace's cousins who lived in Seattle, Mary helped with work details, including notifying everyone in Grace's department, as well as the dean. Is it weird we both came from small families? But it made us even more aware of the importance of our chosen family, and of our relationship. No parents, no siblings, not even close cousins. Just each other. And a huge extended chosen family, spread across the country. Next task: the funeral. Once I determined the order of things and who'd speak, I let Sue and Jordan handle the other details—make the calls to let people know, put an announcement in the local paper, social media god spare us (that was Grace's area. I don't even have a Facebook account.), and generally get the word out. I agree to show up where and when I'm told. And I did give them a list of what I absolutely wouldn't allow—no harps, no Pachelbel's *Canon*, and definitely not what was becoming its poetic equivalent, that Mary Oliver poem that ends *Tell me, what is it you plan to do/ with your one wild and precious life?*

Jordan offered to come with me to the funeral home, but I said I'd go alone. "I'll be fine."

"I'm sorry," she said then, "did you think I was giving you an option?"

As it turned out, I was glad to have her there. If only to confirm my sense of the bizarre world of funeral planning.

It's like we'd entered the Vale of Euphemism. Grace hadn't died—she had "passed." Working in academe, that was a good thing, the opposite of fail. *Congratulations! You passed the class!* When I'd worked in Hollywood, a "pass" was a bad thing. It meant some executive had turned down my script or TV pilot. *I'm sorry. We heard from the studio, and they passed on your idea.*

So when Kyle, the funeral director, asked if we'd made "pre-need" arrangements before you "passed," I just gave him a blank stare.

Not because I didn't have an answer, but because I had too many. Pre-need? Really? So many possibilities my mind raced! I could have riffed for an hour on the concept of need, pre-need, post-need. You would have understood my...*need*—sorry, couldn't resist—to joke about this. Kyle didn't. In just the short time since Grace has died I was learning that not too many people think death is funny.

Not that the Vale of Euphemism was entirely new to me. At least not the concept. Grace and I had already dipped our toes in the Lake of Misdirection when her mother started her decline—see what I did there? Without even thinking I said "decline," instead of when we realized her mother didn't have much longer to live. See—I just did it again. When we realized her mother was dying. We wondered if maybe the best thing would be to bring her here to Ithaca. Not to live with us, but in the town, somewhere nearby, where we could keep an eye on her, be around in case of emergency. So we started to investigate...*places.*

Assisted living facilities. Does anyone still call them old age homes? What euphemism is most appropriate? Many of these "homes" have names. Often nature-related—a tree genus. Elms and pines seem popular. With appropriately soothing adjectives to qualify the experience: shady or quiet or serene. Though you could hardly expect them to name the places "God's Waiting Room."

But why not? Some people must have a sense of humor about this whole process—aging, dying. Or if unable to see the humor in it, at least possess a penchant for telling it like it is.

As awful as I feel today, as much as I ache because I never got to say a real goodbye, wake every morning forgetting for one blissful second my new reality, I wonder if it would have been worse to have to visit Grace in a place like that.

Or move into one together.

Is that what I'm going to have to do one day? How long will I be able to maintain our house and the land on my own?

I never pictured myself old. Or, to be more accurate, if I ever thought about being old, because, really, who does? I just thought of myself as me, but older. Never imagined the lumps, bumps, aches, and vague diminutions that accompany the aging process.

So I'm glad Grace wouldn't have to think about where to put me. Because how can you wish that on anyone? When we were looking at options for her mother, we visited one highly-rated facility. It had elegant, well-appointed public areas, a pleasant dining room where residents could entertain guests. But the residential floors broke my heart—oh, they were clean, but more like a residential hospital, emphasis on the hospital rather than the residence. I couldn't imagine living there because I fear losing my independence, my agency, more than I fear death. I wondered how the residents handled that. And what does it mean to "handle" something like that. Adjust to it? What does it mean to move into a space knowing that it's your last? That this is where you'll die? Do I think it would be better to die there than in one's own home? Or what about in one's car—let me ask Grace.

We can die any moment, at any age (yes, Grace, thank you for that reminder), but we're not expecting it. If we were, wouldn't we be quivering, fearful messes 24/7?

"Um, Hannah?" Jordan's hand is on my arm, bringing me back to the Vale of Euphemism. Poor Kyle probably thinks I'm struggling with my grief which is why it's taking me so long to answer his simple question— had we made "pre-need" arrangements. I'll put the guy out of his misery. "I suppose this is post-need." I look at poor Kyle. No sense of humor. "But I know what she wanted."

I also know what you didn't want. We'd had that conversation one sunny fall afternoon as we readied the garden for winter.

"Where do you want to be buried?" you'd asked me, dirt-caked hands packing down hyacinth bulbs and covering them with soil and mulch.

"Are you planning to do away with me? Should I be worried?"

"I'm serious," you said. "We should know each other's wishes."

"I'm not going to be buried. Cremation for me."

"Me, too," you agreed. "I wonder how that works."

"Well," I start, "you get this big oven..."

"Not cost-effective for just the two of us." At least you have—had—a sense of humor about these things.

"Then we'll simply call Acme Peaches and Crematorium and they'll take care of the rest."

I don't think Poor Kyle would understand this. I couldn't tell who was helping whom as we went through the arrangements to finalize the "disposition" of the body.

No-brainer: Cremation. Only the "no-brainer" was silent.

"It's not like I'm dying to do this," I said. That makes me chuckle. The use of "dying" here in a funeral home. I could use that in class to illustrate irony. Except, it isn't really ironic, is it? What would I call it? Irrelevant, I guess, since I won't be teaching anymore. What *will* I be doing, then? Panic hits me. Luckily I can't fall down that rabbit hole because Poor Kyle is asking me another question. My blank stare makes him repeat it.

"Will you be interning the cremains?"

Cremains? I look at Jordan as if to say, do you believe this guy? Was he serious? Apparently yes, because he just matched my stare with one of his own. So, cremains. That's a word. Well, if craisins exist, why not cremains? This is a comic's goldmine. Maybe that's what I'll do in my retirement. I could work up a solid ten-minute set around this topic. Passing! Pre-need! Cremains! I'd have 'em rolling in the aisles. They'll die laughing!

Poor Kyle was still waiting.

I kept it simple. Nope. I wasn't going to bury your ashes.

And I certainly wasn't going to buy a $500 cremation urn. You weren't going to be in it forever, and I didn't want it sitting around once I'd scattered you. Your ashes.

I don't even know what to call you anymore.

Whatever you like, darling, as long as it's not late for dinner.

Very funny. You and I had joked about the scattering, too. Your parents are in a lovely cemetery—with a nice view and a few famous people buried nearby. "There's room for you, honey," your mother had said as she lay dying.

You didn't have the heart to tell her you planned to be cremated. You had specific instructions for me, however: "You could scatter a few of my ashes on my parents' graves. Surreptitiously."

I said sure, no problem. "I'll just drop your ashes through a hole in my pants pocket. You know, the way prisoners hide the dirt from the escape tunnel they're digging." I demonstrated, looking away nonchalantly as I shook the imaginary ashes out of my cuff, shaking my leg for emphasis.

We'd laughed.

Now I can't decide if it's still funny. Now that I actually have the ashes. And now that I have to actually divvy them up to distribute across the places I determine would most please you. Because you hadn't gotten around to actually writing up the list.

You who was so prepared with your DNR and health proxy and detailed instructions on how far doctors could go should this or that happen. Every eventuality. You who'd tried to spare me having to think in any emergency. And who spared me even that by having a stroke driving to my retirement party.

That harsh reminder wakes me to my surroundings. I'd managed to navigate myself back home.

I pull into the space in front of the garage—which is really the old barn from when this land was part of a working farm—and shut the engine. The little buzz that the Prius makes, then silence after the noise of the road before the sounds of our property fade up. Birds. A rustle of wind in the trees. An alive quiet. I've been all-go since being called to the hospital and haven't had time to think, which I suppose is a good thing, since at this moment I feel truly alone for the first time since you died. Was it only a week ago?

I get out of the car and just stand there. I can't take a step in any direction. I reach for you in the back seat, but can't make myself walk the thirty feet to the house, walk the path we made, through the garden you planted, to our sweet home out in the middle of nowhere. That's why we could have so much land. As motivation I start to count the stones we laid into the earth for our path. Irregular and separated by strips of grass rather than cement. One. Two. Three. Four. Five. But after seven or eight it's too hard to keep track and I give up.

I don't know what to do with the boxes of stuff I've brought home, so leave them in the car and just carry you to the house with me. What a strange weight you've become.

UPS has made a delivery. A big box sits on the porch beside the front door. It's addressed to you. Whatever it is can wait. I take you inside.

I stand at the kitchen counter, the urn—or should I say, you? how do I address this?—near my elbow, and look around. We'd only just finished the re-model a month ago, everything designed to your specifications. State-of-the-art refrigerator, six-burner Wolf range, butcher block island we could eat at. Coffee-prep area—burr grinder, several types of coffee makers, beans of various roasts and complexities, food prep area with its own sink. Food processor, blender, mixer, utensils, knife drawer. Spices galore.

Have I mentioned that I don't cook?

Light pours onto the shiny surfaces. I look at you. Where to now? Beats me.

In a burst of efficiency, I start on what I'm calling the Distribution List. Number one: our land. No matter where we traveled, you said you loved that best, were happiest here. Where's your second favorite spot? Or maybe I shouldn't worry yet about ranking and just come up with the list.

So: our land. Family cemetery plot per your wishes. Herring Cove Beach in P'town. Somewhere in the lake near where we got married.

What about Central Park, where you proposed? Somewhere on campus? You loved your work, but enough to want to spend eternity there? Is there even an eternity?

I vow to stay away from the philosophical weeds and turn back to the list.

Am I supposed to go to Venice? What about Barcelona? Did you love them equally? What about that Italian hill town whose name will come to me eventually? And what about Venice Beach, California? We got our start in L.A., after all.

And should each place get the same amount of...you? How much would I need to leave to feel I'd done right by you? Is there enough of you to go around?

Do I even need to follow through with this? You're not here—you'll never know the difference. I could just keep all of you for myself.

Or is that creepy?

Any creepier than flinging human cremains into a lake or a canal or onto someone else's grave?

For once I welcome the ringing of my cell phone. I haven't answered the landline since last week (meaning since you died), so if this phone rings, it's probably one of only a handful of people. You loved your mobile. (Forgive me, sweetie, but it's been in your bag since I brought it home from the hospital. It hasn't rung for days, so I guess the battery's dead. I will not make a dead joke—too easy.) Generally I've had an adversarial relationship with mine—why do I want to be available wherever and whenever? But this past week I'd taken to carrying it with me at all times, even in the house, in case of emergency. Though your death was the emergency, so what do I care now? But I answer, seeing Sue's name come up on the screen.

"Hey," she says. "Whatcha doing?"

Is complete honesty always the best policy? "Making a list. Trying to organize some things." That's honest enough.

"How are you doing?" she asks. "I'm sorry. That was a dumb question. But. Well. How are you? Do you want me and Annie to bring out dinner? Or just come hang out?"

Pienza! That's the name of the hill town. I knew it would come back to me. Remember how lost we got trying to get there from Siena? Should Siena be on the list?

"Hannah? Are you there?"

I apologize for zoning out and say I'm okay. Whether or not that was a true statement, having someone in the house with me isn't going to make a difference. Sue says she'll check on me tomorrow. I thank her— at least I remember my manners—and hang up.

What little concentration I had was broken now. No more list-making. I start to head to the bedroom to change out of my widow's weeds. Is that what they're called? That sounds so strange. I stop in my tracks in the hall, pull out my phone (Okay, so maybe it is a handy gadget.), and search for the phrase. Yup. Sure enough. Widow's weeds. Comes from Old English "waed" meaning "garment." I call out to you to tell you what I've learned.

Of course you don't answer. You're the reason I'm wearing the fucking widow's weeds. Which is also the reason I'm able to stop in the middle of whatever I'm doing and look up something on my phone. Do I adhere to our no-phone between four and six p.m. policy now that it's just me? I'd instituted this policy to have you all to myself for just a couple of hours, but I guess now I can execute random searches any time I damn well please.

Have I seriously just had this conversation with you in our hallway? Apparently so. Well, with myself, actually, since I've left you on the kitchen counter. I go back and walk with you to find a more appropriate resting place.

Resting place! Ha! I should keep a notebook to jot down potential material for my comedy set. And fuck it, I'd add the dead phone battery joke. Have to start somewhere. Or I'll keep notes on my phone like you used to do. Maybe I'll come to love mine as much as you loved yours. I can hear you add the distinction: I *appreciated* mine, you'd probably say, I *respected* its capabilities; love is different. But I have a more serious concern than your digital allegiances at the moment. I pause at the threshold.

Do you want to be in the living room, so you can look out at the garden and the pond? I don't mean on the mantle, too trite. And no view out the window from there.

Maybe the bedroom? But just the thought creeps me out. Sorry, honey. Not in my study, either, which doubles as the guest room.

The urn looks out of place everywhere I put it down. I've walked you through the whole house, ended up back in the kitchen. I am not keeping you here. I don't care how much you loved the new setup.

When the landline rings I freeze in place, you still in my arms. I have no intention of answering it. I hear the answering machine engage and then your voice instructing the caller to leave a message.

I forget each time that I'm going to hear your voice. Maybe I'm playing at oh, this is just my real, regular life, and in my real regular life I'd let the machine get it.

I don't move, as if whoever's on the other end would sense my presence. I make it through till the beep, almost relieved to hear an automated recording rather than a real person. It's the dentist's office reminding you of your appointment for a cleaning.

Shit. Shit shit shit shit. Now what. I cradle you in one arm and pick up the phone. I hit redial. A relentlessly cheerful woman answers. She's barely finished her spiel before I blurt out that I need to cancel your appointment.

"Do you want to reschedule?"

Everything. I want to reschedule everything. This was supposed to be our year, 2019. Our birthdays are on the 19th, different months, but what are the odds, so 19 became our lucky number. And then this year, 2019, my retirement, your sabbatical. Adventures awaited! We had plans, so many plans!

"Not now," I remember to say before hanging up.

I know I've got a whole other set of lists to make—check both our calendars for appointments and cancel them. Medical checkups, haircuts, what else had we each put off till the end of the semester? I don't have the stamina or the courage to deal with them now.

And to ensure that I don't have to, I yank the cord out of the phone and unplug the machine. The missed calls notification disappears. The blinking new messages light, signal from the outside world, goes blessedly dark. I have a crazy thought: what if you try to call and the line's disconnected? Duh. You'll try my cell.

I'm still clinging to you. And you're getting heavy.

One room I hadn't entered: your study. I haven't been in there since you died. But it seems like the place you'll be happiest for now. Or that I will be happiest having you.

I don't look around when I open the door. I carefully rest you on the small table next to the overstuffed armchair you never sat in but used as a repository for whatever you'd be bringing to campus—books, your briefcase, papers. I still don't look around. I feel like a little kid daring herself to be brave, walking into her dark bedroom and forcing herself to look not just in the closet but under the bed before tucking herself in for the night.

When I step back into the hall, I'm surprised how hard my heart is pounding. I'm not a religious or particularly spiritual person, but the air in that room was different. Charged.

Nah. You're just imagining it, I tell myself.

So go back in, ya big chicken.

I put my hand on the doorknob, but don't turn it. I've had enough stimulation for one day.

Exhausted, I head back to our bedroom.

That charged energy follows me down the hall.

Big chicken.

2

How to Remember

That energy follows me not just down the hall but into our bedroom, where the force of your presence strikes me so hard I have to sit on the bed. But not your presence—how could it be your presence? It is your absence that wallops me—a physical force that rocks me onto the edge of the bed.

Once there, stuck, catching my breath, all I can do is look around. Everything in here—photos on the dresser, art on the walls, your clothes in the closet, magazines and books next to your side of the bed, your iPad on the nightstand—should trigger me, trigger memories of our life together. Something for me to hold on to that would dull this unbearable longing for you. But try as I might, nothing comes—no images or snippets of conversation. Can I even hear your voice?

My gaze lands on the dresser, takes in your jewelry, the tchotchkes, the dried flowers, the beaded bracelets you must have decided against wearing that day but hadn't put away. Why doesn't this let me remember our life together? Why can't I see it? It's only been a week. What barrier lies between me and you?

Other than death.

Oh. That.

We'd been together long enough to go through periods wondering: Shouldn't we do something to pop us out of our rut? Are we tired of each other? Right this minute, I'd settle for boring and rote. Or even the ability, since I can't have you here, to play these memories for a few minutes, a respite from the dark void, just a clip from our daily routine.

But nothing comes. Twenty-five years and I don't remember anything. Not one thing. Not a sound, smell, image. The only thing I do know at the moment is that I can't sleep in our room anymore.

I tried Grace's side of our bed and that just felt wrong. Being in the bedroom feels wrong, period, so I abandoned it. The living room couch is where I sleep every night. It's kind of weird and kind of nice. Like sleeping somewhere else, like being away from home. I suppose my whole life now is like being away from home, since I thought of Grace as home. Living with her was more important than where we lived. Not that we didn't make our place nice, or that my surroundings don't matter to me. Just that she was what grounded me, more than any one place. After twenty-five years, I don't know who I am without Grace. So lesbian of me, I know. Yes, we had separate jobs, separate identities. But we were part of a couple. Grace's aunt called us "The Girls." Plural, but a single unit. And without Grace as my tether, I feel lately that I could just drift off, away. Not literally. Well, maybe literally.

Work always anchored me, so I take my blank self into my study. Since it doubles as our guest room, it isn't overly officelike: a sofa bed, coffee table, you'd hardly notice the small wireless printer unobtrusively placed in the bookcase. There's a cleared space on the desk for my laptop, now covered by a stack of student papers and scripts I need to grade. Soon I'm going to have whatever I bring home from my school office, but my intention had been to finish the semester before I did any rearranging and preparing for my retirement.

But now I'm thinking, preparing for what? I've no plans and no partner. And certainly no guests on the horizon.

What am I going to do with myself now that I'm retired? What had Grace and I discussed about that? About anything?

It's not like I've always had the greatest memory. Since I was young, I've been the person who walks into a room and can't remember why I'm there.

But it's different when you're older. Old. The difference between young-forgetting and old-forgetting is the accumulation of information available to forget when you're older. More weeds to get lost in. That and the retrieval mechanism. Well, there is no retrieval mechanism. As you age, words disappear on you. Gone completely. A black hole in their place, not even a letter to start with. And then they come back to you at the oddest time, often when you've forgotten the context in which you needed them.

Names, forget it. Doesn't matter if it's someone I know or a famous person. For example, if it's an actor, I can describe her, list almost all the films or TV shows she's been in. And their plot lines.

Grace and I would joke about it. Our conversations often bordered on parody.

"I was flipping channels and saw that actor you like. One of his really early movies. He was so young!"

"Which actor?"

"I can't remember his name. Married to the gal in the show about the doctors. She was in the episode where she didn't want to tell her daughter she was dying."

"And they were stuck in the elevator?"

"Right. That one."

"He got better looking as he aged."

"So did she. What *is* his name?"

"It's on the tip of my tongue. They're not together anymore, are they?"

"No. She left him for what's his name."

"Right."

"The brawny one."

"Yes. I always liked him."

Does that count as remembering? Having that snippet of a conversation float around my head? Does that give me anything of Grace? Of our life together? "When was that?" I ask out loud. "What were we doing? Where were we? Out somewhere and you saw something that prompted you to say that? Or had I been the one to say it? What were our days like? Our nights? What did we do? And what *was* that actor's name? I can still see his face, but not you."

On one of our first dates you stopped mid-stride as we hurried toward our cars. Having met at the restaurant, this being L.A. and you being afraid of committing/commitment, we'd come in separate cars. You pressed me against the window of a shop on Melrose and kissed me. A for-real, serious kiss.

I must have looked surprised. Or puzzled. On top of being delighted.

"I think this is going to work out," you'd said.

I remember the precise colors of the sky, that L.A. smog-induced orange-y/persimmon-y palette, the sounds of the cars on the avenue, the neon glow of the shop's sign. And I know you spoke those words.

But the kiss, other than that it happened, the taste of your mouth on mine, the feel of your hands on my face—did you even take my face in your hands?—your body, your weight, your breath—these I do not remember.

It's a different kind of forgetting than not being able to recall an actor's name. Just as there are different kinds of remembering, forgetting has many variations.

I will myself to sit at my desk and at least sort through the pile of papers, arrange them by class, decide which group I'll tackle first. Out of habit, I pick up the top script, and before I realize it, I've picked up a pen and started grading.

This is muscle memory kicking in. Something I no longer have to think about to remember how to do. It's become instinct.

I manage to finish two scripts, notes and everything, before I acknowledge that you're not away at a conference, a trick I've played on myself with varying success. It only lasts so long. Eventually I get up to find you but slam into the truth instead.

Since you left, I've wandered through our house as if its rooms could tell me something.

But I can't put you into it. I can't picture you in that chair or on that couch playing a video game, by the fireplace, stretched out on the bed watching your shows, or curled up with a book. I can't remember what we did during our days together, or how we spent our evenings.

Since I can't remember, tonight, in my infinite wisdom, I decide cleaning is a good idea. Who cares if it's past midnight. It's not like I'm going to wake you. And no way can I rest. All I'm concerned with now is getting the dirt off the windowsills. And the bookcases. When was the last time I took out the books and wiped behind them? I blow a cloud of dust off the top of each volume.

After that, I vacuum the living room rug. One corner keeps curling up, getting caught in the suction. I try anchoring it, straddling the edges and guiding the brush between my feet. Still the little fringes wrap around the floor nozzle.

Banging the machine against the floor doesn't free the threads, but I feel better having done it.

Where's my muscle memory surrounding your death? I have to consistently and constantly remind myself that it actually did happen. But it's not a fact yet. How many reminders will I need?

That I'm cleaning house at two a.m. is certainly one.

This whole week, if I've been lucky enough to fall asleep, I'll have one unconscious and beautiful moment when I wake up and don't remember. This blissful state doesn't last more than a second, if that long, and I resume my training. Self-consciously keeping my eye on the ball. I have to be brutal with myself, or I'll dive into pretending you're off at a conference and never resurface from that make-believe world.

Hey, kiddo. This is your life now. Get on with it.

That sounded like you talking, not me. I mean, like your actual voice. In the room with me. I swear I heard it.

I stand stock still to better focus all my energy on listening. Close my eyes. I even hold my breath for a few seconds.

Nope. Nothing.

All that does is remind me how quiet it is here without you.

I mean, really quiet. Not like when we were each in the house doing our own whatever. This quiet is a sound of its own. The sound of absence? I can't pin it down. But it isn't merely an absence of noise. It's like the hum of a distant freeway. Maybe that's what we become after we die: a sound, a vibrational hum, not matter at all. A disturbance in the atmosphere.

I remember when men I knew—neighbors, co-workers, friends— started getting sick back in the 80s. My day-to-day interactions encompassed hearing news of another seroconversion, working out schedules for meal preparation and delivery, accompanying someone to a doctor's appointment, or just hanging out. AIDS became a sonic disturbance, a dissonant whir in the background, a constant presence under, sometimes over, every other occurrence in my life.

Now I have my own disturbance in my own atmosphere. And in it, I'm aware only of me.

In space.

And the absence of you.

So maybe that—your absence—has its own sound. Maybe.

Or maybe I'm just flipping out from grief.

How normal is it to be having this conversation with you? And is it even a conversation if I'm the only one talking? (Because I couldn't have heard you speak to me, right?)

Maybe I should stop talking to you. But it's not like I've had a lot of other conversations this week. Jordan calls at the end of the day, Sue sometime in the morning. I finally caught on that they're double-teaming me. But it's easier to respond to their calls than to have them lecture me about the importance of connecting with people.

I have no interest in connecting. With anyone. With the exception of Sue and Jordan, I haven't answered the phone in a week. I have nothing to say. Or I'm afraid that if someone asks how I'm doing, I'll lie and say fine (I know myself well enough to acknowledge that). I'll say fine, when what I really want to say is:

What if your worst "what if" came true? Actually happened?

What if you woke to the reality of your spouse, wife, partner, gone, dead? And in those first five seconds of being awake you thought, oh my god—what a terrible dream! that was awful—and you turn to her, not to tell her your dream, just to touch her leg or even just see her there, for reassurance—because how could you tell her that you'd imagined her dead, you couldn't...

Well, you could, but why would you? So you just look to see her, or you just lie back to turn to her to tell her about this awful dream.

But she isn't there.

Because of course, she really did die. And you hadn't forgotten. You don't forget a thing like that. You simply haven't believed it. *Believed* is the wrong word. You haven't incorporated the fact. Haven't learned it. Absorbed it as part of your reality. Not yet.

And you can't even really call it waking up because you're not sure you really got to sleep. Not the way you used to. More like a series of waking dreams, short naps, some real sleep, on top of an awareness of something unpleasant you can't quite put your finger on (that disturbance in the atmosphere).

As you lie there not sleeping you think, I'll get up and do something. And you know from past experience that while lying in bed you feel 100% awake and alert, that you're not really awake at all. But rather than lie there pretending to try to sleep, you resolve to get up and do something non-essential.

And, of course, now everything feels non-essential.

So you can understand why it's easier not to talk to anyone than drone on like that, making no sense.

"Hannah. You have to talk to people."

I spin around, because I *definitely* heard that.

"Write this down."

I hear that, too. I'll worry later whether or not I'm going nuts. Now, I grab a pad and pen, ready to take dictation.

And Grace starts:

How to Talk to People

1. **Not everyone is comfortable with silence**

2. **Use your words.**

3. **Don't assume people know what you're thinking.**

4. **If you start a sentence, finish it. Don't immediately jump into the other one you've realized has popped into your head at the same time.**

5. **Pay attention. You have a tendency to wander, and I'm not here to kick you under the table.**

I study the words, not entirely sure what just happened. I stay on the couch and listen for Grace. A faint hint of that energy, but mostly she's not there.

At least the living room is clean, I think, as I lie back on the fluffed cushions.

The phone wakes me. I wonder why you aren't answering. Tell myself you're dead. I pick up. Not because I want to talk to anyone, but to stubbornly prove to you that I do talk to people. When I want to. Besides, I see it's Sue for her morning check-in. In addition to the usual, she invites me for dinner the next night. "I'm trying a new recipe on Annie and I don't want her to be its sole reviewer."

I've known Sue long enough to know that that's just an excuse. She probably thinks it's time I got out of the house.

"Besides," she adds, "it'd be good for you to get out of the house."

See.

I look at my list. The first point, *Not everyone is comfortable with silence*, prompts me to respond. "Um...I don't think..." What don't I think? And what thinking does a dinner invitation require? None. Idiot.

How long have I been silent? Shit. Point number two: *Use your words.* Or three: *Don't assume people know what you're thinking.*

"I really appreciate the invite, but final grades are due at the end of the week and I've got miles to go still."

"You've got to eat."

Not really, I think, but don't say out loud.

Sue accepts my silence. "Are you okay for food? I'm going shopping and can run some things out for you."

"I'm good," I lie.

All Sue says is, "Okay. Maybe next week, when you're done grading." I sense she wants to say more, try to persuade me. Or tell me they're worried about me. But she lets me go.

I put down the phone and look at Grace's *How to Talk to People* list. She did used to kick me under the table. I hated that.

I can't explain the phenomenon I just experienced hearing and feeling Grace like that, and I know I'm too depleted to figure it out. I leave her instructions on the table near the phone. I know I'll need them again. I also resolve to stop talking to Grace. At least to try.

Tempted as I am to collapse back on the couch, I feel I should be productive in some way. More relaxed now that I know the landline isn't going to ring—before I disconnected it, I had started to think of it more as a land*mine*, Grace's voice exploding my peace—I resolve to tackle the mail.

I haven't looked at it for days. In my frenzied cleaning I'd shoved it all into a paper bag I now dump out onto my clean floor. I set the bills to one side, immediately shift the junk mail and catalogs back into the bag for recycling, and am left with a bunch of condolence cards. At least that's what I assume without opening them. But what else could they be? What kind of commitment am I making if I open them? What's the rule on responding? How long do I have? Am I even obligated to? Is it like wedding gifts—you've got a year to send thank you notes, right? Several envelopes have L.A. addresses I recognize. Word does spread fast. A few business envelopes from colleges and universities, but addressed by hand, so probably from colleagues at those institutions.

I make a deal with myself. I will open one, see how I feel before continuing.

I grab an envelope at random. I open it to find a store-bought condolence card—tasteful photograph, canned message, but a handwritten note in a steady, bold script:

> Hannah – I'm at a loss for words. Grace was such an amazing woman. You were so lucky to have each other. Kit

Early in our relationship, so early that maybe we weren't even officially a relationship yet, Grace had taken me to a party so I could meet some of her friends. At least that was what she told me. I found out later it was really so her friends could vet me. Steph and Alix's house was in the San Fernando Valley, at the top of a steep driveway. We were all sitting outside when a powerful motorcycle rumbled up the hill.

"You invited Hell's Angels?" I joked.

All the women exchanged glances, though only in hindsight did I realize this. No one looked at Grace or me. Then, a huge machine, a Honda Gold Wing, varoomed up the rest of the steep driveway, capably handled by a tall, tan, exceedingly handsome woman, her white shirt billowing over Levi's. Billowing because it was unbuttoned halfway down her chest. She steered the bike right to the gate, which set the two big labs barking furiously as she parked, killed the engine, and removed her helmet to reveal an English schoolboy haircut casually mussed. She entered the gate. The dogs calmed instantly when she addressed each by name. She greeted our hosts, worked the circle of guests, hugging everyone until she reached me and held out her hand. "You must be Hannah. I'm Kit. Welcome to the family."

Her bone-crushing handshake made me feel I'd been lucky to avoid the hug.

Kit moved on. "Gracie," she said.

Wait—what? *Gracie?* No hug or kiss, but that somehow made the greeting more intimate. Call it what you will—butch bristle, whatever— my hackles went up immediately and stayed on alert for the rest of the evening. What did Kit have that I didn't—apart from beauty, charm, swagger, a huge fucking motorcycle, great hair—and clearly a history with my new lover?

Grace and I had our first fight when we got back to her apartment and she said, "You were so quiet tonight. I wanted my friends to get to know you."

"You didn't think to tell me your ex would be there?"

"That's what you're upset about? Alix is also an ex. You don't have a problem with her."

"Alix isn't a secret. You told me about her. And she and Steph are as good as married."

"I didn't know Kit would be there."

"So then you wouldn't have to tell me about her?"

"No. That's not what I meant."

"When were you together?"

Grace, who had been so forthcoming until that moment, suddenly had nothing to say. Her silence, which I interpreted as an answer, as "recently," propelled me out the door and into my car.

Los Angeles is the best place to rage at seventy miles per hour. My thoughts sped equally fast, unspooling a quick-cut film in my mind's eye. Disparate images that morphed from how I'd originally experienced them in the weeks Grace and I had been dating to become answers to my "when were you together" question. Nights Grace had been busy, mornings I couldn't reach her. Events she'd glossed over. Because…she'd been with Kit?

I told myself I was being ridiculous. Grace and I were obviously falling in love. We'd started to talk about moving in together. Did I really have any reason to be concerned? Did this swashbuckling biker even figure? So she was a hotshot PR person and I was an unemployed, scratch that, sporadically employed screenwriter. Why did I care about Kit? She was the past. So what if it was the recent past. Grace couldn't have been the way she was with me if she were seeing someone else at the same time, could she? And if this was over, again, why should I care? No sooner would I calm myself down than I'd hear Kit saying "Gracie" and I'd be fuming again.

This being before ubiquitous cell phones, I arrived home to a slew of messages from Grace on my answering machine. I was still listening to them when she called again. We talked. Made up. I don't remember now how long after that we moved in together, but we did.

For a time, Kit was a bone of contention between us. Even as Grace and I laid the foundations for our life together, I found it hard to let go of my jealousy. I made an honest effort to change—Grace and Kit would go out to dinner or lunch on occasion; I pretended not to care. I even encouraged Grace to attend a museum fundraiser Kit was working because lots of artists would be in attendance and Grace would love that. Grace coached Kit through a breakup (see—she'd been in a relationship, however brief—why couldn't I let go?). I was happiest when Grace coached her through the interview process for a new job that took Kit out of L.A., all the way across the country to New York City, where she'd been recruited by a big PR firm. Good riddance, I thought, and breathed a huge sigh of relief.

I didn't doubt Grace's love for me. We'd exchanged rings, for crying out loud. We were officially "committed." So I made a point of using Kit's name in conversation, pretending to let it roll off my tongue as casually as the names of Grace's other friends until it actually did.

By the time we moved East, my jealousy wasn't even a blip on the radar. I hadn't even thought about Kit until the spring semester of our first year in Ithaca, when Grace went off to a conference in Chicago. She called after her panel to tell me how it went, and midway through told me to hold on a sec. I heard her say, "Whatever toppings you want. I'll be right there." When she came back on the line, Grace said, "Kit's in town to visit her family."

My old jealousy roared to life as if it had been hiding in some dark green corner of my mind waiting for something like this to happen so it could pounce out to say, I told you so! Grace had asked me to go with her to this conference, but I'd declined, thinking it would be easier for her to network if I wasn't tagging along. Had that been a mistake?

"Hannah, are you there?"

"Yes."

"I thought I'd lost you. So anyway, the panel went great. You were absolutely right to tell me to cut the number of slides by half."

Grace went into more detail, and I forced myself to pay attention, to keep my tone normal. "How many more sessions do you have to sit through today?"

"I decided to ditch the conference. Kit's jonesing for deep dish pizza and then we're going on this architectural boat tour."

My jealousy prodded me to ask who else was going to be at lunch and on this boat tour. But I kept the questions I had to myself and instead launched into a detailed rant on the superiority of thin crust over deep dish pizza.

My mantra for the rest of the time Grace was away: Be supportive. Be supportive. You're practically married. If it were legal, you probably would be married. Grace loves you. You're being ridiculous. That was two years ago. Kit. Kit was years ago. Another lifetime.

Grace brought me a present from Chicago, a glass paperweight shaped like an apple. "For my favorite teacher," she said as she handed me the box. I felt ridiculous for my jealous musings.

With time, Kit was gone, not just from our lives, but my consciousness. A year ago we ran into her in the city and agreed to meet for dinner. Kit's girlfriend LeeAnne was supposed to join us but had to cancel at the last minute, so it was just the three of us. We had a nice evening, reminiscing about L.A. people we'd known. Any jealousy or anger I felt had long dissipated. From this distance, I can see how ridiculous I'd been to be jealous. Grace and I were solid almost from the very start. I have twenty-five years' worth of proof.

So today, instead of rising to anger, or moderate butch bristle, I surprise myself by thinking how nice it was of Kit to write to me as I add her card to the small stack of opened mail.

That's the extent of my productivity for the moment. If I'm unable to conjure more recent memories of Grace, I may as well get more grading done. I sit at my desk and let myself go back to pretending she's off at a conference.

3

How to Make Dinner for Yourself

Before I knew Grace, I stayed up late. I'd read or listen to music, organize my desk. I liked the quiet, no phone interruptions. Then, when Grace and I started to spend nights at each other's apartments, I learned she was an early-to-bed person. Not unreasonably early—she just wanted her eight hours. I'd get into bed with her and read till I fell asleep. Gradually I learned to go to bed at a reasonable hour. But if she was out of town for a conference, I'd find myself staying up a little later each night.

In my fugue state, I fall back into my old bad habits. I maintain the fantasy that Grace is away at a conference and I grade. The semester didn't end because Grace's life did, I tell myself as I pull up another script to read. I wake in the morning, light still on, my last note trailing off mid-sentence. And an incredibly stiff neck since I fell asleep propped up on the couch.

It feels like the most normal thing to be doing. When I focus on a student's script, I'm in my old life. No death or loss here. I function purely by rote. My job is to question the logic of a story, help a writer develop their world. *Why* is your character a lawyer? What kind of law do they practice? Why? Or, *Why* did this band of survivors settle in Denver after the apocalypse? Did something about the landscape or climate or altitude draw them? And what *was* the apocalypse? A nuclear blast? The collapse of the electrical grid? A pandemic?

I'd constantly ask that: *Why?* I'd tell them your audience is willing to believe anything as long as you construct a strong foundation. Plant clues along the way. Every story arcs to its logical conclusion, I'd tell them.

Now I look at my own world and think, where's the logic? Can I look back at my own life and point out those clues to the future the way I can with the films and scripts we study in class? Where's the foreshadowing? Was there anything to point to healthy-as-a-horse Grace—Grace who never got a flu shot or the flu, or even a cold, whereas all I had to do was hear that a student was sick and I'd catch whatever—Grace is dead, and I'm here grading scripts? How does this make sense? I remember a book series I'd loved as a kid about Mrs. Piggle-Wiggle, who lived in an upside-down house and solved the neighborhood children's problems. I'm living in an upside-down world. Most days it's dark and dreadful, more *Stranger Things* than Mrs. Piggle-Wiggle, so I choose my students' scripts over thinking, and I'm making steady progress through them. I spend my days following the same routine.

As soon as I wake I make what passes for breakfast: coffee. Breakfast used to be my favorite meal. Now I just drink my coffee, and when I'm finished, I rinse out the cup and the pot, stand at the sink looking out. What would we be doing if Grace were here? Depending on the day— what day is it? I've lost track (which wouldn't happen if Grace were here). But even if I land on a day, I can't remember our time in the house.

Not that our life was always perfect, or we never fought. We went through patches where we'd toss occasional snide comments at each other, bumps in our daily life. In the long run, meaningless. Tiffs about nothing.

When I was going through menopause, or as I came to call it, "Who Invited Her," we'd be having breakfast and I'd hear myself bickering with Grace about something—how much time she had to spend on department chair business, say—and even as my volume raised, I'd be thinking, I don't care about this, I understand her responsibilities, why am I making such a fuss? Not that that stopped me in my "put up yer dukes" mode. It's like someone else had invaded my body. Who invited her? Then I'd spend the afternoon apologizing for my morning behavior.

And now I wish for all of that back, even the tiffs.

Tiff? Who says that?

Old people, that's who.

Old women.

Well. I qualify, don't I?

People tell me I don't look my age. I pride myself on that. If someone didn't react with surprise when I said I'm seventy, I'd probably be a little depressed. Ageism isn't only for the young. Whatever young means. The older I get, the younger everyone else gets. And what I used to think of as "older" these days strikes me as not so old.

But why do I not want to look my age? Who am I trying to fool? I *am* my age. Why do I give a shit?

I have never been an "I don't know what I want to do when I grow up" kind of adult. I am grown up. And I did pretty much what I wanted to do, right up until I decided to retire. The novel I wrote as my MFA thesis didn't get published, but it did get optioned for a movie. That didn't get made. But I followed it to Los Angeles and ended up writing scripts. That also didn't get made. And then I met Grace and we moved east for her job at Hollander College. My MFA plus screenwriting experience made me an attractive plus-one.

I'd been reluctant to start teaching. Correction. I, being of the "those who can't, teach" school of thought, deemed it a fate worse than death. Given the small size of our school, only around two thousand undergraduates, it has no dedicated film program, so screenwriting is housed in the English department. I got to teach screenwriting as well as some creative writing courses. Imagine my surprise when I realized I loved teaching and had found my dream job. I loved getting to know my students, talking to them about their ideas, their responses to what they watched and read. Who else was going to be as interested in talking about movies and television as we were?

Plus, it came with a steady paycheck and benefits. But its biggest bonus I kept secret: tremendous relief at the thought that I'd never have to write again, never have to come up with another story. Every so often I'd play around with an idea. I'd make notes, write some scenes. Sometimes it would be for a movie. Sometimes a series. Sometimes I even imagined it as a novel. Mostly though, I just planned to teach until I retired at seventy.

2019 was supposed to be a spectacular year, our lucky number year. My retirement and Grace's sabbatical falling on this auspicious number could only mean great things.

We had it all planned. First we were going to take a two-week vacation in the Adirondacks as soon as graduation was over. Neither of us had ever been, and we were going to use the vacation to clear our heads after the semester. Grace could start thinking about her sabbatical, and I'd have a clean break between my final teaching semester and retirement. Thanks to Grace's supreme organizational skills, our suitcases are packed and ready to go.

Well, Grace's is packed. Mine only sort of. Every so often, I'd throw in something else—a book I'm determined to read, an extra sweater. Grace never added anything. She'd made her list, packed it, and that was that. "But what about..." I'd ask. "I'll be fine without," she'd say. "If it didn't make it onto the list, I didn't need it."

Both suitcases lie open on the floor of our bedroom. Grace's all tidy, mine less so. Those two packed suitcases, which had represented our excitement for our plans, now are unexploded landmines, serving only to rob me of my anticipated happiness.

I add them to the mental list of what I can't deal with yet. Grace's study. Her game consoles! I'd lost track of which she had. At some point I should plug her phone back in, shouldn't I? Or I'll just cancel her number. No more family, so no more need for a family plan. Her computers! Each time Grace got a new piece of equipment, she'd print a fresh instruction sheet for me on how to access all her devices. I, on the other hand, possess a grand total of two: phone and laptop. And the laptop belongs to the college, so I'll have to return it as soon as I've turned in final grades. Grace was so excited to go computer shopping with me, and all I wanted to do was get it over with. "Why do we need to shop? Can't I just order the same kind I've been using?" I'm such a killjoy.

She'd at least be pleased about our still-unplugged landline. She'd wanted me to get rid of it for years. "Why do we need it?" she'd ask.

"For emergencies," I'd answer.

"The landline won't work if the power is out. And if the power is out, that's the emergency situation. Besides, that's what your cell is for." She'd constantly harp at me to bring it along when we left the house.

Her logic eluded me. "Why, if you're bringing yours?" I'd ask.

"You need to have it."

"Why?"

Round and round we'd go until Grace, completely exasperated, would say, "Because—for emergencies."

"Because," her argument of last resort. She hated "because." She was excellent at explaining—to someone who wanted to listen.

Well, fat lot of good your phone did you in your emergency, I remind her. Ha! I won that round!

I make a victory march to the kitchen.

In my family, the answer to "Are you hungry?" was "I could eat." Occasionally, if we happened to be on vacation in a different time zone, the answer might be "What time is it?", followed by "I could eat."

Food was the answer to many questions. How was your trip? Great—we ate at that restaurant your mother and I discovered the first time we went. How are you doing? Fine. We had pork chops for dinner.

Even though I don't like to cook, I remember events by their meals. When I told my ex I thought she was an alcoholic: lunch of pasta with a fresh tomato and basil sauce. The first time Grace cooked for me in my kitchen: a lovely chicken with lemon, roasted potatoes and vegetables. "Do you remember?" I ask, as if she's standing here next to me. (And who's to say she isn't?) Right before she was ready to serve the meal, she'd said, "Do you want to light the candles now?"

"Candles?" I said, with what I hoped was the right amount of flirtatious innuendo. "This sounds promising."

"It's Shabbat," she said. "I thought you were Jewish."

"I guess we were more cultural than religious. I consider myself a culinary Jew—I've eaten all the food."

Kidding aside, I don't limit myself to the food of my people. I'm far from parochial in my tastes. I don't care if a restaurant is upscale or no-scale, as long as the food is good. That's probably what I regret most about living in a small town, the finite number of restaurants. Grace and I made up for it with a wide-ranging in-house menu. Entertaining at home became an orchestrated event, Grace in charge of the cuisine and food preparation, me of everything else—place settings, lighting, even the music. I enabled her sense of theatre, encouraging her to flambé the Grand Marnier for the poached pears at the table before I served them to our guests.

So I'm surprised that now, for the first time in my life, I can't eat. I've essentially given up any pretense of keeping to a meal schedule. After consuming only coffee for breakfast, at some point in the afternoon I realize I'm weak and light-headed and grab a yogurt, a food I previously never bothered with. Until it ran out, I'd toss in some trail mix.

So many people at the funeral had offered help. "Let me know if you need anything." "Call anytime." "We'll have you over for dinner." Some have followed up, leaving voicemails I don't return.

I slightly regret refusing Sue's offer to shop for me. By now, widow food (the name I gave to the various casseroles and banana breads and cookies people brought me) has just about run out, and I'm down to the last of Grace's supply of snacks. If she were here—

The fridge would be stocked.

"No, Grace. You never let me finish." (I have thrown all pretense of sanity to the wind and keep up a running conversation with her. Well, more of a monologue, since she doesn't always respond to me.) "I was going to say, if you were here, you'd be laughing," I say out loud. "You know how I am about food. It's been almost two weeks since you died. If you were here, we'd mark this kind of occasion with a meal. We'd have people over, you'd cook."

I hear Grace clear her throat.

"I get it," I say. "If you were here, we wouldn't be marking the anniversary of your death."

So basically, my relationship to food—and everything else, actually— has changed. I've lost so much weight I can take off my pants without undoing the zipper.

This is not healthy, you tell me.

"Oh, come on. We always talked about losing a few pounds."

Not healthy, you repeat. **Listen**.

You clearly mean business. I pull out a notebook and write as you dictate:

How to Make Dinner for Yourself

1. **You need a routine. Choose an arbitrary time: 6:30 p.m.**

2. **At 6:30 go into the kitchen and tell yourself it doesn't matter if you're hungry. You need to eat.**

3. **If the fridge presents too great an obstacle (that bottle of champagne you were saving for my birthday), close the door and,**

4. **Move to the cupboards. A can of soup will do fine. You can microwave it right in the bowl; fewer dishes.**

5. **If you want the illusion of cooking, pour the soup into a pot, add some dried herbs. Doesn't matter that you won't really taste anything. The point is to have a plan for nourishing yourself.**

I wait. Nothing more from you. I look over the list, tear the page out, and use a Georgia O'Keefe magnet to stick it on the refrigerator. If anyone asks, though no one's going to ask because I don't have anyone over these days, but, hypothetically, if someone were to ask, I'll say I wrote it myself.

Then I realize that if I intend to adhere to this plan, I'll need to go to the store.

I go to the pad on the fridge to start on a list. My vision blurs when I see Grace's nearly illegible handwriting.

What would you do in this situation? The love of your life has died. You've just found a scrap of paper that has her handwriting on it, her fingerprints, her DNA, right? Invisible to your naked eye, but you know it's there. Do you keep it? Add the items you need to buy to the list and head to the store? Then cross off each item as you drop it into the cart. That's what you do every time you shop, right? That's why you make the list, to cross off as you go along. But now, today, you're holding this flimsy paper in your hand, and you're looking at this distinctive yet illegible handwriting (is that *flowers* or *floss*?), and you know that the love of your life held this very paper in her hand and wrote those indecipherable words—when? A month ago? Three weeks? She was here, alive, in this room, at that time. And it was routine, inconsequential—she may have even kept the paper on the fridge while she wrote. Which could explain the worse-than-usual writing. Maybe you were even with her in the kitchen when she wrote it. Making tea. Or getting lunch ready. Or you were mid-tiff, annoyed with her for no reason that would make any sense to you right now, when you're wanting with every fiber of your being to have it be that moment, that time a month ago or three weeks or whenever it was, and you were both alive and not remotely thinking that something like this could happen.

You'd agree with me that crossing off even a single item in her handwriting is unthinkable.

I open the utility drawer and drop the list on top of a bunch of user manuals for appliances, many of which I don't even know if we own any more.

I'll wing it—no list required. I'll just pick up whatever appeals to me.

Excited to have even a flimsy excuse for a plan of action, I grab my keys, and wallet, and my phone (which has informed me not only of the date, but the day: Wednesday) and head for my super-smart car. I'm halfway into town before I realize I never got dressed. I look down. Sweatpants, an old cotton pullover, running shoes (not that I run). Well, not my usual leaving-the-house attire—I try to always look put together in case I encounter students. But afraid that if I go home to change, I'll lose my resolve, I forge ahead.

I learned years ago to always park in the same aisle of the lot, wanting to never be that person walking up and down repeatedly clicking the unlock button on my remote to find my car. I take only one reusable bag from the trunk—shopping for just myself now—hit the lock button and start to walk away. I don't hear the familiar beep, so hit the button again. Nothing. Try the button on the door. Nope.

The day we'd driven our new Prius off the lot, Grace and I stopped for an afternoon coffee to celebrate. She headed into the café while I fed the meter. I took one last look at our new purchase, proudly hit the lock button on the driver's door handle, and nothing happened. After opening and re-closing all four doors and the trunk, I saw Grace's key fob in the cup holder. Once I had that in my hand, the car locked. Prius prevents me from locking my keys in the car. My first acknowledgment that one of my possessions was smarter than I was.

Now on that list, in addition to the Prius: my phone, my TV, even the heat tape around the pipes in the crawl space has its own thermostat that kicks in so that the pipes won't freeze no matter which way the wind blows in the winter.

I'm not a Luddite. Okay, compared to Grace I am. I just wish some things were simpler and didn't remind me of my own fallibility. Because when I think I'm becoming more digitally savvy, I'll hear how someone's adjusting their heat or turning on their outside lights while they're away on vacation.

We've come a long way from that first day with our new Prius when I marveled at the technological advancements that prevented us from locking ourselves out of the car, running down the battery by leaving the lights on, since they shut off automatically—only after allowing us enough time to safely exit the vehicle and move to the house. Grace figured that by the time we were on our last car, a topic that had come up frequently as I neared retirement, we'd have a self-driving option. "I'll be dead before then," I said. To which she'd responded: "'Then' is already here. Look at Tesla."

Grace loved how technology was improving our lives. I didn't always share her view. And it's only getting worse—or better, depending on your attitude toward the increasing interconnectivity of objects. The Internet of Things. Your phone talking to your thermostat while you're miles away. Or your phone talking to your car when you're not the one driving. Refrigerators. Washer/driers. Alexa and Siri and Google Home. Smart pills containing a drug and an ingestible sensor enabling the pill to transmit data to an app on a smartphone. Data that can be accessed by a doctor or caregiver.

Or maybe your fucking freezer.

Because what if that app was also connected to your smart refrigerator? Say you rebelled, skipped the pill that made you loopy, nauseous, hyper, and instead headed to the kitchen for some ice cream, or even a healthy snack, and your own fridge won't open for you? Sorry, pal, not until you've taken that pill.

Grace didn't fully comprehend how much this terrified me. Or why. She called me a pessimist, always looking on the dim side.

None of this is helping me lock the car. I look at the once-shiny red thing. (I should take it through the car wash.) "Work with me, okay?" No response from the car. It's smart, but not much of a talker.

WWGD. What would Grace do?

I open the driver's side door to see if I'd left the motor running (for not the first time; those silent engines!), but the engine is off. I open and close all the doors and the trunk. That doesn't solve my problem, either.

Not that I can't leave the car unlocked. It's the principle of the thing. If I let something be wrong with the car, that would be the first domino to fall, the first thing I didn't have the interest in fixing, the first thing I let go now that Grace herself is gone.

I contemplate my next move. Drive to the mechanic and have him look the car over to see what's wrong? I take a deep breath. Ask myself again: WWGD? Aha! Check the owner's manual—I might have missed something.

Who's smarter now? Inordinately proud of myself for thinking this through rather than rushing off in a panic, I sit in the passenger seat and open the glove compartment.

Out tumble Grace's keys.

This stupid touristy key ring from Fisherman's Wharf in San Francisco shoots me back to our vacation there, the trip through the wine country, how I had to drive through the hills so I wouldn't get carsick but then couldn't see the spectacular views, getting lost in the forest the time we locked ourselves out of our rental house and had to backtrack twenty windy, dark miles to the nearest motel. The million silly things you remember instead of the one thing you really want to, though even if you could remember, the memory doesn't give you the weight of that person's hand in yours, her breath in your ear when you dance, the sound of her voice.

I stare at the keys a moment longer. I must have shoved them into the glove compartment when I left the hospital and hadn't locked the car since.

Another victory for the car. Smarter than me. (Than I?)

Enough. I clutch Grace's keys—they feel like they weigh a thousand pounds. I lock the damn car and head into the store.

I used to love going to Wegmans. It's huge and has everything. I could buy socks or sockeye salmon. Since she did the cooking, Grace would compose the food list, and I'd fill in the rest and do the shopping. Today, I almost don't make it past the entrance. I'm overwhelmed, paralyzed, by the enormity of the place, the sheer plentitude on display. The Muzak, the smell of the produce, the rattle of other carts. Plus the fear of running into someone I know. Be brave!

I'm being ridiculous. How much courage does it take to go shopping, for god's sake. None. Just great will and determination because the thought of food repels me. Or at least isn't at all tempting. Focus. I'm in the produce section. A few bananas couldn't hurt. Though why they're labeled yellow when they're mostly green. Anyhow, I've gathered the smallest bunch I could find.

"Can I help you, dear?"

The first time I heard myself referred to as "Ma'am"—what a shock. Of course, it was so long ago I don't remember if I was in my thirties or forties. One minute you're so flattered to be carded at twenty-five, then someone calls you "Ma'am." Or "Mrs." But at least those are honorifics, offered out of respect for your age. "Dear," on the other hand, grates because it infantilizes. Today, already on shaky ground being in the store, I choose to ignore it. Which only makes the speaker repeat it. Louder.

"Can I help you, dear?"

I will be polite. "Excuse me?"

"Do you need help with that? I can explain how to use it." The cheerful, round-faced smiling girl points to the scale, as if maybe I didn't know what it was, or how to punch in the item code and print my own label.

I want to slug this kid. What is she, like twelve? "No. I'm fine."

"Are you sure?"

Twelve and deaf? "I've got it." I let it go at that, rather than telling this poor kid off in the middle of the produce aisle that I've been weighing bananas since before you were born. I've been using computers since before your parents were born. Don't assume that just because I have gray hair that I'm technically illiterate. Fucking digital natives think they know everything. And you don't need to raise your voice when you speak to me—nothing's wrong with my hearing. What happened to the customer is always right?

Have I said any of this out loud? Because now there's a manager asking the kid if everything's okay and shooting me a sideways glance, but clearly more concerned about the kid.

I storm out of the store, empty-handed. Except my hand isn't empty. I'm still clutching Grace's keys, which by now feel so heavy I'm practically buckling under their weight, like I should use both hands to carry them.

I dump them on the passenger seat and start the car.

I showed them! I gloat. Calling me "dear." I practically harrumph. I stood up for myself and my whole age cohort.

I also walked out of the store without buying any food.

"Way to go, genius," I chide myself.

4

Get a Dog

I have every intention of going home, yet instead find myself pulling up to Sue and Annie's steep driveway. Their house is right on the main road out of town. No need to use the doorbell since their two big dogs of indeterminate breed, Cagney and Lacey (lesbians of a certain age and their pop culture icons, right?), bark and jump excitedly behind the glass of the storm door as I approach.

Just as I open it, "Watch out for Louie," Annie warns a moment too late, as a grey blur streaks past me out of the house and up the hill, Cagney and Lacey following close behind.

"Oops," I say.

"Don't worry," says Annie, giving me a big hug before going after the dog. She uses the older dogs to round up Louie, whom she scoops up and brings back into the house.

"He's new," I say, following Annie, who plops on the couch holding the little pup. I sit next to her.

"Sue always promises no more dogs, and then she tiptoes home saying, 'But he's sooooo cute.'" In addition to being a vet, Sue's a rescuer.

I have to agree with her assessment, though. Louie's really adorable. "What is he?" I ask, stroking his head.

"Mostly Shih Tzu," Annie says. "But it's the terrier in him that tears up that hill after rabbits. Or squirrels. Or whatever else happens to be around at the time."

"He's really cute," I say.

"Most of the time," Annie says.

"What do Cagney and Lacey think of him?"

"They're getting used to him," she says, kissing the top of his head. "Someone just found him wandering along the highway and brought him to the SPCA. Can you imagine not wanting a little fella like this? He was so skinny and anxious they didn't want to put him in with the other dogs, so Sue said we'd foster him. We'll probably end up keeping him." As we both pet the little fella, Annie says, "Sue's at the market. Are you staying for dinner?"

I don't even know why I'm here, which doesn't seem like an appropriate answer to the question.

"You can think about it while we walk these beasts," Annie says, grabbing leashes. "Here, you take Cagney. I'll take the little guy. He's still learning to behave." She puts a halter on Louie. "Lacey! Come on, girl."

Instead of heading down the driveway, we walk behind the house, which backs onto the old city cemetery. We're in another world, even though just five minutes outside town. It's not like Sue and Annie live in the country like we do. Though coming from New York City, I still think of anything with grass as country. But it is very green and quiet as we walk off the road that winds through the cemetery, between graves dating back to the 1700s and 1800s. Small American flags, freshly planted for Memorial Day, mark veterans of conflicts dating back to the Civil War, including Black soldiers as indicated by the U.S.C.T. on their stones. Some of the markers indicate the presence of a conductor on the underground railroad since Ithaca had been a stop. Others are labeled with names I recognize from local streets and avenues. On past walks through here I've been inspired by history. Today I mostly see the decrepit state of many of the gravesites: broken headstones, memorial pedestals toppled and broken, parts overgrown with grass. Crazy, but I think of the poem *Ozymandias*, the prideful ruler's statue in ruins overlooking a vast desert. So much for the mighty. So much for permanence. So much for teaching all the newest and latest in story structures. Here I am, recalling a poem I studied in high school. But do the people buried here give a shit about any of my unraveling thoughts? Do they care about the mess the country's in, the unbalanced narcissist in the White House? They're lucky they don't have to see this. Maybe Grace had the right idea. Sudden death, no slow goodbyes, lengthy preparations, trying to leave nothing left unsaid.

"Maybe this wasn't the best route to take," Annie says.

I'm jarred from my thoughts. "Sorry?"

"Through the cemetery."

"It's fine," I tell her.

We walk in silence. I focus on breathing in and out, reminding myself I'm alive. The air is fresh, birds swoop and dart. The dogs' tags jingle as they trot alongside us.

When we get back to the house, Sue's home and happy to see me. Doesn't ask, just assumes I'm staying for dinner and assigns me various chopping tasks.

She makes a paella that in my former life I would have found delicious. We eat in the dining nook off the kitchen. Something about being nurtured like this breaks my heart. Well, would break it if it weren't already broken. I feel like one of Sue's strays being incorporated into the family as I listen to her and Annie talk about the dogs, the merits of this paella over one they'd eaten at a restaurant somewhere, what kind of work they're going to do for the presidential campaign once the Democrats have a candidate.

Might as well be the grown-ups talking in a Charlie Brown special— just the wah-wa-wa horn noise, none of the words come through. I mostly space on the conversation until Sue asks, I think for a second time, "Want me to make you a doggie bag to take home?"

"It's delicious," I say. "I just..." I don't know what else to say, so leave it there.

Annie gives my shoulder a squeeze as she takes my plate into the kitchen. In this democratic household, whoever doesn't cook cleans up.

"You're looking kind of thin, my friend," Sue says. "You've got to keep up your strength."

"Leave her alone," Annie calls from the kitchen.

Louie trots over to Sue's side, looking for a little affection. She pats his head.

"Couldn't resist him, could you," I say.

"How could I? Look at that face," she says, hauling him onto her lap. "I could find you one, you know."

"She worries about you out there all alone," Annie calls from the kitchen.

"I'm fine," I say.

Sue won't let me leave empty-handed. I try to refuse the old yogurt container she's filled with paella. "You don't have to return it," she says. I know better than to argue with her.

Big hugs from both women, waves as I drive off.

On the way home, I pull into a gas station and dump the leftovers into the trash.

I drop onto the couch as soon as I'm inside. I don't turn on the TV. I don't change out of my clothes. I just lie back, exhausted at having made it through another day. More exhausted when I think I'll have to go back to the market and actually buy provisions. But I'll arm myself with a list next time.

"The suitcases!"

I'm panicking. It's a huge plane, and the flight is full. I'm jammed into a window seat way at the back of the main cabin. I can tell the doors have just closed by the pressure building in my ears. Seatbelts click closed around me. The flight attendant strolls down the aisle, arms raised, hands checking that overhead bins are shut, a smile plastered on her face, oblivious to my situation. I grab for her. "I have to get off! I left our suitcases in the car!"

She ignores the suitcase problem. "Our?" she asks, like I'm nuts. Repeats it for effect: "Our?"

I bolt upright in bed, arms flinging out to grab the flight attendant. So I'm not on a plane. I'm not even in my bed, a fact I realize when my arm hits the back of the couch.

My heart pounds. I can't catch my breath. I focus to orient myself. Even though I now know that I'm in my living room, I can't quite shake the feeling from the dream. What have I forgotten? Where was I going? I close my eyes, imagine myself on the plane again. Realize the seat next to me is empty. Which explains the attendant's questioning my use of "our." That must have been Grace's seat. I open my eyes. Where were we headed? And why wasn't she there? Maybe that was going to be the next part of the dream. I'd missed a chance to see her again.

Or maybe it doesn't fucking matter because 1) it was a dream, and 2) Grace is dead. And I'm still sleeping on the couch, something I thought I'd only be doing for a few nights, till I got "used to" my new life. Or comfortable sleeping alone in our bedroom. But it's been a month now, and I already know that isn't going to happen. Clearly that isn't the world I live in anymore. Everything is strange.

Like not being able to shake this dream. That uncomfortable feeling that I'd forgotten something has followed me into what passes for my real life. What did my students call it – IRL? In Real Life.

Is there such a thing as IUL? In Unreal Life?

ISL? In Surreal Life?

Life after spouse—that would be LAS.

This meditation isn't getting me anywhere. Certainly not back to sleep.

Was I telling myself I needed to deal with our suitcases, still packed and ready for our trip?

I need a second opinion. "Hey, Grace—want to weigh in on this?"

Since I never know when Grace is going to tell me something, I've put a pad in every room so I'll be ready at a moment's notice. I carry my notebook and a pen with me wherever I go so I can record any messages she has for me.

I listen for her answer. Nothing but the hum of the house and a light rustle of leaves in the wind.

"Fine. Be that way."

I settle back on the couch. I'm hyper-vigilant, on perpetual high alert. Once again, sleep will be impossible. I grab the TV twanger and press power. Meredith Grey and her merry band of interns and residents can keep me company through the night.

I made my breakfast coffee in a fog of exhaustion. I'd finished my grading and resolved to bring my pile of papers to the office. And while I'm there, I'll clean it out. That normally would have happened between finals week and graduation, but I missed all that. And this will be the last cleaning.

So here I am, in my office on campus for the first time since Grace died, sorting through a stack of papers and whatever else has accumulated over the semester. I choose to ignore for now the packing boxes I'd begun to gather as the semester wound down. I start small, recycling notices for events, meetings, and catalogs. I'll leave the graded scripts with Deb for the students to claim. I work quickly and efficiently, another "normal" thing I've done since Grace died, and I lose myself for a good hour.

I get so lost, in fact, that as I'm winding down, it feels perfectly natural to pick up my phone to text Grace an estimate of how much longer I'll be and ask whether I need to pick up anything on my way home. Four words in, I realize what I'm doing. That catapults me out of my chair and across the hall to Deb's office. I sit next to her desk. She's on her computer. After all our years working together, she knows I'll ask if I need anything. But all I need is this companionable silence and to not be in my office for a few minutes.

Frank, who teaches history, stops by with a messy sheaf of papers and receipts. "Deb, can you go over my expense report with me? Something's not making sense." Deb doesn't turn around. She has amazing compartmentalizing skills and is quite capable of ignoring faculty clamoring for her attention until she's at a good stopping point in whatever task she's performing. Frank notices me.

"Hannah, hi." He stops, not sure what comes next. When he sees I'm not going to help him out, he forges ahead. "How are you? I'm so sorry about, you know…"

"My retirement?" Am I being cruel? He's just trying to be nice.

"No. Not your retirement. Your, um, wife. And well, plus your retirement on top of that. What crazy timing."

Is he done?

"I couldn't come to the funeral. I was at a conference." He holds up the folder, out from which drift several small receipts he tries to catch.

Deb, who has no patience for fools, spins around and grabs the papers from Frank's hand. "Let me see what you've got." Rescued, I can slip back to my office.

Can't people ask something other than how are you? How do they think I am? Though maybe I prefer that to the dog suggestion. In voicemails, as well as in my relatively few forays into the world, I can't count the number of times people have told me I should get a dog. They're totally well-meaning, but still, why can't they just keep their mouths shut?

People are so full of advice. Was that always the case? Or do I, now that my spouse is dead, look like someone particularly in need of advice? Not only about companion animals. All sorts of advice. How to spend my time, whether that's traveling or just going to movies or lectures, because, you know, you'll need to get out more. Restaurants I should try, support groups I should join. Meditation would be great. Yoga. Pilates! But most of all, they tell me to get a dog. Sometimes it's just get a pet, any variety would do—cat, ferret (seriously), bird, though only if that bird has the capacity to speak. I'll appreciate the company, they tell me. Tropical fish would be soothing, I'm told. Beautiful to look at, very meditative. But based on my extremely unscientific calculation, dog is mentioned 97.9 percent of the time.

So far I've fended off every suggestion. Not a good idea, I say, if I say anything, because I plan to travel. Which is a lie. I have no intention of going anywhere. The I'm-not-really-a-dog-person excuse doesn't work because then they tell me to get a cat. Or a talking bird. A rabbit. Something so that I'll have company. Another living being to care for. I don't need that, I tell them. I'm fine. They look at me like they don't believe me. I'm doing better every day, I lie again.

In some ways, though, I'm not lying. I can now turn off lights in rooms I'm not in. For the first week or so, I'd leave a light on in the room next to wherever I was at night so I could see it falling in the doorway if I just glanced up from whatever I was doing—grading, or sitting with a plate of food in front of me, trying to force myself to eat—in that quick glance with the light spilling through the doorframe, I could for a split-second think Grace was there, in that other room, bathed in that bright white light.

Obviously when people tell me I should get a dog I don't tell them I already have a companion in the house. Grace's absence is palpable: it takes up space, has weight, volume. Sometimes, uses up all the air in the room so that I can hardly breathe. When that happens, I sit quietly until it—or she—passes. I've even stepped outside onto the porch to gulp in the night air. I don't tell people any of this.

Nor do I tell them I love dogs. Adore them. Could see myself going to the shelter and picking one to bring to its forever home. I'd be that old lesbian who took her dog everywhere. People would recognize it, know its name, even if they didn't know mine. I'd talk to it. We'd watch TV together. Take walks. It would be the kind of dog I could take to hospitals to visit kids. A comfort dog. We'd be inseparable.

I keep all this to myself. I don't tell them the real reason I won't get a dog is because there is no such thing as a "forever" home. Grace's death proved that to me. And I couldn't survive losing another being I love.

I drop into my chair. As preparation, like an athlete stretching before an event, I swivel around, looking out the window onto campus, serene now that the students are gone for the summer, then toward the wall of books, my file cabinet, back to my desk. My walls are cluttered with sayings and cartoons, posters for lectures and presentations long past. A framed photo of Grace and me on our wedding day. I reach for it but stop. She can keep me company while I work.

That makes me sad. I should go home.

No, I can do this.

Start with the easy stuff. Fill some of these book cartons. I pull out individual volumes to decide whether or not I want to keep them. I have hardly any textbooks, mostly novels, comix, poetry collections, screenplays, books about writing. Plus, while I'd done a certain amount of decluttering at home over the last few years, whenever I couldn't quite part with something, whether a book or a piece of art, I'd bring it to school. Grace and I both did. Anything we didn't want, we'd bring to the office. Someone would always take it, whether it was leftover Halloween candy or souvenir mugs. I'm paying for that now. To even get to my books I have to move aside bobbleheads—all three Golden Girls plus Sofia, Princess Leia, Wonder Woman, RBG, Gloria Steinem (are we detecting a theme?)—rocks and stones collected on various beaches and hikes, dream catchers, decorative boxes. Much of the collection came from students.

Maybe I should just pack everything up and sort through it at home. God knows I'll have the time. And the space, once I get rid of the stuff in Grace's study. No, I reprimand myself. Be ruthless.

I peruse the titles, considering each one. I select five for Oliver: Alison Bechdel's graphic novel *Fun Home; Brown Girl Dreaming,* Jacqueline Woodson's memoir in verse; Joan Didion's collection of essays *Slouching Toward Bethlehem*; Jewelle Gomez's *The Gilda Stories*. I have my own copies at home, and those volumes have my notes.

When that's done, it takes me all of eight minutes to scoop up two shelves worth of books and load them into boxes. I dust the shelves, then turn to grab another box. Somehow looking at what I've done fills me with such—I can't call it grief because that's all taken up with Grace— but—maybe regret to be leaving this behind? I haven't thought too much about being retired. I won't be teaching these books, or pulling them off the shelf to illustrate a point I'm making to a student during my office hours. What did all those years mean? What am I going to do now? Who will I be? A writer? Wasn't that what I was supposed to do? But even at my best, I felt ambivalent about writing and have no intention of going back to it.

Rather than feeling accomplished at my progress, I'm more than a little sad. And can I even call this progress? Rather than empty shelves, despite the number of boxes I've filled, I see items I couldn't bring myself to pack away, gifts from former students. Shouldn't I keep this painted box from Bolivia? Or the Turkish candy tin? I give myself permission not to decide today.

I turn back to my desk. Let's start small, I think. But still be ruthless. I pull open a side drawer. It's fairly well-organized. Department letterhead and envelopes, department mailing labels, plain envelopes. I put them in a pile on one of the cleared bookshelves. Deb can use all this. I'm developing a system. This is easy! This is progress! Back to the drawer. I gather the assortment of pens and pencils and grab a rubber band from a tangle in the same drawer to put around the pencils to keep them together on the shelf. The band snaps. As do three others that I try. So. Rubber bands that have lost their elasticity—right into the trash. Loose paper clips at the bottom of the drawer, right into recycling. Do not pass go. A few notepads. I'll keep these. I start filling a bankers box with stuff I'll bring home. I'll allow myself just this one box, no more.

I add a few things I know I want to keep: a ceramic tray a student from Mexico gave me; some good pens. I hold my apple paperweight in my hands for a moment before putting it in the box. I find its heft solid and comforting.

I'm on a roll now, ready to move on. Except I see a piece of paper stuck way in the back, caught in the crack under the drawer's divider. Probably nothing important, but my goal is one hundred percent empty and cleaned, so I tug it back and forth to work it loose. It's a memo from the Dean dated eleven years earlier thanking me for my service on a curriculum committee. I had looked for that when putting together my promotion file that year. I have no idea how it landed in this drawer, which clearly was for writing supplies. Into recycle this goes. And boom! One drawer done!

Encouraged, I slide open the next one. This presents more of a challenge, as it doesn't have an immediate organizing principle. Pen refills (why weren't they with the pens?), lens cleaning cloths, staples, a box of paper clips, chopsticks, a pepper mill, napkins, and a small baggie containing packets of salt and pepper. Loose business cards, both mine and a stack of others I'd collected over the years, names I no longer recognize. I'm relieved I don't have to make sense of or organize this. I just have to clean it out. Which I do, starting from the front. Most of the stuff is junk I can toss. I find more department envelopes, and a surprise under them.

Grace was a romantic. She'd slide a postcard under my door on the first and last day of each semester. She didn't write much on them— knock 'em dead; made it through another one—but that wasn't the point. The images were of places we'd visited, or photographs of artists, writers, musicians. They were a reminder of the invisible thread that connected us at work. And now I've got a whole stack of them, tossed carelessly into this drawer year after year. They're coming home with me. Into the bankers box they go.

But wait—there's more.

I dig out a plastic photo album, three-quarters filled with 4x6 prints of students in their caps and gowns. I flip through it, marveling at the images of these exuberant young men and women. I find two more of these albums. I'm mesmerized. First of all, who remembered they existed? Second, when did I stop taking pictures? What had changed? Had the novelty worn off? I certainly didn't love my students any less as time went on—just the opposite. They were the main reason I hadn't retired sooner. Probably digital photography is what changed. I stopped making prints. And then stopped using a camera because I wasn't making prints, and my phone was good enough. Whatever the reason, it was a shame, because these are great. I'm seeing students I hadn't thought about in years. With each photo, I remember the stories they wrote, some of the conversations we had during my office hours, details they'd shared with me about their personal lives. I have to keep these.

Another album contains pictures of colleagues. Several of Grace and me in our offices, together on campus, with students and their parents at graduation, both of us in our academic regalia (closest either of us ever got to wearing a dress). A few loose photos fall out and I examine these. Grace and me out on the lake at the helm of a friend's sailboat. Grace standing at the wheel, me sitting next to her. Sun shining, water glinting behind us. "We were happy, weren't we," I say out loud to Grace in our wedding photo, the lone object left on my wall.

I repeat it, aloud again, to Grace in the atmosphere around me.

And with that, I'm done for today. I leave everything in this half-packed state. I'll come back tomorrow, see if I feel differently about wanting any of this stuff I've left behind. And then I'll be able to declare myself moved out.

5
Organizing Principles

I follow Grace's dinner instructions when I get back from my office. I heat up a can of soup. Yum. But at least I've eaten something. Then I shower because Sue told me that doing so changes your body chemistry, something about all those negative ions being a mood elevator. And my mood could definitely use some elevating. Also, the process takes up time. If I go to bed too early, I'll be up in the middle of the night, the worst time to be alone with my thoughts. I pop two Advil PM to help me at least fall asleep and stretch out on the couch. I dream that Grace has been living in an apartment near campus, but wake up before I find out why she didn't tell me she was going to do this.

Wake up is a relative term. It's 4:00 a.m. and I'm logy from the diphenhydramine, the PM part of Advil PM. I think I'll get up, but keep just lying on the couch. Not that this inertia is new to me since Grace died.

When this happens, day or night, I let my thoughts wander. That's a euphemism for: I just lie there. I'm not aware of thinking anything. Minutes pass. An hour. Sometimes I will myself to get up. Sometimes I just want to die. Not to be confused with wanting to kill myself. I simply don't want to feel this pain anymore. I believe the pain would diminish if I could remember my life with Grace, if I could just lose myself in those memories. But nothing. Still nothing.

This morning I feel a tinge of motivation because I'm determined to start on Grace's campus office. After my encounter with Frank, I wonder if there's a way for me to avoid everyone, just slip in and out unnoticed, not have to interact, make conversation, lie to people about how I'm doing today.

Maybe I should wait and go in over the weekend. Less chance of running into anyone. Is that actually a good idea, or an excuse to just lie here some more?

And when were weekends invented? Were they invented?

Weekends have a different meaning, no meaning, now that I'm alone. Not just alone—*retired* and alone. Wow. Is that even me? My bio could read: seventy-year-old widow, retired, lives alone. I hear those words, because, yes, I've spoken them out loud, and picture someone very different than me. A sweet old lady in a shapeless floral dress, cardigan held at the neck by one of those little sweater clasps, palsied, liver-spotted hand fluttering to her throat to check the clasp.

Ageist much?

Well, what comes into your mind if I say seventy, retired? Hardly an old butch dressed like a teenaged boy in a worn polo shirt and board shorts.

Oh please. Are you still on this age thing? Give me a break. This is so boring!

I may still be lying down, but Grace is definitely up.

Pull yourself together, she says. **Get a grip.**

I don't need to leave the couch. I've got a pad handy. Pen poised, I wait for Grace's dictation, which I know will come if I quiet my thoughts. Sure enough:

Now that you've got dinner down, try this:

How to Keep It Simple

1. **Make a routine and stick to it. Such as:**

2. **Determine the order of morning activities. For example:**

    a. **Meds & vitamins**

    b. **Exercise**

    c. **Breakfast**

3. **Once you've done that, set your alarm for the same time each morning. When it rings:**

4. GET OUT OF BED. DO NOT WALLOW.

Wallow? Who's wallowing? Though I know better than to argue with Grace, even if she's dead. Death has made her bossy.

5. Do those morning activities in order. Every day. Without fail.

6. The less you have to plan, the better off you are.

I'm a quick study. I list my morning activities—take my meds, eat breakfast. Don't get all worried about the meds. They're just for hypothyroid. I'm not actively dying, at least not any more or less than all of us who are nominally healthy. Since I haven't been able to get myself to the gym—I only went because Grace went and now don't go at all— I'll figure out later what will replace exercise. In the meantime, I get right to work, starting with breakfast. I'd better choose wisely, because that's what I'll eat for the foreseeable future.

Easy answers first: coffee. Not as fanatic as Grace about this, I've allowed myself to buy pre-ground. I move on.

Since breakfast is a meal, I should eat something. Keep it simple. Toast.

Is that all I have? Is that what all my days will be? Coffee and toast? (Once I go to the store and buy bread.) What routine am I supposed to stick to? And isn't being retired all about *not* having a routine? Isn't this when people travel? Where am I supposed to go?

I realize it isn't so much the where, but the why. Shouldn't I want to go somewhere? I'm retired. Single. Not responsible to anyone anymore. No commitments. I have all the time in the world to travel. To do...anything.

Maybe I should take up a hobby. If I ever regain my appetite, I could take up cooking. I hear Grace laughing at me, and I laugh a little, too.

Grace was an excellent cook.

On the few occasions I've tried to cook, well, let's just say that as a cook, I lack imagination. I'd spread the ingredients out in front of me, and I'd follow the recipe, but I didn't know why I should be slicing thick or thin, why cubing, and is that the same as dicing? And is dicing bigger than mincing? I had no sense of what it was going to do when I put it all together, so I was always surprised how a dish I had cooked turned out. I'd experience a childlike wonder every time I saw ingredients behaving just like the recipe said they would—onions turning translucent, garlic popping in the pan as it browned. But the process didn't give me pleasure, so I basically just gave up, especially since Grace enjoyed it so much. I was a grateful audience and consumer.

Every once in a while, after I'd ceded the kitchen to Grace, I'd see a recipe that looked relatively easy—my easy criteria: few ingredients, no complicated preparations, everything had to cook in the same pan— think to myself, I could make that. Then immediately think better of it and turn the page.

Without admitting that Grace was right about my wallowing, I've hauled myself off the couch and into the kitchen. I dig a loaf of banana bread out of the freezer—the absolute last of the widow food—thinking I can have a slice with my coffee. That would count as toast, right? But not if I'm going to break a knife trying to saw through it. I don't have the patience to thaw it. Much less any real desire to eat it. I promise Grace I'll start on the breakfast plan tomorrow, after I've bought some bread. Then I head for the shower and more negative ions to prepare me for facing Grace's office.

I stop at my own office to pick up the bankers box with the items I want to bring home. The place is a mess. I thought I'd made progress but it mostly looks like I'd emptied all the drawers and distributed their contents evenly between the desk and the no longer denuded bookshelves. I'm tempted to finish here, make my final decisions on what to keep, but know that that's only a stalling tactic to avoid Grace's office. I toss the photo albums into the box, leaving room for anything I might find in Grace's office. Then I take down our wedding photo and add it, put the lid on, and head out.

When I arrive at the art history offices, I'm relieved Mary isn't at her desk so I don't have to interact. I don't know if I'd survive another hug like the one she gave me at the funeral. The floor is quiet since most faculty don't come in during the summer. I go straight across the hall and let myself into Grace's office. I'm hit with such a powerful jolt of her that I have to steady myself against the bookcase.

This is the space of someone who's in the middle of multiple projects.

Sticky notes surround her twenty-four-inch monitor. Two pads, one white, one yellow, lie next to her keyboard. That was Grace's method—white for the draft of whatever she was writing, yellow for notes, facts, references to check. No pages torn off until she'd finished with them. Assorted sizes of colored sticky notes to mark her place in books, journals, even on her own notes. A stack of books on the desk, more on the floor to the left of her chair. A bankers box full of draft pages, X'd out because she'd either already put them into her chapter or decided not to use them. But Grace always keeps everything until the article is published. And beyond, as towers of bankers boxes in our barn attest. She once threw out her notes after a conference presentation, then needed them later for an article, and spent days of her tight deadline reconstructing the missing section. Since then, she's kept it all, methodically indexed and labeled.

It looks like she's just gone down the hall and will be back any second. I expect her to pop back in to admonish me not to touch anything. "I know where everything is," she was always telling me.

This is going to be harder than I thought.

Well, duh.

I pick up the office phone and punch in Jordan's extension before Grace can get in another word. Unlike faculty, associate deans are on twelve-month contracts, so I'm pretty sure she'll be in her office.

"Hey," she answers. "I hear you had dinner at Sue and Annie's."

The four of them, Jordan and Janey, Sue and Annie, are close friends. In the time-honored tradition of lesbian interrelationships, Sue and Janey are exes who stayed close long after their relationship ended. They'd become lovers when they were both in vet school, started their practice together afterwards. Sue left Janey for Annie, who'd been part of the group they ran with. By then, Jordan had moved to town, starting in a faculty position at the college, and was embraced by the group of women who'd basically come up and out at the same time. Even though Grace and I were welcomed and accepted and loved, we never felt like we'd overcome a certain impenetrability of the group who had such a long history. Even twenty-plus years later, I feel like we're still the "new" friends.

Jordan's going on about how Sue thinks I need to eat more, but I don't have time for a lecture. "I'm on campus. In Grace's office."

I almost don't get my sentence finished before she says, "I'm on my way."

I put down the phone and sit in Grace's chair. Where am I supposed to start? I flip through the pages of her white pad. Even if I took the time to decipher her handwriting, I would need several readings to fully understand what she was talking about. While Grace could explain her ideas to me in plain English, she wrote in academese. Since I like the feeling that these were the most recent thoughts occupying her mind, I take a look. She must have been having a hard time with this piece, because she hadn't written anything, just a few doodles before printing in big block letters: ART IS THE LIE THAT TELLS THE TRUTH. Picasso had said that. We'd talked about this idea many times over the years, both for her discipline and mine. Whether it's a painting, sculpture, or novel, all art is after a truer truth than whatever inspired a particular piece. Sometimes truer even than what the creator thinks about it. This idea had changed the course of Grace's life.

She'd entered college as a computer science major. In an art history class taken solely to fulfill distribution requirements, she had to write a paper about Van Gogh. As part of her research, she started reading his letters. The intensity of his beliefs and his fervor to express what he felt and saw took hold of Grace. She read the letters and several books about him. Made trips to the Museum of Modern Art and the Metropolitan Museum in New York City to stand in front of his paintings. In her paper, she focused on the discrepancy between the peace of mind Van Gogh described in his letters toward the end of his life and the increasingly violent brushstrokes and thickness of the paint on his canvases. The truth was not in the peace the artist described in his letters. (And she'd read every single one of them, not an abridged version, the complete editions.) The truth was in the movement of the brushstrokes. The truth was the swirling mass of the petals of the sunflowers, the thick impasto of the crows over the field. Her professor told Grace she should publish her paper. Grace had switched her major to art history that semester.

Art is the lie that tells the truth.

I look at the sentence. Had Grace been planning to revisit her earliest work? Investigate Van Gogh again? Amsterdam was one of the places she'd been considering for her sabbatical. Did she want to go to the Van Gogh Museum? His passion had ignited something in her college-age self, this desire to experience life so intensely. His ability to turn the everyday into something extraordinary. She told me that when she went to MoMA to look at his work, she'd stand as close as allowed, marvelling that he'd actually touched this canvas.

Her connection to him lasted long past her transition to other topics she was passionate about, topics that fed her soul as a feminist, a lesbian, and a queer activist. If she was returning to him now, maybe it was less about Van Gogh himself than about a way to connect to the person she'd been. Age will make you think about shit like that. Or maybe it was related to the effect his work still had. What is it about his paintings that they still affect people so profoundly? What made them more than simply a picture of a wheat field with crows, what turned them into art, or Art? How did what he painted somehow become so accessible and also so extraordinary?

Did Grace think any of these thoughts? Why am I even trying to reconstruct her creative process? What will it get me?

I pick up one of the yellow pads, its pages a jumble of ideas about passages in a painting by Degas, notes about the influence of photography on his work, references she needs to check. This was from earlier in the semester. I remember her talking to me about the topic— the beginnings of photography, the mundane subject matter. I can hear her lecture—she'd throw in personal anecdotes, the impression of seeing these works in person for the first time, their size and scope. How you think they're familiar because you've studied them, but then how standing before them changes everything. "Van Gogh's 'Starry Night' is so small!" I can hear her telling them.

It's almost like spending time with her, watching her warm to her subject, her enthusiasm building and transferring to her students. "I can't imagine not being involved with people this age," she said one night. It was right after spring break. We were both on the couch, and she'd just finished grading one of her papers. Whatever she'd read inspired the remark. She'd get so excited for her students and their potential to change the world. I see the spark in her eyes, her renewed energy. I feel her presence. But not like when she's lecturing me on how to pick up my life without her. This is a glimpse at *our* life.

I realize I've remembered something. I can't get to the time before that memory, or after, but that glimpse is something I can hold onto. I don't know if it's being here in her space, one we didn't share, touching her things, but maybe if I keep at it, not just here but back at the house, I'll be able to reclaim the full picture of our life.

I turn back to the pad with new hope.

After the Degas notes, she'd started a new page and written, centered on the top line, RELIGION. This surprises me. I may be a culinary Jew, but Grace doesn't identify with any religion. Nothing else on the page. On the next page she'd written VIOLENCE. The rest of that page also left blank. The last page on which she'd written was a list of video games, no commentary, just the list.

I may not know where Grace was heading with these topics, but some notes in the margin of the video game page are perfectly clear to me: "Pick up mulch at Agway." "Pay bills Friday." "Order congrats cake for H." That one's too much for me. No more pad right now.

Grace doesn't hang pictures on her walls, which some thought odd for an art historian. The wall above her desk is bare save for a stand-alone shelf about three feet wide on which she features one artist, stacking books about them, monographs, sometimes with a volume open to a particular image. She rotates the display every few weeks. Sometimes it isn't an individual artist, but a grouping around a theme. The current one is a fascinating assortment: books about Hieronymus Bosch, the Sistine Chapel, the Italian Renaissance, a volume about medieval monsters, and the video game *Assassins Creed II*. Propped alongside the game is a bunch of postcards featuring gruesome illustrations of naked humans being tortured by horned and winged demons. I flip one over, handling it gingerly—these are really disturbing images—and learn they're frescoes by Taddeo di Bartolo depicting the seven deadly sins, painted in 1396 for a church in San Gimignano, Italy.

Grace has only one other piece of "art": a large circuit board, at least twelve inches square, pinned on the wall to the left of her desk. She may have chosen art history, but Grace was still a computer geek at heart, fascinated by function dictating form. If she was sitting at her computer and happened to glance up, there would be a reminder both of her first love, computers, and of how much that world had changed over the years. "To get all this information onto a chip today, do you know how big it would be?" Grace had told me more than once. I'd indicate a tiny space between my thumb and forefinger. "Exactly. Teeny." She keeps a few circuit boards in her office at home, too. I actually love looking at them. "Change happens so fast," she was fond of saying.

No shit.

Back on task, I slide open a desk drawer, cautiously, as if something's going to spring out at me. I don't know why I'm so jumpy. I mean, all I'm looking at are pencils, rubber bands, an emery board, loose stamps, an ATM receipt, a valentine I'd sent her three years earlier. But this feels so intimate, so private. This is the mess you hide from the world, that only you are going to see. Unless you die suddenly and your wife has to empty your office.

I'd better stick to the external surfaces today. I close the drawer.

A light knock on the door and Jordan enters. She takes one look around and lets out a whistle of overwhelm.

I glance at the clock on Grace's desk, which reads eleven-fifteen. "I've been here since about ten-fifteen." I've lost track of time, so it comes out more like a question than a statement.

"Oh," is all Jordan says. But the look she gives me is oh-poor-baby-this-must-be-so-hard-for-you.

I realize why: The office looks almost the same as when I came in. Books in their piles on the floor. Notepads on the desk. The only difference is that now Grace's pens and pencils are neatly aligned, put back in their proper place, ready to go when she is, right next to her notepads. Idiot. No wonder Jordan looks dismayed. What have I been doing all this time? I'm supposed to be packing up all this shit, not tidying it for Grace's return.

But I had a memory! At least a snippet of one. Which wouldn't mean anything to Jordan, so I don't mention it. Because then I'd have to confess that I have little recollection of the last twenty-five years of my life.

Whatever her interpretation, Jordan's no dummy. Her administrator's brain quickly sized up the situation. "I'm going to get some cartons from Mary so we can pack up the books. Do you know what you want to do with them?"

My blank look is all the answer Jordan needs.

"No problem. I'll get Mary."

After she leaves, I stand and look at the bookshelves. They cover the entire wall opposite Grace's desk. She may not have much above her desk, but these cases are packed. The titles reflect her scholarly interests and the reason she loved her discipline, because it could expand to anything. She's got artists' monographs, volumes on the Renaissance, the Baroque period, the pre-, the post-, as well as the plain old Impressionists. Feminist art. Queer art. Architecture. Tattooing. Plus philosophy, politics, social history, and design. I don't know where to start. I don't know which, if any, of these books I might want. What *am* I going to do with all this? At least there aren't *tchotchkes* all over, like in my office. But I had a hard enough time figuring out which of my own belongings I want to keep—what the fuck, Grace?

And the circuit board—what about that?

I take it off the wall carefully. The back resembles a topographical map of an imaginary world, a green surface with silver solder lines to mark highways and rivers. The electronic components on the other side represent a three-dimensional view of the same world, a strange cityscape: transistors become water towers; integrated circuits represent buildings, or long low factories, maybe; inductors are power plants; LEDs are the streetlights, of course. And printed directly on the board are route numbers and street names marked in tiny, precise print.

I bend down to place the board next to my bag and car keys. Sitting back up, I have to laugh. Scotch-taped to the wall under where it had hung is a tiny 256 MB MicroSD card, a rectangle all of maybe 5/8" x 7/8". I imagine a puzzled student sitting patiently as Grace demonstrates Moore's Law—that overall processing power for computers will double every two years—by simply lifting the huge circuit board off the wall and revealing its infinitely more powerful replacement at a fraction of the size.

A great visual. But still, the student probably thought, what does this have to do with art history?

Jordan comes back with Mary right behind her. Both carry empty boxes. Mary drops hers and gives me that big hug. Doesn't ask. Just swoops.

I let this happen for as long as I can stand it without dissolving in a heap. We used to joke about how Mary was the "other woman" in Grace's life, given how much time Grace had to spend at work and on department business.

"We miss her so much. It's just not the same…" Mary's mouth quivers a little. I know she means, "*I* miss her so much." But Mary's too practical to wallow. "We'll box these up and store them. Once you decide which books you're keeping, we can just have the library pick up whatever's left. They'll keep anything they want, and figure out what to do with the rest."

Jordan's been examining the circuit board.

"Grace loves those," I say. "Do you know how much the information on this board would take up now?" I point to the MicroSD card taped to the wall. "Actually, that tiny card can do more." I have no idea if that's true, but what do either of us care.

"Excuse me." A voice so soft its owner has to repeat herself. I look up to see a student, dressed for summer in a worn Wonder Woman (old school, Lynda Carter, not the 2017 incarnation) T-shirt and cut-off shorts, hand tentatively poised to knock on the door, clearly intimidated by three adults. "I'm sorry," she says. "I can come back."

"Megan, hi," says Mary.

Megan looks relieved that she can now speak directly to someone. "I just wanted to drop this off." She holds up a small grey envelope. Megan isn't facing me, but I can smell a condolence card from where I'm sitting. "I just…I mean, I didn't…" nothing else as Megan breaks down and Mary swoops her into a hug as she simultaneously takes the card and passes it to me. Over Megan's shaking shoulders, Mary explains, "Grace was Megan's advisor."

Megan straightens up and turns to me, dabbing at her eyes with a tissue Mary magically provided her. "She was just the best. She let me do an independent study on art and video games."

A hazy picture emerges: Grace on the couch, game console in hand, typed pages and pen next to her. She maneuvers her avatar through a devastated landscape. Stops. Makes a note on the paper. I can see she's impressed by what she's read. Maybe the paper she was grading was Megan's. This is another memory!

In my excitement, I stand up and grab the circuit board. "Thank you," I say, putting it in her hands.

"But it's her Moore's Law board."

I can see how much this means to Megan, even as she tries to protest that she can't take it. "I insist. Please. She'd want you to have it." Did I really just say that? How corny is that? And is it even true? Am I in a bad movie? Or am I rewarding Megan for helping spark another memory?

After Megan leaves, circuit board clutched to her chest, Jordan turns to me. "Why don't you call it a day? Mary and I can take care of the books." Jordan's too diplomatic, too good a friend, to tell me I am no use at all here.

"Okay," I concede. "Leave her desk for me. I'll finish it another day." I sound like I'm saving them some work, but in reality I'm thinking that maybe the only way I'll be able to piece together my life is to hold more of these objects as I sort through Grace's possessions. Use tactile evidence as a path to memory.

"When we're done with the books, we'll start on the file cabinet, and leave out anything we have questions about," Mary says.

"Thank you both," I say.

This time I'm the one who goes in for the hug with Mary. "You're fine," she whispers. I don't believe her, but I appreciate the encouragement.

"Mary, I'm going for lunch. I'll—," the speaker stops mid-sentence when she sees me. "Hannah. I didn't know you were here. I'm sorry. I can come back."

Ava wears a loose blouse over tight jeans and bright blue high-top Chucks. Her hair is in well-styled box braids. She could easily pass for a student, but is actually in her mid-forties, an accomplished art history scholar, and now interim department chair.

"Ava, hi. I was just leaving." Perfect cue to disentangle myself from Mary's embrace and make my exit. I pick up my bankers box, wave goodbye to Jordan and Mary, and move past Ava into the hall.

Instead of staying to talk to Mary, Ava follows me. "Can you join me for lunch?"

My new life is full of these dilemmas. Normally one wouldn't have to think about a proposition like that. You're either hungry or you're not, have the time, or don't. But while Grace has seen to my morning and evening meals, she hasn't yet provided me with any rules governing midday, so I'm on my own here and don't think fast enough to come up with a way to refuse. "Sure," I say, making a note to work up a set of excuses I can pull up on the spot so I don't get caught again.

"Great! Are you okay staying on campus? I have to meet some students after."

"That's fine."

"Do you want to leave that here?" Ava indicates the bankers box.

"Nah, it's not heavy." At least not physically. And I've had enough for one day and don't want to have to return to Grace's office.

"How are you doing?" Ava asks as we head down the hall. "That's probably a stupid question, isn't it. Forget I asked."

Ava is genuinely warm and considerate, and after that one slip, very good about keeping the conversation off my "situation" and on various school-related topics as we walk over to the campus center. "As if being interim chair weren't keeping me busy enough, some of my rising seniors want to organize a multimedia exhibit about the experience of Black and Brown students on campus for the fall semester. I said I'd help them brainstorm ideas. They're who I'm meeting today." Like many of the faculty of color on our predominantly white campus, Ava does more than seems humanly possible. On top of advising several student organizations, she's called on to serve on numerous committees related to diversity, equity, and inclusion.

By the time we're at the food court, I'm not even thinking about my "situation" because I'm too focused on what I'm going to have for lunch. So many choices, none of them excellent, but still, overwhelming to me.

"I'm going to get on the sandwich line," Ava says. "I find that to be the safest option."

Crisis averted, I get on line right behind her. She orders turkey on rye with cheddar, lettuce, tomatoes, mayo. I order the same thing, but with mustard instead of mayo, just to prove I can think for myself.

Settled at our table, Ava rips open a bag of chips. "God, I'm hungry. I run early in the morning, and then forget to have breakfast. By the time I've put in my two hours writing, I'm ravenous." She sips her iced tea. "Do you want any chips? I'll never finish all these." She holds out the bag for me.

"Thanks. I'm good."

"Are you? Good? There I go again. You don't have to answer that. Would you rather I kept talking? I can also shut up. You may not believe that, the way I've rattled on, but I can just as easily eat in silence."

Something about her tone and easy presence makes me believe her. "This is nice, actually," I say. "I haven't been out much since…"

"Is there anything I can do to help? Sort through the office, anything?"

I tell her she's welcome to any of the books Mary and Jordan are packing up. I know Grace would be happy for her to have them. Grace had hired and mentored Ava and had encouraged her to be interim chair of the art department while Grace was on sabbatical, even though Ava already heads up the African Diaspora Studies minor. Grace believes Ava is the only person alive who has actually mastered the ability to be in two places at once.

"Well, really, if there's anything I can do…" Ava says.

"You've got plenty on your plate," I say. "Lots of chair duties over the summer."

"I can't say Grace didn't warn me."

"And yet you manage to put in two hours of writing," I say.

"Every morning. I was hoping to have a very, and I mean very, rough draft of a paper by the end of the summer for a conference I'm presenting at in the fall. But since my term as interim chair started earlier than it was supposed to—," she cuts herself off, Grace's death being the cause for the interruption of her plans. Ava reaches across the table, touches my forearm for a second, then pulls her hand back as if she hadn't meant to overstep. "There I go again."

"You're fine, really," I say. To show her I mean it, and I do—I know how carefully academics monitor their research time—I ask her about her work.

"Are you familiar with the artist Bisa Butler?" Ava's as eager to change the subject as I am. "That's who I'm writing about now. She makes quilts—not that that descriptor does justice to her work—she makes portraits, life-sized, out of fabric. Since you could call them quilts, Faith Ringgold keeps coming into the piece, so I'm going to have to say something about her, also, though there's already a lot out there about Ringgold. But mostly I'm envisioning a whole series of essays about these Black women artists of the same generation. I already have one about Mickalene Thomas. And do you know Ellen Gallagher's work? She's next, I think."

"Sounds like the making of a book."

"From your lips to some university press's ear."

Ava's excitement reminds me of Grace's when she got onto a new project. She'd be telling me about it and it would be like hearing her think out loud. A rush of topics to explore, ideas for papers to deliver at conferences. A million thoughts coming out at once, flashes of inspiration sparking new ideas. I swear I'm paying attention to Ava, but Grace shimmers in the background. Grace coming home late one night, too keyed up to get into bed, so we sit in the living room while she tells me about this amazing job candidate, her choice for the position, who blew the other two finalists out of the water. "She's brilliant. Her area of study fits right in with my vision for making our department truly interdisciplinary. She can teach about the African Diaspora, popular culture, social change. She reminds me of me. Except younger. And Black." Grace collapses back, adrenaline gone now that she's said all that.

I see Grace, alive and vibrant, so completely present. And I hear Ava's voice telling me she'll send links to the artists she's been talking about.

I walk back to my car feeling better than I've felt since I got the call from the ER and my life exploded, pulverized into pieces I'd believed impossible to put back together. But today, between dealing with Grace's office and talking to Ava, I'm beginning to remember.

"Hannah!"

And Grace is calling to me. Wow. This memory thing is really powerful.

But apparently this is real, because I hear my name again, and louder this time. "Hannah! Wait up!" I turn to see a lively woman about Grace's age hurrying toward me.

"Ellen, hi," I say, one hand on my door handle, the other balancing the bankers box against the car while I open the back door. Ellen teaches women's and gender studies. We've served together on various committees over the years. She dresses in arty tops and skirts and one-of-a-kind necklaces. She's smart and opinionated and a force to be reckoned with.

"Here, let me help you." Ellen tries to take the box from me, but I'm very reluctant to let it go. In our pulling, the top slips off, the box tips sideways, and out spill forty semesters' worth of postcards from Grace. Plus the photo albums, the loose photos scattered. Plus the good pens. Plus the small ceramic tray, which breaks. And the apple paperweight, which shatters. The framed wedding photo remains in the box, wedged under the notepads. The happy couple looks up at me because I'm still holding the box by one handle.

Ellen lets out a cry of dismay and immediately stoops to gather up what's salvageable. "Oh my god. I'm so sorry."

She's scooping the cards together, trying to be careful, but scraping them against the pavement. I'm sure they're going to be covered with grit. Same with the loose photos. I'm powerless to move, have to perch on the backseat, my feet still on the ground, box at a precarious angle.

Ellen rises with a handful of cards and photos and ever so gently levels the box in my lap so she can replace the items. She gets on her hands and knees to look under the car, rises shaking her head. "I'm afraid some things broke. But here," she hands me three pens she was able to salvage. "There's a few more under the car."

I don't bother to look. I'm numb, but Ellen's face reveals the devastation I probably should be feeling. She's still apologizing. I tell her I'm fine, really, but she stands by the Prius for a few moments before finally heading toward her own car. She turns back abruptly and says, "No more apology, but at least let me take you to dinner."

"Okay." I say it to end our exchange. But Ellen just stands there. What else does she want?

"Are you free tomorrow night?"

A commitment is what she wants.

She takes my silence as an answer. "Great. How about seven?" Ellen hesitates, and I sense she wants to apologize again, but instead she turns and waves goodbye. "I'll text you tomorrow afternoon and we can decide where to go."

I secure the box on the backseat as best I can—a little like closing the barn door after the cows got out. Then I get behind the wheel and drive off.

I don't know if I'm sad about what broke or thrilled that I've recalled some scenes from my life with Grace, all of which I had thought was lost to me. But what if what broke held the key to full recall?

In my mind's eye, I see the tiny pieces of the shattered glass apple glittering on the pavement. I hear Grace all those years ago when she returned from that conference in Chicago: "Close your eyes."

I obey.

"Put out your hands."

I hold them open, palms raised.

Grace moves them together, cups my palms, places a heavy, solid object in them. "Okay. Open."

And the weight is revealed. "An apple for my favorite teacher."

I look at Grace. She has tears in her eyes. She looks so sincere.

And then she's gone again, and I see where I really am, in the present. Today. Here. Still in my car, now parked at the house. My cupped hands are empty. And I am bereft.

When I can finally open the car door and head to the house, I go straight inside. I don't even bring the bankers box. What are a few paltry snippets of memory out of twenty-five years of a life together?

6

A Thousand Words

Our house is small, but we made sure we'd each have our own workspace in it. Those rooms were sacred, private. And while we shared housecleaning responsibilities, we were each responsible for our own study. Since mine doubles as the guest room, in addition to a desk and functional bookcase, it contains a sofa and coffee table. Grace and I were compatible in that we tolerated the same amount of clutter, but our home offices could range from pristine to storm-ravaged depending on where we were in the semester, or if one of us had a looming deadline.

I still haven't entered Grace's space. Yes, I put the urn in there. And before that, right after the accident—the death, let's be accurate—Mary had come by to pick up a set of graded papers to distribute to Grace's students, and I ventured in to get them for her. But that was just a quick in and out. I didn't have to look around or rummage through stacks of books or papers—her course folder was ready to go. I thought then that I might tackle the space, but if her papers and books weren't enough to deter me, her dark computer monitor was. A maze of passwords and documents and paperless billing awaited. I was at the bottom of a sheer cliff with no visible route to the top. What do I even do with all this, I thought as I backed out of the room closing the door. I'd spent the rest of that evening in front of the television.

Today, fortified by my modest success on campus, I resolve to at least make a start on Grace's study. I want to trigger more memories. At least I think I do.

Though once I'm standing outside the door, avoidance seems a reasonable option.

No, it really isn't. Go ahead. Be brave.

For whatever crazy reason, I knock first, something we always did when the other was working and we were going to interrupt. Given my running conversations with her, it isn't all that strange that I don't want to disturb her.

Well, yes, it is, I remind myself. Grace is dead. So yes, I do worry just a little that I'm talking to my dead spouse, more concerned when I believe she's actually talking to me. I hope that I'm merely talking to myself, walking myself through this awful, awful time, and not cracking up.

I take a few steps into the room and look around. Like her campus office, Grace's study is in productive disarray, waiting for its occupant to return to work any moment. Piled onto the comfortable armchair she rarely sat in because she was always at her desk: the briefcase she sometimes carried, two tote bags, four neatly labeled file folders, five books half-hidden by a sweater tossed carelessly over everything, probably removed in the heat of some task, Grace too absorbed to pay attention to where it landed. Three pairs of drugstore reading glasses: on the table next to the chair, on her desk, hooked on the handle of the briefcase. One glass of water, its contents long evaporated.

Oh, and one funeral urn.

Unlike her more ordered campus office, I avoid the over-crowded bookcases, these shelves stuffed with memorabilia and photographs.

I'd like to say I'm undaunted, but I'm just the opposite. I'm very, very daunted. What am I going to do with all this? Maybe I don't have to do anything yet. Just keep breathing and being in this room. Which is when I realize I've also been holding my breath. I exhale. Inhale. Exhale slowly. I still haven't stepped an inch further into the space.

Come on, ya big chicken. You made it this far. You're here to mine memories, remember?

Okay. But first: Grace. "Sorry, honey. I don't want you to watch while I do this." I pick up the urn and take it to our bedroom. Since I'm only in there to get dressed these days, that feels the safest place for her. Or makes me feel safer. I leave the urn on the dresser.

When I return to Grace's study, odd, but I feel alone now. I cross to her desk chair, take a deep breath and sit down, careful not to touch anything.

I sit for a long time that way, hands on the arms of the chair, like I'm braced for takeoff. I have to really focus my breathing to slow my pulse.

A couple of times my hand moves as if I'm going to start a task, maybe sort through the pile of papers to the left of her computer. That would be her most recent stack. I could learn what she was working on before she left the house. What kept her from driving in with me as she normally would have on a day when we had social plans. But my hand doesn't budge. I don't align the mess of papers or create neat stacks I could examine. I'm afraid to move even a loose paper clip. Since I started cleaning out our offices, everything I've done feels like one step further into my new life. One detail more in solidifying the reality of Grace's death. I've kept myself in this dark, narrow tunnel that connects my life with Grace, my past, to what is to come, my life without her.

What lies behind me, where I've come from, is rich with experience and memories, even if I can't access them at the moment. Ahead is a vast blank area. Or maybe it's filled in, but it's all blurry. I can't recognize anything. As long as I stay within the confines of this restrictive tunnel, the present, I can manage. Just barely. But that counts, doesn't it?

And vast is probably the wrong word—there's a lot less ahead of me than behind.

Focus. Grace's study.

Since our studies were our sacred spaces, you didn't disturb anything without specific permission. Didn't dust, tidy, or organize. Didn't shut off or turn on a machine. Everything was right where it was supposed to be, no matter what it looked like to the other person. But that's not why I'm afraid to disturb the organized mess in front of me. Not just habit: respect for Grace's process. She always needs a certain amount of disarray to feel productive. I realize that I'm afraid to move anything because when she comes back, she won't be able to find whatever she's looking for. Of course, that isn't a conscious rationale on my part.

"Or a rational rationale," I say out loud.

I keep catching myself in this strange middle ground of doing what I always do—saving up things to tell Grace when she comes home, like how I gave her student Megan the big circuit board. And that Ava is already department chair. I even want to tell her about her death—she'd get a kick out of some of the stories. All of them, really. It doesn't make sense. That thought strikes me a thousand times a day. How little sense all this makes. I would never sit at Grace's desk if she were home. No.

Not home—alive. Not that I wouldn't come into the room to talk to her, or to leave a note or letter on her keyboard where I knew she'd see it. But I never sat here when she was out, certainly not when she was home. This room is her private space. It's so ingrained that I don't belong here—I keep slipping in and out of what's real.

Focus. The only reason I'm sitting at Grace's desk now is because she's dead, and I need to deal with this shit. Also: I want my memories back.

I take a deep, cleansing breath and pull the chair closer. When I bump into the desk by accident, the computer sparks to life, and the dark screen is replaced by Grace's home screen.

I scan the dock at the bottom to see what apps she had open. Maybe they'd provide clues I could use. Use to what end? What am I even looking for?

I've pondered so long that Grace's screen saver comes on. The stunning display startles me. I'm used to my thirteen-inch laptop screen, and this monitor is a ginormous twenty-seven-inches.

Instead of a stock screensaver, Grace had chosen random photos she took—places we visited, the garden in all different seasons, the way light fell across a flower arrangement in the living room. Pictures that wouldn't make sense to anyone but us, some only to her. Why'd you take that, they'd probably ask if they saw the image of croissant flakes on a section of the *New York Times*, jammy knife on the saucer of an empty coffee cup. To us, it meant our Sunday breakfast routine. Or hyacinth bulbs lying in shallow holes in rich soil, a marker of how she'd arranged them before covering them up with dirt. A photographic note to herself, a reminder of where they were in case she wanted to put in some annuals. The images crowd each other on the screen, then fold over or down before giving way to the next set. I sit transfixed, letting them cycle through more than once. It's like looking into Grace's memory. Not that I believe Grace has achieved singularity with her computer—though if anybody could, it'd be Grace, given how much respect she had for the machine's capabilities. I feel closer to her than I have since she died—on the cusp of remembering more details of our life. Maybe her photos will help me in my quest.

I tap the mouse to restore the home screen in order to begin my investigation. Grace had several tabs open: email, a search engine, news articles. I scan the dock at the bottom of the screen. Black dots under applications indicate which are running: Safari, Google, Word, Excel, her calendar, Spotify. I'm surprised to see Photo Booth is open. When I click on it, my face pops on the screen. I look a lot surprised, a little puzzled. Now I see the green light indicating the computer's camera is on.

I grab a pen and use it as a microphone. "Hannah Greene, coming to you live from Professor Grace Black's office." Then I drop the pretense. "Hey," I say. "Hey Grace." It sounds so right, so familiar to say those words. It's how we always started our emails, phone messages. "Hey Hannah." "Hey Grace." It was a joke at first, coming out of our laments at students' lack of respect for their faculty, too often starting their emails with "Hey" rather than "Professor" or, in Grace's case, "Doctor."

I look only at the little green dot, because then I'm not looking at myself. In some crazy way, I feel like I'm communicating directly with Grace. I'm oddly comforted by the act of talking to this device that holds so much of who my love is. Was. Her words, her correspondence, her course files, her credit card statements. Her books and articles. Notes and memos. Games. Those photographs. God knows what else. What her new project is going to be. I know at some point I'll have to dig around, and then both god and I will know all that this mighty machine holds. But not today. Not right now. Right now, all I want to do is talk to Grace.

I'm comfortable for the first time since she died. And I keep talking. I give myself permission, carte blanche, no concern for whether or not this is crazy.

I tell Grace everything. What happened in the hospital. The funeral home. The funeral. I fill her in on the day's activities—the broken paperweight. And the moderate progress I'm making in my office at school. And that I have to return to hers. How I can't remember our life—what we did, how it felt. How I don't know how to get it back.

Some of this stuff I've already told her, but it feels different in here. Official. When I finally run out of steam, I sit back in her chair. I exhale. And only then do I notice the row of pictures under the big image of my face. There she is. My Grace. Very much alive. A whole row of her. I click on one where she's mugging for the camera, head tossed back and to the side, eyes looking up. I'm sure she's imitating some famous portrait, but

I can't remember which. I study her. I lean as close to the screen as possible. Can I detect any signs of ill health, weakness, anything that would foreshadow what happened? I see nothing. The next is a variation on that pose. The third is a video. I impulsively press play. There's my Grace. Alive. In motion. Her voice comes across loud and clear.

"Unaccustomed as I am to public speaking..." she cracks herself up. Her laughter is infectious, catches me unaware. Delight reaches right through my grief and astonishment at hearing her, seeing her. She starts talking again, and after a few false starts and resets, she launches into a serious acknowledgment of the momentous occasion that is my retirement. I realize she's rehearsing what she's planning to say at my party.

Grace hates speaking in public. Giving a lecture or a talk is one thing, but something like this would tie her in knots, so she always prepared. I see her look down and cross out some words. I want to find the piece of paper she was writing on, but I'm too focused on Grace. Grace alive. Grace going about her day. She finishes writing and starts talking again. Then she pauses for a second, tilts her head. I'm surprised to hear myself calling to her from offscreen: "Hey, Grace! Come on. We'll be late." Do I detect annoyance in my voice?

Without pausing the recording, Grace yells over her shoulder: "I need to finish up here. I'll drive in later. You go ahead without me."

"You're the one who doesn't like ending up with two cars." Yes. Clearly annoyance. "We're supposed to go out with the J's after."

"For dinner. I know," Grace answers patiently.

I'm caught in a time warp, want to turn around and yell to myself on the other side of the door, "Don't you know this is your last conversation? And you want to be annoyed? At *nothing*. This was *nothing*."

"I know, sweetie. I really need to finish this." She tilts her head, waiting for my response. When none comes, she calls out, "Bye! Love you!" Then she turns back to her notes, forgetting the camera. I watch her write, mouth the words, edit. She finally looks up at the camera. "Who needs you?" she says and shuts it off.

I'm too stunned to move. She isn't speaking to me, who needs you— she'd clearly finished her speech and didn't need the machine. But I need her. I simply hit "play" again. And again. Again.

As I watch and re-watch, I can't help but think: What if she'd stopped rehearsing and driven in with me that morning. What if I'd insisted? Stuck my head in and demanded she come now—it was my fucking retirement party, after all. Would things have ended differently? Would I have been able to get her to the hospital, or summon paramedics? Not according to what the doctor said. But maybe, maybe it wouldn't have happened at all. What if one slight variation in the fabric had changed the design completely?

Seeing Grace ends my memory hunt for the moment. I wander through the house, unable to land anywhere, unsure what to do next. I plop on the couch, turn on the television, and navigate to the recorded shows.

For the life of me, I could never see what Grace saw in *Grey's Anatomy*. She'd record the show during the semester so she could catch up during the summer. She knew it was soapy, corny. Cheesy, our students would say. Grace referred to the characters as her people. They're not my people. My people is Grace, and she's now nothing but bits of bone and oily ashes. So I watch because she watched. I find I do care about these people and their mixed-up lives and their episodic, serial calamities. I can't keep track of all the plane crashes and accidents and who lost which lover through death, abandonment, infidelity, or geography. But I can't bring myself to erase any of the episodes she recorded. I've started to watch one or two a night, in addition to sporadic insomniac viewings. Or like now, when I don't know what else to do.

Have I mentioned that I haven't cried since Grace died?

I didn't cry at the hospital when she died. I went home alone and stretched out on the couch in my study—couldn't imagine going into our bedroom—and lay there, waiting for the tears to come. But I couldn't be calm, couldn't even manage counting. And then my heart raced and the air around me shimmied and vibrated. I felt like Grace was there, or maybe like she was saying a final goodbye.

Almost immediately, I fell into a black hole. Not literally. I was lying on the couch, but I could feel myself falling. Grace wasn't there. I had no memories. I wasn't missing this thing about her, or that, or her voice. She wasn't there. I was barely there. Just this wild plummet into an abyss. And still no tears. It's not that I'm not sad, not devastated. I'm just not a crier.

It's been five tearless weeks now, and I'm not sure I've climbed out of that abyss yet. The *Grey's Anatomy* characters are still not my people, but now I want them all to get what they want because I know what it means to have had what you wanted, and to have realized it at the time, not taken it for granted. I just want them to be happy, I realize. And at some point in each episode, for a split second, tears well in my eyes. Huh, I think, isn't that interesting.

I allow myself one episode then force myself to be productive. I open the front door to confront the package that had been waiting for Grace the day of her funeral. I circle it warily a few times, then shove it with my foot. It's big, maybe two feet by three feet, but not that heavy. I dig my little knife out of my pocket—you know the old lesbian joke: how can you tell the butches from the femmes? The femmes carry their Swiss Army knives in their purses. Ha ha—slice through the packing tape, take a deep breath, and dig out a top layer of packing material.

That Grace. She loved her coffee. Was obsessed with finding the right gadgets—though I couldn't get away with calling them that in her presence. Appliance, tool, system—with which to brew, steep, press, pour-over, whatever, the perfect cup of Joe. I'll bet we have an entire section of the barn filled with the seemingly infinite numbers of grinders, pots, makers, filters, storage containers, foamers, frothers, and assorted coffee-related gewgaws she'd accumulated over the years.

So now the joke's on me. Or on her. I can't tell which. Here's the latest in a long and now finite line of appliances. Because this buck stops with me. I mean really, it's just coffee, right?

I lift the box out of the plain brown shipping package. It's a glossy, deluxe four-color job, showing the machine prominent in the background, but foregrounded by a luscious-looking display of the many possible coffee beverages you can now produce in your own home.

Don't get me wrong. It's not that I don't like coffee. I just don't pay it as much attention as Grace does. Did. But I must have known when I opened its package that I wasn't going to return this machine, out of some loyalty or mixed-up sense of if she were alive she'd be so excited to set it up and demonstrate to me all that it can do.

I confess, once I get the thing out of its box, it's quite handsome. And doesn't take up a lot of room. Grace would tell me it has a small footprint—that would be her way of trying to convince me that it isn't going to clutter up the coffee area. Yes, our kitchen has a designated coffee area. And it's a large footprint. This new machine fits right in. It's black. Not just black, but *piano* black. Discreet and unobtrusive. I look at the instructions. It comes with a separate stylish device for foaming hot or cold milk, because, turns out, all it does is make espresso.

Maybe because I feel like I just spent time with Grace, I decide I need an espresso right now. I don't care if it's past 4:00 p.m., my caffeine cutoff hour. It's not like I sleep through the night anyway.

I lug the machine into the kitchen. I follow the setup instructions, which are pretty simple, and soon am watching the syrupy liquid fill an espresso cup. (Just because Grace isn't here doesn't mean I'm going to ignore protocol and use a *regular* cup. I have some standards, after all. And she trained me well). The foam at the top, the *crema*, is thick and perfect. Looks just like what you get at a café. Impressed, I take a cautious sip.

It's fucking delicious. So delicious that I make myself another cup and march with it straight into Grace's office and drop into her desk chair, palm the mouse. I look directly into the green light, hold up the cup to show her and say, "Hey Grace. I don't know if you planned to keep this machine at home or bring it to your office or what, but it's staying right where it is."

Two sips and I've finished the drink. Reluctant to leave Grace—and possibly a little amped on the caffeine—I open her Spotify and hit play. Jazz piano fills the room. I check what I'm listening to. Ahmad Jamal. Nice. Grace compiled this playlist called "Music to Work By." I'm comfortable enough now to look around. A small package neatly wrapped in plain red paper sits on a pile of books stacked by her armchair. I pick it up. It feels like a tiny book, not much bigger than a pack of 3x5 index cards. And it's very light.

The music has changed to something more upbeat. "Golden Days" by King Pleasure, whom I've never heard of, but what a great name. I screw up my courage and carefully peel open the wrapping to preserve the paper, keeping it intact so I can pass this along to whomever Grace had intended it for.

Turns out, it's for me. When we were in Venice the year before, we'd wandered across the Accademia Bridge into a quiet neighborhood and stumbled into a shop filled with gorgeous handmade paper. This had been one of several notebooks I'd admired and yet declined to buy.

"Why not?" Grace wanted to know.

"How many blank journals do I need?"

"What, there's a limit?"

"No. But—"

"How many blank journals from Venice do you have?"

She had a point there.

"With handmade paper—look at these details. Check out the binding."

"I don't need it, Grace."

"This isn't about need, honey. You could use it to write down ideas."

I gave her a hard stare. She knew how I felt about writing. About not writing.

"Ideas for your retirement."

She knew I was anxious about that.

"Then I'll get one closer to the time I'm going to need it. It's over a year away."

Grace had known better than to argue with me.

Though who actually won that argument, since here I am holding this tiny blank book in my hands. She'd obviously gone back and bought it for me.

I flip through its ivory pages. Only then do I see Grace's precise handwriting at the front of the book: Hannah's Retirement Planner. She even dated it: May 2019. No re-gifting this.

Whether it was the easy swing of the music or the tactile prodding of the little book, I've had another memory. Which triggers a fleeting image of Grace, reading glasses perched on her nose, listening to music and reading, pencil in hand to make notes in the margins of the book. A memory *and* a sighting!

Inspired, I grab one of Grace's pens, open a new page in my beautiful journal, and write the number one, a period, and then...what? GET OVER G's DEATH. I cross that out as soon as I've written it. SCATTER G's ASHES. That gets a line through it as well. START A NEW LIFE. Scratch that. REMEMBER YOUR OLD LIFE! That's more like it.

Inspired by my progress at home, I've gone to my office determined to make actual headway.

I have King Pleasure playing loudly on my computer, the door open to facilitate my passage down the hall to the large recycling bin.

I'm sorting through old syllabi, student evals, handouts, on the odd chance there's something I actually want to keep, when someone passes my door. I see this in my peripheral vision, so it's natural to distrust what I think I saw. Still, I stand in my doorway and look down the hall.

How could this be?

"Hey, Grace!" I call out.

The figure stops, turns around, and walks back toward me. I am stunned to see her because, well, because she's dead.

Yet here she is, large as life, moving toward me.

"Grace, where have you been?"

"I moved into student housing."

I'm stunned. So happy because here she is. Puzzled because she hadn't told me she was doing this. Relieved. Then furious. Then wide awake, bolt upright in the chair in Grace's office. At home.

It takes me a little time to come back to the present, to realize I'd been dreaming.

But the dream was so real I still smell her perfume. Now I feel betrayed. Then pissed off.

"Cut that out!" I yell at her, looking around the room. "It's one thing for me to talk to you when I'm awake." How could I explain this to her? What logic covered the ecosystem I've been living in—feeling her presence, getting those messages from her. Even writing them down. Starting to remember things. Maybe that's why the dream felt so real, made sense. When she was alive, we didn't have to be in the same place to be connected.

Not only had I not encountered Grace, who is still dead, I hadn't actually gone back to my office on campus, a fact I'm reminded of by the crick in my neck.

I move from Grace's armchair to her desk chair, address her computer. "Hey Grace," I start. And I lay into her for playing a mean trick on me, showing up in my dream like that. Dreams, actually, since this was at least the second time I'd had it. But really, dying was the meanest trick.

I return to the kitchen and cross off "coffee" on my How to Keep It Simple list and write "espresso." Then I unplug and/or dismantle every other coffee appliance. I manage to fit most of them into the shipping box and original box the new machine came in and schlep it all to the back door, ready to bring to school where someone will find a use for each item.

And now it's dinner time. Grace's photos must have inspired me since I add some dried basil to my canned tomato soup. "That makes me a chef, right?"

Right, Grace chuckles, **a lazy chef.**

That strikes me immediately: what a perfect name for a blog—The Lazy Chef. That's what I can do in my retirement: start a blog! Here's how the Lazy Chef makes...guacamole. Then I'll give 'em the recipe.

LAZY CHEF becomes the first official entry in my planner.

I'm not sure who's laughing at that, me or Grace.

That night I dream that Grace is going to teach me how to cook, but I don't have my apron so I go look for it in the attic, and when I come back, Grace isn't there.

I've given up trying to decipher the meaning of my dreams. Our house has no attic. No Grace anymore, either.

7

Dinner Out

The next morning, I have my retirement planner open in front of me. Pen poised over the page, again I'm at a loss for what to write. So far I've got a bunch of crossed-out lines and **1. Lazy Chef**. I stare at that for a while. A long while apparently, since I've made no further progress twenty minutes later.

It's not that I'm not curious. Or interested in things. Or have no ambition. Though how ambitious are seventy-year-olds these days, unless they're politicians? I was having trouble imagining my retirement before Grace died. Now, forget about it. But what do I think about all day? Grace? I guess. Maybe.

Not 100 percent true. Right now, I'm trying to come up with a way to get out of my dinner date with Ellen.

Maybe I should use the planner to brainstorm situations that could arise so that I have a prepared list of excuses for any eventuality: *We're going berry picking!* Love to, but, allergies. *Hiking in Watkins Glen!* Darn—my back's been bothering me. (An advantage of being old: people accept excuses like that, no questions asked.) *Just a few people over for dinner and game night—it'll be fun!* Alas, I already have plans.

Actually, that one could be my go-to. I wish I had landed on that elegant solution when Ellen asked me to dinner. Instead, I'd felt caught between the proverbial rock and a hard place. Saying no would have meant an extended conversation right there in the parking lot, which would probably have involved more apologizing on her part, so I put her off by accepting, knowing I'd cancel before having to meet her. Which I need to do in the next few minutes.

I walk through my silent house—first time I've named it mine. The rooms I spend time in are festooned with scraps of paper, post-its stuck to lamps or tables, books, framed photos. Reminders to do something, read something, find something. Tell Grace something. Maybe my little book would be a good repository for all these notes. Or a grief journal. Or evidence of my mental disintegration.

I force myself to cut some peonies and put them on the kitchen table, in the glass vase Ellen sent us when she heard we'd gotten married. Which reminds me: cancel dinner. I'm glad I was able to make myself do something "extra" to dress up the space even though no one would see it but me. Their fragrance swirls around me when I walk by. I also put some in the blue vase on the dresser in our bedroom, next to Grace. Peonies are her favorite. I hope she's happy in here. I know I'm happier with her in here, out of the way, where I won't run into her. I generally confine my activities to only three rooms, so the rest of the place stays just the way I like it. I have done everything in my power to maintain...what? Myself? The house?

Part of that upkeep is trying to eat. So I'm staring into the refrigerator when my phone vibrates in my pocket. I haven't been without it since I missed the call from the paramedics about Grace, even if I mostly let everything go to voicemail.

I check the screen and see a missed call from Ellen, but no message. I could tell her I was just thinking about her because I looked at the vase and remembered that I had a prior engagement for tonight. Maybe better, or easier, to do in a text. But I need to think about how I'm going to phrase it.

I re-pocket the phone and go back to the fridge. I've stocked it with the few things I've managed to stomach. Turns out yogurt isn't so bad after all. I have worked hard at feeding myself. It's almost routine again. At least the timing is, thanks to Grace. If I make a very thorough and specific list, I can manage the supermarket. But I can't always force myself to eat—except for the six-thirty dinner time. A deal's a deal.

This is one of those times when I just can't force myself. I close the fridge.

Now what?

That thought still hits me if I haven't made a firm enough plan for my day. How am I going to pull myself from one end of it to the other? Can I keep making busywork? I don't know, and Grace isn't offering any suggestions.

It's a pleasant enough afternoon. I could sit on the porch and read. Well, if I could manage reading. What if I sat out there and tried reading? I promised myself that I would be "productive." Which means what, now that I'm retired? I need to redefine productive.

The phone vibrates. Ellen again. Shit. I've dithered so long I never texted back to cancel our dinner. A slight breeze—unsourced—crosses my face. I turn to look back down the hall. Only someone crossing my path—someone's presence—could have stirred the air. Grace has her way of telling me what to do. As I said, she's bossier now that she's dead.

I take the hint. I swipe answer and bring the vibrating phone to my ear. "Hello?"

"Hi," Ellen says. "We never set a time for dinner."

"Actually," I start to make an excuse.

But my moment passes because Ellen doesn't really pause for a response. "How about six?"

I honor my commitment to Grace by asking if we can make it six-thirty.

Ithaca and its environs are a haven for foodies. Pizza, Mexican, Korean, Vietnamese, Chinese, Indian, Middle Eastern, and Italian restaurants abound. Plus every fast and fast-casual chain. But Ellen and I choose the only French restaurant in town. We have a big booth to ourselves.

The restaurant has a more urban than Ithaca feel. It's narrow and deep. Six booths along the wall, three of them opposite the kitchen. The other three, one of which is ours this evening, have a view of the well-stocked bar. Six stools to accommodate patrons for either drinks or food service, three of which are occupied by hipsters whose tight jeans, short hair, and deliberate beards wouldn't be out of place in Brooklyn.

Ellen orders a cocktail, so I go for a Negroni, which is Grace's favorite. We share a plate of olives as we study the menu.

At least I study the menu. I look up to see Ellen studying me. Or maybe I'm just imagining that. I ask her what she's going to have.

"The steak frites. I always think I'll get something else, but I never do."

Also Grace's favorite. "I'll get that, too."

"Are you always this easy?" Ellen asks.

She's smiling. Was that a serious question? Or is she flirting with me? Why would she do that? When the waiter arrives and Ellen orders for both of us, I don't mind. Maybe I am easy? I'm very happy with my drink. It's smooth and not quite sweet. And it does take the edge off my anxiety about being out with a woman who isn't Grace.

Not out. I mean, we're out, but it's not like a date.

Date? Why would that word even enter my mind?

Another sip. Remember Grace's rules about how to talk to people: Use your words; pay attention! Since I'm not talking, I focus on what Ellen is saying.

"I used to love running into you and Grace. You always seemed so happy together. I don't mean bubbly, bouncy happy. Just like you really enjoyed each other and whatever you were doing."

She's not looking to me for a response, so I sip my drink as she talks. Did we run into Ellen a lot? Possibly. I guess at school functions. And parties. Maybe. I never noticed other women. I mean, of course I did. I was married, not dead. My relationship, even before we got married, shielded me. Not from temptation, infidelity never occurred to me, but made me able to just be. Made situations not fraught. Not that I'd have noticed anyway. I was never good at picking up if someone was coming on to me.

Ellen talks. The bartender mixes sophisticated cocktails, squeezes a twist of orange rind around the rim of a glass before dropping it in. He carries the drink to a booth at the back. The scent of orange wafts in his wake and triggers an almost memory—Los Angeles, driving the 405 at night, windows open. Am I alone? Is Grace with me? Is she driving, or am I?

A hand on my arm. I'm not in a car.

"Are you okay?" Ellen asks.

"Can you smell that?" I scoop my hand in front of my face as if to move the scent closer, turn to follow the bartender and his nostalgic cocktail.

"What? I'm afraid I can't."

"From the orange rind."

Ellen looks at me like *Oh, poor dear*. Then returns to what she was saying, which was something about finding me funny, always something to lighten the mood if discussions got tense.

I don't remember, which doesn't surprise me, especially these days.

Stop drifting! Pay attention.

"I put all my energy into my work," Ellen says. "My writing projects and my teaching. And I love to travel. You can find conferences just about anywhere in the world if you're determined enough."

"And you are?"

"So determined. And it was wonderful."

"Was? It got old?"

"No. My mother got old. After my father died. Mom was still pretty independent, but keeping up the house got harder for her. That's why I took the job at Hollander, so I could be closer to her. I grew up about ten minutes from the school. She still lives in the same house."

I make a note to tell Grace, who'd always wondered why someone with Ellen's credentials wasn't teaching at a big university. Then remember that there would be no telling Grace anything anymore. Though that hasn't stopped her from telling me things: Use your words. Don't assume people know what you're thinking. I venture, "Do you spend a lot of time with your mother?" It's been years since I've had to take parents into consideration.

"I do. We have dinner a few nights a week now. During the semester, I only go out there on Sundays. But I check in with her just about every day. Whenever I think about retiring, I remember I'm my mother's sole support and have to keep at it a while longer. You're lucky."

Those last words have hardly crossed the table when she reaches over and grabs my forearm. "I'm so sorry. I didn't mean...I meant...you're lucky you could retire."

"No. It's fine. I mean...I am lucky. Or was lucky." I grab my drink, but it's just a huge fancy ice ball that bangs against my nose when I sip.

"I'm sorry." Ellen pulls her hand back. "I'm doing a lot of apologizing, aren't I. You think I'd know better at my age. I'm going to be sixty-two next month."

I mock sigh. "Ah, I remember when I was your age."

"I thought we were the same age."

"I'm seventy."

Ellen looks genuinely surprised. "I had no idea."

I risk exposing myself as shallow and ageist: "I confess I love that response."

"You certainly don't look it. You look great. Though why wouldn't you, I mean…" And her hand shoots out again.

I shouldn't read anything into this. She's just a touchy sort of person.

"I feel like I missed my relationship window and now I'm just here and trying to figure out what's next," Ellen says. "Which is okay. Overall, I really like my life."

What's that supposed to mean? Is there a "but" lurking, as in "I really like my life but…" I still feel her hand on my arm even though she's using both her hands to hold the wine list.

The waiter arrives with our food. After a brief discussion with him, Ellen orders us each a glass of Primitivo.

"I hope you don't mind," she says when he leaves. "I think it'll be really nice with our steak. And I remember you like red."

"You do?"

"When we were both on the dean's search committee and were all taken out to dinner at the end. You ordered red even though you were having fish, and Frank teased you about it."

I don't remember the occasion at all. I didn't even remember that Ellen had been on the committee. But that's something I'd definitely do. And Frank's an idiot.

As I said, I have never been very good at reading the signs, even when I was young and single, but despite my distracted state of mind I can pick up on the way Ellen has been taking care of me. The ordering. The touching. And in a strange way, I feel I'm being unfaithful to Grace.

Which is ridiculous because, well, do I even need to say why that makes no sense?

Whether it's the Negroni plus the Primitivo—which is truly delicious, big and chewy and rich, a gorgeous deep red—or just the fact that I'm out for dinner with a beautiful woman—and yes, I may be in mourning but I'm not dead, I have eyes—I hear conversation and realize that it's not coming from any of the other tables, but is one that Ellen and I are having. I'm surprised I'm able to participate as much as I do. We've covered the usual—origin stories (when we came out, how many times), discussed people and politics on campus—and somehow got around to the rise of the internet and how our lives changed because of it. We have the same love-hate relationship with our gadgets. Ellen says, "I remember when I thought it was crazy to email someone who worked on the same floor. Why wouldn't you just walk down the hall and talk to the person?"

"Right?"

"And now it's not even email. Texts."

"Grace and I text each other when we're in different rooms at home."

Big pause after Ellen and I both catch my use of the present tense. I go somewhere as dark and complex as my wine. Or what's left of my wine. Ellen starts to reach across the table to me but stops. She's got a concerned look on her face, but also concentrated, like she's trying to do the right thing, read me and take care without crossing any lines or being misinterpreted.

I surprise myself by being the one who breaks the silence. "I need to get out of my head and more into my body." I don't know if I'm the blushing type, but if I were, that's when I would have. "That didn't come out right. I'm not used to talking these days. I meant, do some exercise. I spend a lot of time alone. I'm not sure exactly what I do all day, but I wake up and then eventually it's time to go to bed. I don't really have a routine anymore. I try to get myself to come into town, but it's a schlep. And there's no reason to. I'm trying to figure out what to do so I don't spend all my time in my head. Rather than doing something. That's what I meant by 'in my body.'"

Ellen doesn't say anything.

I gulp the last sip of my wine. "I used to play tennis. I stopped after college."

Ellen latches onto that theme. "I saw Martina play at a tournament in Palm Springs. She could barely get through the crush of her lesbian fans to make it to the court. There's a whole group that follow the women's tennis circuit."

"Did she use her racquet like a machete?" I make a swinging motion.

We each laugh more than the remark warrants, but we're back on course. I make it through dinner, decline the offer to share a dessert, and when Ellen tries to pay for my meal, I protest.

"Come on," she says. "This was supposed to be me making up for breaking your stuff."

"You don't need to. Really."

"You're on a fixed income now," she says with a smile. Then, more serious, "Please."

We compromise—how lesbian of us!—and I pay the tip. And then we're outside the restaurant. I'm holding a box of leftover steak and frites which I know I don't ever want to see again, but I'd felt too guilty to return my half-eaten food to the kitchen.

"Thanks for coming out," Ellen says. "I hope we can do this again."

I don't have time to respond before Ellen closes in and gives me a big hug.

Though it feels very good, being held by this woman who missed her relationship window, I can't let myself relax completely, and extricate myself from her embrace.

Ellen nods, as if to say, I understand. "Are you okay to drive? I'm just a few blocks away. I've got a guest room."

"I'm fine. Really."

But as soon as I get in my car, I realize I'm not fine at all. This was the first time I've spent outside our inner circle. I did okay, didn't I? But what was that body remark? Dumb. Did I give the wrong impression? How many other gaffes had I made? Did I comment out loud about the guys whose beards I wanted to shave off? When did our little town become hipster haven? Did I say that out loud, too?

I resort to counting: Three men with beards I wanted to shave off. Six booths. Six stools at the bar. Two tables in the front window. One fragrance. Four times Ellen touched my arm. One almost memory.

Stone cold sober now, aching for Grace, I drive as fast as I can to return to the safety of my couch.

8
Arrivals

A few mornings after my dinner with Ellen, I'm half asleep and still in my blissful split-second of forgetting Grace has died, so it's perfectly natural for me to hear her voice: **"What's up with the garden?"**

"Huh?" I murmur, only half awake.

"It's practically summer, and what have you done?"

Is she serious?

"Did you do *any* raking?"

Apparently very serious. I grab my pad and pen.

"You should have done this already. Get the top layer of matted leaves and old mulch off the places where I've planted bulbs. But do it carefully. You might be able to rescue what's already started to come up."

I just want to reclaim some memories, not turn into Farmer Joan. If the garden means so much to you, you take care of it.

Boom.

I'm fully awake now. No sense lying in bed.

"Bed" being a metaphor, since I'm still sleeping on the couch in the living room. And "sleeping" being a euphemism for making myself lie there for a certain amount of time, no fewer than four hours. Four *consecutive* hours.

Don't judge. This is a marked improvement.

I've also tried to be better about communicating with friends. I told Jordan about my dinner with Ellen. Not a blow-by-blow, just that it happened. She takes that as a sign I'm "doing better." I'm not sure what "doing better" means exactly. I lump it in the same category as having a good day. Grief is not linear. That much I do know.

I down my first espresso while waiting for the toast to pop. I can almost eat a whole piece. Yay. Progress. That's "doing better." I let the Lazy Chef take over and spread some pre-packaged guacamole on it—way to improvise! More Progress! I write down as much as I remember of Grace's orders, not because I want to do the work. I'm hoping it might trigger some memories. Where did she plant bulbs? Did I help with that? Didn't I see some pictures on her computer? I'll have to check. I eat my toast standing at the counter. I'm allowed to do all sorts of things like that now, not set a table, or even use a table. Then I make a double espresso and take it onto the front porch, where I eye the garden as if sizing up an opponent.

Our house—my house—sits on a couple of acres of land, most of which we leave as is. Once the grass starts growing, a neighbor's son will ride over on his mower every couple of weeks. We have our own riding mower that Grace loved using but had to give up when she became department chair because what she called "administrative caca" ate up too much of her time. I won't touch the thing. I suppose I'm going to sell it now. But that's way down on the priority list. Only slightly higher at this moment is the garden. Grace had sectioned off a small patch that's a formal, well, informal, garden with flowers and vines. That's what she woke me up about—as well as an adjacent herb and vegetable garden. That one is fenced in to protect it from deer. Though they're perfectly happy eating the flowers, so why we don't just let them have it all, I'll never know.

No matter how much I tried to muster the enthusiasm for the gardens, not to match Grace's, but at least to be her companion in the work, I never managed to. I took a certain amount of pride in being an adequate sous gardener, doing whatever Grace instructed. But I don't have the instinct nor the inclination to get out there on my own. And since Grace died, it's been the furthest thing from my mind.

Even this morning, after Grace's directive and specific instructions, I can't muster the energy to do more than survey our land. A path connects the two gardens and leads past the barn/garage and to our pond. I can't think past the barn yet, and don't force myself to.

It's a glorious day. Gorgeous clouds in a bright blue sky. Cumulus clouds, I believe. The big puffy ones. High up. Does that make them altocumulus? What are the other kinds? Stratus. Nimbus? Is that a cloud or just a word? Nimbostratus? And there's cirrus. And I think fog is clouds.

But Grace is right—summer is arriving. What once would thrill me about the season—the greens, the richness, the slower pace—is playing out in front of me and leaves me numb.

Is that true? Even with that blue sky? Does that spark anything in me?

Despite having lived out here all these years, I'm always a little surprised how much I like it. Growing up in a city, I never believed I'd be happy outside one, so I couldn't imagine appreciating the quiet or, more importantly, the solitude of being in the country. Granted, we're – I'm – just thirty minutes outside an active college town, which is very civilized for its size. A perk of our jobs was that they afforded us the ability to leave every so often for vacations as well as academic conferences, sometimes combining the two. Whenever Grace and I traveled to a big city, we'd think of moving back to one. So much to do, so much excitement. The noise! The crowds! And for Grace especially, the art. Yet after a few days, or a week, no matter how much we'd enjoyed ourselves, we'd be ready to leave. Mostly, we liked being home and figured there'd be plenty of time later to think about retiring somewhere else.

So much for that.

Can I be happy here again? Or anywhere, ever again? What does it mean, to be happy? Maybe being happy isn't the only happiness.

I let my mind fill with what's in front of me: our garden and our property as it slopes down to the road.

What I appreciate about our road is that no one uses it. There's only ours and three other houses on it. It doesn't lead anywhere, just loops off and back around to a county road that intersects with the main route into town. The most traffic we get is the mail truck, the occasional delivery service, and our neighbors.

So I'm very surprised to see a green Subaru Forester come down the road.

More than surprised. I mean, we have a green Subaru Forester. In a split second, I go from thinking it's Grace coming home, and this has all been a dream, to can't be. Grace drove our green Forester the day she died. It was towed to the body shop, where I would have left it indefinitely because I knew I could never get into it again. But Jordan picked it up and drove it out to her lake house, where it still sits.

So then, whose car is this?

The not-our Forester slows as it reaches our mailbox, then turns up the driveway.

I see now it's a later model than ours, so it couldn't have been Grace. And of course Grace is dead. But man, in that split second, hoo boy, I didn't know what to think.

Only a few yards in it stalls. Starts up again and pulls forward. Lurches, actually, a few jolting beats at a time, till it jerks to a stop a car's length shy of the path to the house. It's got California plates. The two women inside exchange words. I figure they must be lost and have stopped to ask directions. What else would they be doing here?

Then the passenger side door opens, and out springs—that's really the only accurate way to describe her energetic egress—a lively thirty-something woman with close-cropped black hair and an excited smile. "I'm teaching Nicky to drive a shift!" It's like her whole body is smiling.

I haven't moved. So much enthusiasm exhausts me. Even with my espresso.

Undeterred, the woman throws her arms wide and bursts forward toward me. I have no idea who she is or why she's here, but this ebullient being looks at me like we've known each other for years. "Hannah! I am so excited to finally meet you!" Everything about her is an exclamation point. "I'm Cristina!" She rolls the R, makes it Spanish.

I am gobsmacked by a bolt of memory. Oh my god. Which comes to me as #OMG with that Munch's-*The Scream*-like emoji followed by an exclamation point. Make that five exclamation points. Ten.

The new hire! Grace was so excited about her. Her areas of specialization rounded out the department. She could teach interdisciplinary courses. "She's Chicana! And a lesbian! With a partner!" Maybe exclamation points are contagious. "I said they could stay with us while they looked for a place to live."

That detail had completely slipped my mind. All the details, actually—the hire, that she and her partner would be staying with us. I swig what's left in my cup and step off the porch to greet my guests. And to deliver some bad news.

I probably could have been more tactful. But I'm still very new at telling people about Grace's death. When Cristina bounded out of her car and said something about wanting to say hello to Grace—so excited she could hardly wait—I thought a straightforward response would be best. Short, to the point, no beating around the bush, no euphemism.

So I delivered the news that Grace had died just as Cristina wrapped her arms around me. She would have fallen if I weren't there. More details come back to me as I hold her up. Grace had chaired the committee that hired Cristina. "She's amazing, Hannah. Very accomplished, lots of published articles. She's working on her first book. She and Gustavo are going to team-teach Art and Social Change." My joy at finding another memory is muted somewhat by the circumstances.

Her partner properly introduces herself to me across Cristina's back. "Sorry to meet under these circumstances. I'm Nicole," she says as she half-holds/half-carries Cristina, who's in shock and unsteady on her feet. "I think maybe we'll just walk around a little, if that's okay," Nicole says. "Let her catch her breath."

Excellent idea, I think, because I need time to clean up.

I go inside and try to see the place as someone entering for the first time. Does it look like the house of a crazy person? Crumpled sheet and blanket on the couch, glass of water that's been on the coffee table for god knows how many days next to books, magazines and newspapers, a stack of unopened mail and accumulated condolence cards.

Not to mention that it looks like I've decorated for some holiday involving Tibetan prayer flags. Either that, or it's like a permanent Day of the Dead shrine but with multi-colored sticky notes instead of papel picado.

As I hustle from room to room de-cluttering, I thank god I've pretty much confined myself to just the living room and the kitchen in the time since Grace died. The kitchen is neat since I'm basically only making coffee there, and it's easy enough to grab whatever else I've left lying around and dump it on the floor of Grace's office—sorry, honey—and peel notes off tables, bookcases, mirrors.

I still can't bring myself to throw out the notes, especially if they're messages from Grace. Do I have to take down the reminder at eye level on the back door? "Recycling to end of driveway. Don't forget the tag." A sane person would do something like that, wouldn't they?

"Wouldn't they?" I call out loud. "Grace, honey? I could use some guidance here." I pause to give her a chance to answer me. Of course I'm greeted by silence.

Fine. I'll figure it out myself. I make an executive decision: The recycling reminder can stay, but I compromise and stuff all the others into a kitchen drawer. I can always write new ones. I've got an ample supply of Post-its. Thanks to Grace's obsession with them, I've got a rainbow assortment: in the original yellow, pastels, also the neon hues. Every shape and size. A lifetime supply.

How much is that? On game shows back in the day, contestants would win a "lifetime supply" of junk they'd never need but seemed thrilled to be getting. What were Lee's Press-On Nails, anyway? I wasn't the kind of girl who would know, or care. I used to wonder what I would have done with them, what the contestants did with all that stuff they'd won. And how did they get it? Did a package come monthly? Weekly? Or did they arrive in a one-time delivery? I imagined a big truck pulling up to someone's house, the driver hopping out to ring the doorbell. What if the people didn't want them? Or wanted just a week's or a month's supply? That's a hell of a commitment, a lifetime supply.

Although I see now that the term is relative. In those back-in-the-day days, a lifetime supply seemed...well, a lifetime. Infinite. Something that would never run out.

I've got a whole new concept of lifetime.

Is this what it means to be old? So much more behind you than ahead. But because you're old, people think you know things, have wisdom. Well, that's if they think of you at all. Mostly you're invisible. Someone with no needs, no desires.

One of the first things Grace said to me after she died (I'll make a note to NOT say that out loud to anyone): **"Don't buy things you don't need. Nothing will bring me back."**

But there isn't any particular thing I want. Except my memories. It would have been helpful to remember these women were coming. What else have I lost?

Even while I was in the ICU holding Grace's hand, I had flashes of thinking, Shit! I have to organize our supplies for the Adirondacks trip, or get the car tuned up before we leave, buy the super-powered insect repellant, stop the mail. Whatever. And then I'd remember there wasn't going to be a trip. I'd get stuck in these time loops, pressed to respond to something that would no longer happen, then pivot back to the present, each twist interrupted by the fact of Grace's death and a return to reality, only to be sucked back into the vortex.

These past weeks have not been my best period for staying focused. Forget focus—not my best period for anything. I'm not making Progress. Who am I kidding? I can feel myself withdrawing further and further, retreating into myself and thinking there's nothing wrong with that.

A knock at the door startles me. My guests! I hope I've made the place presentable. As I open the door, I think, fuck, am *I* presentable? What am I wearing? That's been the last thing on my mind these days. A quick glance tells me I'm in my cotton shorts and baggy Elizabeth Warren "nevertheless she persisted" T-shirt. Presentable enough.

Though I don't think either of these gals even notice right now. Cristina still looks a mess, holding a wad of crumpled tissues. Even with that, she's striking-looking. She's got style—I mean, they're from L.A. after all—her dark hair in a funky cut, appropriately retro bowling shirt, baggy shorts, and sneakers hipper than Chucks. Behind their very stylish frames, her eyes are red from crying. Nicole—who is gorgeous—is the femme equivalent. Sporting equally statement-making sunglasses, she wears flowing pants and a top that looks like maybe it wraps. And jewelry. Who wears jewelry driving cross-country?

Cristina apologizes for her meltdown. "I was so excited to be working with Grace..." she has to stop because she's teared up again.

"Where should I put our things?" Nicole asks. She's pretty sharp, and has picked up on my inability to stay present. We're still standing at the front door, waiting for someone to tell us what to do.

Oh shit. I hadn't thought about that. Is their arrival enough to embarrass me into moving back into our—my—room. I mean, really, how can I keep sleeping on the living room couch when there are guests in the house? They could sleep in the bedroom—someone might as well. But would they think it strange if I offered that? I could make sure they knew that Grace hadn't died in there. Would that be creepy? What—convincing them that it was okay to sleep in a dead woman's bedroom because she had died somewhere else? Okay. No. Just why would I offer them the bedroom? Oy. Who am I trying to convince of what? And how long have I been standing here not saying anything?

"Here you go." I show them to my study.

Then I show them where the extra towels are in their bathroom. After I help them unload the car, I leave them alone to unpack.

I plan to hide out in Grace's office for the rest of the afternoon. I don't want to have to talk to anyone, a risk if I sit in the living room. And I won't spend any time in our bedroom. Maybe it's good to be in here, where I can take my mind off...itself, basically.

I straighten the stuff I'd dumped in here—magazines, mail, my sheet and pillows. While I'm folding the blanket, I catch sight of an orange lacquer box on the bookcase. I don't remember this. Curious, I open it—maybe I'll find some secret stash of...what? Grace didn't keep secrets from me. Still, I open the box. Inside is another box. Inside of which is another. When I have all five boxes lined up, no secret treasure in sight, I remember: when you buy a set of something here, dishes, cups, whatever, they come in fours. But in Japan, sets are five because the number four is associated with death. Where did I learn that fun fact?

I'm on a numerical roll now. The five stages of grief: Denial, anger, bargaining, depression, and acceptance. DABDA! Yabba dabba dooooo!

Are they the emotional equivalent of narrative structure? The stages of three-act structure are, to state the obvious: Act I, Act II, and Act III. Each act has its purpose, its own sequence of events, that have been defined at great length and in numerous ways, but they are, essentially, beginning, middle, end.

There are something like twelve stages to the Hero's Journey. Can I remember them all? Shouldn't I be able to, having taught them for years? The Ordinary World. Call to Adventure. Into the Special World. There are more. I know you're supposed to Return with the Elixir.

The point is, every story is a journey made up of stages, however you define them.

So where am I in my journey? Bumfuck nowhere. And it isn't linear.

I read that memory has its own stages. Who knew. Encoding, storage, retrieval. I'm okay for the first one, and possibly storage as well. I just can't make the retrieval mechanism work.

Could it be that I'm choosing not to remember? Or that I'm fighting a battle between what I want to remember but can't, and what I want to forget, but can't.

Who cares. And I probably didn't read that about the stages of memory. Grace probably told me. And about the number five in Japanese. She knew so much about so much. And she retained everything she learned. I counted on her to explain everything to me. Just look at the number of books she has in here. It's not like I don't have books, or read them. But Grace had a scholar's mind.

I turn my focus to organizing the papers strewn about her desk and am immediately distracted by a postcard of a David Hockney painting, *A Bigger Splash*. I put down the papers and pick up the card. I move over to Grace's chair and study the picture.

I love Hockney. A year or so ago we went down to the city when The Met had a big retrospective, and I spent a long time in front of this very painting. It's huge—almost eight feet square. A lot to take in. It's also stark and simple: a modern split-level house, a strip of pavement between it and a blue swimming pool.

The house is bare of decoration, with a tiny fringe of shrubs to the right of sliding glass doors reflecting buildings and palm trees. A lone director's chair sits in front of the doors. A yellow diving board juts into the frame from the lower right corner, and below it, a big splash of white water leaps up. That swoosh of white signifies the only motion in the picture. We can't see who just dove or jumped off that board, and this splash, immortalized here, in actuality would have taken, what, two seconds to materialize and settle.

The picture makes me miss L.A. Even when I lived there, I wondered whether L.A. was a place or a feeling. I mean, of course it was a place. A place with ugly strip malls and smog and impossible traffic. But it was also sun-drenched and magical, making us feel we were all participants in and contributors to its mythology, and Hockney's pictures synthesized that for me. Especially his swimming pools.

Does any of this count as memory?

I lean back in Grace's chair and close my eyes.

I hear my guests talking, though I can't make out what they're saying. Then I hear the shower running. It's strange having other people in the house.

I don't realize I've fallen asleep until I hear someone moving around in the kitchen.

I head out to see what's going on. Nicole, looking fresh and put together—stunning, actually—in tight black pants and a brilliant red blouse, is admiring my espresso machine. "This is impressive," she says.

"Shall I make you a latte?"

"Yes, please." She sits at the counter while I foam the milk to make her drink. "Cristina's asleep," she says. "She totally crashed. I know she wanted to shower, but I didn't want to wake her yet."

I hand her her coffee. She takes a sip, nods approvingly.

Nicole tells me Cristina had left several messages on Grace's cell. "Starting around Kansas, I think. She wanted to update Grace on when we'd be arriving. She said Grace had told her you might be traveling—to the Adirondacks? Is that right? —so we figured that's why we didn't hear back."

I don't confess to having shut off the phone. Doesn't seem like necessary information at this point.

"Cristina did most of the driving, all the way from L.A. It's not like I don't drive. I mean, L.A., right? You've gotta drive. But I don't normally drive a stick. I'm fine on the highway, but starting and slowing down, not so much. I guess you saw that. Cristina had very," she searches for the right word, "specific ideas for our new car. Like needing a manual transmission for winter."

"Are you going to get a second car?"

Nicole nods emphatically. "And mine will be an automatic."

I learn Nicole's a native Angeleno. "We both are, actually. Though I grew up in the Valley and Cristina in East L.A." She tells me she's an editor.

"Grace always had me read early drafts of her writing. She called me her in-house editor."

"Not that kind of editor. Film and video."

"Oh. You're in the industry."

"Only peripherally. I do commercials and industrials."

"Will you be commuting between here and L.A., or can you work remotely?"

"I'm taking a break," Nicole says. "I've bought myself some time to think. I was getting burnt out, and this move was a good excuse to see what else I might want to do." She looks out the window at the garden. "The light's so different here. I live in sunny southern California and spend most of my time in windowless rooms. Dark, windowless rooms."

Maybe Nicole following Cristina here is a little like me following Grace. I thought I'd found paradise in sunny Southern California, even if my career hadn't taken off. I thought all I wanted was the sun and the ocean. Then it turned out what I truly wanted was Grace, and I couldn't be the reason she passed up the offer for her dream job, even if it meant I'd be living through winters again.

"This is a great kitchen," Nicole says.

"It's all Grace. She's the cook. Was."

Nicole admires the Wolf range. "I'd love to make us dinner tonight," she says.

"I don't know that you'd have much to work with," I say.

"Oh, you'd be surprised how much I can do with how little," she says.

"Have at it," I say, motioning for her to open the refrigerator.

"Hmm..." is her response. "Not that I have anything against yogurt and trail mix...Are we," she hesitates, "close to any stores out here?"

My, isn't she diplomatic for city folk.

Just then, Cristina stumbles in, clearly not fully awake, wearing boxers and a sleeveless T that reveals an intricate web of tattoos snaking down each arm. "Man. I was really out. What time is it?" She puts her arms around Nicole, her head on Nicole's shoulder.

"You slept a long time," Nicole says, kissing the top of Cristina's head and offering her a sip of the latte. "You needed that."

Cristina tries to apologize again for falling apart. I brush it off. But now we're in an awkward silence.

Nicole leaps into the breach and tells Cristina to get dressed. "We're taking Hannah out to dinner."

"I'll jump in the shower and be ready in twenty minutes," says Cristina. She gives Nicole a quick kiss and leaves us. "Grace took me to a great Thai restaurant when I was here for my interview," she says as she moves down the hall. "I don't remember what it was called."

"I'll bet I know which one," I say to Nicole.

She looks at me. "Am I okay to go like this?"

"Absolutely," I say. "This town's pretty casual."

But then I realize she didn't need my approval of her outfit. She was giving me a subtle hint about mine. "Maybe not this casual," I say.

As long as I'm going to change into real clothes, not just a T-shirt and cotton shorts, I might as well shower. I stand under the hot water and think I'm going to have to step up my dressing game, or at least pay some attention to what I wear. I've got roommates now. Living people, not just Grace. Who, I know, is dead.

9
Trailing Spouse

Academe is a strange place to live. To succeed in its arcane rules and caste system, you have to have a certain temperament, the right blend of equanimity and priorities, to ensure you'll get through it with your faith in humankind intact. So much depends on rank, I learned when I first met Grace. Lecturer. Instructor. Assistant Professor. Associate Professor. Full Professor. All the jokes about academic fights being so bitter because the stakes are so low hit the nail on the head. When I started at Hollander, I watched the internecine power struggles from a bemused distance. How could I take them seriously? I was in my forties when I started working there and considered "junior" faculty though I was older than most of my colleagues in the department. I'd landed here by chance, simply because I followed Grace. And because they were so eager to have Grace, the school found me a position. That made me a "trailing spouse," even though marriage was far from our minds back then, not to mention not legal, either. It helped that I had a graduate degree and could teach creative writing as well as screenwriting. Once I got over myself—being a teacher instead of a writer, the shame!—I had a great time. I was interested in what my students thought and took them more seriously than I could many of my colleagues. After the first semester, I couldn't believe my luck at where I'd landed.

I don't know for sure which type of academic Cristina is: pedantic and insufferable, the type that can only speak academese? Or enthusiastic about what she teaches and relishes the opportunity to spend her life digging into it and discussing it with students, some of whom may be as passionate as she is? I guess I'll find out this evening.

I'd grabbed a bottle of rosé on our way out, since the restaurant we're going to doesn't have a liquor license. It's a no-atmosphere place with the best green curry in town. I'm sure this is where Grace took Cristina. My guess is confirmed when we walk in, and Cristina says to Nicole, "You're going to love this."

The host leads us to a table in the back. On our way, we pass a solitary diner at a table for two. Maybe people eating alone are happy, there by choice, but I always find it kind of sad. I can't see myself doing it. I worry what people would think—that's the poor widow, they'd whisper behind my back.

Oh, don't be ridiculous. No one would even notice you.

"Hannah," the solitary diner says as I pass.

I turn back. "Ellen, hi." I stop to talk as Cristina and Nicole continue on to our table.

"I'm glad to see you out," Ellen says.

"That's the new art history hire, Cristina Flores," I say. As if that's a response. "And her girlfriend. She's a film editor."

Ellen smiles at me. "I was on Cristina's search committee."

"Of course. Yes. Sure." Why am I such a dope? Ellen looks perfectly comfortable and relaxed dining alone. I don't know if I'm embarrassed for sounding like an idiot, or for my thoughts about eating alone in a restaurant. Or for my remarks at our dinner. At least I remember my manners. "Would you like to join us?"

"I'm waiting for the check. But I'll come over in a minute, just to say hello."

I join Cristina and Nicole at our table. After we've ordered our food and opened the wine—easy, since it's just a twist-off cap—Ellen stops by, carrying a to-go container. Cristina stands to greet her, but Ellen motions her to sit, then reaches her free hand across the table to Nicole. "Ellen Monroe. Women and gender studies."

"Nicole Speaker. Civilian."

"Welcome." Ellen tells Cristina to be in touch once she's on campus. "I'd be happy to show you around, tell you whom to avoid, that kind of thing, though I'm sure you'll get the skinny from Hannah here." Then she puts her hand on my shoulder. "And you—let's make another dinner date."

She says it with such certainty, all I can do is nod in response. Then she's gone.

My table mates look at me. Smile knowingly.

"We had dinner last week," I say.

"You don't owe us an explanation," Cristina says.

Why did I feel like I did? And who are they to judge? I chafe at the idea of living under a microscope—another reason to avoid eating out alone.

Our food arrives. The green curry doesn't disappoint. "Fantástico!" Cristina exclaims after the first bite. "Just as good as when Grace brought me the first time."

I don't know either of these women, but I'm sensing that Cristina, at least, is a little subdued around me now. Nicole had told me how excited she was about working with Grace. Now, no Grace, and Cristina probably wonders how much she can talk about her with me. I think that's how everyone is around me these days, whether friends or colleagues. Even the owner of the restaurant had put her hand on my arm when we came in. "I'm very sorry about your friend," she said. I mumbled something appropriate in response.

Grace is She Who Cannot Be Mentioned, death is That Which Cannot Be Mentioned.

There's always the weather. "Are you prepared for winter?" I ask, out of nowhere. We'd been eating in silence, which I took as a sign that everyone enjoyed the food. Or, see above, didn't want to talk about anything painful. I continue. "Moving here was an adjustment, even though I grew up in the east. I'd lived in L.A. long enough to think sixty degrees was cold."

Nicole answers. "Once we're settled, we have a whole list of what to order—from silk long johns to down jackets."

I nod approvingly. "I'm impressed."

"After I accepted the position," Cristina says, "Grace gave me advice about how to dress for winter. More like a treatise."

I don't flinch. I merely smile. What I really want to do is ask what exactly she said, tell me everything. And how did she sound? Did she go into detail about the kind of down, synthetic versus real, the brand of silk underwear—she had her preferences. Did she say that after we moved back East, she understood layering in a whole new way?

"She said after you moved here, she understood layering in a whole new way."

Yes, she did. In L.A., layering was a style. Here, a necessity.

Rather than press for more details about her meeting with Grace, I force myself into the present. "So how did you two meet?" I ask. It always gets around to origin stories with lesbians.

Cristina is eager to oblige. "I'd just broken up with someone and friends brought me to a party. They promised they weren't setting me up, but later I found out they knew that someone they wanted me to meet would be there."

I look at Nicole. "And that was you?"

"Actually, no," Nicole says.

"But Nicole thought I was hot," Cristina says.

"I thought you were cute," Nicole corrects her.

"And hot. Come on. It's been five years. We're still together. You can admit it."

"You were flirting with every woman at that party. I wanted to stay away from you."

"You played hard to get." Cristina takes Nicole's hand, raises it to her lips, kisses it while looking into her eyes. "And it worked. Here we are." Nicole pulls her hand away. Cristina looks at me. "I wore her down."

I'm ready to ask more questions, but the restaurant owner comes over to check on us and see that everything was okay. Cristina raves about the food.

"I hope that means you'll be back," the owner says.

"Absolutely! We live here now," Cristina says, pointing to herself and Nicole. "You'll be seeing a lot of us." She puts her hand on Nicole's shoulder. "And she's a terrific cook. Her green curry is almost as good as this was."

Nicole doesn't seem thrilled to be on display like this, but Cristina is so enthusiastic, just like she was when she jumped out of the car to greet me. She's like a happy, friendly big dog.

Nicole must be used to it, because when the owner walks away, she doesn't say anything to Cristina or chide her at all. But Cristina's on a roll now. "She's such a good cook. I keep telling her she should write a blog."

"Honey..." Nicole protests. She is not a friendly big dog and isn't into doing tricks.

This doesn't stop Cristina, who can barely contain her excitement. "You could include some of your photographs." She turns to me. "There's a pretty serious food scene here, am I right?"

Nicole turns to Cristina. "I'm not starting a blog."

"We had that whole conversation—"

"Stop," Nicole says. "That's your idea, not mine."

They're saved by the check, which is delivered as Cristina tries to coax Nicole into talking more. But Nicole is firm, and simply tells Cristina to figure out the tip and pay up.

They don't let me chip in. I'm apparently still on the "widows eat free" plan.

Back home, when I've parked the Prius, we're getting out of the car and Cristina says, "Oh, when Nicole and I were walking around earlier—that place out past the barn is so cute! And you've got a pond! Can you swim in it?"

"Yes," I say. We go inside, and I'm distracted now as I show them where to find extra blankets or towels should they need them. The whole time, I'm thinking about what Cristina said about "that place."

Have you ever had a dream where you added a room to the house you live in? When I first lived in Los Angeles, I dated an actress. We talked about living together, but she didn't want to move into my apartment because it wasn't big enough for her piano. One night, I dreamt that there was an extra room that I'd forgotten about, definitely big enough for her piano, her music, plus whatever else she wanted to bring. How could I forget about this room, I wondered in the dream.

And now, in real life, or what's passing for my real life these days, I've had the opposite experience. I remember only what I need to at the moment—have managed to get this far by focusing on what's directly in front of me. I've lived in a circumscribed space, the living room mostly, gradually branching out to Grace's office, and just barely starting to think about what's immediately outside the house. But Cristina's remark gave me an idea that excites me. I say goodnight to them and head down the hall, pretending that I'll be sleeping in the bedroom. When I'm sure they're in their room, I sneak back to Grace's office and spread my blanket on the floor.

Of course I can't sleep. Only partly because I'm on the floor. I'm aware of strangers in the house. Friendly strangers, but strangers. I can hear them talking. Someone goes into the bathroom. More talking. Arguing? Maybe—is someone crying? Then silence.

But not silence like when I'm alone, just me and Grace (who's dead, I know). I'm not sure I like it. I mean, I'm sleeping on the fucking floor, for god's sake. In my own home. But that's not Cristina and Nicole's fault. These young women remind me a little of me and Grace when we were younger. I think of Grace's aunt who called us The Girls. Only partly because she couldn't officially acknowledge our relationship. But she accepted us. We were, in her mind, a unit. I'm already starting to think of Nicole and Cristina as The Girls.

So, as I was saying, they're here, and this creates a different kind of silence than I've been used to. I'm not sure I like it. Nor am I sure I don't like it.

I do my best to get some rest, but the idea forming in my brain wakes me each time I drift into almost-sleep. Finally, I give up. I throw on sweats and a hoodie and head outside before first light.

10
The Little House

I haven't been to the Little House since Grace died. We'd chosen the spot years earlier, but only finished construction on it this fall. It's small, not a tiny house like in the Netflix docuseries, but a streamlined, well-designed, fully winterized dwelling with a main living area, fully loaded galley kitchen, bathroom with a great shower, utility room with washer/dryer hookup, and two small rooms with big picture windows, one an office for Grace, the other a workspace for me. Not that I had any work plans. "You'll come up with something. I know you," Grace kept assuring me. Either could have been a bedroom. Possibly for our caretaker when the time came. Our plan had been to use it ourselves for the next few years, then maybe rent it out to have extra income after we both retired. It would make a great space for a person living alone—a young faculty member, artist, a single mom. A compatible couple. Whatever, lots of possibilities.

I open the door. It's a little stuffy. Every surface could probably use a good dusting, but overall, the place looks great. "We did good, honey," I say to Grace. The big L-shaped sofa was as far as we'd gotten with furnishing the living area. Each work area had the basics—desk and chair. We'd just added the final touches—cable and wi-fi—over our spring break.

Standing by the sliding glass door, looking out onto our pond before the sun is up, I feel calm. I don't have the urge to remember what our life was like, what we did, how the light fell across Grace's face when she lay reading on the couch. I just...I just *am*. I don't have to worry about having strangers in our house. My house. I breathe easily. To test this, I close my eyes and keep breathing. In for four. Hold for four. Out for six. When I open my eyes, I'm alone. No Grace. Just me.

I close my eyes again. Bask in the peace that's come over me, for however briefly it may last. I think again: Being happy isn't the only happiness.

My phone pings. Jordan's moved from morning check-in phone calls to texts:

> *how r u?*
>
> *K*, I respond. *I've got company.*
>
> *!?!?!?!?!?!*
>
> *Grace's new hire + her girlfriend arrived yesterday. Staying with me.*

The dots indicating Jordan's typing hover on my screen. Stop. The phone rings. As soon as I answer, Jordan says, "Are you sure you want them there?"

"It's fine," I say. I don't say that it hadn't even occurred to me to think about whether or not I wanted them here. Or that I could have said no. Grace had set it up, they had arrived, and that was that.

"Okay," Jordan says. "But it's only temporary, right?"

How do I know? But I don't say that. Nor do I tell her that I feel a plan forming in the back of my mind, inchoate but present. I'll let it sit and percolate.

"Just take care of yourself, okay?" Jordan won't let me off the phone until I promise.

Not that I even know what taking care of myself means anymore. I head back to the Big House.

Keep in mind that "big" is relative here. The Big House weighs in at a whopping twelve hundred square feet, give or take. We'd started calling it that when we conceived the other place, which is about seven hundred square feet sopping wet.

I hear that The Girls are up, so I make myself a coffee. Knock on the door to the guest room and announce: "I feel like eggs. Anyone else?"

"Yes, please!" Cristina answers.

When they come out, looking L.A. hip in artsy shirts and pants, cool sandals, and Nicole in her funky jewelry, I've almost finished the eggs, toast is on the table, and I'm ready to take orders for espresso drinks.

"I thought you said you hated to cook," says Nicole. "I'm impressed."

"Even a Lazy Chef can make eggs." I sound almost chipper, a word I've never used in conjunction with myself, even before Grace died. "You'll need a good breakfast to fortify you for apartment hunting."

After The Girls leave, I clean up the kitchen. Once that's done, I'm at a loss for what to do next. Best thing would be to tackle Grace's study. Or her half of the dresser. Or go through the mail I've let pile up. At least dig out the bills. Maybe I should call the phone company and cancel the landline. Am I ready to do that? What am I waiting for? I haven't plugged it back in. I don't want to talk to anyone. Mostly I don't want to be asked how I'm doing, how I'm feeling. Maybe I should just go through Grace's calendar and cancel any appointments she's made.

I can't even go into my study because The Girls' stuff is in there. I mean, I could if I wanted to. They're very good about keeping it neat, putting their things to the side in case I want to get to my desk. But it doesn't feel like mine.

There's the rub. Nothing feels like mine anymore. Mine was always part of ours. And now ours no longer exists.

That realization drives me outside, where I feel safe in the expansive space that I don't have to claim or reclaim. I can just sit on the porch and do nothing.

Four minutes later I'm walking down the driveway. Turns out sitting still is not something I'm suited for at present. I need to move. I really do want to get back into my body. I could go for a jog. Once I get to the road, I stop. Who am I kidding? I turn back toward the house.

The Girls come home discouraged.

"I can't believe how high rents are here!" Cristina exclaims. "It's almost as bad as L.A.! And you don't get a lot of bang for your buck." She holds up a list. "We have a few more places to look at tomorrow."

"Don't feel you have to rush," I say.

"We don't want to impose," Nicole says.

I wave that off. "Don't worry about it."

Nicole thanks me, then says, "We stopped at the market on the way home. I thought I'd make dinner. If that's okay with you."

"You had my full repertoire this morning," I say. "Tell me what you're making and I'll pick an appropriate wine. I'm also a good prep person."

Cristina turns to Nicole. "That means you don't need me, right?"

Nicole responds like this is a familiar dynamic between them. "Yes. Go work."

Cristina gives Nicole a quick kiss. "Thank you. If I'm not out before then, give me a five-minute warning."

As soon as she's gone, Nicole starts laying out ingredients on the counter. "Cristina's writing her first book and her deadline is approaching. We may not see a lot of her." She holds up a big bag of spinach. "Saw this at a farm stand and couldn't resist. Isn't it beautiful?" Indicating the other ingredients, which include garlic and kalamata olives, she turns to me. "This is a very simple recipe. I hope you don't mind."

"That you're making a beautiful dinner?"

"That I'm taking over your kitchen to do it."

Do I tell her that it never felt like mine? That I'd probably be fine with just a mini-fridge and a microwave? And my espresso machine. Gesturing expansively, I say, "Someday, this could all be yours."

Nicole doesn't miss a beat. "What? The curtains?"

I crack up. *Monty Python and the Holy Grail* was a touchstone for me and Grace. I can't remember the last time I laughed like that. When I've recovered, Nicole asks if I wouldn't mind chopping some garlic. "Yes, chef!" I snap.

We toss quotes from the film back and forth as we work. Nicole inspects my progress. "A little finer, please."

"Yes, chef!"

I feel almost normal. Someone's writing in another room, dinner's being made. Evidence of life in this house. I could pretend Grace was at the office, that she'd be stopping on her way home to pick up dessert.

Nicole opens a cupboard and frowns at the sight of glasses and plates. "What do you need?" I ask.

"Mixing bowls?"

I show her the mixing bowls, and then open the drawer with the knives, show her where everything else is. Now that she's got the lay of the land, it's like watching Grace move around the kitchen. Even in this unfamiliar space, Nicole looks completely at home.

"What do you usually serve pasta in?"

I go to the sideboard in the dining room and return with a bowl Grace and I picked up at a crafts fair in the Catskills.

"This is beautiful," Nicole says. She starts chopping the olives and placing them right in the bowl. When she's covered the bottom, she adds my finely chopped garlic. Then she pours extra virgin olive oil till it covers everything. "Are you okay with this?" She holds up a jar of crushed red pepper flakes. I nod. She sprinkles some in.

"Okay," she says. "We'll let that sit while we have some wine and cheese."

I remember that's my job. "Do you have a wine preference? Red? White?"

"We drink both."

When I return with a Chianti and a Barbera, Nicole's setting out a plate with some herb-crusted cheese and crackers. I hold up each bottle, and she points to the Barbera. As I'm opening it, "Try this," she encourages me, just like Grace used to, holding out a cracker she's smeared. She makes one for herself and pops the whole thing in her mouth. She closes her eyes as she chews. "Isn't that amazing? I feel like I'm in a meadow in Provence." She opens her eyes and looks at me. "Am I right?" She closes her eyes again.

I take a bite. The cheese is great, light and fresh, and the herbs give it a lovely flavor. "It's delicious," I say.

"*Tomme fleur verte*," she says with an unpretentious French accent. "A very fresh, young goat cheese. Aged only a few days, so it doesn't have that overpowering goat-cheesy taste. And the dried herbs and pink peppercorns add such a nice contrast to the creamy texture, yes?" She spreads us each another cracker. I bite into mine, and try to travel somewhere, but I'm pretty much right here in the kitchen.

Nicole turns on the flame under the water for the pasta. She's already learned where various paraphernalia is, and pulls out a box grater and starts on the parmesan.

Cristina joins us then. "Isn't my timing impeccable! You've even opened the wine." She pours herself a generous amount, raises her glass.

"I'd like to make a toast. To Hannah." She pauses briefly before adding, "And to Grace."

"To Grace," Nicole echoes.

They drink. I'm a little stuck for a moment.

Cristina helps herself to cheese. "Que rico!" she says, spreading another cracker which, she pops into her mouth. "Riquísimo!"

When we sit down to eat, I know the food is delicious, but I can't make myself care. I try to eat. I try to engage in conversation, but even that's too much effort, so I pull out more of their story. It's easy enough to get people talking about themselves. I can drift in and out of the conversation. I drink more wine. Cristina drinks more wine.

"I'll open the other bottle," I say.

"I'll get it," says Cristina. She pulls open a drawer and finds the opener on the first try. I guess some people just know their way around kitchens. As she's opening the wine, she asks me how my day was.

"Fine," I lie.

Cristina has a positive outlook on everything—so excited about starting the new semester! Seeing what the students are like! She has a good feeling she and Nicole will find a place tomorrow!

"And now I have to get back to work," Cristina says, rising from the table. She gives me a hug. "It feels really good here. Thanks for letting us stay," she says to me. To Nicole, "Sweetie, I'll do the dishes later." She kisses the back of Nicole's neck and is gone.

"She's so optimistic," I say.

"Hopelessly."

"And she works a lot."

"Constantly."

"I guess as long as she likes it…"

"She's passionate about it." Nicole starts clearing plates.

"This I'm good at," I say, carrying dirty dishes into the kitchen.

"Cristina really will come back and clean up after she's worked for a while."

"I feel strange leaving the dishes in my own house."

Nicole leans against the counter finishing her wine while I rinse plates and put them in the dishwasher. I thank her for a great dinner.

"You didn't eat very much of it," she says.

"But it was delicious."

We say goodnight, and I head off to the bedroom. But instead of sneaking into Grace's study, I go back to the Little House. I want to see what it's like at night.

As I walk over, I wonder if this is going to work. I let myself in. Again that peace settles over me. Again I think it's not that I don't like having The Girls around, just maybe not so close. My plan is maybe I could offer them the Little House. Let them stay there while they settle into their new life. I walk through the rooms, imagining the two of them inhabiting the space. I think they could make it work. It would be easy enough to install a washer and dryer. I sit on the couch to strategize. I'll wait till they come back from their apartment hunting tomorrow before I say anything. I can absolutely promise to not interfere with their lives, but be a resource as they adjust to the East Coast. And I'll—what'll I do?

I'll fall asleep, apparently. Because the next thing I know, it's morning and I'm sprawled out on the couch. Wow. My first full night's sleep since Grace died.

When I slip back into the Big House, The Girls are already up. "You were out early," Cristina says. "Great time to exercise." Nicole doesn't say anything, but I think she's on to me.

I make myself an espresso and join them at the table as they talk about their day.

"I told the owner we could be there at eleven," Nicole says.

"That's when I'm meeting with the dean."

"I thought you said that wasn't until one."

"She changed the time."

"And you didn't tell me?"

"I thought I did."

"Well, you didn't."

"Can't you go without me? I trust your judgement."

"That's not the point."

Time for an intervention. "I'll take you, Nicole," I offer. "I can bring you to campus after."

"Really?"

"Yes. I need to finish clearing out my office and keep putting it off. This'll get me there."

"That would be great," she says. Cristina agrees. "If you see anything you like, I can go back with you to check it out."

"That's it, then," I say.

This is good, I tell myself. Tricked myself into doing something productive. And helping out The Girls.

I plan my outfit while I take a quick shower. My retirement wardrobe has been extremely limited—sweats or shorts and T-shirts. Always clean, or clean enough. But really—who's going to care? And who cares if I waste time or don't accomplish anything? What's to accomplish?

Is that retirement, or grief?

"Wow," I say to Grace. "I haven't heard from you in a long time."

No response.

"Really?" I say to her. "You're just going to leave it there? You know I hate when you do that—make some statement or exclamation and then don't say what the fuss was about."

Silence.

"Fine. Be that way."

I make sure to put on a nice button-down shirt and clean black pants. A cool pair of socks decorated with a cool Chinese dragon. These socks deserve real shoes, not sneakers. I finish it all off with a silver bracelet Grace bought me in New Mexico.

"How do I look?" I ask her. But I'm still on my own.

Nicole's waiting for me in the living room. "You look nice," she says.

"I keep telling Cristina," Nicole says as she pulls her seatbelt across her body, snaps it in place, "You can take the girl out of the city—"

"But you can't interest her in learning to drive a stick," I finish.

"Cristina wants me to understand how this," she motions to the dash and the front of the car, "all works."

I smile. "That sounds familiar."

"Grace was like that?"

I sense her hesitancy, like maybe we shouldn't talk about Grace. But I find I want to, and hope my tone conveys that. "Very much so." And today, rather than understanding how my car's engine works, I focus all my attention on the road directly in front of me, forcing myself to ignore anything in my peripheral vision as we pass where Grace's car went off the road.

She really must be pissed to not be here now. She and Cristina could explain everything to me and Nicole. Like Cristina, Grace understood how things worked and was always trying to get me to share her enthusiasm. This Prius, for example. She wanted me to appreciate the sophistication and elegance of its engine. But not like you turn on the engine, push the accelerator, and the car goes, sometimes using gas and sometimes running on electric. Grace wanted me to understand it the way she did, the principle behind a hybrid engine.

That was never going to happen about anything, no matter what the technology. I told her so as early as our second or third date, which was pretty much when I realized I wanted us to be a thing for however long it lasted. We were at her office on campus because Grace had to photocopy some articles for one of her classes. We stood near the big copy machine as it rattled off double-sided, collated and stapled copies, and Grace said, "Do you know how complicated this is?" I probably responded less than enthusiastically. "But you appreciate beauty," she said.

"Yes, when you tell me about a painting you'll be dealing with in class. I love when you talk about 'passages' in a painting. Or how an artist achieved a certain effect using color or perspective."

"Exactly," she said, excited now. "Don't you want to see how the workings of this machine are just as beautiful? It's such a complex system."

Let me count the ways "no" was my answer. But I stood patiently while she went on about exactly how the image of the page was transferred onto the paper. Something about drums and rollers. What really fascinated her, however, was how each piece of paper followed a path through the machine and couldn't touch or interfere with the next piece of paper also flying on its own path. I didn't really care. She'd lost me back at the drums and rollers. As she talked, I would focus on her bright eyes, the curve of her lip, how she used her hands for emphasis.

No matter how hard she tried, how clear her explanations—and I know they were clear—I never really appreciated what she was saying. Whether it was the copier, the elegance of the Nintendo Wii and later the Switch game consoles, or a hybrid engine, it didn't matter. All I needed to understand about any of these things was how to use them. (Well, not the game consoles.) It was Grace's passion for them that mattered to me.

That, and just being with Grace. And having our life together. I'd been looking forward to traveling with her on her sabbatical. It was going to be a good way for me to transition to retirement, my new life.

Oh god. My new life.

Between my pension and Grace's salary, I would have the luxury of not having to think about earning money. At least that was what Grace kept telling me. We'd couldn't spend lavishly but could live quite comfortably. If she was correct, all I have to do now is come up with meaningful ways to spend my time.

I turn to Grace to have her remind me why I retired. What did she think I wanted to do? I'm a little surprised to see Nicole in the passenger seat.

As if she understands something about where I've just been, Nicole says, "I'm so sorry I didn't get to meet her."

"She's probably so pissed she's missing you two."

Since I know this to be true, I smile a little. I'm also smiling because I've unlocked another memory.

Nicole returns to our discussion. "I'm sure we'll get another car," she says. "Or I could take public transportation." She looks out the window at the fields and farms we're passing. "There is public transportation, isn't there?"

"Yes. As well as lighted streets at night *and* running water. And soon I hear we'll have something called telephones."

Nicole smiles. "Okay. I get it. I'm a provincial city gal."

"I was the same way when we first moved to town."

Nicole swivels in her seat to stay focused on a herd of buffalo grazing peacefully in the field we're passing. "Really?" she asks, referring to the buffalo.

I nod.

"It's beautiful here."

I nod again.

"Wait till Cristina sees this." Nicole takes a picture with her phone. "When she was little, her grandparents had a big farm in the Central Valley, and Cristina loved spending time there. This area reminds her of that, which is part of why she was so excited about moving."

I can almost see this scene from a newcomer's eyes. Farms, fields, picture-perfect clouds scudding against the blue-blue sky. It is a beautiful part of the world. I lower my visor against the glare.

As we approach town, I point down a road we pass. "That's a shortcut to the college. Also the fastest way to the supermarket, liquor store, bank." I tell her which restaurants to try, which to avoid, where the students hang out. "I don't expect you to remember any of this. I'm just giving you a general lay of the land."

Nicole takes it all in. "It was hard to leave L.A., but Cristina was so excited at the prospect of working with Grace, I couldn't refuse her." She stops there, either to gauge my reaction to another mention of Grace or because she's trying to think of a way out of the hole she felt she was digging around herself.

I give the kid a break. "The things we do for love, right?"

We stop outside the first address on her list. It's a gloomy, rundown duplex on a busy street. I see Nicole study it from the safety of the car.

"Just because it's on the list, do you have to go look at it?" I ask.

She turns to me, relieved, and crosses that off on the page.

Once we've established eliminating dim prospects as an option, we cut our hunting time by one-third. We do get out and look at two places, both pretty dismal.

"You used to live in Los Angeles, right?" Nicole asks.

"I did."

"Was it hard to adjust to life here?"

"There were times I felt like I was living in Cicely, Alaska."

Nicole gives me a blank stare.

"*Northern Exposure?*"

Still blank.

Well, of course—she's young. I explain the reference. "It was a TV show about a new doctor who had to start practicing in Alaska because the state had subsidized his med school. And he ends up in this tiny town. And of course he's neurotic and Jewish and from New York." Rather than explain more, I say, "It was a great show," and leave it at that. "And yes, moving here from L.A. was quite an adjustment."

Nicole directs us to a street only a few blocks from where Grace and I first lived when we arrived. "I've saved the most promising for last. Mary, from the department, gave us this woman's name. Lillian Hayes," Nicole says.

For some reason, the name is familiar to me, though I can't place it. I park in front of a duplex set back from the street. Well-maintained lawn, a sweet patch of flowers planted around a bird bath. This is familiar, too.

"This is a good location, right?" Nicole asks. "She said to call when we arrived—she's home all day." Nicole takes out her phone, but there's no need to call. The owner must have been watching from her window, since she steps outside as Nicole and I make our way down the walk.

I recognize her at once, even though it's been years. That's why the name rang a bell. Lillian Hayes, everyone called her Miss Lillian, had been a seamstress. There'd been a time, when we first arrived in town, that we'd taken some of our clothes to her for alterations. A thin Black woman, stylish though casually dressed, Miss Lillian walks with a cane, which she treats as more of an annoyance than an aid, as if it can't keep up with her brisk pace. "Which one of you is Nicole?"

"That's me. Good morning, Miss Lillian." Nicole motions to me. "And this is Hannah. Cristina and I are staying with her."

"I have a no pets policy," Miss Lillian says without turning from opening the door. "But I'd let you bring your cats." She ushers us into the apartment, which is empty and very clean. "But no more than two."

"We don't have any cats," Nicole says.

Miss Lillian looks skeptical. "Have a look around. Utilities are included. There's two cable outlets, one here," she points to a wall in the living room, "the other in the bedroom. I'll let you poke around by yourselves. Just knock on my door when you're leaving. Front door'll lock behind you."

After she leaves, Nicole turns to me. "Does she assume all lesbians have cats?"

I shrug. "Clearly we're the outliers."

Nicole and I wander through the rooms. Nothing special about them, but the front room and the kitchen have great light, the appliances are new, and everything is impeccably clean. And it's a great location, right in town. I can tell Nicole likes what she sees because this is the most time we've spent in any place we've been to.

Nicole stops to tell Miss Lillian she'll be in touch after talking to her partner, then we head back to the car. Miss Lillian waves to us from her front window.

As she buckles her seatbelt, Nicole says, "This was the best place so far. And I like the idea of renting from Miss Lillian. It's very...white...around here."

"I can't deny that. You definitely have to work to create the community you want, but it is possible. Despite its reputation as a liberal college town, a magazine once dubbed it 'enlightened'—Grace called it smugly enlightened—I understand how hard it must be for you two to move from a very diverse city, cross country, to our little town." I don't add, especially for you, Nicole, whose only reason for being here is Cristina.

Just goes to show—being happy isn't the only happiness.

This whole day, I'm seeing the town through a newcomer's eyes. Though I wonder—maybe I'm also seeing it differently for myself, my vision affected by grief. A few flickering images passed through my mind, more sparks than actual memories. I don't usually make as many associations as I've made today as we drove around: This is where we used to live; we took our clothes to Miss Lillian for alterations; feeling like I lived in *Northern Exposure.*

"I think we've earned lunch," I say and point us toward the Ithaca Bakery on Route 13. This time, I insist on paying.

When we get to campus, Nicole heads off to find Cristina and I go to my office, firm in my resolutions to finish up here once and for all.

Normally I'd drop my keys and bag (if I had one) on the bookcase near the door. But now I have to fight for space since the top shelf is covered with stuff I plan to give away or bring home. I will be ruthless in my culling.

11
Boys and Girls

Despite my good intentions to get right to work, I dig into one of my boxes to find the script for *Monty Python and the Holy Grail*. Nicole and I talked more about it at lunch, and I need to see it on the page. So much of it cracks me up. The whole could-a-swallow-carry-a-coconut digression after the already hysterical King Arthur prancing around the countryside pretending to be riding. Which the audience thinks at first, too, because we heard hoofbeats. Which turned out to be coconuts knocked together to sound like hoofbeats. I crack up again just thinking about it. And then those robed monks parading through the medieval village, chanting, self-flagellating, whacking themselves in the forehead with their bibles. I could "and then" myself with clips from the film all day. The cart with the dead bodies and the crier: "Bring out your dead!" Townspeople obliging. And the frail old man draped over his son's shoulders, about to be dumped on the cart, moaning plaintively, "I'm not dead yet." Hysterical.

Standing in my almost packed-up office, having reconsidered what's coming home and what isn't, I can't completely separate that plea from my own life. Specifically, my own no-longer-gainfully-employed life. I've got that "I'm not dead yet" refrain as an earworm. It was anxiety-provoking enough before Grace died, but now: What will this mean for me? What will I do? Who will I be? Retired. And a widow!

Various pathetic scenarios play out in my head until I have to literally shake them away and tell myself: You're here. You're slogging forward. Being happy isn't the only happiness, remember? Even if you're merely going through the motions rather than the emotions, this is progress. Right?

Whatever sense of progress I feel, I attribute to clearing out the past and making room for who knows what. When I'm finished in my office,

I will head over to Grace's and be done with campus once and for all. I tell myself this is a good thing.

I'm interrupted by a light knock on the door, even though it's open, and a friendly "Hey stranger" from Oliver. Normally he'd come in for a hug, but today he keeps a physical distance to better size me up. His eyes show his concern. "How're you doing?"

I appraise my surroundings and answer, "I think I'm almost done."

Clearly that isn't what he was asking about, but Oliver accepts my cue and surveys the boxes I've accumulated. "I'm going to be in my office for a while if you need help getting this stuff to your car."

"Thanks. I'm trying to be selective."

His phone pings with an incoming text. He ignores it while eyeing some books left on my shelf.

"Yes," I say. "These are for you. If you want them." I hand him the stack. "They're my favorites to teach."

"Ooo, *Fun Home*! You don't want this?" His phone pings again.

"We have a copy at home. *The Gilda Stories* also. Well, all of them."

He looks through the others. "Wonderful." All this time, his phone is pinging like crazy.

"Do you need to check that?"

"I'm working with a colleague from UCLA. We're proposing a paper for a conference."

He holds up the books. "These are amazing! Thank you." He doesn't hesitate to hug me now.

Now his phone rings. He answers. "Leslie—can I call you back in a minute? I'm not in my office."

"A girl Leslie or a boy Leslie?" I ask when he's off the phone. He looks puzzled, so I clarify. "I knew one of each in L.A."

"This one's a very demanding cisgender heterosexual girl. And if you think *I'm* high maintenance. I'll be in my office for a while. Let me know if you need a big, strong man to carry those boxes, little lady." He flexes his biceps and calls Leslie as he walks down the hall.

I'm left thinking of my Leslies. Girl Leslie was one of the first people I met in L.A. In fact, she was the one who introduced me to Boy Leslie. I actually listed them in my address book—does anyone still use an address book? —as Girl Leslie and Boy Leslie. We met in the late '70s, and our friendship grew as we three marched and phone-banked and stuffed envelopes for the No On 6 campaign. (An idiot assemblyman wanted to pass a bill making it legal to fire teachers for being homosexual.)

Boy Leslie had grown up in and then fled Dike, Iowa— "Yes, really," he'd always add—where a big night out meant heading to Waterloo. He knew from the age of five that he'd have to escape.

Ironically, given lesbians' penchant for serial monogamy, Boy Leslie was the only one of us in a stable relationship when we all met. His boyfriend Patrick was a partner in a big L.A. law firm and had given Leslie a year to write his book, a mystery with a gay protagonist. Boy Leslie had been working on it for a couple of years already. He had a low-wage job at A Different Light, the gay and lesbian bookstore in Silver Lake, and Patrick generously said he could have this time to finish it.

I didn't have a Patrick to support me, but I did have a friend, Jonathan, an agent with a small weekend house in Palm Springs. Jonathan was very generous with the place. He figured if he wasn't using it—and given his crazy hours and long days, he didn't get out of L.A. all that much—at least someone should enjoy it. Often I'd go down with my Leslies for a weekend. Boy Leslie was newly sober, and very determined to finish his book. He'd bring his pages and write. Girl Leslie and I would spend the day lying by the pool.

She and I had very different MOs. I'd wear a baseball cap and read a book or the trades. Girl Leslie would lie perfectly still, eyes closed, adjusting the angle of her chaise to follow the sun. At the end of the first day we'd done this, I compared my arm to hers. "You've got this golden glow, and I look like I've spent all my time inside," I complained.

"You were reading," Leslie said.

"What?"

"You need to focus."

"The sun didn't know I was reading."

She tilted her head toward her tanned arm and my pale one. "I'm just saying."

"Well, that's ridiculous."

Over time, I accepted the inferior results of my bronzing technique. I enjoyed the weekends we spent in the desert. When it was just the three of us, my two Leslies and me, we'd all have dinner together, then Boy Leslie would go back to his writing, and Girl Leslie and I would go out dancing. Remember, this was back when there actually were lesbian bars. The '80s were lively, with lots of partying. Often chemically enhanced. Personally, I liked cocaine or quaaludes. Coke let you feel in charge and in control. My first agent described its industry-wide popularity this way: "L.A. is a town that makes you feel bad about yourself. Cocaine is a drug that makes you feel good about yourself." Quaaludes were entirely different. The right amount loosened you up, let you slip inside the music, move along with it. I never understood the attraction to amyl nitrate. Poppers made my heart race, my pulse pound. I hated that feeling. And they left me with a splitting headache. Plus, they smelled like a locker room. A stuffy locker room. A stuffy boys' locker room. But to each her own.

One crazy evening, eight of us down from L.A. had arranged to meet up at a bar. Our friend Emily was going through a breakup, and we were determined to cheer her up with an evening of dancing.

For the record, I never dated anyone I'd met in a bar. Probably because I'd never met anyone in a bar. Never picked anyone up, never even recognized if someone was hitting on me. So I don't know why I went. Or why, when I did, I felt this anticipation that something might happen. Maybe it was just seeing all those women in one place. Back then, both here in the desert and up in L.A., lesbians were invisible most of the time, whether in or out of the closet. Going about our lives under cover during the day, definitely not a critical mass. But at night, in the bars, we saw each other. Each venue became ripe with possibility and promise.

But did I really think I'd meet someone there? Did I believe deep down? No. I just loved being around all those women. And I did love to dance.

That night in the desert, we did our best to bolster Emily's spirits. We danced as one big group. After a while, I was sweaty and needed a break. I stood by the edge of the dance floor. A sweet-looking young woman a few feet from me motioned to a couple dancing right in front of her. She said something to me that was impossible to hear over the pounding music, so I simply answered with a nod-laugh, like I knew what she meant.

Then Emily came over. Rather, our friends AJ and Jen dragged Emily, an arm draped over each of their shoulders, to me. "I have to go home," Emily told me. "I don't want to go home. But I don't have any bones."

Ah, quaaludes. While the right amount loosened you up, too much turned you to rubber.

By this time, leaving seemed like a good idea to me, too. AJ said they could drop me off, so I looked for Girl Leslie and spotted her dancing with a tall, athletic woman she'd been eyeing since we arrived. I gave Girl Leslie the sign that I was ready to head out. She spoke into her dance partner's ear and then came over to me.

"AJ's giving me a ride home," I said, handing Girl Leslie my car keys.

"Thanks. I'll stay and get to know Tanya better," Girl Leslie said, waving at the woman who hadn't stopped dancing but waved back.

"I'll bet you will," I smiled, waving to Tanya.

Girl Leslie punched my arm.

Outside, I breathed in the quiet of the desert night after the pulsing of the loud music. My head felt encased in a pillow. As always, I experienced a twinge of regret at leaving before something good happened. Even though I knew it never would.

Boy Leslie was smoking a cigarette outside by the pool when I got back to the house. I joined him. We sat in silence for a while, just looking at the stars.

"How'd the writing go tonight?" I asked. He was making final revisions, and his manuscript chapters covered the dining room table. "Looks like you were productive."

He made a so-so motion with his hand. "Was your mission successful?"

"Emily certainly was feeling no pain by the end of the evening." Then I told him what had happened. "She's still in love with Pam."

"So why don't they get back together?"

"Because Pam slept with Jackie."

"What is it with you girls and monogamy?"

This was a frequent topic of conversation between us. I didn't understand how gay men could have sex with other men and not consider that being unfaithful, but I didn't have the energy to debate tonight. Monogamy had little relevance to someone not in a relationship.

Boy Leslie patted my leg. "Look at all the stars. Let's each wish for something. But it needs to be something real. And important."

We both looked up. He pointed toward one constellation. "I choose that one."

I scanned the sky and found a bright cluster. "What's that one?"

Boy Leslie shrugged. "They all look like the Big Dipper to me."

"Okay. I'll take that."

We each tilted our heads back and were silent for about a minute.

"I wished that my book sells," Boy Leslie said. "What about you?"

"Are we allowed to tell?"

"Of course," he said. "Our game, our rules."

"Don't laugh." I looked at him.

He crossed his heart. "I promise."

"I've been thinking I might want to have a baby."

"You'd be such a great mom," Boy Leslie said.

I told him I hadn't done anything about this yet, it was a very nascent thought. But I did have friends who'd been through the process, which for two women is a process. Tests to see if they could conceive, choosing a donor, then the actual inseminations. It would be a costly undertaking, even before there was a baby. "Back when I slept with men," I said to Boy Leslie, "getting pregnant wouldn't have cost me a cent."

He took my hand. "You should go for it."

"Maybe I should wait till I'm in a relationship?"

We sat in silence a while longer.

"Who am I kidding?" I scoffed. "I'll never find anyone. I can't even manage a conversation with a woman." I told him about the sweet young thing who'd spoken to me from the dance floor sidelines. Then I burst out laughing.

"What?" Boy Leslie asked.

"I just realized—she was asking if I wanted to dance. I'm hopeless." Reeking of cigarette smoke—not only did a lot of people smoke back then, but they could do so in bars and restaurants—I sat under the desert stars and stewed about my inadequacies.

Boy Leslie said, "Patrick doesn't believe I'll ever finish. Maybe he's right."

Good. We can talk about someone else's problems. You couldn't really blame Patrick for being jaded. Everyone in L.A. was writing something. When I pulled into a gas station to fill up before heading to the desert, the attendant had been tapping away on a portable typewriter (not to be confused with a laptop computer).

"My year's almost up. I'm going to have to get a job soon."

"Your book is good," I reassured Boy Leslie. I'd already read his first draft, and he was just about done with the revisions. "Don't listen to Patrick. You'll get it published. And when my kid is old enough, I'll let her read it."

"It'll be a whole series by then," he added.

"That's the spirit," I said.

Girl Leslie came home while we were still sitting out there.

"I'm surprised to see you," I said. "What happened to Tanya?"

"Not interesting once you got her off the dance floor. God, all my clothes stink! And my hair. I'm going in," she said, indicating the pool. "Who's with me?"

As inviting as the water looked, lit from below, its clear blue lapping against the tiled sides of the pool, neither Boy Leslie nor I moved. "It's too much work to change into a suit," I said.

"Who said anything about a suit?" Girl Leslie asked, stripping down to her underpants and then shedding them before diving in, her evenly tanned body cutting through the water. She pulled herself underwater the length of the pool before surfacing at the other end. "You're both poops." She swam back toward us and hauled herself out in one smooth motion. She picked up her clothes, made a face at their smell. "I'm going to bed."

All that was left of her presence were her wet footprints on the deck and the motion of the water.

"That girl's got spunk," said Boy Leslie.

He and I sat together a while longer before heading inside. Boy Leslie stopped at his door. He gave me a big hug. Still holding on, he whispered, "You could join me." He let go, stepped back, and waited.

I miss cues from women, so I certainly wasn't attuned to anything coming from a man. Especially a gay man. Especially this gay man. It took me a long moment to realize what he was offering. This nice-looking guy—that's how my parents would have described him, nice-looking, meaning not so handsome he'd break your heart—and he had money; well, Patrick did, and they shared everything—was offering to father my child.

In case I didn't get it, he added, "It'd be just like the old days. Won't cost you anything."

Don't think I wasn't tempted. Whatever kind of mother I'd have been, Boy Leslie would have made a terrific father—so would Patrick— and many of my other male friends. I could see all the guys taking my kid to the theatre, ballet, concerts. And my dyke friends teaching my kid how to throw a ball, set up a campsite, build something.

"Just know the offer's there," he said. Then we went off to bed. Separately.

Boy Leslie and I took a rather hungover Girl Leslie out to breakfast the next morning. When we returned to the house, Jonathan's Mercedes convertible was in the driveway. We thought we'd find him in the pool. But he was seated at the dining table, reading Boy Leslie's manuscript. "This is fantastic! I couldn't stop reading!" Jonathan said as we walked in. "Promise I'll be the first to see it when it's finished."

I don't know who was more surprised, Boy Leslie or Patrick, when Jonathan offered to represent Leslie a few months later. And then got him a two-book deal plus talk of a film adaptation. No job-hunting for him.

To celebrate, Girl Leslie, Patrick, and I toasted Boy Leslie with champagne. The honoree stuck to sparkling cider. It had been a great week for him—learning about the book deal and celebrating his one-year AA birthday. Matt and Dennis, best friends who had taken him to his first meeting, were there also. Boy Leslie thanked us individually before saying, "I'm so grateful for each of you. I feel so lucky—this is going to be a great year."

And it was. Our chosen family saw each other several times a month for dinner or brunch. We were in on each other's triumphs and trials, big and little decisions: Do we buy a house? Should I paint the living room? We celebrated holidays together, often with Matt and Dennis, and other friends. Girl Leslie and I had a brief...I can't call it a relationship, but we did end up in bed together and going out on a few legit dates until we realized we were meant to be best friends. Then Girl Leslie started seeing Diane, her first serious girlfriend in years, and luckily we all loved her.

We were all having a great year. Boy Leslie's book was about to come out and he was almost finished with the second. Diane and Girl Leslie moved in together, started talking about having children. That was wonderful news to me, because by then I had realized that what I really wanted to be was an aunt, not a mother.

Like the false resolutions early in a film—you know, in a romcom when the meet-cute couple seem to be getting along great before the blow up, or when a problem has been solved so early that you know bigger trouble lies ahead—we moved along not suspecting that Boy Leslie would be dead two years later. They all were: Boy Leslie, Patrick, Jonathan. Matt. Dennis. And so many of the others I'd marched with and worked with and met at Leslie and Patrick's holiday parties. Patrick was diagnosed first. Then Boy Leslie's A.A. sponsor died. Boy Leslie died a month after Patrick.

A pall had fallen over the city, and the phone had become an instrument of death notices. You'd be talking to a friend, hear the stutter tone to indicate a call waiting, ask your friend to hold, press the receiver button, say hello, then hear, "Is this Hannah?" A tentative voice I wouldn't recognize.

I'd be tentative right back. "Yes?" My voice rising, making it a question, more of a please-don't-be-what-I-think-this-is than an acknowledgment of my identity.

"Hi. I'm Jennifer Johnson. I'm Leslie's sister."

How many of those calls did we get, from sisters or cousins, people we'd never met who'd been delegated the unenviable task of going through their dead brother's/cousin's/friend's address book to announce another death from AIDS complications. How many condolence letters had I written? Some to men who themselves would be dead in a matter of months. If not weeks.

Girl Leslie, Diane, and I were practically inseparable after that. Then we folded Grace into the family. Leslie and Diane threw us a huge going-away party. Leslie joked it was her way of making sure I actually left.

Grace and I were halfway cross country when we found out Leslie had been diagnosed with breast cancer. "Very treatable," she assured us over the phone. I could see her brushing it off like it was nothing.

I remembered Boy Leslie's comment— "She's got spunk." I held on to that assessment. She'd be okay. And she was. After aggressive treatment, she had a couple of years in remission until, well, no more remission. No more treatment. Grace and I booked a flight out to be with her and Diane, say a proper goodbye. But by the time we arrived, instead of going to their house where we'd be staying, we went straight to the hospital where Leslie had been admitted that morning. The cancer had spread to her brain, so she didn't recognize either of us, didn't even really see us, because she was too intent on getting out of bed so she could go home.

Grace and I waited up that night until Diane came in, too exhausted and depleted to do more than sit between us on the couch. We never got our real goodbye.

My Leslies and I were all supposed to get old together. Twenty-five years after these losses, I'm the only one left.

Oliver understands that. In some ways, he understands more than my lesbian friends because he lost people, too. Which of course makes me think of Oscar Wilde's "To lose one parent may be regarded as misfortune; to lose both looks like carelessness."

A knock on my door interrupts my reverie. I expect Oliver and am ready to tell him the long version of how I came to know Boy and Girl Leslie. Tell him how I miss not only Grace but all the people I lost. How I want to talk to someone who experienced some of this, the same losses I did, who would understand just how deep this went, who could converse with me using the shorthand of devastation and death.

There is no way to fully process certain losses. Grief is not linear, and being happy isn't the only happiness, and all these ideas are in my head at once, and I don't know which will pop out first, but Oliver will understand. He'll also understand this burgeoning sense of, not adventure, but of making the most of whatever time is left, that's come over me. I look up to try to start somewhere.

But it's not Oliver. Ellen stands in my doorway.

She must recognize something on my face. "Are you okay?"

It takes me a moment to come back to the present. "I am." As if to convince myself, I motion to the mostly packed-up state of my office.

Even though she doesn't look convinced, Ellen says, "Very impressive."

"Would you like to grab dinner tonight?" That's me asking. What's taken over my brain? "I'm planning to finish here, then head over to clear out Grace's office. It'd be nice to have something to look forward to after."

Seriously, who's talking? My sense of adventure isn't really about adventure, just about being present, being here now. Is that supposed to include other people? Having to make conversation?

"Sure," says Ellen.

"Six-thirty okay with you?" Listen to me, sounding like a functioning adult.

"Perfect." She AirDrops her contact info to my phone so I'll have her address. "Come by, and we can walk downtown."

As soon as she leaves, I'm back in my dark place, as if I hadn't been interrupted. And out of that void emerges an image of Boy Leslie's writing chair.

Before anyone got sick, I'd go over to the swanky condo Patrick had moved them into, part of a complex of townhouses near Century City, and Boy Leslie and I would read each other's pages.

The place was big enough for him to have his own study, but Leslie preferred a green leather wingback chair set in what had been intended as an eating nook off the kitchen that he made into a writing space.

Is it strange that I call up that tableau before I see an image of Leslie himself? A pad and pen on the empty chair, a worn pair of brown penny loafers tossed off on the floor next to it, an assortment of pens and more pads at the ready. That empty chair and those kicked-off loafers spring to mind every time I think of Boy Leslie—each represents him, as if they were a foreshadow of his death.

If I were an artist, I'd create a piece in honor of each of my lost men and women. I'd recreate Boy Leslie's chair with his loafers and pads and pens. Maybe a whole row of chairs. All empty. For Girl Leslie, the rippling water of a cool blue California pool. For Grace—too soon to know.

12
Evidence

I'm still a little stuck in Palm Springs with my Leslies. I keep seeing the pool that night after Girl Leslie pulled herself out. I flash to the swimming pools in David Hockney's paintings and understand in that instant how he captured not just the movement of the water but its capacity to be both seen and seen through. I want to share this observation with Grace, tell her how I've never been able to look at pools the same way since seeing this work. It would be the most natural thing in the world to do that. And then we'd probably have a conversation about the power of art to make us see the world anew.

Instead, I shake myself out of the past and check my watch. Four-fifteen. That gives me about two hours to get over to Grace's office and accomplish as much as possible before heading to meet Ellen. I no longer feel that impetus to be present, have no sense of adventure, wonder if I should cancel. Tough. You made the plan. Follow through.

I gather my newly arranged and sorted possessions and make a neat stack of boxes. Then I head down the hall to Oliver's office.

The sounds of Oscar Peterson's piano drift from his open door. Too few of our colleagues understand the importance of how their offices feel. Not just look. Because it's not only about neatness or what's hanging on the walls, but how it fits together. The gestalt. Can a room have a gestalt? Whatever. You walk into Oliver's and immediately feel calm. Informally organized shelves, nice prints hanging. He's even got a plant. No wonder there's always a bunch of students sitting in the hallway outside his door waiting to meet with him during his office hours.

"I'm ready if your offer still holds," I say.

We grab a rolling cart from the mail room and Oliver follows me back to my office. Right off he notices a photo I'd left tacked on the wall near a small mirror. "This is great," he says. "I remember that day. Grace was such a powerhouse."

I was so used to its being there I hadn't taken it down. It was taken on National Coming Out Day at least ten years ago. Maybe longer. We'd had a big rally on campus, and out faculty lined up to start it off. Grace had been the first to speak. You can see the fire in her eyes, the sheer joy she took in being able to stand in front of a crowd and state who she was. This was nothing new. She was like that when I first met her.

"It's so liberating, Hannah! Come with me." This was way before moving East and when we were still in L.A. ACT-UP was sponsoring protests against a piece of anti-gay legislation moving through the California assembly. Grace had just come from one. Everyone had gathered on a corner of a busy intersection in the Valley at rush hour. They held signs, paraded in a tight circle on the sidewalk. At the appointed time, they'd all gathered at the curb, waiting for a signal from the leader. When his arm dropped, everyone stepped off the curb into traffic. Grace had come home exhilarated. "Come with me tomorrow," she said again. There was another march planned for Hollywood the next day. "Boy Leslie would want you to."

That wasn't fair, and Grace knew it. She even apologized to me. Though she'd never met him—or Patrick, any of them—she knew how much these men had meant to me and how we'd met fighting for our rights.

"Earth to Hannah. Do you read me?" Oliver's waving his hand between me and the photograph.

I return to the present, marveling at the power of that photograph to prompt memory. That had been my goal. I've loosened something, cracked the hard shell encasing my old life and now memories are oozing out. What if they all come at once and I can't staunch the flow? I should be careful what I wish for.

"Do all of these go?" Oliver's motioning to a stack of boxes.

I nod. I'm only partly here. I grab the photo off the wall and add it to the box. Then I stand in my office as Oliver loads the boxes onto the cart. After he's left, I look around. Desk is cleared. Shelves also. I can't gauge my feelings about vacating this space I've inhabited for so many years because they're all tied in with, no, subsumed by, Grace. By not-Grace. By Grace's death.

I grab the floor lamp and a bag of stuff, turn out the light, and shut the door behind me.

Oliver is standing by my car as I walk out of the building. I pop the trunk and he loads the boxes. We have to fold down the back seat (more Prius ingenuity) to fit everything. We manage to balance the lamp on top of it all.

I put a bankers box on the front passenger seat. It's got the picture of Grace from the campus rally. I like the idea of having company.

"You're good to go," Oliver says.

We look at each other for a moment. At the same time we open our arms for a hug. What kind of good-bye is this? Who knows. He's been a great colleague, but we never socialized much outside of school events. And now I'm retired and there's no more Grace to gather colleagues at the house for a meal over which we'd brainstorm or strategize about a new school policy or have an informal salon, people sharing work, talking about ideas.

"You take care of yourself," he whispers. "Let me know if there's anything Gustavo or I can do. And let's grab dinner sometime."

I nod into his shoulder and then we break apart.

I drive to Grace's building, park, and head to her office. I'm determined to finish up there today. To be present, to handle some items that might prompt more memories. I'm trying to just *do*, not think.

I have the rest of my life to think, I think as I climb the stairs to Grace's floor.

Mary and Jordan have done a great job with the bookcases and the big file cabinet. Grace's shelves are totally cleared, even dusted. Book boxes are labeled for easy identification. Despite my resolve to keep my space clean and spare, I dig through "ARTISTS A-E. BIOS/MONOGRAPHS" and pull out a few Hockney books. I also have to decide what to do with the video game and the Seven Deadly Sins postcards that still sit on the display shelf. They're held together with a rubber band and labeled with an acid green post-it marked: <u>???</u>

Good question.

I put off answering and turn to the big file cabinet. Three of its four drawers are empty. The last one has a sticky note attached: "We didn't know if you'd want any of this. Take what you do—I'll deal with the rest. M." Bless Mary's organized heart.

Given how much everything hurt when I was last here, how raw I was, I start to pull open the drawer very slowly to give myself the most time to prepare for any triggers I might find. Then I remember I'm here expressly to find those triggers. Bring it!

There's not much left. I start with grade books. They're from at least fifteen years earlier, nothing more recent. That must have been when Grace switched to digital record keeping. Into recycle they go.

Next up: Conference and convention badges, their lanyards and clips neatly sorted. I don't even look at these. Toss.

Mugs and utensils. After a five-second debate about whether to keep Grace's favorite mug, with an image of the *Pac-Man* screen that changes when you pour in hot liquid, I decide to leave them all as a contribution to the faculty lounge.

A few small jewelry boxes. I recognize these, since I have my own collection. They contain pins for years of service to the college. Who cares. Since I can't bring myself to toss them, I place the boxes on an empty bookshelf along with the mugs.

I return to the *Pac-Man* mug. Maybe I still care about this. We'd seen it on a trip to a conference. "Check this out," Grace called to me from the aisle where she'd found it. *Pac-Man* took each of us back to our early, early days when arcade games like *Pac-Man, Asteroids,* and *Space Invaders* stood near the pool tables in all the lesbian bars. I'd returned to the store to buy it when Grace was at a panel and hid it in my luggage. I planned to surprise her with it when it felt right. We'd each do that, give each other little presents for no particular occasion—maybe it was the first day of the semester, or to cheer the other up, or to celebrate making it through finals. I had pulled out the mug when Grace was elected department chair and made her promise to use it at every meeting she ran. I didn't want her taking herself too seriously.

I look at it now, the blue grid of the game the only visible image. I could go to the faculty lounge, boil some water, and watch the board come to life—the yellow dots light up, the ghosts appear. And I could bring it home and watch that every day. But then I think: My goal is to simplify my life. This will allow clutter back in. Once it's home, I won't ever be able to get rid of it. And I don't need any more ghosts showing up.

Back on the shelf it goes.

And that's that. I check my watch. I've only been here for fifteen minutes. With the exception of that little *Pac-Man* detour, this has been a breeze. I can be done in plenty of time to meet Ellen. I find myself looking forward to the evening. And immediately feel guilty, like I'm being unfaithful to Grace.

I argue back and forth with myself about this. Why should I feel guilty? It's not a date. Not a date date. Just dinner with someone I'm getting to know better as a friend. And what if it were a date? Which it isn't. I look around the office, listen for her. But Grace is silent on the subject. Has been silent for a while, come to think of it. No messages, no dictated lists. Have I pushed her away? Is she angry with me because of Ellen? It's not a date!

Now I'm just being silly. Grace has nothing to say because she's dead. Still and always. But again: maybe she's happy for me that I'm regaining some memories, interacting with living people. Maybe she thinks I'm making Progress! The Girls, Oliver, Ellen. Maybe it was even Grace who pushed me to suggest dinner.

Focus on the task at hand.

I sit at Grace's desk. Once I've cleaned it out, our official connection with the college will be over. I take a deep breath. I'm ready.

I pull open the bottom drawer on the right. Hanging files. Very organized—clearly labeled folders containing student information, department and college rules and regulations, department business.

Probably recyclable since this is all available online, but Mary can decide. I slide that drawer shut. Easy.

Left bottom drawer. Same hanging file setup, but these folders contain course information, handouts, articles. Old conference programs with notes and (probably defunct) phone numbers scribbled in the margins. Having been through my own desk, I understand how easy it is to keep this shit. You don't even think about it. Just shove it in a drawer to get it out of the way, knowing you'll deal with it later. (I have a whole new concept of later.) How easy to accumulate stuff to fill up any size space. I'm pretty sure all this can be recycled, but don't want to make any mistakes in case any of the course information is relevant, and write a note to that effect to Mary.

Two drawers down, four to go. I opt for the middle left. Clearly this was Grace's food drawer. A pepper mill. Hand wipes. A stack of napkins, lots of take-out chopsticks. Coffee pods. A few plastic plates, more utensils. Three kinds of hot sauce. A half-empty pack of birthday candles and a Bic lighter that actually works. I'll keep that. This is easy. I'm on a roll.

Top left drawer: department envelopes, letterhead, paper clips, staples, butterfly clips. I box it up and leave it all for Mary. This is too easy! What am I going to do with all my extra time before I have to meet Ellen? Maybe take a walk around campus, sort of a farewell tour.

I turn to the final two drawers. Top right is a veritable rainbow of sticky notes in assorted shapes, colors, and sizes. Pens and markers in two colors only: blue and black. Lots of pencils and erasers. Notepads. A pencil sharpener. Grace was nothing if not organized.

Even though I've got plenty at home, I grab one pad of neon pink sticky notes and shove it in my pocket along with the Bic lighter. Tactile triggers. Or representational talismans that won't take up too much room. Maybe I'll make a little shrine.

I open the last drawer. This contains fresh letter-size lined pads. Underneath those are notebooks and pads with Grace's distinct handwriting. She wrote notes for her classes in longhand as a way to organize her thoughts, even though she didn't refer to them in class. Same for her articles, draft after draft until she was ready to type them up. I look through a few and recognize key words and themes she'd talked to me about, some as recently as the morning of my retirement party—ideas for future articles. One pad is filled with notes for her sabbatical project, not only ideas, but towns to visit, even restaurants to try. Is this her legacy? Did she want a legacy? We never talked about that. What would she have wanted me to do with her unpublished work? Save it? Pass it along to—whom? We have wills, but never talked about literary remains. I look around the room hoping to see Grace standing there ready to give me instructions. If anything would bring her around, this oughta do it. "Come on. A hint. Keep? Pass along to…Ava? Cristina?"

I allow ample time for her to respond. Surely she has opinions. Her work. Her projects. Her thoughts. I sit perfectly still, listening. I even hold my breath. Nothing. Gulls soar past the window. "Okay then," I say out loud. "If you're sure."

But I'm not sure. I realize I don't have to figure it out here. I can just throw everything into a box, or five boxes, and bring it all home. Sort through it at my leisure, or just dump it without looking. Decide later. Because something about these notebooks, the very present-tenseness of them, the sense that they're living documents, this was for the future. No hint of illness or anything that would prevent Grace from finishing these articles, delivering these lectures, writing her book, sharing this information with her students, visiting these places with me—it's the closest I'll get to what we used to have, when Grace would share an idea with me, or the germ of an idea. I want to preserve that time with her for just a little longer. I pull over a bankers box and start loading it up.

As I transfer one of the last notebooks from the drawer a bunch of photographs spill out. What are the odds we'd each have the same forgotten stack? Maybe I'll find some to add to the shrine I've envisioned. I look through them. Some are, in fact, duplicates of ones I'd found in my office. But: Grace and me when we'd just moved, in front of our respective offices, at the entrance to the college. Definite keepers. I toss these into the box. Next batch: water. We'd taken several trips through the Finger Lakes. This is Cayuga Lake and some of the gorges in fall and winter. Stark contrast to the next one, shot in the bright sun of Venice Beach, Grace and me on bicycles. God we were young! I remember that day. That whole time. Which proves to me I was right to do this excavation. I can almost smell the suntan lotion. The salt air. More memories.

Then a different body of water. A beach. But not the ocean; high-rise apartments in the background. I recognize Chicago, its own waterways depicted in various shots. These must be from the architectural boat tour Grace and Kit took when she was at that conference. There Grace is, standing with her colleague Jean, both smiling, splashing in the fountains in Millennium Park, posing arms around each other in front of the Silver Bean. I can make out Kit's distorted reflection in the sculpture as she takes the picture.

I study Grace. Mid-thirties, thrilled to be teaching, set to deliver an important paper, excited to be sharing her research with colleagues at this conference. Everything about it excited her. I feel guilty now for giving her such a hard time about Kit when she came home.

Speak of the devil. The next photo is of Grace and Kit. They're not touching, no comradely arms around each other. They're merely leaning into each other, hands in pants pockets, each looking directly into the camera. I drop the photo into the trash. I'm willing to sacrifice one photo of Grace. I don't need another reminder of my petty jealousy from all those years ago, nor do I need a picture of Kit. I continue to flip through the stack. Like the others, they're in no particular order—chronological or geographical. Many are here in town, shots of the campus under a blanket of snow, crab apple trees in bloom, spring buds pushing through dead leaves. I find one of Grace and me on a beach in Mexico. I remember that trip, swimming every morning before breakfast, walking on the beach, immensely grateful to be able to escape winter for a few days. Another one of the two of us, arms around each other. But the clear blue of the Caribbean waters doesn't calm this nagging feeling I have, a sharp tug in the middle of my chest. Against my better judgment I pull the photo of Grace and Kit out of the trash.

I had tossed it without turning it over. Now I see a note in Kit's handwriting. And she fucking signed it "K." Not Kit, just K. Like when she called Grace Gracie the first night I met her. The years telescope. I'm filled with rage and shame as I read: *Thank you!*

How many ways do I parse that sentence. The two words—thank you—innocuous, innocent. But with an exclamation point? That changes the meaning entirely.

I look at the photo again. This time I read the Thank you! and the exclamation into it. That changes how they look. The way they lean into each other. Both with the same smile. At first I can't put my finger on it.

Then I can.

I know it as surely as if I'd read it in one of the notebooks I'd just packed away, or if Kit had written it in her inscription.

They'd slept together.

I never asked outright, though I had shown my jealousy when Grace came back from Chicago and I detected a certain awkwardness whenever Kit was mentioned. Grace picked up immediately on my discomfort and tried to reassure me. But presenting me with that glass apple paperweight and taking me out to dinner wasn't really an answer to my unasked question, was it.

But I shouldn't have had to ask outright. Or even had to think about it, am I right?

I'm being ridiculous. Twenty-five years we had together. Twenty-five. We'd been happy. Could she have lived a lie all that time? No. We'd been through surgeries, 9/11, disasters, gay marriage, and in the last few years the most disastrous, dangerous, lunatic of a president. You can't fake it for so many years. Talk of Kit had faded. My thoughts about Kit had faded. Grace and I had had a full, rich, committed life. So, no. It wasn't a lie. Then why am I still thinking about this? I wrack my brain trying to remember what happened in the months after Chicago, or the rest of that year. What did we do? What am I forgetting? I fan through the memories I've been able to recover. No sign, no tell, nothing to indicate Grace was hiding anything, keeping a secret. Of course she wasn't. We didn't keep secrets from each other.

I'm rocketed back to that evening on the hill when Kit roared up on her Gold Wing. Her intimacy with Grace. Gracie.

Focus, Hannah. Come back. Grace and I had been together so long it became hard to distinguish one year from another. But not in a rote way. Just...we'd built such a life together. So many highlights. Was the year of the Chicago conference the same year we sold the car we'd driven here from L.A.? I think that was the year we started house-hunting for real.

I curse my depleted memory bank.

If I picture us driving around looking at neighborhoods, meeting with realtors until we found the one we went with, can I detect any hint of— of what? What am I looking for? Signs of guilt? Distance from me? Disinterest in me, or us? All this time I'm looking for triggers, fingering items I come across as if my memories resided in this mug, that pencil.

Nothing's helping.

"Fuck you!" I say it out loud. "I've spent the entire time since you died trying to remember our precious life together, realizing what a luxury to just take us for granted because we were going to go on until I died. Until *I died. Me. My* death was going to be the end. Not yours. And now this? I followed you off that curb at the ACT-UP demonstration and it *was* liberating. I followed you to fucking New York State, for fuck's sake. I would have walked through fire for you. And I learn this? Now? You're dead and I learn this? Are you fucking kidding me?"

My rant leaves me out of breath. Under my rasping inhales I hear a faint sound. Or feel a ripple in the air. I try to still my breathing. Is Grace asking me to forgive her?

Seriously?

I look at the photograph again. Both Grace and Kit are smiling. They're not super close or clingy. But now that I've seen their connection it's the first thing I notice. The only thing. It jumps out and would be apparent to anyone who looked. I can't not see it.

My vision tunnels, bores into their faces in the photo, everything around me a swirl of dark energy. Their features so alive I swear I can hear the sounds of the park around them. Children screaming with delight in the splashing fountains, their footsteps pounding as they run around the sculpture. My rage is so intense I feel its heat. As if the picture were on fire.

Which, turns out, it is. Because I've taken the Bic lighter to it. I drop the photo onto the carpet, stomp it out. Stomp more than a flimsy piece of paper warrants. Stomp till I'm out of breath again.

A wave of nausea sweeps over me. I drop into Grace's chair. How could I not have known? What distracted me from noticing one tiny clue planted early in our years together, the equivalent of the gun in act one that would have to go off later? And how could Grace not tell me? How long did their affair last? How could she live all those years without telling? Was our whole life together a lie?

My thoughts spiral into a tight spring that propels me forward.

Next thing I know I'm in my car. Parked. But not on campus. A residential street. I have no recollection of leaving Grace's office. Or driving.

I still hold the lighter.

A knock on my window startles me.

13

Close Calls

"Are you all right? Hannah?"

The voice, muted, comes from a great distance. I look to the source. Ellen leans over slightly so she can see into my car. Her voice is soft because the window is closed. It appeared to come from a great distance because I'm at a great distance from everything, still inside the tunnel at the end of which stand Grace and Kit, smiling. Or are they laughing at me, at how dense I am?

Ellen raps again—motions for me to exit the car.

I do as I'm told.

"Mission accomplished, I'm guessing," she says, looking at all the boxes stuffed in the back.

A beat late, I look at the contents, then back at Ellen.

"Are you okay?" she asks.

I manage to shake my head.

Ellen takes my arm, moves me away from the door, which is still open, and closes it. "You should lock it."

I do.

Ellen steers me into her house. She makes small talk as we go. Telling me I'm early, but that's okay. Telling me we don't have to go out. Telling me if we don't go out, I should still maybe sit for a while till I'm okay to drive home.

This brings us safely up her steps and into her thoughtfully decorated living room. Original art on the walls, furniture that goes well together but isn't all matchy-matchy. She guides me to a very comfortable couch and sits next to me. She still holds my arm in a firm, steadying grip. After a brief moment, maybe she's making sure I'm not going to fall over onto the coffee table where a book lies open next to a glass of red wine, Ellen gets up and leaves the room. When she returns, she's holding a box of Kleenex, having already plucked a few which she offers to me.

I'm not crying, but I take the tissues anyway. Then I think Ellen's looking at me with such concern I wonder if maybe I should be crying. Or if she thinks I have good reason to cry, given all I've had to deal with on top of Grace's death—removing everything from Grace's office, and from my own. It must make me realize that I'm retiring and won't be teaching or meeting with students, won't have a place to go to, a reason to get up in the morning.

I'm not a mind reader. Ellen is actually saying some of these things to me. Maybe not in those exact words, but that's her intention. And she's rubbing my back while she's talking. And I find it very comforting. And sad, too. And then Ellen wraps both her arms around me, strictly for comfort, I'm sure of that. But where I've just come from, what I've just realized, well, seize the fucking moment. Right, Grace? Isn't that what you did?

I move away a little, take my head from Ellen's shoulder, look into her eyes for a split second, and move in for a kiss. She's surprised. Tries to pull back, but I'm persistent. My hand has snaked its way up her back to her neck, and I hold her against me as our kiss deepens, and I'm still not thinking, just sensing: my lips on hers, our mouths opening. I ask Grace: how does it feel?

I leap up.

Ellen remains on the couch, not looking at me, still holding the Kleenex box. She runs a hand through her hair.

"I'm so sorry," I say. "I didn't mean that." I feel terrible. "It's been...I've had...I ..." I can't seem to finish a sentence, and certainly can't explain myself. I settle for "rough day" and mumble something about a rain check.

I take myself out of the house and want to start the car the moment I sit behind the wheel and peel away with a screech of tires, except for a second I forget how this works. I go to put the key in the ignition, except I don't have the key. Shit! Did I leave it on Ellen's coffee table? Then I remember this is the Prius—no key to insert. The key never came out of my pocket. Okay. I've got it. Step on the brake, push the power button. Okay. We're good to go.

Once I'm in motion, I yell at the top of my lungs. Some incoherent screams to start with, a warmup. But then words. Stupid! Stupidstupidstupid! Stupid! I pound the wheel for emphasis.

Am I yelling at myself? At Grace? Does it matter?

Stupid!

But Grace wasn't stupid. She was a traitor.

I was the one who'd been stupid when I kissed Ellen. Stupid because that wasn't a kiss. That was a weapon I'd wielded against Grace. Against Kit. I won't put their names together—they weren't a pair.

I owe Ellen an apology.

Shit! Stupid!

My rant lasts the whole ride home.

I storm into the house, relieved the Girls aren't home yet. I need privacy now. I need to yell. I pace the living room. Now that I've had my Kit realization, I have something to focus my anger at, rather than just at Grace for having died.

I rage at her for cheating on me.

So what if it was over twenty years ago.

If it even happened...

Oh, it happened all right—look at the identical smiles on their faces in that photo. But I can't look at the photo because it's ashes. Thank you!

I'm furious. Livid. I wrap my arms tight around myself so I don't throw things and then have to explain the mess to the Girls. What am I supposed to do with all this anger? I can't have it out with Grace, can't ask her what Kit meant to her, what anything meant, what our life together after that betrayal meant. Or before, even—had she been lying the whole time since we started? Otherwise how could she do that to me? To us. I'd been bereft when Ellen broke the glass apple Grace brought me from Chicago. Now I wish I could break it myself.

I'm such an idiot. I'd been trying to make our house my own, a near-impossible project—and now I know that will never happen.

I storm into the bedroom. I've been yelling at Grace this whole time, but now I can look at her while I shout. "What did you do! How could you! And you didn't tell me! What am I supposed to do with this information? Who were we? Who were you? What am I supposed to believe? What does this do to...everything!" I say words, I curse, I yell. I won't go into Grace's office, won't give her a chance to answer me. I don't want to hear what she has to say. And that only reminds me that anything she might say wouldn't really be coming from her because she's dead and isn't going to say anything ever again. About anything. And here I am yelling at a stainless steel urn in a room that's feeling more and more claustrophobic.

I pause long enough to change out of my nice clothes and then hop back into the loop of anger that Grace is dead, anger that she slept with Kit, fury, incomprehension, grief.

I hope at some point I'll run out of steam, collapse on the couch, and wake up with the sun on my face and maybe the strength to deal with this. I would like a little oblivion. But the Girls will be home soon and I don't want them to find me there. More to the point, I don't want to see anyone right now.

I take myself to the Little House where I can vent and scream to my broken heart's content. I wear myself out storming the perimeter of the front room and force myself to lie on the couch where I fall into a fitful sleep, only to wake after an hour. I repeat that pattern a few times and then I'm on my feet again.

I pace in tighter and tighter circles until an idea explodes in my head, and I'm back out the door and in the car before I can talk myself down from it.

I drive like a maniac, one goal, one goal only. It's like a beat in my head to the rhythm of the wheels on the road. Until I discover that what I'm actually hearing is a steady knocking against the window behind me.

The floor lamp has been rolling from one side of the car to the other ever since I'd swung onto Route 81. A few miles back, it finally locked in place between a box and the window behind me, which was a huge relief until I hit a bump on 380 that loosened it and started the rattling again.

When I can stand it no longer, I pull off at a rest stop. I've no intention of resting. I don't even turn off the engine, just get out and open the hatchback and try to work the lamp loose from whatever it's stuck on. I'm working in the dark, almost blind, because I was too dumb to park under one of the streetlamps in the area. But that's fine with me. I can feel the hook of the neck is caught. I turn, I twist. Never force, a mechanic once told me. But maybe he'd never been cheated on. Anger plus frustration give me super strength. I yank the pole hard and I'm able to pull the lamp out of the car. Whatever I'd done dislodged a box lid, scattering some of the contents. I stand the lamp on the ground while I rummage in the dim light to put everything back, reconfigure all the boxes for a tighter fit.

I slam the hatchback and get into the car.

Back on the road, hurtling through the night once again, pleased to hear only the hum of the tires on the pavement, I pride myself on my engineering genius. Grace would be proud of me. Then I remember I'm mad at Grace. Mad at myself.

And then I realize the reason the lamp no longer rattles against the window or anything else is because it's standing where I left it, twenty-five miles back at the rest stop.

I don't care. I'm laser-focused on my goal.

The average drive time from our house to New York City is four hours. Stops for food and gas, breaks for stretching or peeing, add to that. But if you're obsessive and enraged, you can hit the West Side Highway in three and a half hours. Especially if you're driving at night, even if your night vision isn't what it used to be. Your rage has honed your focus; you're speeding, and the car has never handled so well.

I'm in the Village at 4:45 a.m. and pull over by a hydrant (the only empty spot) on a tree-lined side street. I need a moment to lose the feeling I'm still moving, to just be still. I hardly know how I got here. I'm not entirely sure of the address I want, but I'll recognize the building when I see it. I desperately need to pee. First, find a legal place to park. I nose back into the street and begin the hunt.

The sun isn't up yet, but it's already starting to get light. I turn off the a/c and open the windows. I love the heavy air of the city in summer. Whenever my L.A. friends complained about the humidity, I'd just laugh at them. They didn't know from humid. This is what it feels like, like you're conscious of the atmosphere. The streets are still empty. I hear trucks bouncing up 6th Avenue, but the leafy side streets are quiet. Unidentified nostalgia weighs on me. I shut it down. I can't let myself be distracted by any of this. I'm on a mission.

I drive around until by some miracle I find a space on West 4th. I turn off the engine. When I close my eyes, I feel like I'm still in motion. I breathe in, out, calmly, until my body, if not my brain, is at rest.

I get out of the car, resolved to accomplish what I've come for. This is going to fix—I don't know what it's going to fix, or if this is fixable, I only know I need to do this. I'm going to find the brownstone Grace and I visited once, many years ago. I'm going to walk up its steps, ring the bell. Then I'm going to confront Kit.

I detour into a 24-hour diner. I sit at the counter, order coffee and a cheese Danish, then head to the bathroom. By the time I'm back, having peed, washed my hands, and splashed water on my face, my order's ready. I drink the coffee, eat as much of the pastry as I can handle, leave payment plus tip, and head back outside.

I stand a moment to orient myself, then cross 6th Avenue to head west. Not only do I not have an address for Kit, I don't even know if she still lives here—though who'd be foolish enough to give up a rent-controlled apartment in the city? Or is it rent-stabilized? I can't be bothered with that now. It's going to take a while to find her building, a systematic walking of each block. I remember its position on the north side of the street, midway down the block. I see it clearly in my mind's eye.

Now I set out to find it.

All the clear logic of the Manhattan street grid goes out the window in the Village. Avenues go at crazy angles rather than on a straight north-south line, some streets have names rather than numbers, and even the numbered streets don't let you know where you really are, since West 4th intersects with West 10th, West 11th, West 12th, and West 13th. The illogic suits my mood. That unspecified nostalgia accompanies me on my methodical search. I don't let myself be charmed by the brownstones and small apartment buildings I pass. A few times I think, this must be the one. But the butterflies in my stomach pass when I realize, no, that isn't it.

By now the sun is up and it's dog-walking time. I observe women in yoga pants or tights, coffee tumbler in one hand, leash in the other, scrolling through their phones, paying little to no attention to Fido. Gay men in tight shorts and tank tops, designer slides, their perfectly groomed pets reflections of their tight-muscled selves. These Villagers go about their mornings as if this day were ordinary. Just another hot summer's day slog through the routine. For me, this day is anything but routine.

Especially now that I've spotted Kit's brownstone.

My pulse races. I'm thinking about what I'm going to say to her. What I'm going to do. I want to flatten her. Will I throw a punch? Or let her have it in a speech? I've been inarticulate with rage thus far, what would change? Am I a woman of action?

We'll find out soon enough.

"Fucking Kansas, Grace?"

"It's not Kansas-Kansas. Lawrence is a university town. It's progressive, like Ithaca."

"Kansas is Kansas is Kansas," I counter. "Do you not remember?"

When we'd driven cross country from California to Ithaca, Grace and I had made a point of stopping to eat in "real" places, not just fast-food chains off the Interstate. Looking for local diners or restaurants had been our policy till Kansas, where a man had made me so uncomfortable with the dirty stares he gave us that I swear I thought he was going to come over and harass us. I still believed that if it hadn't been for his wife's presence, he'd have done something to show his son how a real man behaved. Anyway, I'd been so intimidated we gave up on sampling a flavor of whatever town we were in. Easy on, easy off the Interstate it was for the rest of the trip.

And now Grace had come back from Chicago all fired up about applying for a position at the University of Kansas. I couldn't understand it. "That school is everything you didn't want." I punctuate each item with a finger: "A major research institution. They get grants from the defense department. And you'd be teaching grad students, who would be your TAs."

Whether or not Grace remembers Kansas, I do. I remember lots of brown food. In one restaurant, two women who in L.A. would be ordering their salads with dressing on the side so as not to be in the vicinity of fat, here in Russell, Kansas, dug into chicken-fried steak, biscuits and gravy. And they were smoking. I remember everyone smoked.

"It wasn't that bad. And Lawrence isn't Russell. It's a college town, like Ithaca," Grace pleaded, quoting the popular description: "Ten square miles surrounded by reality."

"Right," I harrumphed. "Except Lawrence would be more like ten square miles surrounded by homophobic pro-lifers who can't see the irony in also being in favor of the death penalty."

"Well, Kansas or not, it's an amazing offer."

I wasn't going to let Grace off the hook so easily. "Lawrence is where we watched the crazy anti-abortionists."

This couple, formally dressed, he in suit and tie, she in a dress, probably with stockings, had stood in the already-hot sun—I remembered the oppressive heat and humidity—across the street from a women's health clinic that wasn't even open for business at this hour. He held up a sign that read "Abortion is Murder," sweat running down his face. She held up her arms, praying a steady, mumbled stream of words, eyes shut tight as if that would beam her words directly to God, who would then smite a deadly beam upon the sinners across the street. Though Grace and I were the only sinners in sight as we headed toward our parked car about to get back on the road. That couple had stood stock still, the only motion her lips and his dripping sweat.

"So we'll volunteer at Planned Parenthood," Grace said. When she dug in, she was immovable. "The university has a tremendous art gallery, way more funding for my research."

"Do you really want to leave Ithaca?"

"It's not about leaving Ithaca."

"Then where is this coming from? I'm sure it was flattering to get the offer, but why on earth are you even considering it?"

Grace had waited until I opened my present, the glass apple paperweight, before dropping this bomb on me. I couldn't make sense of it. She'd jumped at the offer from Hollander because she wanted to work with students, undergraduate students, students she could fire up about what was possible for their future, and for possibly changing the art world. She wanted to be able to get to them before they made their grad school decisions, involve them in her research. She wanted a relatively small campus and small student body.

Grace parried my every objection with a "but." We didn't often fight, and when we did, we fought fair. This go-round, however, felt off. While every statement Grace made followed the previous one, her entire argument rested on an unstable foundation. I couldn't see its logic.

I kept coming back to "What is this about?"

"A job offer. An *amazing* job offer."

"I didn't know you'd been on the market."

"I'm not. I wasn't."

"Is this something you'd been thinking about and didn't mention to me?"

"No. Of course not. They approached me at the conference. I was totally surprised."

"Just because it's flattering doesn't mean you have to consider it."

"You don't understand."

"Then help me understand, Grace. Explain it in words that will make me see why this makes sense—why it's something you want. And why I'd follow you—again—to some place I have no desire to live in."

And then the foundation crumpled. Or exploded.

"So I made you come here?" Grace was yelling now. "It's my 'fault' you have this life? You'd rather be back in L.A. not making a living from your writing?"

Ouch. That was a low blow. And I know Grace saw the effect her words had on me, because I actually flinched when she threw them in my face. I think she even flinched a little. She was fighting dirty. And we didn't do that. Or hadn't, until then. I had no comeback. Even if I'd managed one, I'd have nowhere to deliver it. Grace had grabbed her car keys and flown out the door. "I've got to get out of here."

She left me standing in our kitchen, still not knowing what hit me. We were renting a one-bedroom near downtown even though it was close quarters. The living room was huge, so we'd carved out a corner to use as office space and traded off with each other between that and the top of a low bookcase in our bedroom. We were economizing on rent to speed up accumulating enough savings for a down payment on a house once we knew where we'd want to start looking. We were working on a five-year plan. A five-year Ithaca-is-the-forever-place-for-us plan. Though after what had just happened, I didn't know that we'd still be living together in five days, forget where.

When Grace came back two hours later, she lugged her pillow and some blankets into the living room. "You can have the bedroom."

We spent a tense week living in the same space, but not talking. We drove to campus separately, even on Tuesday and Thursday, the days our schedules overlapped and we usually drove in together. We ate at different times, didn't watch TV or read together in the evenings. I don't know how well Grace slept, but I managed only a couple of hours a night.

I'd lie awake examining my behavior, reliving what I remembered about what had happened, trying to see my part in this fight. And was this just a fight, or something bigger? No matter how I thought about it, I couldn't honestly see that it was my doing. Maybe I had to go back further than the argument. Had I been too jealous of Grace's time with

Kit? But I'd apologized, even before Grace returned from Chicago. No. This wasn't on me.

I spent most of my days at school. I ate dinner in my office and went straight to my bedroom when I came home. I used Grace's side of the bed as my staging area, separate piles for each course. I stayed away from Grace because I felt it was her job to tell me what was really going on. And to apologize.

I stayed away also because, deep down, I was afraid I'd lost her. Feared I was doomed to a series of two- and three-year relationships, never landing the one that was forever. Or as forever as relationships get, the ones that last till death. I had thought that's what Grace and I had. How had I misread her, us, so completely?

On the evening of the eighth day of our Troubles, as we referred to them later, Grace knocked on the door of the bedroom. I was propped up on the bed grading, student papers strewn around me. I laid down my pen.

Grace opened the door enough to let me see her. "May I come in?"

I sat up straight and motioned her in. She perched on what normally would be her side of the bed.

"You were right. I let my ego get the better of me. I don't want to work anywhere else. Or be anywhere else." She carefully moved my papers to the low bookcase, not disturbing their order, took my pad and pen from me and stacked them on top. "I want to be here. With you." Then she came back to the bed, our bed again, kissed me gently, lay down beside me, and proceeded to apologize.

After the Troubles passed, we dove back into our lives and were more solidly together than ever. Once we got out of bed, that is. Grace's apology hadn't only been delivered in words, and had renewed our sex life. Obviously we taught our classes, held our office hours. But once back home, we'd start out working, reading at opposite ends of the couch, but soon would be all over each other, ending up in bed, where we'd stay. We ordered food in or made eggs. We talked. Planned our future. Eventually we ventured out, starting with a couple of hours on Sundays to explore neighborhoods we might want to live in.

Grace didn't pursue the Kansas job offer. We'd survived a major upheaval and come out of it stronger. We never talked about our

Troubles again. And the rest of our life was about as perfect as you'd want your life to be. Not conflict-free, but real and honest.

At least that's what I'd thought all these years. Right now, standing on West 11th Street, near the corner of West 4th, in what is already a scorcher of a day and it's only eight-thirty in the morning, of course I understand what had gotten into Grace, why she'd come back from Chicago ready to jump out of our life and into a job she didn't really want. I understand now why she couldn't explain to me her desire to take that amazing offer—because that amazing offer wasn't what had motivated her actions. She'd felt guilty about having slept with Kit, couldn't cop to being unfaithful, and needed the fight to gain distance and process her emotions.

Of course, since Grace is still dead and I'm standing in the hot sun like those crazy anti-abortion fanatics in Kansas, laser-focused at the building across the street, not holding up a sign saying "Kit is a homewrecker," not mumbling incoherent prayers (Though it's quite possible that I have done some of my thinking aloud. I hope I haven't, but I wouldn't put it past me.), this is all conjecture on my part.

And Kit hadn't, in fact, wrecked my home. Grace's return, not from the conference, but to me, felt complete, total. As part of our future planning we opened a joint savings account for a house fund. And we bought rings to exchange in our own private commitment ceremony. I still wore mine along with the newer one we exchanged at our legal wedding. I twisted them both now, a way to fortify myself for what I was about to do: march across the street to that brownstone with the lovely planters dripping coleus and sweet potato vine, ring the bell or bang the knocker, and tell Kit I know what she did.

"Hannah."

I'd been wondering if Grace would show up to talk me through or out of this. I'm about to warn her away when I hear my name again, as a question this time.

"Hannah? Is that you?"

Okay, those of you who don't believe in coincidence can explain this any way you want. I'll leave you to it. I can hardly believe it myself when I turn around to see if someone is really talking to me on this steaming summer-in-the-city morning and find myself three feet from Kit and a very cute dog. Did I do a spit take? Is my head swiveling back and forth between her and the brownstone I'd focused on so intently? She stands right behind me. I don't know how she got there. How did I miss seeing her leave her building? How zoned out had I been? I stoop down to pet the dog, partly because it's cute, mostly to see if it's real. And it gives me time to think about my response. You're probably wondering what thinking does "Is that you" require. Mostly I have to ascertain that this is, in fact, real and not something I've conjured in my beseeching whatever to help me figure out how to confront Kit.

If it isn't real, I can always pretend to be bending down to tie my shoe.

The dog seems real enough. He has short fur, not exactly soft. And maybe he isn't the cleanest dog around. My fingers feel a little, dusty. Okay, then. This is not a hallucination.

I stand. Kit and I move awkwardly into a handshake that maybe should be a hug, but there's the dog's leash, and neither of us knows how to be physical with the other.

"What are you doing here?" Kit asks.

It's an innocent question. Perfectly natural for her to ask. I took "here" to mean the city, why was I in the city, not why was I standing staring at her brownstone.

I give a vague "tying up loose ends" answer, which seems to satisfy her.

"How are you? Did you get—"

"Yes, thanks for your card."

Fantasizing about what I'd do to Kit is one thing. Standing face to face with the woman I'd driven 260 miles through the night to eviscerate is another. Kit looks great. She's closer to Grace's age than mine, maybe even a little younger. She's maybe a little softer, rounder than when I'd last seen her all those years ago when she'd first moved to the city, but still has that butch swagger about her, and a perfect short haircut. My jealousy flares up. As a stalling tactic, I look at my watch, as if to calculate how much time I have before I need to be somewhere.

"Do you have time for a coffee? You could come up and meet LeeAnne."

I'm now vaguely remembering Grace telling me Kit had started seeing someone. This was a few years ago—a record for Kit.

"We're just around the corner, a few blocks over on 4th." Kit points behind us.

"What?"

"We live around the corner. I think you and Grace visited once, when I first moved in. I didn't realize how lucky I was to find the place when I did. It's a little small for two of us, but rents have skyrocketed."

I'm too stunned to speak. Too stunned even to be jealous. If she lives around the corner, whose building have I been laser-focused on? I'd been so sure that's where Kit lived.

Clearly I've been silent for too long. "If you don't have time..." Kit says.

I feel as if I've just woken up. I look at the brownstone I thought was hers, then back at Kit, who lives on a different street. The longer we stand there, the more I see her as she was when she'd roared up that driveway on her Gold Wing all those years ago. Still handsome. She sports a different look than the rebel she was back then, but holds the same dashing swagger. Today she's college-boy casual, wearing loose khaki shorts, an un-ironed blue and white striped oxford shirt, sleeves rolled to her elbows. Black low-top Chucks, no socks.

That appraisal makes me realize I have no idea what I'm wearing. I know I got dressed yesterday to go to the office. Yesterday feels like eight years ago. Didn't I change into sweats and a T-shirt at some point in my late-night ranting?

You know that dream where you show up to some important event naked?

I glance at my watch again, surreptitiously checking my attire.

Phew. I'm in shorts, an almost-clean T-shirt, off-white low-top Chucks. The irony of our similar outfits is not lost on me. Under different circumstances, Kit and I could have been pals.

"I need to get back home." I say it before I even realize how true it is.

That's fine with Kit. "Let me know in advance next time you're going to be down," she says. "We could grab a drink, or dinner." A large rottweiler and its owner walk by, and Kit's dog goes berserk, barking up a storm, straining at its leash. "That's our cue." Kit pulls her dog away, back toward home. Which is not the lovely brownstone across the street.

The rottweiler, for whom Kit's dog would be a snack, bares its teeth. Kit's trying to tell me something as she walks away, dragging her dog down the sidewalk. She's yelling her address and something else, but her words are lost under the snarling, barking racket.

I give a semi-wave and walk in the opposite direction, like I know just where I'm going, like I have a purpose.

I take myself back to the same diner I'd stopped at for coffee. This time, I order a proper breakfast of eggs, crisp bacon, rye toast. I even manage to eat most of it. I sit for a few minutes with my coffee. Not really thinking. Just watching people walk by outside. The heat and humidity tamp down any remaining nostalgia, and I know it's time to get back on the road.

14

Return with the Elixir

The whole point of the hero's journey, when you get right down to it, is their coming back with whatever they went in search of in the first place. The solution to their problem. But I'm returning with...*bupkis*. Not only sans elixir, which in this case would have been, what? Confirmation? Certainty? Catharsis? Ah, yes. Catharsis. Giving Kit a piece of my mind. That would have done it. But I hadn't even been standing in the right place to have it out with Kit. That was sheer coincidence running into her.

Face-to-face with my nemesis, my puffed-up bravado deflated. I realized I didn't want proof. I declined Kit's invitation because I was afraid she'd confess to me about her and Grace. It's human nature. She'd feel better for getting that off her chest. And I knew that I would feel worse. She might even figure that Grace had already told me about them, so it wouldn't be news. But I figured if Grace could go all those years without confessing, I don't need to process with Kit. Kit isn't the important factor in that equation. And I'll process when I'm back on my own turf. No. Make that when I'm damn good and ready.

Normally when I'm on a long drive, I play a lot of loud music, something that stands up to road noise, that I can sing along to. Today, though, I need the relative silence, just the hum of tires. Every half hour, I open all the windows for an air bath.

On my way back to the West Side Highway I detoured past Kit's actual address, the one she'd shouted at me. I had gotten everything wrong about it—not just the street, but the style, size, color, everything. It faced south, I had it north. It wasn't a brownstone, but a small multi-unit building.

What did that mean for the trustworthiness of the rest of my memories? Clearly I suck at the retrieval stage. Did I just make things up out of whole cloth, like moving Kit into that lovely brownstone? And then obliterate others—I'd forgotten about the Troubles, for crying out loud. Does eliminating the bad completely erase the good? Can you have selective amnesia? Had I elevated dead Grace to sainthood? Do I have to reevaluate the snippets and flashes I've managed to dredge up? If I can't trust them, what am I left with? Then I wonder: Does it matter if I get every detail just right? Or do I simply need the feelings they bring up for me? What am I looking for from them? Feeling loved, that I'd loved and been loved, my life had mattered to someone? Is that what makes a life worthwhile?

Some catharsis.

Clearly Grace is sitting this out, waiting for me to come around to what's really important. A clue wouldn't kill you, would it?

Art is the lie that tells the truth.

That's it? No apology?

Okay then. If art represents a truer truth of its subject, can we extend that same principle to memory? As in, the exact details of what we remember aren't what matters because we're going for something more profound, not the exact details, but what it felt like at that precise moment in time? The essence of the event rather than the exact number of people at the party. And if we measure by the accumulation of those moments, what was more real—Grace's sleeping with Kit, or the sum of events of the twenty-plus years Grace and I had after that? Buying our house. Shopping for a new water heater. Paying off loans. Designing and building the Little House. Determining which cable plan we wanted. The truth is in the life we built, not an indiscretion early on.

Indiscretion? Isn't that letting her off way too easily? I can rage at her all I want.

And that will get me what, exactly?

Does it really even matter anymore?

Maybe I've been looking at it all wrong. I mean, what did I teach my students all those years: The heroine returns with the elixir, but that doesn't mean it's the elixir she thought she'd been searching for. Often it's something at least as good, if not better, because our heroines and heroes don't always go after the right thing. A character might want one thing, but, in actuality, need another. Like they think they want to stay on the farm, when in reality, they need to go off to fight the Empire. Or they think this high-paying job is what they want when what they really need is a job that makes them happy.

Whatever I thought I'd accomplish by confronting Kit has been replaced with an odd sense of, I can't call it contentment. Being happy isn't the only happiness? Whatever I'm going to call it, I'd definitely gotten something out of my system. Grace is still dead, and I still have to face the rest of my life.

I'm relieved that The Girls aren't home when I pull into the driveway. I've got all sorts of ideas spinning around my brain, one of which involves them, but I'm in no shape to carry on a conversation with such major consequences.

I'm so loathe to think/process/sort my thoughts that I don't hesitate when Jordan calls to ask me to meet her for dinner in town. "Sure," I say. I answer so fast I think I surprised her. I'm not eager to spend more time in my car, but dinner's hours away. And this is my new life.

I collapse on the couch for a minute, just to be still. Next thing I know, it's two hours later. I jump in the shower, pay attention to the outfit I put on after, clean shorts and a polo, and head off to dinner, relieved The Girls still haven't come home. I need time to formulate my offer. I want to make sure I get it right.

One block of Aurora Street is Ithaca's restaurant row, with an impressive number of eateries lining both sides of the street. It's cool enough to sit outside, and Jordan's snagged us a table at our favorite Italian restaurant. She gives me a big hug when I arrive. "It's so good to see you," she says, like it's been a long time. We've eaten here often enough that we don't even need to look at the menu. Black pepper fettuccine for me, chicken marsala for Jordan. Red wine all around. The interrogation doesn't start until after the waiter leaves.

"So," she starts. "How are you?"

I sort of answer. Tell her I'm fine, I'm out of my office, almost done with Grace's. That part's true. I omit anything about my discovery of the photograph or my impulsive drive into the city. I'm being dishonest, but my behavior is starting to feel crazy to me and not something I want to broadcast.

"Ellen told me you two had dinner," Jordan says. Though she leaves it there, it sounds to me like she wants to say something else.

"And?" I prompt.

"And, she said she doesn't know you that well, but wondered if you were okay." Jordan plays with her fork. "So I guess I'm asking—are you okay?"

I glare at her.

"What?" she asks. "I can't be concerned?"

I take a big sip of my wine. "I just don't like everyone knowing my business."

"You didn't think anyone would know you're seeing Ellen?"

"What is this, high school? And I'm not 'seeing' anyone. We had dinner. Once." I hold up my index finger for emphasis. "One time." I don't count our aborted date, act indignant to hide it and any hint of my bad behavior.

"Down, girl," Jordan says. "I'm just happy that you're getting out of the house."

I'm so relieved Jordan didn't bring up anything about the kiss—and if she'd gotten even a whiff of that, she would have—I feel I owe her something. I share with her my plan to let the Girls stay with me.

"That's a great idea," she says.

"That's a switch from the other day."

"It is. I've been thinking about it, and I think it's good that you're not alone right now."

I bristle a little at that. I'm fine on my own. Or I will be, once I figure out what I'll be doing with my time. And how am I going to figure that out? I can't land anywhere long enough to think. Even my grief, which had been my refuge since Grace died, my safe place, is closed to me because I'm still angry at her. So much for thinking I was getting past that.

"I hope you come for just a little," Jordan is saying. So much for my staying present. What's she talking about? "We bought some new floats." That's my clue. She and Janey have an annual 4th of July party at their lake house, an all-day event. "You don't have to bring anything—everyone knew Grace made the potato salad, even though you claimed it as yours."

"Well, I did give her the recipe." Actually, it was Boy Leslie's recipe. He called it Iowa potato salad. "Did everyone know, really?"

"Anyone who knew you well."

"No secrets in this town," I said.

Jordan grabs the check before I have a chance to. "You'll get the next one."

Back at our cars, Jordan says, "I already invited Cristina and Nicole. They're coming. And Ellen will be there." That last said with a certain tone.

I give Jordan a look.

"What?" she says, all innocence.

"Very funny," I say, waving as I turn around and head to the Prius.

Driving home, I acknowledge to myself that I owe Ellen an apology. That kiss hadn't been fair to her, and it had done nothing to change my feelings about Grace, about what Grace had done to me. My indignation boils up—Grace is dead. I'm not. I'm free to see anyone. Be with anyone. And if I were twenty, make that thirty, all right, forty, if I were forty years younger, I'd have thrown myself into other women till my hurt subsided. At my age, despite my atavistic action with Ellen, I know I don't want to be with anyone.

When I get home, I'm too keyed up to go to bed. I need something soothing. I head to the kitchen and put on water for tea and get out an herbal sampler. As soon as the water starts to boil, I think, who am I kidding? I hate herbal tea. I shut off the flame and pour myself a whiskey.

All the drama I've stirred up makes me think about *Grey's Anatomy*. I see that big strapping gal who plays the…shit. I can't remember the word. She's a bone doc, but all I get is chiropractor, and I know that's not right.

And I also know if I try to conjure up the word, I won't get it, so I try to let it go, and still chiropractor floats around my head like an annoying fly that won't land.

The only way to remember is not to try to remember. To distract myself, I look at the photo of Grace on the windowsill above the sink. Taken on our first trip to Mexico, she's standing thigh-deep in the clear turquoise water of the Caribbean, hands on her hips. She's telling me to put the camera away. She's feigning annoyance, but really smiling and squinting into the sun, animated, motioning me to join her.

This isn't helping me get past "chiropractor."

At first, my memory losses scared me. Aside from not wanting to seem old, I didn't want to seem like I was losing it, especially in the classroom. I'd gotten good at substituting a phrase when I couldn't remember a familiar word that was lost in some black abyss. And not being able to remember my life with Grace terrified me. Then look where my excavations got me—discovering Grace's betrayal. And I'd been so sure I knew where I was this morning in the Village but had gotten everything wrong. What else might I be forgetting?

Maybe I should be grateful I have no memory. I can just settle into a peaceful oblivion in the home Grace and I made. Memory is overrated, and being happy isn't the only happiness.

ORTHOPEDIST! Callie is an orthopedic surgeon. Ha! I knew if I let go it would come back to me.

I stand at the counter with my drink, looking into the living room, and have another altered point of view moment. The idea that had been forming on my drive home from the city percolated while I napped, bubbled up during dinner with Jordan, now bursts out of my mouth in one declarative sentence: "I can't live in this house."

All this time I'd been thinking I could make the Big House more mine. Who was I kidding? It would always be ours, mine and Grace's.

At that precise moment, The Girls walk in.

"What a day!" Cristina flops on the couch. "It's so good to be home!"

Boom. Of course. Face-palm emoji—of course!

"We looked at four more places today," Cristina says. "We didn't like any of them. Nicole's going to take me to see Miss Lillian's tomorrow. I really want to get settled somewhere before the semester starts."

Before I can propose anything, Nicole says to me, "You must be tired. You were up and out early today."

As soon as she says it, I realize I am. Not just tired. Bone-tired. "Yes. I'm off to bed."

I'm so tired I don't even sneak out of the bedroom. I spend what I know will be one of the last nights in our house on top of the covers on our bed. I claim a space in the middle, not my side, not Grace's side.

My last conscious thought of this life-changing day is: The Girls would be cramped in the Little House. I, on the other hand, will fit perfectly there.

15
The Offer

I wake the next morning in an almost good mood. I don't dwell on or dissect this fact. To avoid thinking, I get up and shower before I even make coffee. Nicole comes into the kitchen—how can she look so together already, not even dressed for the day, just in yoga pants and a loose-fitting shirt—and opens the fridge. "I was thinking I'd make eggs. Would you prefer scrambled or an omelet?"

"Chef's choice," I say. Listen to me, being decisive.

Nicole opts for scrambled but adds fresh herbs—dill and thyme. I make us each a double espresso.

Cristina stumbles out in boxers and a tank top, her tattoos radiant. I make her a coffee.

At Nicole's signal, I start the toast.

By the time Nicole's plated our eggs, we're all awake enough to have conversation.

"What's on your docket for today?" I ask.

"We're going to take another look at Miss Lillian's apartment," Cristina says.

Nicole adds, "Someone else is interested, so we have to make our decision by tomorrow."

I listen to them talk about the plusses of that apartment, the advantages of living in Ithaca proper, being able to walk to restaurants, something they really couldn't do in L.A. They'd have a longer commute to school, but the trade-off would be worth it. Nicole isn't so sure about being out in the country, which is how she thinks about the Big House. "Isn't it ironic that Cristina feels perfectly at home out here, in the middle of nowhere, and I, the white girl, find it scary?" She looks at me. "No offense."

I shrug. "None taken. I'm used to it."

"It just feels like when I was—" Cristina starts, but Nicole cuts her off: "At your abuelita's. I know."

Cristina backs off. "Miss Lillian's is smaller than our apartment in L.A. I'm a little worried we won't have enough workspace."

"I have another option for you," I say. "Follow me." Nicole starts to clear the table, but I say, "Leave it for now." Not only decisive—in command!

As we walk over to the Little House together, I realize how perfect this solution is. And throughout the tour I give them, which only takes two minutes since there isn't much to see, I feel something I don't quite recognize. A sense of a future. Maybe that's what my better mood was about when I woke up.

Tour concluded, we sit in the big front room, each on a section of the huge couch. That's what Grace and I had wanted, something we could sprawl out on and not be in each other's way.

"What a sweet setup!" Cristina says.

I get right to the point. "We all seem to get along well," I say. When I pause, they look at each other, then to me, nod. "So here's what I'm thinking. I like having people around, but not too close around."

The Girls look at each other, sensing something's coming.

"I'm going to move over here. You can have the Big House." I hold my hand up to prevent Cristina from talking. "Hear me out. For as long as you need."

Again, they look at each other. I can't tell if they like the idea or not.

To allay anyone's fears, I continue. "Let's say just for the academic year to start. You don't have to decide right this minute. Go look at the apartment again. Take your time to think about it. Clearly you're not right in the middle of things out here like you would be in town. It's a little closer to school, but a pain in the ass if you forget something at the store." Shush, I tell myself. You don't have to persuade them, but don't talk them out of it, either. Let them decide on their own. "If you want the place, we'll come up with a specific agreement…"

"And a fair rent," Cristina interjects.

"Sure," I agree. "We can work all that out." I'm making this up as I go along. I guess that's what my life is now, one big improvisation. But this doesn't feel crazy, like my drive to the city did.

I look at them, they look at each other, then back at me. No one knows what to say next.

I've made my offer, now I make my exit. "What time do you have to be at Miss Lillian's?"

Cristina looks at her watch. "Shit! We'd better get a move on."

We head back to the Big House. I tell The Girls I'll clean up breakfast so they can shower and hit the road. As I do the dishes, I wonder if they'll take me up on my offer. But the feeling that I can't stay in the Big House is stronger than the fear of what will happen if The Girls move out.

After they've left, I head right for the bedroom and zip up my suitcase, still packed for the Adirondacks. I have to sit on it to get it to close because of all those little extras I'd tossed on top. I'll worry later about what to do with Grace's—which is also when I'll worry about all her clothes and everything else in the house. One task at a time.

With my laptop in one hand, I use the other to wheel the suitcase across the lawn and past the barn to the Little House, where I leave it all on the floor in Grace's office because I've decided that will eventually be my bedroom. Then I go back for bed linens and towels. I can make do with the toiletries in my travel bag for now. I suppose I could have just loaded up the car and driven everything over in one trip, but the physical exertion keeps me from thinking, and also debating with myself whether or not this is a good idea. I don't even know if The Girls will accept my offer. This is just a trial run for myself. After a few trips, I've got everything I want. Well, everything I need. For now.

I sit on the couch to contemplate my next move. The big windows behind me look out on views of the pond, the open fields beyond, and the path to the barn. I suppose now the Little House is mine to furnish as I wish. In my own taste. Do I even know what that is? The Big House is filled with a combination of furniture and art Grace and I had brought from our L.A. house, which had been a melding of our individual apartments. Pieces we'd thought of as stopgap till we found the perfect chair or side table or bookcase ended up being what we'd lived with for years. On top of those came items inherited, in college-town-transitional fashion, from friends who had to move when they got jobs at other schools. It all worked together in a harmonious, if haphazard, kind of way. No one particular style, but an overall sensibility that broadcast "real people live here and you don't have to worry about putting your glass on the coffee table."

The Little House will be deliberate. And I can take my time with it, which is good, because I'm in no frame of mind to make any more momentous decisions.

In the meantime, I get to work putting the few things I brought with me in their proper place. I put towels in the bathroom along with my travel toilet kit. I put a few extra towels and sheets in the linen closet, which is also the storage closet since it's the only hall closet. That's about as much as I can unpack since we don't have dressers and there are no hangers in the closets. We'd left all those details for when Grace was on sabbatical. I leave my suitcase on the floor for now. No bed to make. At some point, I'll have to shop for a big girl bed, but in the meantime, I seem to do just fine sleeping on a couch.

I step out onto the back porch to take a break. I sit in one of the two plastic Adirondack chairs.

Closing my eyes, I feel just as calm as I do in Grace's study. Calmer, I realize. Another surprise of this day. Sun warming my face, a light breeze rustling the leaves, birds chirping. After a month of confinement within a few rooms, now I'm opening a door to the outside.

Well, you are actually sitting outside, after all.

So much for the metaphor and my reflective moment.

I look to the empty chair next to me. If I close my eyes, I can see Grace there. She's holding a bottle of Anchor Steam. We've just finished construction on the Little House and have brought over a six-pack to celebrate. We'd also schlepped these plastic Adirondack chairs with us, which are surprisingly comfortable, and positioned them to catch the sunset over the pond.

This is a memory, I tell myself. We were happy. I return to that day on this porch.

"How perfect is this?" Grace had said.

"Pretty damn," I agreed.

She reached over then and took my hand and kissed it. "It's a good life," she'd said.

I had realized then that this was my favorite place to be on our property. Not because of the sweeping view of the fields beyond the pond. I think I like it here because it's the detail that reveals the essence of our land. I can't see the house from where I sit, but like a painting that lets the viewer enter its landscape, I can see the path that leads to the house, reassuring me by its presence that there is something at the end of it. Something at the end that used to mean Grace, but now doesn't.

Again, I can't say I'm happy. But calm is good. And, let's all sing the chorus together: Being happy isn't the only happiness. Maybe I have made a good decision.

This calls for a celebration. Had we left the rest of the six-pack in the fridge? I go inside to find out. Eureka! Four left! I grab one along with the Day of the Dead bottle opener and return to my chair. I pop the cap and take a few celebratory sips. Looking to put the bottle down, I realize there's nowhere to put it other than the ground. I know we bought a few plastic folding tables that matched these chairs. They must be in the barn. Even if I can't trust my memory about the tables (Exhibit A: Kit's building; Exhibit B: The Troubles), who knows what else I'll find that might be useful.

Sorting through the mess that is our barn I think, how did we accumulate all this stuff? Maybe old barns, like nature, abhor a vacuum. But this is ridiculous. Beach chairs galore. We set them out when we had summer parties. Winter gear: snow shoes, a sled, shovels. Boxes. Many boxes. Those containing Grace's notepads are neatly labeled and stacked. Maybe this is where I'll start digging around to find what Grace had been working on. But what's in the other boxes? Why didn't we label them? I peek into one. Her aunt's china! Grace had said she'd donate that. Oh, brother. Once I've set up in the Little House, I need to come back and sort through all this shit.

And there is a lot of it to sort through. I dig around some more. So that's what happened to the bocce set. I thought we gave away those cross-country skis years ago. I'm getting off track, not to mention it's dirty and spider-webby in here.

I make one last scan and still don't find the tables I'm looking for, but I do find a dusty old safe, the size of a file box. I remember when Grace bought it.

"What are you going to do with that?" I'd asked.

"Put papers in it," she said, keeping the "duh" silent.

"Isn't that why we have a safe deposit box at the bank?"

"Yes, but who wants to drive into town every time we want to look at something?"

"So these aren't for important papers?" I asked.

"They'll be important to me."

"How secure is this, really?"

"It's got a lock," Grace said. "But I won't need to lock it. Mostly I want to keep things safe from fire."

I knew better than to argue with her. "Knock yourself out," I'd said.

And now I'm excited by the possible treasures I'll find in it.

The thing weighs at least twenty-five pounds. I lug it out onto the grass so I can peruse its contents in the sunshine. Once I've caught my breath, I prepare myself for whatever I might find when I open it. Maybe Grace updated her will without telling me. Or she stored whatever manuscript she was working on. No, not if it's out here in the barn gathering dust. It has to be important papers she wanted to keep safe. But what would those be? What did she need to keep safe and separated from her other stuff? Which of course I read as—away from me.

I've got it. Letters. It's secret correspondence that will answer all my questions about Kit. Maybe even the letter Kit sent that contained the photograph I'd destroyed. Maybe even more photographs.

Oh, just open it already!

Fine.

What do you mean, it's locked? Didn't Grace say she said she wasn't going to lock it? Did she need to make sure I didn't see what was in here? More incriminating photos?

Of more immediate relevance: where's the key?

Because now it's imperative that I find out what's inside.

On a nail just inside the barn door hang a spare key for the house, an extra set of car keys, keys to whatever we kept in the barn that had a lock, plus random keys to who knows what. Precisely the kind of shit I need to clean out. But after carefully trying every possible option, Grace's secrets are still safe from me. Okay then. I figure the key must be somewhere in the house.

Almost an hour later, having searched every drawer and cabinet and little box of forgotten objects I can think of, starting in the logical place, Grace's office, and widening the perimeter to include every room in the house, I haven't found the key. I have, however, found: a lapel pin from the 1994 25th Anniversary of Stonewall, an ACT UP Silence = Death pin, a gajillion lead refills, both .5 and .7 mm., and a Kuru Toga mechanical pencil Grace had spent two days searching for because it was her favorite.

I've also found and stowed for later the realization that at some point I'm going to have to deal with all the boxes and accumulated detritus of my life, and now, gee thanks, honey, Grace's. What the fuck do I do with this shit? You know how you're only supposed to handle a piece of paper once? Pick it up and deal with it is the point of that rule. I bent that to accommodate two handlings: the first to see if it needed dealing with at all, the second would be when I picked it up again, ready to reply or edit or whatever. That's what it was like with some of the items I'd come across in my search for the key. Two used-up Blaster Balls that had belonged to Girl Leslie. I remember the day we each got a set. How much time had we spent tossing one up so it would land on the other and make that satisfying crack, the smell of caps permeating the air until finally, Diane made us go outside to play so she could read in peace. I toss one up to see if they'll still pop. I get a couple of cracks, a whiff of powder, but no smoke. Now what? I haven't touched these in years, but can't part with them.

Who's going to deal with this stuff after I die? No one will understand its significance. Should I just throw it all away? Have a garage sale? The mere thought exhausts and depresses me.

As does the realization that now I've lost an hour and gained a sense of futility that'll take years to untangle. Or maybe just a few sessions with a really good shrink?

Whichever, I still don't have the key.

I'm back outside staring at the box as if my willpower could flip the lock when The Girls drive up.

Cristina bounds out of the car and does some Julie Andrews in *The Sound of Music* spins. "I love it out here!" She stampedes over to me. "We accept your offer!" She gives me a bone-crushing hug, then goes on about how they could have made the apartment work, but they've never lived anywhere like our place before. "I mean, with all this," she looks around and gestures, "land. We realized what an amazing opportunity this was going to be! It's like my abuelita's watching over me."

Nicole joins us after putting the groceries on the porch. "Are you sure about your offer?"

"Absolutely," I say.

Cristina wraps her arms around Nicole and says, "That's because Nicky's not as sure, but she'll learn to love it."

Nicole pulls away and points to the safe. "What's in it?"

"I'm wondering the same thing myself. It's locked. And no, I don't know where the key is. I'm going to have to bring it to a locksmith." Because now I'm sure that the contents of this box are vital to my recovery and my moving forward.

"Try Google first."

"What?"

"Seriously. Just type in how to break into a safe without a key."

Why didn't I think of that? Put that on the list for the therapist, right after memory loss and overwhelming sense of futility: Disintegration of problem-solving capabilities. Inability to think through to a solution. Look that up in your DSM.

When I move to lift the safe, Nicole says, "Don't. That's heavy." She turns to Cristina, "Get that for her. I'm going to put the groceries away."

Cristina hefts the safe. "Where to?"

I indicate the Little House. As we walk over, I think of Nicole's concern for me and am reminded I'm old. Does their decision to accept my offer have anything to do with their thinking I need looking after?

I direct Cristina to the kitchen counter. After she places the safe, we both stare at it.

"Any idea what you'll find in there?"

"Not a clue," I lie.

"Ooh, her secret diary! Wouldn't that be cool!"

I don't admit I'm hoping for just that.

"Or maybe it's her long-lost Van Gogh manuscript."

"She told you about that?"

Cristina nods. "We kind of shared our what-got-us-started-in-art-history stories." She's lost in thought for a moment before adding, "Do you need anything else?"

Why is she being so solicitous? Again I'm reminded we're not the same age. Euphemism police: you're old enough to be her mother. "I'm good," I say in what I hope is a robust, youthful voice.

"I'd better get back. Nicole's making dinner, and I'm sous chef."

I point at the safe. "I'm going to spend some time researching how to get into this. I'll be over in a little bit."

Amazing how one thing leads to another to another to another. All I'd wanted when I went out to the barn was to find those little folding tables. That was three hours ago. Now I'm standing at the kitchen counter in the Little House ready to begin my search for a way to open the box that contains the key to my future.

I imagine Grace faced with this problem. To say she'd approach it differently is a gross understatement. First she'd need to understand everything about a lock—its components and mechanisms, the basic principles on which a lock operates. She'd study diagrams, read an article or two.

I don't care about that. In the month or however long it's been since Grace died, I've learned that aging is about priorities—what I need to know, what I don't care about knowing. My interests have narrowed rather than broadened. I care less about experimentation—

Oh please. Who am I kidding? All I really care about these days is making it through each one. And today, that involves breaking into this fucking safe.

Back on task, I type my request into the search box. In less than a second, I'm presented with over 200,000 options from which to choose. All right then. At least one is bound to work. I open YouTube and dive in.

The first video I come across is far too professional. This guy's a pro who uses two kinds of picks. No way I'm shopping for tools. Onward. The next one looks equally complicated. This guy uses a straightened paper clip that he strips of its plastic coating and bends with needle-nose pliers to form a pick, which he combines with a screwdriver to jimmy the lock. I'm already discouraged, and I've got over 199,998 more to go. I pull up the next video.

Same close shot on a safe, not the exact model as mine, but same brand. When the voice comes on, I lose my shit. I miss the beginning of his introduction because I'm laughing so hard. Some ten-year-old is going to tell me how to crack my home safe with a pair of scissors. A pair of child scissors. No tools, no stripped paper clips. I watch his pudgy little hands manipulate the lock till, click, it's open. He then walks us through the reverse process, locking the safe.

I love the internet!

I'm excited until I realize I don't have scissors—a reminder that I need to stock the Little House. Still, forget those old professional dudes. I hone in on the amateurs. I have hope now. Another kid—how many pre-teens have their own YouTube channels? —opens his safe with a paper clip and a ballpoint pen. (I'm tempted to contact the needle-nose pliers guy to tell him you don't have to go through all that trouble to bend the clip—straight works just as well.) A young woman with a southern accent uses a nail clippers. So I have hope plus options.

Confident that I've got the hang of this, I dig out my trusty little Swiss Army knife, unfold the teeny nail file, and go to work on the lock. I insert and jiggle. Apply more pressure as I jiggle. No luck. I stop. Pull the file out, frustrated. This is not acceptable. I need to get into this fucking box, and I will not be deterred. Forget William Carlos Williams' little red wheelbarrow in the rain—so much depends on this safe. Not merely getting to the bottom of Grace's affair with Kit, but also proving to the world that I can take care of myself. If a ten-year-old can crack this, shouldn't I be seven times more likely to be successful?

Deep breath. Another thrust. Lots of jiggling. Voilà! As they say on NCIS, I'm in!

I don't rest on my laurels, however proud of myself. I had a purpose, which I'd briefly forgotten in my quest to become adept at safecracking. Having achieved my goal, I ignore anything I may associate with Pandora's box—who remembers the actual story, anyway, just that she unleashed...what, exactly?—or anything about being careful what you wish for.

I put a hand on either side of the lid. Okay, Grace, time to talk to me. Please.

I lift the lid.

If I were editing this film, would I show my face first, let the viewer see the reaction shot before showing them what it's reacting to, the contents of the safe? Which would be more important? Do we want to create suspense, or reveal information?

But I'm not editing a film. And I'm the audience here, dying for new information.

I look down into the now-open safe and find...nothing.

Dust. A dead fly.

Are you fucking kidding me? Really? After all that?

I want to laugh, but I can't yet.

I return to the Big House and ask Nicole if I have time to take a shower before dinner. "Kind of dirty out in the barn," I offer as an excuse. But what I really need is time to transition out of my disappointment—if that's even what I'm feeling—before I can be with people again.

What does it mean that the safe was empty? A metaphor for my life? Or was all that just a distraction? Had I been looking for something that never existed in the first place. Hmmm...

Whether it was the shower or the excellent champagne The Girls bought to celebrate our deal, I'm able to turn my safecracking into a funny story at dinner, omitting my hopes for the contents, not touching on my fury at Grace for leaving me like that, burying my roiling thoughts of her and Kit.

Because they don't know what's going on with me, the Girls are able to change the subject easily, concerned as they are with working out the terms of our arrangement. How much will I charge them, do we need to set ground rules for living on the same land but also ensuring everyone's privacy. "And how much we'll be paying you," Cristina repeats.

They've sublet their place in L.A., so have relatively few things to ship east. "Basically books, clothes, and some kitchen items Nicole can't be without," Cristina says. They want to know what I'll be moving to the Little House, offer to help with that, assure me I can take as long as I want to clear out. Which is not how they put it—they'd never say "clear out." They're deferential and considerate (because I'm old?) and don't want me to feel like they're pushing me out of my own home.

They don't know that the longer I'm in the Big House the more I need to escape it, as if that will enable me to leave behind the life Grace and I lived here, even if I can't remember it.

16

Sitting Here in Limbo

I wake the next morning and for a second can't place where I am. I reach my hand out for Grace, who isn't there, which brings me into reality and reminds me why I no longer sleep in our bedroom. And that she's still on the dresser, right where I'd left her. I'd tried to camouflage the urn, stowing it between an 8x10 framed photo of us in front of our L.A. apartment building and a small set of drawers that held Grace's jewelry. I'd even placed the blue vase Ellen gave us in front of it. But the urn's like a portrait where the eyes follow you no matter where you stand. Maybe I should drape a scarf over it. Then I remember that I'll be moving soon so I can find her a place where I'll be out of her sight. Though she can probably float wherever she wants these days. I'm the one stuck in the material world. And still sleeping in this room. Only knowing that I'm leaving has made that possible. I still occupy the middle of the bed. No one's side. Liminal, transitional, temporary.

Rather than drift into that metaphysical realm, I get out of bed and wander into the kitchen. The Girls are already up. Cristina's scrolling through emails on her phone as she eats her cereal. Nicole has coffee and a book in front of her, but offers to fix me breakfast. Tempting, but, "I'm just going to make some toast," I say.

We're all a little awkward with each other. Kind of like the first morning with a new lover. Take your mind out of the gutter. That's not a sexual reference. We're a unit now and have to get to know each other for real. We understand that something about our relationship has changed, and we're going to have to see how this will play out. Will we still like each other? How are we going to manage the day-to-day? Did we make the right decision?

"I have to go to campus," Cristina says. "Nicole's coming with me and we're going out to Taughannock after. Time to do some sightseeing."

"Did you get there when you came for your interview?" I ask. Sometimes prospective hires would get impromptu tours of the area—the natural beauty of the Finger Lakes region is as big a selling point for the college as its proximity to Ithaca—small city convenience but plenty of amenities and cultural activities because of all the colleges and universities in the area.

"No. But everyone says it's beautiful."

"It's actually higher than Niagra Falls. Not as wide, but pretty spectacular. It's an easy walk into the falls. And be sure to check out the overlook. Then a few miles up 89, you can't miss it: excellent ice cream."

"Why don't you come with us?" Cristina asks.

See what I mean? This is where it's awkward. It isn't that they wouldn't want me to come, just that she doesn't know what our relationship is or should be. Are they guests still? Neighbors? Friends? The Girls and I hadn't set a timetable for our arrangement, but I figure I should begin the moving process sooner rather than later. "I think I'm going to get started on packing. Maybe take a few things over to the Little House." And just like that I've come up with a plan for my day. Brava.

After they've left, it occurs to me that they haven't spent a lot of time together since they arrived. I hadn't paid enough attention to know if that was simply because Cristina had business at school—new faculty orientation, setting up her office, getting her ID, and signing up for health insurance—or if it was more deliberate and personal. Since Grace died, I've spent a lot of time in my own head. Though underwater might be more accurate. It's like I'm pulling myself upstream, against the current, and now have surfaced to look around.

While it was easy enough to declare my intentions to start on my move, actually putting the plan into motion is a lot harder than I'd thought it would be. First off, I don't know where to begin. Clothes? Objects? And what do I want over there? More importantly, what don't I want? This is my chance to start fresh, uncluttered.

So much freedom has immobilized me. I sit with my retirement book, ready to make a list.

Grace prompts me: **Keep it simple.**

"Go away," I tell her. Then I start with the basics. I write: clothes. As if I need more specific reminding, I then add: shirts, shorts, underwear. Shoes, jackets, hats.

That was easy enough. Next. "Things" goes on the list. I'll need plates, utensils. I pause—where does that leave The Girls? What do they have coming from California? Am I renting them a completely furnished house? I put that decision aside for now. I'll have enough to keep myself busy with my clothes.

I open the closet and shove Grace's clothes to one side. I don't bury my face in them to catch her scent. (I don't need to. I'm surrounded by it.) I don't lovingly touch her favorite shirt. I am tunnel-visioned. I grab an armful of my belongings, keeping them on their hangers, and schlep them to the Prius, which I've parked by the front door. I lay the first load in the back, realizing I probably should have put a sheet down first. Oh well. I'm doing the best I can. Back in the bedroom, I dump my shoes into black plastic trash bags and bring them out to the car.

I drive to the Little House and start ferrying my things into what would have been Grace's office, which I need to start calling my bedroom. After I've hung up my clothes, I dump my shoes out of the bag and arrange them on the floor of the closet.

I hoist my suitcase onto the desk, which will serve as my dresser until I buy a real one. And that will happen when I buy a bed? I'm also going to need a dining table and chairs, a coffee table. End tables. Lamps. Or I can just dismantle the Big House room by room and reconfigure it over here. But that's precisely what I didn't want to do, even if the Girls won't need furniture. I stop my spiraling thoughts. This was to be my clean-slate dwelling. I don't have to rush into anything. I can give myself time.

Back in the Big House, I empty my half of the dresser into a suitcase and throw that in the car, then go back inside for one last look around. Not a lingering look, even though I know that when I step out of this room, despite the fact that I'm not done in here, I'm crossing some point of no return. I can't think about any of that. I start to grab the lamp from my nightstand to use in my new office, but instead opt for the blue vase.

Decoration over practicality. Which of course reminds me that I need to figure out what to do with Grace.

Not today. She can wait. My boiling rage has subsided, simmers just under the surface. I tamp it down, afraid I'll do something stupid again if I let anything out, especially now that I know exactly where Kit lives. I pour all my energy into the move, no more memory dredging, no more revenge fantasies.

Sitting on the big couch in the Little House, clothes in my closet, blue vase on the kitchen counter, I wonder what comes next.

Kitchen. Hmm. Even if I'm not ready to stock the pantry, I could at least buy some food. And it'll get me out of the house.

I drive to town and head into Wegmans feeling sure of myself. I've had a productive day. I've made a move. Progress!

Only a few minutes in, I realize I was being overly ambitious. Far from being ready to stock my kitchen, I can't think of even one thing I want to eat. I grab a few items and hurry back home, not sure what I've picked up in my haste to escape.

Force of habit, I park in my old spot by the barn rather than in front of the Little House. I'm halfway to the Big House before I realize what I've done. I stand at the path to the front door, grocery bag in my arms, about to turn back to my car when The Girls drive up.

Cristina is beside herself, raving about the beauty of the area. They now have an expanding list of other places to explore—state parks, wineries, Harriet Tubman's house! "Did you know there's a Museum of Play in Rochester? A museum. Of play! How far is Rochester?"

"How was your day?" Nicole asks.

"I didn't get as much done as I'd hoped," I say. "My clothes are out, but that's about it."

"Take your time," Cristina says. "Really."

"We're fine in the guest room till you're settled over there," Nicole says. "We've been thinking that ultimately we'll move into the back bedroom and use the guest room as Cristina's office. We thought you might like to keep Grace's study intact until you've figured out where everything's going to go."

"Are you sure about that?" I ask. I catch her tactful use of "back bedroom" and the implied suggestion of using Grace's office as a storage space. I could just dump things in there until I was ready to deal. That would be handy. And a great place to keep her. The urn. The her in the urn. The "hern." I crack myself up. Hern. Even Grace would chuckle.

"That's more room than we had in L.A., so yes," Nicole says. "Plus I may have to go back for a while."

I look at her. "To L.A.?"

Cristina jumps in to answer. "Our friend Cara's directing her first feature, and she begged Nicky to cut it!"

"Just when I think I'm out..." Nicole shrugs.

"Come on, it's exciting!" Cristina says. "It's what you always wanted."

"It's a long time away from each other," Nicole says.

"Well, it'll give me a chance to settle into the semester without worrying about you," Cristina says to her. Then turns to me. "Fewer distractions."

I feel like I watched a tennis match, a long rally between two strong players. Maybe I should be wondering if everything's all right between The Girls, but selfishly I'm relieved that I know what I'm going to do with the hern.

17

Insomnia

I'm on the couch in the living room of the Little House. It's my first night sleeping here. Well, staying here, since I'm definitely not sleeping.

I fuss with my pillow, settle onto my back, and close my eyes.

They pop open immediately.

Okay. Close them. Focus. Count.

I can't make it past ten.

Okay. Try another tactic. Picture a place you like.

The beach in Costa Rica. Sand as soft as talcum powder that burned your feet unless you wore sandals. Pelicans flying low over the water. I reach back to remember the sound of the waves. I can't conjure it.

Emails light up my phone. I don't have to look to know they're not from friends. It's the middle of the night. These are sent automatically from lists I'm on. Or from stores. From the college. From political organizations ramping up for next year's elections. Even though I'll delete them all in the morning, I find these oddly reassuring. They're proof of an outside world, one I don't need to engage with.

I pad over to the kitchen, stubbing my toe against a stack of unpacked boxes. The Girls were happy to let me take a set of dishes and some flatware, a few pots and pans (how optimistic of me!). Nicole packed it all up while I sorted through things in my study. With help from her and Cristina, I mustered the energy to bring the boxes over here, but that's all. I switch on the light over the cooktop, set the empty dishwasher for a light wash, and start it. I find the noise reassuring, like this is a real house and I'm living a real life. Shuffle back to the couch and stretch out.

Back to the beach. I will myself to feel the sand under my feet, hear the gulls and the rustle of wind in the palm trees.

But the palms I see aren't in Costa Rica. They're in Los Angeles.

When people hear "Los Angeles," they think palm trees. They think Hollywood. They see an establishing shot in a film, towering palms silhouetted against a blue sky as a fancy convertible travels down a wide street in the flats of Beverly Hills. They think beaches, too, and the iconic Hollywood sign nestled in the hills. Am I right? The Walk of Fame, its terrazzo and brass stars imbedded in the sidewalks of Hollywood Boulevard imprinted with names of film, TV, radio stars, or the movie stars' hand- and footprints in front of Grauman's Chinese Theatre—still referred to as Grauman's despite an actual Chinese company having bought naming rights. TLC Chinese Theatre doesn't roll trippingly off the tongue or conjure the glamour of Hollywood in quite the same way. Still, yes to all those images that contribute to the mythology of the place. But really, first the palm trees.

No one ever mentions the pumpjacks. They're what struck me when I first saw them en route from the airport into Hollywood. Oil wells! They look like erector-set dinosaurs, perpetual motion machines bobbing in the Inglewood Oil Field. Only later did I learn that this is one of the country's largest urban oil fields, 1,000 acres spread below the fancy houses of Baldwin Hills (nicknamed the Black Beverly Hills). That controversy surrounds the industry, which extracts millions of barrels a year from these and from the actual oil derricks scattered around Los Angeles and its environs, some camouflaged to look like nondescript towers, office buildings so unremarkable you wouldn't think to wonder why there were no windows. The derrick on the Beverly Hills High School grounds is disguised and colorfully painted to resemble an abstract art monolith.

But that knowledge came later. I spent my first year in L.A. trying to be nonchalant about everything that, in actuality, seemed strange and wondrous to me. The sun and the perpetual flowers distracted from the very regular lives being lived, drew attention away from huge, ugly stretches of the city, with its end-on-end strip malls, no thought given to design aesthetics. Plus all the ills facing every city, large or small, in America—income disparity, systemic racism, an increasing homeless population. The seemingly idyllic weather lulled you into forgetting you lived in a desert. Months of no rain followed by fires followed by floods. And of course you'd want to forget the earthquakes. But the flowers! The scents! The light! The weather! You can go from the beach to skiing in two hours. All this contributes to the mythology, not just "Hollywood."

I'd sometimes be driving in L.A. and have a moment of panic because I couldn't remember what season we were in. But the moment would pass. As would any momentary thought that I missed winter or wanted to feel cold air.

January 1994 was the kind of month L.A. homeowners gloated about. While the eastern half of the country shivered, dug their cars out of the snow, and knocked icicles off their gutters, we were smug and warm in the California sun. Hot, even, as temperatures soared into the 90s.

Until an earthquake woke us up. Literally.

A word about earthquakes. By that time, I'd lived in L.A. long enough to have experienced my share. Each had its own personality: gentle sometimes—did you feel that?—sometimes rolling, or like a sudden sharp slap against the side of the house followed by one beat of perfect stillness broken by car alarms and dogs barking. Some quakes were bouncy-jiggly, others swaying. But this one, the biggest I'd felt, magnitude 6.7, big enough that it got its own name, the Northridge Quake, was angry. Enraged. Determined to shake us out of our complacency, as well as out of bed at 4:31 a.m. PST.

The rest of the morning was surreal. I sat outside later in 90-degree heat, shut off from the rest of the world, trying to hold the contrasts of the experience in my mind. I had thought I was going to die, buried in the rubble of my rented house. Now here I was. No power. No phone service. But alive. Birds, heat, and glorious sun in mid-January. This beautiful Southern California day had sprung from that violent start. I didn't know yet how many people had died (fifty-seven, though some say more, if you included heart attacks), or structures destroyed. I just soaked up the glorious heat while I could because I'd already made up my mind. "Maybe you want to stay in this town," I'd say to my friends, "but I don't." Of course I had no idea where I wanted to go or what I'd do there, but the Northridge Quake made me—and hundreds of others—rethink whether I wanted to be living anywhere near a major faultline.

Isn't it amazing what a person can forget—the absolute terror that angry temblor caused. Weeks later I'd find myself observing people in restaurants, supermarkets, on the Venice Boardwalk. They weren't going anywhere. They were staying. They weren't even stocking their earthquake kits, not buying a single extra battery. I could feel my own resolve waver.

Then Diane said, "I have someone for you to meet."

"Nah. You know I don't do well with set-ups."

"Leslie and I are having a party. You'll come. She'll come. Lots of other people will come. No pressure."

Wavering resolve or not, I was still planning to leave L.A. So I clearly wasn't in the market to meet anyone.

The night of the party followed a particularly warm day—eighty degrees in February. Leslie greeted me at the door with an exuberant, "How about this weather! I'll bet our property value went up today!"

I never liked parties. I'd only come because Leslie wouldn't allow me to decline their invitation, so I was playing this game under protest. I poured myself some wine, planted myself in the corner of a couch while everyone else stood around the dining room table where the food was. One woman left the group to ask if she could get me anything.

"I'm fine," I said. And because I'm polite, added, "Thank you."

"Don't like parties?" she asked. She wore dangly earrings that looked more like sculpture than jewelry.

"No. It's just…" oh, what the hell, I thought. I don't have to be polite. It's not her party. I can answer honestly. "Does anyone?"

"I kind of do," she said, and proceeded to tell me why, something about enjoying being with her friends, good food, good conversation.

"What if you don't know anyone?" I challenged.

"You mean if somehow I'm at a party out of some obligation?"

I nodded.

"If I know that's going to be the case, I tell myself I can leave after an hour, but first I have to talk to at least three people."

"So am I one of those three tonight?"

She smiled and was just about to reply when Diane swept past us with a cheese platter, glanced at me, and said, "Oh, great, you've met."

The woman looked at me. "Well, not officially." She extended her hand to me. "Grace Black."

And that, as they say, was that.

Right off the bat, on an early date, I had confessed my new fear of earthquakes, but Grace was more sanguine. Fatalistic. "Hey, when it's your time, it's your time." I told her that was her youth talking. "You're ten years younger than I am. You still think anything's possible at thirty-five," I said. But by then, it didn't matter. I knew I'd have followed her anywhere. And I did.

Tonight, lying in the dark, my phone a semaphore reminding me there's a world outside the Little House, I think about what makes us move. Or stay. I think about Nicole following Cristina. I think about those pumpjacks bobbing in the oilfield. My phone illuminates the room for a few seconds. A pulse of light, then darkness. The dishwasher's hum gives me a sense of stability, normalcy. Lets me pretend I'm living a regular life. Which for me means my old life. My life in which Grace was alive. Is alive. I don't know about her betrayal. I'm sleeping in our room, on my side of the bed. She's next to me. We've turned off the lights but lie together talking, planning her sabbatical. That's when I sleep.

And then the sun shining on my face wakes me.

18
Wellness Check

It's hot. Really hot. Unseasonably hot. And humid. Not even a breeze to relieve the weight of early summer air that wraps around you the moment you step outside. I'm proficient now at my morning three, as I've taken to calling them: meds, espresso, toast. Skipped chores this morning because chores have become unpacking and I can't face that. And because it's too goddamn hot to be productive. Instead, I'm sprawled on the inner tube floating around the pond, thinking I should get out now and do...what? What should I do? Unpack? But then what comes after that? I dip a hand into the water to half-heartedly splash some on my face and body, wash away the guilt I feel at not being productive.

I hear a faint "Hola!" from the front of the Little House.

"Back here," I call.

Cristina walks around the house and makes her way to the edge of the pond. "That's a great idea."

"Come on in," I say. "There's more than enough floats."

"Can't. I need to finish my syllabus."

Even this early in the summer Grace and I would be thinking about the new academic year. Grace would start to prep her chair duties—schedule department meetings, organize committees, whatever—and I would think about revising my syllabi, rearranging modules, or changing up the reading lists. This wasn't supposed to be a normal summer, however. We'd had so many plans for this particular summer—get ready for Grace's sabbatical! My retirement! New adventures! How strange now to have nothing to do, to be able to float aimlessly.

"Sorry to bother you," Cristina says. "I called a few times and texted, but you didn't respond."

I'd been making such progress—where is my phone?

"Nicole and I wondered if you'd like to come for dinner tonight."

"This isn't part of our arrangement," I say. "You're not obligated—"

"We really want to say thank you for everything, and this is how we can show our appreciation. Though it does feel a little weird inviting you to your own house."

"Don't be silly. I told you that you weren't supposed to think like that. It's your place now."

"Then let us host you tonight."

"Okay. What can I bring?" Which sounds strange to me now, so I understand what Cristina must have felt inviting me. Strange also because I still have a lot of stuff over there.

"Just yourself," Cristina says.

We agree on seven, and Cristina returns to her syllabus and I return to floating and wallowing. Only now I have a purpose—figuring out what I'll bring to dinner. Like any Jewish person could ever show up to a meal empty-handed. Really. I dry myself off and head inside. I'm motivated.

I'll definitely bring a bottle of wine. I should have asked what we were having. But is that rude? I'll bring something versatile. Rosé, I think. Something crisp. I feel the need to contribute more to this meal to compensate for being just me, alone, no longer part of a pair.

Then I remember, with forehead-slapping realization—I don't even have wine. It's all still at the Big House. The Lazy Chef is also the lazy mover. I'll need to go buy something. I collapse onto the couch, momentum frozen. Next to impossible to stay motivated about anything—unpacking, deciding what to bring tonight, determining the course of the rest of my life.

All my friends have the answer for me. Everyone's an expert, ready to offer the solution to my "problem." Thing is, I haven't asked a question. And I'm not the one with the problem. Grace has a problem—she's dead. I'm right here. No one's in my position. None of my closest friends, anyway. Whoopee. I'm the first in my circle! Tell the lucky lady what she's won!

They're right about one thing, though. I need to get back on track. Or at least find a track, which won't happen from my current position sprawled on the couch surrounded by boxes that I'm supposed to unpack.

I'd wanted to pare down my living space, have a spare clean environment in which to rebuild my life. Instead, I've brought it all with me.

Grace played a video game called *Katamari Damacy*, about this little prince (not to be confused with *The Little Prince*) whose father, the King of All Cosmos, basically destroyed the stars and the moon and the prince is tasked with rebuilding them. He does this by rolling a magical, highly adhesive ball called a *katamari* around the game world. The *katamari* picks up everything it rolls over—candy, thumbtacks, coins, playing cards, increasingly larger objects like batteries, all the way up to animals and trees—until the ball's big enough to become a star.

The mess in front of me feels that big. Most of the boxes are straightforward and labeled: books, kitchen utensils and bowls, linens. One box contains anything I didn't know what to do with when I was packing up. Items culled from my childhood home, augmented by various tchotchkes collected in college, grad school, and beyond. Girl Leslie's blaster balls. Stuff I've lugged across the country and back. I cleverly labeled the box: STUFF.

Am I going to be carrying this junk around with me for the rest of my life? I didn't think about that when I was in my thirties and forties. I was still accumulating.

But now, who's going to care if I keep any of it or toss all of it? What am I cleaning up for? And for whom? Have I just been keeping up appearances—going through the wrapping and packing and stuffing boxes because this is what a sane person who moves to a new place brings with her? Why don't I just seal all the boxes and donate them! Will people think I'm crazy?

I'm debating whether or not I care when a car pulls up in front of the Little House. Given where we, where I, live, people can't just swing by on their way somewhere. I raise myself enough to see Jordan's Volvo come to a stop. At least with her I don't have to pretend to be in a good mood.

I open the door just as she comes up the two steps of the porch carrying a large paper bag.

"I thought you could use some company. And maybe some lunch." She holds up the bag as well as a pint of strawberries. "Look—first of the season!"

I'm not sure I trust this visit. (Who have I become that I question my friends' motives?) Still, I step aside to let Jordan in.

She surveys the room, wanting to approve, but not quite able to. If I imagine how it looks to her, I see boxes stacked up, winter jackets and coats on hangers in a not-neat pile on the floor. Definitely not the home of someone in complete control of her environment. The view is nice, though. Everything greening, flowers, lilacs. Further out, newly plowed fields of what will be corn.

I know Jordan's here to check up on me. Not that she'd cop to that. "Did Janey put you up to this?" I ask.

"I can't stop in to see you on my own?" She puts the bag on the kitchen counter, then checks the fridge, casually, like I'm not going to notice she's making sure it's stocked. Which it isn't.

"Don't judge," I say.

"It's just, like, you don't have any food," Jordan says, still holding the door open.

"I'm fine," I insist. "Really."

Jordan doesn't look convinced.

"Besides, The Girls have invited me to dinner tonight, so that meal's taken care of."

Jordan knows better than to harp on the topic, so she just holds up the bag she brought.

"We can eat on the couch," I offer. "Or outside, if you can stand the heat."

When we're settled in our chairs on the porch, Jordan looks around approvingly. "It's really nice back here," she says. "I can see why you wanted to move." She gestures in the general direction of the Big House. "How's that working out?"

"The Girls? Fine," I answer. "They're going to stay. At least for the school year."

"It won't be weird to have them living in your house?"

I shrug. I can't explain how I feel I no longer belong there. "I'm happy to know that technically I'm not alone, and equally happy not actually living under the same roof with anyone."

My answer seems to satisfy Jordan, since she moves on to ask, "What time is your dinner?"

"Seven. They said I didn't have to bring anything, but that just doesn't feel right. And all my wine's still over there."

"Take those." Jordan motions to the strawberries.

"You brought them for us. You should get to enjoy. I can head over to the farm stand later and pick some up."

"I know you. You won't go till it's too late and there's none left."

I want to protest, but she's right.

"Take these."

I give each of us one. They're amazingly sweet.

"Have you given any more thought to the 4th?" Jordan tries to sound casual, like, oh-by-the-way, but I know better.

"So Janey did put you up to this visit."

"She just keeps asking me how you're doing—have I spoken to you? Are you okay?" She looks out at the pond. "It wouldn't hurt you to pick up a phone. I know you still own one."

I pull my cell out of my pocket, thankful I'd grabbed it when I saw her car, and wave it at her. See that I've got five unread texts, a few phone calls, and three voicemails. Oops. "It was on silent. Sorry."

"Mary told me she's been fielding calls about Grace's appointments. They eventually call her work number when she doesn't answer her cell."

I want to care but can't. And I'm not ready to cancel the landline, nor plug it back in. The Girls don't need it, they both just use their mobile numbers. The phone itself is in Grace's office, along with whatever else I'd dumped in there. As well as the hern.

"And your friends would like to hear from you," Jordan says. "Not just me and Sue."

I don't ask how she knows. I can't talk about this. But I feel I need to give Jordan something, so I say, "I'll be there."

Jordan looks at me.

"I'll come to your party. I promise."

Once that's out of the way, we both relax. Jordan digs into the bag she brought and pulls out large containers of grape leaves, tabouleh, hummus, kalamata olives, pita bread. But wait—there's more. "I wasn't sure what we'd be in the mood for." Out come some limes, avocados, salsa, chips. Bottles of sparkling water. "Lemon? Lime? Orange?"

"How many people did you think you'd find here?" I ask, eyeing the stunning amount of food, and grabbing a lemon water.

"I had a hunch your fridge would be empty. I wanted to make sure you had leftovers."

Being with Jordan is easy. I feel a little guilty having questioned her motives. She doesn't push me to talk or make me feel I need to keep up my end of a conversation.

After we've eaten in silence for a while, she asks, "Are you going to be okay?"

I know she's genuinely concerned. She deserves an honest response, so I think before I answer. "I guess. Maybe. I don't even know what that means anymore."

I get up to take our plates inside. Jordan offers to help, but I tell her to stay put. I leave the dishes in the sink and grab two beach towels on my way back outside.

Jordan's leaned back in her chair, eyes closed, but she's heard me. "I'm too happy just like this. I was almost asleep."

I toss one of the towels on her lap. "In case you want to go for a swim." Then I sit down, lean back, and close my eyes. Neither of us makes a move to do anything. I'm content to just hang like this with someone who isn't going to make me talk or feel or process.

I don't realize I've dozed off until a splash wakes me. Jordan's in the water, her clothes neatly folded on the ground.

"Oh, I needed this," she says, toweling off before pulling her chair into the sun and sitting down. "You going in?"

"I'm good." And for the moment, I pretty much am.

I decide to shower before I go over for dinner. Makes me feel like I'm actually going somewhere, and I want to show my hosts that I've treated this like a special occasion. An acknowledgment that the Big House is their new home.

Dressed in linen shorts and a short-sleeved shirt, sweater over my shoulders, I pause on the porch for a moment, holding the strawberries, not quite able to leave my Little House, the stillness over the pond. I feel content. Well, not quite—I think I feel content, but then it's like I'm forgetting something. Oh. Right. Can I be content if I don't feel complete? I don't have to decide now. Being happy isn't the only happiness.

On my way to the Big House I stop at the herb patch for some mint to decorate the strawberries. I pat myself on the back: this is the kind of thing Grace would have thought to do. Though by this time in the season she'd also have cleared the ground, cut back the dead branches, and the area would be flourishing, not this we're-here-despite-your-neglect chaos I find. Still, better than nothing. I tear off a sprig of mint. The action scents the air, adds a layer on top of the existing fragrances. I take a moment to breathe it all in, and to listen. Birds, a dog barking in the distance. For a fraction of a second I feel at peace again, whole, calm. The moment I take notice of that it's gone, because I've caught myself thinking how for that brief time I wasn't aware of being alone, of being without Grace. But for that moment, I had a sense that maybe I would be okay.

I look around our land. The Little House behind the barn, the paths to the vegetable garden, the pond, the Big House. Everything so green and lush and warm, the day's heat still held in the plants and leaves. A soft breeze teases a hint of the season to come. I look at the Big House. The front porch light isn't on yet, still the place looks warm and inviting. Light pours from the living room. The kitchen is bright. Is that what Grace's and my guests saw when they approached? They'd drive up, park, and on their walk to our door, would they see Grace through the window, see me come to her, put my arms around her, see Grace turn to me, whisper something? I can almost see us there, but in actuality, Nicole is framed in the window.

She's turned away, facing into the living room, talking. She's animated. I can't hear her words, but she looks agitated, waving her arms as she talks. Then Cristina moves into the frame. Tries to take Nicole into her arms. Nicole jerks away. The women face each other. Cristina is talking. Nicole interrupts. More arm-waving. Cristina takes one of Nicole's hands in hers, pulls it to her. I can only imagine what's happening below the frame. Cristina's other hand moves to Nicole's face. Each woman leans forward so their foreheads touch.

I feel guilty for witnessing a moment that feels more intimate than a kiss.

I walk slowly the rest of the way to the house to make sure I've given The Girls enough time to settle whatever is happening between them.

19
Neighbors

When I reach the front door, I face a dilemma. We don't have a doorbell. How shall I announce my arrival?

The main door is open, so I can see through the screen into the living room, but I feel strange just walking in. I contemplate an entrance line. I nix "Honey, I'm home" as too loaded. I'd jokingly announce that to Grace when I walked in after work. If I said it now, would The Girls think I was reminding them of the fact that this wasn't their home, but mine? We don't know each other's sense of humor yet. Maybe after a few more dinners. Which makes me wonder if I need to invite them over to the Little House soon. Or soon-ish. Just as I raise my arm to knock on the door frame, Nicole walks past carrying a dish in each hand.

"Hannah! How long have you been standing there? Come on in."

I extend the bowl of strawberries, like an idiot, since obviously she can't take them as her hands are full. Cristina swoops in then, all poise and charm and excitement. "Oh, are these real, like not from the supermarket? Can I taste?" She doesn't wait for an answer, just plucks one from the bowl at the same time as she takes my offering. "Oh my god, delicious!" she says. "And they're gorgeous! They can be our centerpiece." She sets the dish on the table.

I step into the house. Our house. My house. But Cristina and Nicole's now. It feels completely transformed, even though outwardly, nothing major has been moved or replaced.

"What would you like to drink?" Cristina asks. "Nicole's the chef, I'm the bartender. I can make margaritas. We've got wine and beer." She doesn't wait for me to answer. "Or something nonalcoholic?"

"If you've got a red open..."

"We do. And we bought it. Your supply is intact." She motions to the full wine rack on the floor by the bookcase. "Do you want to take that over to your place? We can put it in the car after dinner if—"

"She doesn't need it tonight," Nicole interrupts. "Let Hannah enjoy her evening." To me she says, "Obviously take anything you want, whenever you want."

I'm still frozen at the threshold. My eyes have scanned the room, though, noticing everything. The couch now serving its original purpose, no longer a bed. Fresh flowers on the dining table and on the end table near the couch. Everything neat and tidy. Not a sticky note in sight. I'm a little out of my body. This is Grace's and my house, but not. I step inside. Only after I'm seated do I realize I'm on a side of the couch I never sat on. Not a conscious decision, that's just where I find myself.

Nicole has set out olives, cheese, and crackers. She's found matching dishes that I'm about to compliment her on until I remember that Grace and I brought them back from a trip to Spain.

Cristina brings me a generous pour of wine. "It's not a local red. I've heard we're supposed to stick with Finger Lakes whites. We may go on a self-guided wine tour later this week."

I can't call what I'm experiencing déjà vu, but it's akin to that. Maybe a parallel reality. Everything's the same and everything's different. Furniture hasn't been moved or rearranged. Even our art is on the walls. I go in and out of realizing where I am and why it feels so familiar and so completely different at the same time. I'm aware of the forced intimacy of our situation. Not just that they're living in the Big House, but that I'm set up nearby.

"You're welcome to replace anything—furniture, plates, whatever. Just store it in the barn," I say. "Don't feel obligated to live with art we picked out." The Girls exchange a quick look, as if they'd discussed this but didn't know how to bring it up. I can tell they don't want to offend me by looking relieved. "Really. I mean it." It's easy to say that, harder to explain how unattached I feel to all of this, how my attachment to things has changed.

Our conversation comes in bursts followed by intervals of silence. We're still getting to know each other, after all. Nicole pops up to check on dinner. Cristina lists a few wineries they plan to visit, asks if I recommend any others.

"You've done your research," I say. "You know there are some distilleries worth checking out as well."

"Did you hear that, Nicky?"

"I did," says Nicole, coming back in and refilling my glass, which I don't remember finishing, nor do I feel the effects of what I've already consumed. Should I cut myself off? It's not like I have to drive anywhere.

I ask Cristina how she's settling in on campus.

"Everyone's been really nice," she says. "Mary in particular."

"Stay on her good side and she'll make sure you're okay. I'll introduce you to some other faculty, outside the department. It's good to have allies across campus." Only after I offer this do I remember that I don't work there anymore, so it's not like I'll be around to make introductions. "But you're probably already meeting people and don't need me." Which is a perfect segue to: "And you'll meet others at Jordan and Janey's Fourth of July party. Jordan wanted me to remind you about that."

"Do people really go all day?" Nicole wants to know. She offers me the plate of cheese and more wine, which I decline.

"Some do. Not everyone. Some folks leave mid-afternoon, others don't show up till dinner time. It's very casual."

Nicole moves to put the bottle back on the dining room table.

"Hey," Cristina holds up her own glass. "What about me?"

Nicole just keeps walking into the kitchen.

Cristina gets up to refill her glass, as if it's no big deal she's been ignored.

"I've never swum in a lake," says Cristina, like nothing happened. "I can't wait!"

"Is it a dish to pass?" Nicole calls from the kitchen.

"Grace and I used to bring potato salad."

"I can make a potato salad," Nicole says, grabbing the cheese and crackers to bring back to the kitchen. "And dinner's ready. Come eat."

As we're settling in at the table, Nicole says, "Unless you'd rather I didn't? I mean, if the potato salad's your specialty."

"Believe me, I don't have a specialty. That would be great. It was a friend's recipe. I'll just bring wine this year." I plan to milk this widow's dispensation as long as I can.

Nicole has gone silent again. Thinking about her recipe? Grace would do that sometimes. I'd ask where she was, and she'd give me some combination of ingredients, or a flavor to add to a dish. I realize I'd gone silent, also. "Under other circumstances, I'd offer to drive us all, but I don't know how long I'm going to stay, so I think it's best we go in separate cars." That seems a pretty compact statement to me. I leave out that I'm dreading the party for any number of reasons, not the least of which is that it will be my first big social gathering since Grace's funeral.

Dinner is simple, roast chicken and vegetables, a salad. But absolutely delicious.

"This is all local," Cristina says, diving into the silence. She praises Nicole's cooking. Just like I used to go on about Grace's food. "She's an amazing cook."

"Cristina," Nicole warns.

"What? I can't have an opinion?"

"You can. But just because you want me to do something—"

"I know you're not going to start a blog. I know you're going to edit this film. But you're the one who says that isn't your passion."

I feel caught in the middle of some argument, the basis of which I'm not privy to. I break it up by saying, "This is truly delicious."

Cristina pours herself more wine.

"It's pretty easy," says Nicole. "I can tell you how to make it."

"That would be so wasted on me. I'm inordinately proud when I cook something and it doesn't suck. The kitchen was Grace's realm."

The chill doesn't dissipate, and we finish our food in silence. Cristina clears the table. Then Nicole brings out homemade chocolate cake. I take a bite. It's amazing. As good as Grace's, which she was famous for. Inspired, I go to the liquor cabinet (I ask permission first, which feels a little odd) and dig around till I find a small bottle of California dessert wine which I bring back to the table. "This would be a perfect accompaniment. I generally don't like sweet wines, but Grace and I were introduced to this on a trip to Napa a couple of years ago. We were saving it…" My unresolved anger at Grace interferes with my ability to finish the sentence. I switch topics, ready to recite all I'd learned about botrytis mold, how it's called noble rot, how we learned about chemical compounds called terpenes, and how they affect the flavor of the wine, the multiple adjectives used to describe the flavor—honeyed, citrusy, floral—but I can't finish that, either.

Their argument shoved aside, The Girls unite in their effort to rescue me from whatever pit I've fallen into. Cristina leaps up and brings a corkscrew. Nicole finds appropriate glasses. Cristina pours for us. We take careful sips. The Girls wax poetic—the wine really is the perfect match for the rich chocolate cake. I know it's all marvelous, but I can no longer taste a thing.

I walk slowly back to the Little House a little after nine o'clock. Nicole insisted I take a plate of food and a piece of cake. Cristina wanted me to take the dessert wine, but I told her to keep it. And then I conveniently "forgot" to bring the leftovers Nicole had wrapped neatly for me.

It's only just dark, and the fireflies are out in force. I want to tell Grace that. I want to tell Grace that Cristina and Nicole seem like they'll take really good care of our house if they decide to stay. That she'd like them. I want to ask her if she felt the tension between them. I want to tell her that she and Nicole could have talked about cooking and food, that she could have drawn Nicole out about her long-range plans. And that I'm trying to get along, trying to figure out my life.

Then I want to take it all back. I want to tell Grace that I'm still mad at her. For dying. For cheating all those years ago and making me question everything.

This is not how I thought I'd be easing into my retirement. That's for damn sure.

I flip on the lights once I get inside. I'd just spent two hours in a house that was perfectly in order. Why couldn't my place be like that, I wonder. And shake my head to remind myself that *was* my place, even if I wasn't living in it. It pretty much looked like that back in my real life, the one with Grace.

I change into boxers and a T-shirt, thinking maybe I'll do some unpacking. I take one look at the boxes, say "Who am I kidding," and curl up on the couch for the night.

Cristina and Nicole drive over the next afternoon with the wine rack, the wine, and whatever liquor had been in the cabinet, even the dessert wine, but I insist they keep that. Cristina drives off for an appointment on campus and Nicole helps me carry things into the house. "I'm sorry about last night," she says, handing me bottles that I place into the rack. "Cristina has very definite opinions about what I should be doing. We don't always agree."

I think about Grace wanting me to write. "I'm sure she only wants you to be happy." Really, Hannah, that's the best you can come up with?

"I feel like going back to work on this film is giving up on a dream I hadn't even defined yet."

"It's not forever," I say.

"But it's not here. And it's familiar. I wanted our move to be a complete break from L.A. and my work. A chance to think about what comes next." She pauses. "I wanted what I do next to make a difference." She looks at me. "That sounds stupid, doesn't it."

"Not at all."

"I can't really explain what I want. I was hoping to be able to figure that out here."

I sense a big "but" hovering at the end of that sentence. I don't press, and Nicole doesn't offer more.

20
The Wall

After Nicole leaves, I arrange the liquor bottles at one end of the kitchen counter, my bar for the time being. Aside from that major accomplishment, well, that and rotating the wine bottles in the rack so all labels are facing up, I've managed to fritter away a day doing—what have I done? Ordered a washer and dryer to be delivered. Looked at furniture online and retreated back to the couch, rationalizing this as necessary to study the layout of the room. I want to be decisive. I want to be productive. I want Grace back. I remember the T-shirts we wore in the '90s: I don't just want a cure for AIDS—I want all my friends back.

If Grace were here, would I know what I want to do? I wouldn't want to kill her because I wouldn't know about her and Kit. I wouldn't have found the photo because I wouldn't have had to clean out her office. Right now we'd have been, where? Still in the Adirondacks? No. Back home for a while, getting ready to leave the country. I'm tempted to go over to the Big House and check Grace's master calendar but don't want the Girls to think I'll be in their lives every other minute.

Is this grief or retirement? Does it matter?

It's already five-thirty. Not six-thirty, but close enough. I allow myself to move to the next activity: meal prep.

I open the fridge as if I'd be inspired by what I find there. Close it after a long peruse of the mostly empty, save for Jordan's leftovers, shelves. Probably should have given this more thought before I went to the market so that now I could just gather the ingredients I needed to make a flavorful, nutritious, sustaining, or whatever other MadLib-worthy adjective, meal in minutes. All you have to do is have the right ingredients on hand.

Enough of this seesawing between purpose and despair. Summoning another of Grace's admonitions, I'm going to keep it simple. I proclaim loudly to my audience of no one: "I, the Lazy Chef, shall attempt to attempt the impossible." I make a grand gesture as I open the refrigerator and announce, "The Lazy Chef shall not be daunted by the poorly provisioned kitchen. She shall prevail!"

For kicks, I prop my phone on the stand Grace used for her iPad if she wanted to keep a recipe handy for guidance. I never understood my students' reliance on their phone's camera for conversations. But I got used to talking to Grace's computer, then to her phone—actually, any Apple device will do—and this makes me feel less lonely. So fuck it. Besides, it's not me—it's the Lazy Chef.

I open the camera, start recording video, then turn back to the fridge to dig for a few items that will enable me to produce something that I will call dinner. An avocado, limes, a jar of salsa. That works. Then I go to the other end of the counter, my bar, and set out my other ingredients.

Call me crazy, but I think I stand up just a little taller as the Lazy Chef, and my voice takes on a Julia Child quality, if Julia Child sounded like Dame Judi Dench. And if Dame Judi had a New York accent. I turn toward an imaginary camera crew. "Are we ready?"

As if given the go-ahead, I speak to my audience.

"My wife Grace makes—made, she died recently—excellent margaritas. I, the Lazy Chef, have assembled the ingredients on the counter." I take down a glass, drop in four ice cubes, and resume. "She was the love of my life, and I'm having a hard time moving on. Well, you can see that for yourselves, can't you? I mean, here I am talking to you. We're going through a rough patch right now, Grace and me. Turns out she cheated on me. It was many years ago, very early in our relationship, and I'm not sure what to do with this information, where to put it. So maybe this will help." I rattle the ice in my glass. "Or not. Anyhoo—The Lazy Chef will forge valiantly ahead and make her dead wife's margarita. She's had it enough times to know the ingredients by heart. Well, that's easy, since there are only three. Four if you like your margarita with salt on the rim. But the Lazy Chef being, well, lazy, only three. And the Lazy Chef can't be bothered with the juicer and the blender."

The Lazy Chef squeezes in a lot, a *lot*, of lime juice, pours some tequila and an equal amount, maybe just a teeny bit more, of Cointreau into the glass, stirs it all with her finger, and takes a sip. "Tasty. Very tasty."

Fortified by a few more sips, the Lazy Chef smiles for the camera, turns her attention to the other ingredients she'd gathered, and continues:

"Next: the Lazy Chef is making guacamole. It's an excellent accompaniment to this most excellent of summer drinks, the margarita. I would have called this the Gracerita, but that was before I knew about the infidelity. So now, I present to you, Oblivion!" I reach for my glass and hold it up to the camera. "Salud!" I take a sip. "You don't want to drink too much of this on an empty stomach. So make sure you have plenty of chips on hand." I hold up a bag of blue corn chips, bless Jordan for bringing them as part of her lunch extravaganza.

"Let's make guacamole! You'll start with a ripe avocado, fresh lime, or a lemon if you've used all your limes in the margarita, and salsa."

I demonstrate the rest of the process, keeping up a running commentary as I work. "First, cut the avocado in half, whack the blade into the pit so it comes right out with a twist of the knife. I learned a lot about avocados when I lived in L.A. That's where Grace and I met. And courted. That's an old-fashioned word, isn't it. Does anyone still use that? Actually, I probably shouldn't either. It doesn't accurately describe our beginning, which was hot and sexy and political. Okay. Back to our topic. The avocado. Cut up and scoop out the inside, squeeze in lime juice, or lemon, mash and stir it all with a fork."

Then I hold up the unopened jar of salsa. "The Lazy Chef prefers medium heat for this—don't want to drown the avocado flavor—but it's your choice. Before you add the salsa, taste to see if you've got the right amount of lime." I sample my avocado mash. "Perfect." When I open the salsa jar it makes a satisfying pop. I dump a few big spoonfuls into the avocado/lime juice. "Take it easy at first. If you like, you can add a few dashes of hot sauce. If you've got any, which I don't. Then mash and stir some more till it's the consistency you want, adding more salsa if needed." I taste as I go, adding a few hefty dollops of salsa. "Of course when Grace made guacamole, she made it from scratch. She varied the ingredients and sometimes roasted the tomatoes. She was fearless in the kitchen. Actually, everywhere. Very inspiring to her students and her colleagues. And to me. But I digress. And this is *my* guac."

But then I digress even further, my phone's camera serving as my audience. Or more accurately, as a good therapist whose patient silence pulls the truth out of me. Turning from extolling her virtues, I unload on Grace, yell at her for betraying me, for destroying my trust in us, first by sleeping with Kit and then by not telling me. I blame her for my inability to move forward, my insomnia. My embarrassing drive into the city. How I feel I'm on the edge of an abyss.

When I'm finally talked out, the Lazy Chef rips open the bag, dips a chip into the guac, pops the whole thing into her mouth. "Delicious!" she proclaims. She dips another chip, holds it up to the camera. "Buen provecho!"

I turn to my imaginary crew. "And, cut," I say, feeling strangely satisfied as I shut off the camera and scoop more guacamole with another chip.

I feel silly and proud and sad and wrung out. Grace would have loved that I've started to express myself.

"Fuck you," I say to her. "I'm still mad at you."

I take my dinner and drink out to the porch so I can focus on the landscape and settle in to enjoy my meal in peace.

Too restless to sit once I've finished my drink—which did not provide the oblivion its name offered—I head back inside, determined to be productive.

Grace always told me I'd figure out my retirement. I shouldn't worry about it. Let yourself get bored for a while, she'd say. You've earned a rest, she'd say. But I knew what she left unsaid: She wanted me to write. To go back to writing.

One day when we were painting what would be my room in the Little House, she exclaimed, "Wow!" followed by silence.

One or the other of us was always doing that—exclaiming like she'd discovered something fabulous, and then not finishing her sentence. That particular day we'd just had a long discussion on whether we'd chosen the right color, the subtle variations on shades of white— "What's the difference between Cloud White and Simply White?" I asked when we were in the store deciding. "They all look the same to me."—so I thought maybe she was pointing out why we'd made the right decision.

But no. Grace continued without prompting from me, "I was just thinking what a great view of the pond and the field. Very inspiring."

I joined her at the window, careful to hold my brush up so it wouldn't drip Cloud White everywhere. "It is beautiful," I agreed.

Not that it mattered, because I never had my desk face a window. Always a blank wall. Not that that mattered, either, since I didn't plan to be writing. And I knew that's what she had meant. "Very inspiring" was code for "perfect for writing."

And here I am looking out at that view and I have no intention of writing and I'm not inspired to write. I'm not inspired to do anything. It's enough that I got myself out of the Big House, isn't it? Given that I'd just spent half an hour performing for my phone, I think, maybe no, it's not enough. Just because I've retired doesn't mean I can't be a productive member of society. But before I cast about for activities out in the world, let's start close in, shall we? I've been living in just one room since I moved into the Little House and I need to branch out. I'm going to make this my own place once and for all.

I walk away from the window and sit down at my desk to get a feel for the space. I stare at the blank wall. The blank Cloud White wall. Except I don't see our excellent paint job. I see Grace at her computer, textbooks and pads spread around her, absorbed in her research or preparing a lecture. I see Grace asleep on the couch, a book on her chest. I see Grace across the table from me at breakfast, at lunch, or reading the Sunday *New York Times*. I see Grace at a dinner party, making sure our friends have enough food, their glasses are filled, sharing how she'd adjusted a recipe to create an entirely new dish. I see Grace coming in from the garden with a bouquet of freshly cut peonies. The bare wall teems with life—my life, our life, all our years together. Are these memories?

And then I see Kit that evening twenty-five years ago as she roared up the driveway on her motorcycle. I see her greeting Grace. Gracie. I see their familiarity. And then I see Grace and Kit leaning into each other in the photo from Chicago. This is not a memory I want.

If I'm not ready for the hard ones, I'll sacrifice the good ones.

I jump up and drag my desk to the other side of the room, line it up so I'll be sitting facing the window, able to look up to see not a blank wall but what actually exists: the pond, the trees, the fields beyond. Only what's real. I don't want to make up anything.

21
Partay

After I moved my desk under the window, I made a concerted effort to look online for a bed and a dresser as well as chairs for the living room. Okay, so maybe half-hearted is more accurate than concerted. But I needed a distraction from what I have dubbed the War of Memories, a battle with myself to quash those I don't want to remember so they don't filter through along with those I do want to remember. Easier in the Little House, or less frustrating, since I'm not forced to stare at objects we lived with every day, but that didn't help me remember what our daily life felt like. I vowed to move forward. I knew e-tail wasn't going to work for me, so I went to a downtown store that has beautiful furniture. Lots of Danish modern. Beautiful and expensive. And more of a commitment than I was ready to make, so I left the store and hightailed it to Best Buy and bought a big TV, big and smart. And a rolling stand to keep it on. What else do I need at this point, anyway? The couch is huge and provides multiple seating options. I dragged the table and desk chair out of what will be my bedroom and put them in what will be the dining area. I'm not entertaining guests in the foreseeable future. I have a place to sleep, eat, and entertain myself. This suits me fine.

I can wait to buy furniture. For the present, at least. I'd already dug a big suitcase out of the barn and dumped my underwear and socks into it, eliminating the need for a dresser. This'll be fine for now.

"Fine for now" has become another mantra I can alternate with "being happy isn't the only happiness."

I need to come up with a third one to cover today's issue. It's July 4th, and I've got a party to go to. Given that I didn't like parties when I was living my real life, this event is particularly charged.

I need to find ways to keep myself busy this morning so I don't have to think that I'm going to my first party without Grace. That this is my first holiday without Grace. I don't count Memorial Day, since I was too grief-stricken to even take notice of it.

If I weren't retired, I could busy myself with re-designing a syllabus or revising a reading list. If Grace weren't dead, we'd be on our way to Europe by now, or already there. Instead, I'm re-folding each shirt, pair of socks, and underwear I own. Living out of a suitcase can get messy. I really need to revisit my furniture decision. Or at least put shelves in the closet. As with every other project I've undertaken, I'm so over re-folding halfway through that I just stuff everything back on the pile I'd been trying to put in order, defeated.

Being unable to accomplish even that small task has left me cranky and out of sorts. I shouldn't blame Jordan, but why the hell not. If she hadn't made me promise, I wouldn't have to go to this stupid party. I feel like I'm seven and my mother's forcing me to wear these fancy underpants she bought me. If it's possible for a seven-year-old to hate something, I hate those underpants. They're stupid and they're scratchy. My mother's getting me ready for a classmate's birthday party and is insisting I wear them. It's bad enough she's forcing me to wear a dress. The underpants have ruffles! I didn't get it. What's the point of wearing something fancy that no one will see? "So you can feel all dressed up from the inside out," my mother had said, as if that explained anything. It made absolutely no sense to me. Butches, raise your hands if you can relate.

Something must have sunk in, however, because here I am, sixty-three years later, taking my mother's advice. I shower and dress in nice shorts and a clean polo shirt, careful to avoid any hint of a red-white-and-blue theme. I can only celebrate the 4th so far, especially with an unbalanced lunatic in the White House and his sycophants running DC. No fancy underpants. I'm wearing my bathing suit under my shorts. Not that I imagine I'll be going in the water. But I promised Jordan I'd come, and I'm keeping my promise. I never said how long I'd stay. Or that I'd have a good time. But a deal's a deal.

Cristina texts at eleven-thirty and says they're ready when I am. We'd arranged to leave at the same time but drive separately so the Girls could follow me to the lake. I text back a thumbs-up, though I'm feeling more like the Munch scream emoji. After learning that no one ever believed

I'd made the potato salad, I'm completely comfortable dropping the charade. Fully owning my culinary incompetence, I'm bringing three bottles of wine—a red, a white, and a rosé. I lay them on top of my towel, grab the *Fun Home* baseball cap Grace bought me when we saw the musical on Broadway, and head out to the car.

Cristina's already behind the wheel when I drive to the Big House and pull alongside their car. "Nicole said she was ready. Now I don't know where she is." She taps the horn twice, looking annoyed.

"There's no rush," I say. That's an understatement. I'd be happy to wait another year. Or two. But I pull the Prius in front of her car and open Spotify on my phone to choose some driving music to help get me in the mood. Or to drown out my thoughts.

Nicole comes out of the house carrying a huge bowl. She'd said if she brought potato salad, she'd tell people I made it. I like her sense of humor. She sees me and gives a wave. Cristina pops her head through the sunroof. She doesn't look happy. "Where's the bag with all our stuff?"

"I thought you had it," Nicole says, coming down the steps.

"No. You were supposed to bring it."

"How could I carry that and this?" Nicole asks, raising the bowl.

Cristina exits the car, leaving the door open. The persistent chime indicating the keys are in the ignition punctuates her hostile mood.

Nicole pays this no mind. She opens the back door and arranges the bowl on the floor, then settles in the front passenger seat. Cristina comes back out with two canvas bags, a beach towel folded on top of each. "How about practicing driving?" But it doesn't come out like friendly encouragement, rather a veiled threat, or a reminder of a failure. Nicole answers by fastening her seatbelt.

What have I been doing during all this? Trying to mind my own business, trying unsuccessfully to keep my eyes on a playlist rather than the drama playing out in my rearview mirror.

Cristina gets behind the wheel. When she closes her door, finally, that horrible beeping stops. She taps the horn twice and waves out the window to let me know they're ready.

So much for my playlist. Time to move out.

Last year at this time Grace and I were driving to Jordan and Janey's party talking excitedly about what we'd be doing next 4th of July. We found long car rides especially conducive to planning her sabbatical, imagining side trips, how we'd divide our time, how we were going to combine her work with a celebration of my retirement. And a year ago, even though we were smack into summer, we knew how fast the academic year flew by, that it'd be over before we knew it. She'd be deep into her research, and I'd be settling into my new life.

"So much for that," I say out loud, as though Grace were in the passenger seat. "I'm supposed to be sipping an espresso in Europe, not driving to this party." I raise my voice for emphasis: "By. My. Self."

"It's good for you to get out and see people," Grace tells me.

So we're talking again? I don't remember making up. Grace has tried to reach out to me a few times since I moved out of the Big House, but I've pushed her away every time. I don't want to talk to her. And I don't want memories.

And I have no desire to see people. I have no desire to do anything. And would prefer to do that alone.

It's not like I haven't tried various activities. Read a book, I'd tell myself.

Why? I'd ask.

To which I'd answer, Why not?

Because I don't want to read fiction. Or, it turns out, non-fiction.

Then watch your new TV. Or a movie.

I can't focus.

So, organize your shelves.

Well, if I had shelves, maybe. But every time I try browsing for furniture online, I just quit. Perhaps the perfect activity is out there, but I have yet to land on it.

"Just try to enjoy the party. They're all your friends. They'll take care of you."

Go away. I don't want to be taken care of by them. I want the new life you and I had planned, not this one. Or that's what I used to want. Before I learned you betrayed me.

So maybe it's good that I'm in the car, windows open, speeding through a gorgeous summer day. I don't have to think—just pay attention to the road ahead. Which I need to do because Grace always had to alert me to the turnoff, which I always missed, and that should be coming up—shit. That was it. The Girls are going to think I'm nuts. I slow, put on my left blinker, and make a careful U-turn, waving to them as our cars come parallel to each other. "Sorry, I missed the turn. It's just up there," I say, pointing in the general direction. Cristina gives me a thumbs up.

Once we're off the county road we drive past dairy farms and fields of—well, how should I know of what. If it isn't corn or, later on in the fall, pumpkins, I can't tell one crop from another. I'm not proud of this, it's just how it is. You can take the girl out of the city…

Luckily just one more left turn and we're on the road to the lake.

Years ago, Grace and I had talked about buying a teeny place on the lake, but then we saw the Big House, and the land that came with it, and opted for that and dreams of the Little House instead.

Even in my terrible mood, I can appreciate the beauty before me. A slight haze drifts over the lake, but visibility still seems endless. The Finger Lakes region doesn't provide the majestic, rugged, humbling drama of the Grand Canyon. Instead, you get a landscape created over millions of years as glaciers formed, moved, and melted to create the hills and moraines, gorges and waterfalls. A calming vista of farmland nestled in rolling hills behind which stretch more rolling hills unto the horizon. Be patient, they tell me.

I slow to turn into the parking area across from Jordan and Janey's house, and my apprehension is immediately replaced by shock at the sight of our green Forester. I can't articulate how many thoughts flood my brain in an instant. Grace! No. Impossible. She isn't here. But how did she get here ahead of me? But she can't be here. Think. Remember. Oh, right. Jordan had picked up the car.

I don't park next to it. I turn off the Prius but don't move, just try to calm my breathing.

I count the other cars I recognize. Oliver and Gustavo are already here. So are Sue and Annie. And Donna and Gina. Ugh. I'm going to have to deal with a lot of people. Makes me wish I smoked, or had some edibles—being a little high might make this easier. I take a deep breath before grabbing my bag from the back seat.

Cristina is out of her car and looks thrilled, her irritation vanished. "How fabulous is this! I still can't believe we live here!" Cristina's excitement at the scene before us doesn't completely mask Nicole's stony silence as she retrieves her bowl from the back. Cristina happily carries their bags over to where I stand. "What a great setting!"

If I weren't me, her excitement would be contagious. We gather our things and head inside.

Though it's not much to look at from the street, I love this house. Wood-paneled inside and very 1950s feeling. And by that I don't mean hip, mid-century modern. I mean dated. The furniture is comfortable and not fussy. Jordan and Janey did minimal remodeling of the interior, focusing instead on bringing the plumbing and heating up to present-day standards, buying new appliances, and putting on a new roof.

The entryway is a mess of beach bags and sweatshirts. One of Janey's old cats has made himself comfortable, curled up on someone's stuff. We leave our bags with all the others and bring our food and wine through the living room toward the kitchen.

Despite the beautiful weather, a small group sits inside having a loud discussion which halts the moment the three of us traipse through. "Hannah, hi," says Gina. She teaches history. I dislike her, but not as much as I dislike her wife, Donna, who's in my department and says something pleasant but manages to make it sound snide. I guide Cristina and Nicole through to the kitchen, and the living room conversation resumes.

Of course I can't resist eavesdropping. Plus, Gina and Donna talk loud. From what I can gather, the topic is zero-waste. "I mean, we're not fanatic about it or anything," Gina says. Which to me is a dead giveaway for fanaticism. Turns out the topic isn't merely zero-waste, but conservation as it applies to death. They're talking about green funerals. And being buried in forests. Gina goes into detail about how you can have your ashes mixed into the roots of a tree.

Donna jumps in. "That doesn't solve the carbon-footprint problem," she says. "Cremation is the equivalent of a 500-mile-journey worth of emissions. I've been reading about water cremation. No flames. No toxic mercury released into the air. Of course, only a few states allow it."

"Want me to go shut them up?" Cristina offers.

"Nah," I say. "You're going to need to stay on their good side—they're all senior faculty." For a moment I toy with the idea of walking in, casually asking what they're talking about, see how fast that shuts them up. Or I'll come up with a line about doing something to compensate for the pollution I caused by having Grace cremated. Better yet, I'll invite them to an ash-scattering party. My own variation on the lesbian potluck. I envision Birkenstock-clad women of a certain age arriving bearing, instead of a dish-to-pass, a container ready to fill with Grace's cremains. I restrain myself. Besides, they've switched topics to our awful president. Donna is pontificating in a long riff about Marxist ideology and neoliberalism. I learned to tune her out long ago.

Nicole looks at me. "What's her area?"

"Polysyllabic obfuscation. Though that's probably not what's on her CV." I open the fridge, which is packed. "Not much room for your salad, Nicole."

Janey walks in just then, a towel wrapped sarong-style around her waist. Her big dog Xena trots happily next to her. "Perfect timing! I was going to start putting stuff out for lunch." She gives me a big, full-bodied lesbian hug. Then an exaggeratedly noisy kiss on my cheek. "I'm so glad you came." My shirt's a little wet from the imprint of her bathing suit. She then turns to the Girls. "You must be Nicole and Cristina." Cristina says her name and reaches out her hand to shake, but Janey goes in for a hug. "Welcome!" She then turns and approaches Nicole.

"I'm so glad you both came." She gives Nicole the same welcoming hug and sneaks a peek under the tin foil covering the bowl. "Terrific. I wondered what we were going to do without Hannah's," she gives a fake cough to emphasize my name, "potato salad." She sees my wine bottles. "The red can go on the table outside. The other bottles can go in the big cooler by the tree. But let's bring this stuff out first." She gives me and Cristina platters of food to carry, Nicole takes the bowl of potato salad.

As I walk through the door Janey holds for me, she whispers, "You can do this. We've got you."

I chant my new mantra—made up on the spot, right then: here goes nothing—and step outside into the next stage of my life without Grace.

22
Fireworks

I've crossed that threshold and come out alive. No thunder crashes, lightning strikes, bolts from the blue. (What does that mean, anyway? What kind of bolt comes from the blue? There's a research activity to add to my something-to-occupy-my-time list.)

Unlike many lakefront properties where you have to descend steep stairs to get to a narrow, rocky beach, the houses in this cove all have a little bit of land between them and the water. Jordan and Janey's house sits back from the lake, a swath of grass sloping down to the water and the dock extending out past the rocky shoreline. There's room enough for a large picnic table and chairs and a fire pit. On special occasions like today, cornhole boards and bocce balls wait for players. Nicole is charmed by the place. Cristina can barely contain her excitement.

Luckily the other guests are already in the water so I don't have to deal with awkward greetings. I can busy myself nestling the white and rosé in with the other beverages in the crowded cooler and then ferrying more food from the house.

By the time we're finished with that, Jordan's returned from kayaking. She's with Cass, the women's crew coach, a tan, trim, handsome woman in her thirties. I go to introduce The Girls, but Cristina and Cass greet each other like long-lost comrades. "We met on campus," Cristina says. Then to Nicole, "Cass is the one who's going to take us out on her boat!" Cass then turns and says, "You must be Nicole," all suave and debonair, like she's going to kiss Nicole's hand or something. She reminds me of Kit. I shake off the impulse to growl at her.

Cass sees Jordan fussing with the arrangement of food on the table. "Need me to help with anything?"

"We're good," says Jordan.

"Great. Then I'm going to run over and pick up Sandy and her kid." She turns to The Girls. "Sandy lives on the other side of the lake. There's room in the boat if you want to come."

The Girls answer at the same time: Cristina with "Yes, please!" while Nicole says, "I'll stay here."

As soon as Cristina and Cass head for the boat, Nicole says, "I'll see if Janey needs anything."

"Are you okay?" I ask.

"Fine," she answers, and heads up to the house.

Jordan looks at me. I shrug. "I don't know."

"Ah, youth," she sighs, as if that explains everything. Then she gives me a big hug. "You made it. Good for you."

"Remains to be seen," I grumble.

"You just need a job. Sue and Annie are still out in the kayak. Help me get the fire started."

Back in the days of their old charcoal grill, getting the fire started was a more arduous process, a ritual involving coal, kindling, and patience. Jordan had invested in a massive Weber last summer, so now with a press of the starter, a few clicks and a whoosh as the burners ignite, we're cooking with propane. Waiting for the grill to heat is only going to buy me limited time separated from everyone else. My need to hide takes on more urgency as a new group of people show up, a batch of younger faculty with kids who go charging down to the dock as soon as they're released from their T-shirts and shorts. Two teens, barely able to contain their scorn for the children, deign to pick up the cornhole bean bags and play an ironic game. Several people have brought their dogs, so there's a friendly pack trotting around. Oliver and Gustavo drag a canoe out of the water and wave as soon as they see me. The inside group has emerged to gather chairs and spread out towels, staking claim to prime real estate. Panic rises in me. I turn to Jordan and offer to grill. "I may not be a cook, but I do know how to flip burgers and dogs." She senses my distress, passes me the long tongs and spatula, and instructs me in the geography of the grill.

"Like Gaul," she says, motioning as she explains, "this is divided into three parts: meat, vegetarian, vegan."

She doesn't trust me to get it all started on my own, but once the grill is crowded with burgers, dogs, veggie burgers, and vegan dogs, her work here is done. "Don't mix the areas," she warns me.

"Aye-aye, Captain!" I salute her.

She adds a final admonition: "And don't feed any of the dogs."

I see then that Cagney, Lacey, and Louie sit patiently at my feet as if we're grilling just for them. As if on cue, Xena joins the pack. Jordan gives us all a stern look before heading off to her other responsibilities.

As soon as she's gone, I tug my phone out of my shorts pocket, turn on the video, and announce: "The Lazy Chef is hella good at flipping burgers."

I'm prepared to explain what it's like to be here without Grace when Nicole approaches with two glasses of rosé and offers to take over flipping if I need to take a call. Busted, I confess to her that I talk to myself and just use the phone as a beard. Though is that less crazy than admitting I'm sometimes talking to Grace? "I don't need help," I say. I motion her off. "You go enjoy the party."

She doesn't budge. "I hate parties," she says, handing me a glass.

"Okay, then." We clink our glasses and sip. "This is nice," I say about the wine. Nicole agrees. Once I've instructed her in the grill geography, I hand her the spatula, keeping the tongs for myself, and we stand watch over the food.

Thus armed, we parry all approaches. Sue and Annie sneak up when my back is to the lake. I introduce them to Nicole. They're careful to not make a big deal of my being somewhere other than my house and hang with us for a few minutes until the first batch of protein is ready to come off the grill. They help us arrange the food on platters and tell me I have to come for dinner soon.

Cass's motorboat pulls up. Cass, still long, lean, and dashing, and, if possible, even more tan, hops out and ties onto the dock. Cristina helps Sandy and Ricky, Sandy's six-year-old, out. Cristina's already fast friends with the kid, and they perform an elaborate handshake. Ricky sees me at the grill and comes charging over. We've known his moms since before he was born. Grace would hang out with them and play video games, a practice that continued with Ricky. The kid loves Grace.

"Hey, Ricky. Hit a lot of traffic on the way over?"

He skips right over my attempt at humor to ask, "Is Auntie Grace here?"

I really have to think about that. Grace likes parties much more than I do and would have been one of the first people in the water today. So if there's any conceivable way for her to be a presence here, she is. And I guess, well, her car is here. Before I can compose my answer, Sandy has swooped Ricky up. "I'm so sorry, Hannah. We told him, but..." she trails off.

"No problem," I say. "Have you met Nicole?"

They shake hands, and Sandy leaves to pull Ricky away from disrupting the teen's game. Cristina rushes over and puts her arms around Nicole. "That was so awesome! You should have come." Nicole doesn't have a chance to respond because Cristina catches sight of Oliver and Gustavo and says, "Come—I want you to meet these guys."

I sense Nicole's reluctance as Cristina drags her away, but I tell her it's okay. "I've got this covered." She hands over the spatula.

Once the last batch of food is cooked and loaded onto platters, I, too, am forced to leave the safety of my station.

I do a good job impersonating a person at a party. I pour myself another glass of rosé and join the festivities. Only after I've lowered myself next to Oliver and Gustavo who are sitting with The Girls do I realize the group I've joined includes Donna and Gina. And Ellen. I'm not fast enough to come up with an excuse, much less hoist myself back up off the grass, so I nibble at the burger I've served myself and try to remain inconspicuous. I taste Nicole's potato salad, which is amazing, and plot my escape. I've done my due diligence. I'll finish eating and excuse myself gracefully. I can be home within the hour.

Once that's decided, I tune in to the conversation, which is really a Donna monologue, the gist of which I'm only now realizing is a treatise on how video games are contributing to the demise of civilization.

I can barely stand to be in this woman's presence under normal circumstances, and nothing about my present life is normal. Donna has disdain for pretty much everyone, including the students she's supposed to educate. I look around at this intelligent group, eyes glazed, given no room even to comment since Donna scarcely pauses for breath. She must work with a vocal coach.

I remind myself I don't have to engage. I'm fine looking out at the lake, checking my watch to see how much longer I need to stay, or how soon I can leave now that I've fulfilled my promise to attend. Matter of fact, I could leave now. Why not? No point waiting for a break in the monologue since there won't be one. I'm gathering my plate and cup in preparation for standing when Donna exclaims, "They lower the IQ of anyone who plays. They're just a waste of time."

I see Grace in front of the television, game controller in hand, the most intense look of concentration on her face as she navigates the visually sumptuous world in front of her, plotting her strategy. Some of the games she played took a great emotional toll on her, required difficult decisions that determined the fate of characters and affected the rest of the game. I know she wouldn't waste her time. Ever. I may be privately furious with her, but I'm itching to rise to her defense.

"And don't even get me started on the violence," Donna's voice rings out.

"Then don't get started," I say.

"Excuse me?"

"Don't get started. Games aren't a waste of time. They're art. They're story come to life, allowing players to participate in the action, affect how the story changes, create meaning from the world." I pray for Grace to feed me more lines to contradict Donna's arguments.

I go on, not even sure what I'm saying, whether or not it's correct. But I see Grace, and I know she didn't waste her time. I understand in an instant that the list she'd been compiling—religion, violence, video games; and the gruesome postcards—were for her sabbatical. I am compelled to defend, no, to honor whatever that was about.

And mostly I think I'm glad to tangle with this insufferable "intellectual" who lives to hear herself speak. "Video game art is an interdisciplinary mix of digital technologies and traditional art forms. Games are a complex form of narrative delivery."

I'm sure Grace said that. I hope I've gotten it right. It's not like I'm a gamer, or understand that world, and it's quite possible that I'm just in this to let off steam, but I've had enough of pretentious academics and what have I got to lose. I let Donna have it. "You want to talk about violence? Stick with religion. The crucifixion. The martyrdom of the saints. Stoning people to death."

I recite scenes from frescoes, list every preserved body part of every saint I can remember. Throw in a display we'd seen in some church of hair shirts the monks wore under their robes. Every decapitated martyr, crucified saint, tortured soul depicted in countless paintings, frescoes, friezes, on walls of churches and cathedrals. I don't know what all I'm saying. Oliver has to pull me off Donna. Not literally, though I would have welcomed the opportunity. He simply offers to get drinks for everyone.

After he and Gustavo leave to get the beverages, I deliver one more line. "I mean, who invented the Catherine wheel, for fuck's sake? Not Shigeru Miyamoto, that's for damn sure."

So maybe Grace is here after all, because I don't know where else I'd have gotten the name of the head of Nintendo, creator of Mario and Zelda, two of the most popular video game franchises in the world. The WORLD, Donna.

Having declined Oliver's drink offer, Donna and Gina stand, announcing they have another party to go to.

When they've left, we finish eating, everyone relishing the relative silence punctuated by delighted shrieks of kids playing in the water, splashing as Ricky cannonballs off the dock. Rather than wait for someone to comment on what just happened, I start picking up empty plates and soda cans. I dump everything into large plastic bags in the kitchen, then head back outside to see if there's anything else to bring in before I leave.

Like a lull in a group conversation, we've hit a lull in the party. Several guests have gone home or on to other parties, the dinner guests haven't arrived yet, Oliver and Gustavo are napping on their towels. Ellen's sitting on the dock, legs in the water. I head over and sit down next to her. Neither of us speaks.

I wonder how long I could stay just like this. I hear party chatter behind us, exclamations from folks playing cornhole, the sharp knock of bocce balls hitting each other. Gentle lap of the water on the shore, a motorboat somewhere out of sight. Before I realize it, I'm turning to

Ellen, she's turned to me, and we speak at the same time. She stops, says, "Go ahead."

"I owe you an apology." It's easier to just say it than come up with a prologue. "I shouldn't have kissed you."

She puts her hand on my leg. Just a pat, an acknowledgment. "I appreciate that." She doesn't say she understands what an awful time this has been for me. She doesn't say she can't imagine losing the person who meant the most to you. At least she doesn't say it in words. And that is fine with me.

"I'm off to my next event," she says. "I have to make an appearance at my department chair's party. I'm afraid it's the same one Donna and Gina left for." She stands up. "I love how you took her on." She starts to head back to the house, turns around, and says, "Maybe we can try dinner again sometime. When you're ready."

I stay right there on the dock. I like feeling the warm, rough wood under my hands, the cool lake water around my legs. I think this might be the perfect moment to make my getaway. I've stayed a good amount of time, considering I was ready to leave the second I arrived. I'm feeling pretty proud of myself for having lasted as long as I have. I'm about to tell Grace as much, that I stood up for her even though I'm still mad at her, when I hear laughter and pounding footsteps. Cristina and Cass come charging down from the house, laughing and goading each other as they run.

Nicole trails behind at a walk.

Cass jumps into the boat. Cristina leaps in behind her. By this time, Nicole has reached the dock. Cristina reaches out a hand for her. "Hop in."

"No."

Cass tries to mediate. "Come on. It'll be fun!"

I want to knock her into the water.

"Thanks. No," Nicole says.

"Come on, babe," Cristina adds. "We're going to swim in a lake!"

"Cristina..." Nicole warns.

I hardly know her and I can feel her anger.

"Hannah, a hand?" Cass asks as she starts the engine.

As soon as I've untied the rope and tossed it into the cockpit, Cass backs the boat out, swings it around, and they're off, leaving Nicole and me on the undulating dock.

"I've got to get out of here," she says.

Music to my ears, though I'm sorry for whatever pain Nicole is experiencing. "I'm ready to go myself." I turn back for one last glance at the water, to say goodbye to Grace, before heading back to the house with Nicole.

We find Jordan and Janey in the kitchen doing a quick clean-up to make room for the dinner rush. I tell them we're heading out.

"It was so nice getting to finally meet both of you," Janey says to Nicole, wiping her hands on a towel. She gives Nicole a hug.

"Maybe you two will come out again with Hannah and we can actually spend time together," Jordan says.

"Yes, please," Janey agrees. "Let me come say goodbye to Cristina." She and Jordan move with us to the door.

"She's not leaving yet," Nicole says. "I'm going to get my bag." She leaves the room.

"Cristina's with Cass on the boat," I explain.

Janey raises an eyebrow.

"You know as much as I do." Kind of a lie, but I feel protective of Nicole.

"And they just moved here," Jordan says.

"Does Nicole have a job?" Janey asks.

"Not here," I say. "She's going back to L.A. to work on a picture. She's an editor," I say. I hug my friends and leave.

Nicole's waiting for me at the car. "I'm sorry. I just couldn't stay in there another minute. They seem like a really nice couple, but we just met, and here my life is unraveling in front of them."

Since I don't know what to say, I offer Nicole the car keys. "I lost track of how many glasses of rosé I had." She gets behind the wheel, I take the passenger seat. I remind her she needs to have her foot on the brake when she starts the car, and we're off.

I love the afternoon light. It's five-thirty, but the sun won't set till after nine. We've got the windows down, whether to let in the soft warm air or to prevent conversation, doesn't matter. Nicole's driving too fast for these windy country roads, but I don't say anything, merely tighten my seatbelt an extra inch. I can relate to Nicole's need to fly out of her pain, to go fast enough to loop into the space-time continuum and catch up to where she started, where none of this would have happened, where Cristina isn't leaving her. If that's even what's happening.

I watch the grasses blur by, proud of myself for having survived the gathering. Then I close my eyes, get lost in my own thoughts. It felt good to let Donna have it. I feel no remorse. Though maybe I'm more angry at Grace? And maybe at Cristina, who I don't know well enough to be mad at, but I see her cruising toward a big mistake. The motion of the car soothes me. I indulge myself in an illusion that Nicole and I are speeding toward something that might heal each of us.

"Just because I don't care about swimming in a fucking lake," Nicole declares. She makes it sound like a challenge.

Okay then. I open my eyes and look at her. Is this the first thing she's said? Did I miss some conversation, too caught up in my own interior monologue? Or was that the punchline to some silent conversation she'd been conducting with Cristina?

"No offense," she finally says.

"None taken," I say. I wait for more, amplification, or a tirade, a litany of what else Cristina might have done to prompt this. I'd certainly understand, given my own impulsive wild ride down to the city. I hope whoever picked up my lamp is getting good light from it.

"You okay to drive?" I ask.

"I'm good," Nicole replies.

I'm not convinced.

We spend the rest of the ride in silence. Nicole mostly obeys the speed limit. Zooms by the buffalo herd without a remark. Closer to home, we pass the place where Grace went off the road. High above us a hawk makes wide circles, hunting. I don't point it out; don't mention that the corn is starting to come up. Then we'd be talking about the future, and I'm not sure how much either of us wants to think about that.

23

The Big Reveal

"I'm thinking we start off in Amsterdam." Grace is at the dining table, maps and guidebooks spread in front of her. It's summer a year ago, and she's already planning her sabbatical.

I'm on the couch only half paying attention as I thumb through a Magellan catalog looking for the perfect bag for our trip. This is a perpetual search for me: While I understand the convenience of a good bag, I have yet to find one that suits me. Or that I'll actually carry. "Amsterdam? So you can visit your boy Vincent...again?"

"Very funny. I mean, as long as we're there, yes," Grace says. "But where I really want to go," she pauses and motions me over, her finger on a dot a little below Amsterdam. "Here."

I try to sound out: 's-Hertogenbosch.

"You can just call it Den Bosch," she says.

"As in Hieronymus?"

Grace nods.

"Creepy, trippy *Garden of Earthly Delights* Hieronymus Bosch?"

"Precisely."

The triptych is done in meticulous, realistic detail, but the images are surreal, like a visual representation of a bad acid trip, but from the late 15th century. A three-headed bird, a winged fish about to fly out of the water, a fish-bodied-duck-headed creature half submerged in water reading a book. Plus images of hell that could give you nightmares, unimaginable tortures—only Bosch has imagined and depicted them.

"Is this a new interest?" I ask.

Grace nods again. "It's where he lived. There's a museum. I've been thinking about some things."

I knew not to ask. We'd been together long enough for me to know that whatever it was, she'd tell me about it when she was ready. (Of course that's what I believed then, B.K., 'Before Kit.') When a project idea was too new, Grace couldn't articulate it clearly enough to discuss it and worried she'd jettison something good before giving it a chance to coalesce into something of substance. She needed time to read, look at images, mull, and take long walks before she was ready to talk about anything.

I study the map again. "And after Den Bosch?"

Grace pulls a map of Italy out from under her pile of papers. She may have been the consummate early adopter of anything tech, but the computer scientist in her loved a good physical map to give her the lay of the land before we ventured off anywhere. "Venezia. Then Tuscany—Firenze, Siena, some of the hill towns."

I'm a little surprised we're returning to Italy so soon after our last trip. Not a complaint, mind you. Really, who could complain about being "forced" to spend time in these places? A sabbatical year puts pressure on its recipient, who'd better have something to show for it at the end. I know Grace is preparing to buckle down on her research while we're abroad. I'm envisioning long afternoons entertaining myself while she works. I can think of worse ways to start one's retirement than in leisurely strolls down narrow hill town streets, reading at cafés.

"I'm researching who's got the best reliquaries," Grace says.

I look at this person I've lived with for over twenty years.

"Siena has Saint Catherine's head," she says, engrossed in her map.

"I can hardly wait?"

Grace pays me no mind. "We'll see her foot first, because that's in Venice. And here," she plops a finger onto San Gimignano, "they've got a torture museum."

You think you know someone. "O-kay," I'd drawn it out. I'm sensing a theme. I'll bet that's why she dragged us to that medieval monsters exhibit at the Morgan Library in the city a year ago. The monsters included those you'd immediately think of—dragons, demons, and the like—but also "aliens," as in foreigners and marginalized groups of people—the poor, the mentally ill, women, Jews, Muslims. Afterward, we sat in the lovely atrium café having coffee and sharing a piece of cake.

I couldn't shake some of the gruesome images we'd just seen and was about to say I hoped the chocolate would help when Grace launched. "And people complain about video games! Haven't they ever seen a painting of the crucifixion? Not to mention all the truly horrifying depictions of hell and what goes on there. Like any of this is new. It's just a different delivery system."

I'm remembering all this because it's two days after the July 4th party, and I'm still churning over my engagement with Donna, coming up with zingers I wished I'd delivered—isn't that always how it works? And because I picked up the mail and got the latest version of the Magellan catalog I'd been thumbing through that day last summer. It brings back the talk of body parts and torture, the rants about the puritanical nature of our culture and willful ignorance. I think that angered Grace more than anything. People up in arms—often literally—about things they refused to be educated or informed about.

My own inadequacy in the situation frustrates me. I wanted Grace to be the one to let Donna have it at the party. And I want to talk to Grace. Real Grace, not her computer or my phone. I want her to talk to me. Explain how all this is connected. Because I can't stop thinking about it, making associations. The items displayed on her shelf at school—the video game, and what else? Was the book about medieval monsters there also? I curse my sporadic memory and close my eyes to better visualize her office, but all I pull up is the charred spot on the carpet where I stomped out the burning photograph of Grace and Kit.

I don't know if I want to stir up more memories or just forget everything.

I don't know why it's so important to me to know what Grace might have been working on now and throughout her sabbatical, but it's all I can think about.

I text The Girls: Hey—ok if I come over and go thru some things in Grace's study?

Nicole's thumbs-up pings immediately.

I'm halfway out the door before I think to check what I'm wearing. Baggy shorts and T-shirt. Good enough. I head on over to the Big House. I hear rustling off the side of the path, catch a glimpse of a dog turning to watch me. Aw. Cute. Must belong to the neighbors. I move to say hello, but when I step toward it, it takes off in the other direction.

Nicole asks if I want anything. Still strange to be treated like a guest here. I really just want to lock myself in Grace's study and get to my investigation, but that would be rude. Wouldn't it? What are the rules? Is Nicole as unclear on them as I am? Is that why she feels compelled to offer me something? Whatever the answer, here we are in the kitchen.

I lean against the counter as Nicole busies herself making us tea, setting some cookies on a little plate. "Cristina's not home?" I hope I sound casual rather than snoopy.

"She went out on Cass's boat."

I wait for Nicole to explain why she didn't go along. Not that I can't make my own guesses. But she just keeps her focus on our tea. She sets a mug in front of each of us, pushes the plate of cookies toward me.

"Did you make these?" I try one. "Oh my god. Fabulous."

Now that I'm taken care of, Nicole speaks. "I agreed to move here with her because, well, because I love her, and also because I was willing to commit to us. Like not just to her, but to our relationship. We were at a turning point, or a crossroads. And it seemed to me that either we'd go deeper with each other or, I guess, just split up. Not that I believed it would be as easy as that, to just go our separate ways. But those seemed like the only two options. I was at a good point to leave work. And I'm not getting any younger."

She's not even in her mid-thirties yet; what's she worried about? The old biological clock imperative? Do I tell her to be patient? Should I share my experience? Tell her that after my conversation with Boy Leslie my moment passed, and Grace never wanted kids.

That's clearly not the situation for The Girls, because Nicole says, "We haven't ruled out having kids. Haven't ruled it in, just…I don't know."

I've grabbed another cookie—they really are fantastic—which I try to chew as quietly as possible so I don't interrupt Nicole's flow.

"Cristina is," Nicole searches for the language, "well, she's a lot. A big presence. She loves life. She loves people. You know that already. She's got big appetites. She's up for almost anything. Except commitment, which is difficult for her. There's always something else just over there," Nicole makes a vague gesture with her hand. "She says she understands what I want, but…"

I know what I want. I want Grace to be here. She'd know what to say. I just keep eating cookies and hoping that maybe Nicole just needs to talk.

"I understand her point of view. She gets offered this job, and it's so exciting to her. I mean, of course it is, it's really perfect, like tailor-made, plus she'll get to work with her mentor. And I say I'm game if she's willing to put in the work. The work for us, not the job. I know she'll be great at that. And then we're here and find out Grace has died. But there's still this amazing job and your wonderful house and this new community. And somewhere in all this I've become a weight she has to drag along. She knew I needed time to figure out what I want, and that was okay with her when we were in L.A. and I had work and we were planning all this out. Now I'm this wishy-washy unemployed burden and someone like Cass comes along, and she works at the college and she's hot and she's got a boat and we live near a lake and everything's new and shiny."

I want to counter half the things she's said—you're hot, you're going to be editing a feature—but all I do is pass her my napkin. "Here. It's clean."

Nicole looks surprised for a second, like she hadn't realized she'd been crying. She takes the napkin and dabs at her eyes.

She reminds me of myself, throwing everything aside to follow Grace East and commit to a new life.

"Cristina promised after the last time that this wouldn't happen again. I'm such an idiot."

After last time? This has happened before?

Nicole's recovered a little. "I knew I should have trusted my instincts. Cristina's not ready for commitment. I knew it. I just wanted to believe something else."

"Does she know how you feel?"

"She says she does. But…," Nicole shrugs the rest of her answer. She takes a small bite of one of her cookies. "These are good, aren't they."

Nicole apologizes to me, given what's going on in my life. She starts to clean up. "I've been waiting for Cristina to ask me to stay. Who am I kidding. That isn't going to happen. I'm going to book my flight." She brings our mugs to the sink. "And you didn't come over to hear me go on." She shoos me out of the kitchen.

Whether for Nicole's privacy or my own, I close the door to Grace's study before I sit at her desk. I contemplate my approach. I need to be methodical, rational.

Grace didn't keep a journal or diary but was meticulous in the upkeep of both of her calendars. Would I find what I was looking for in either of those? Hollander requires all faculty to keep an updated electronic calendar, but the physical planner was the one Grace used most. Would I be able to glean anything from the record of daily activities, deadlines and due dates, meeting reminders and to-do lists?

If the calendars don't help, the closest thing to a record of her thoughts would be her notepads. Those would contain projects she was working on, ideas for redesigning a syllabus, inspirational quotes. More accurate clues for me to follow. I'd dumped a bunch of pads into boxes and brought them home. Now I'm going to find out if they were worth keeping. (Sacrilege! How could you think anything of hers wouldn't be worth keeping?)

I pull out a pad labeled "sab research." "Sab" equals sabbatical, right? The first page is a list of names of people to contact, their areas of interest. Next: hotel and restaurant recommendations, detailed down to mention of specific rooms to ask for, dishes to order. Places to visit, from Amsterdam to cities and towns in Italy, Spain (I remember that Bosch's *Garden of Earthly Delights* is in the Prado), Ireland, Scotland. Greece. Greece? How many countries was she planning to visit?

On another pad I find entire pages crossed out, big X's that were clear to her, maybe. But to me, not clear at all. Had she already transcribed the thoughts contained here? Would I find documents that made order out of this chaos? Or are these paths she wasn't going to pursue? Notes on the Day of the Dead, articles about Oaxaca. And while that's a trip I'd like to take, so far my investigation isn't getting me any closer to what I'm looking for. Not that I know what that is. The thought of trying to decipher Grace's handwriting, searching for I wasn't sure what, drives me to her computer. It will be easier to look for information from her folders and clearly labeled documents. At least I hope it will.

"Honey," I say to her computer, "if you're here, I could use a little help." I turn on the machine, pull up Finder and scroll through her folders.

Eureka! One folder is labeled SABBATIC. I click on it and then start going through the documents it contains, some of which are transcribed versions of what I'd just looked at on her notepads. She'd want to be able to pull these up on her phone when we were traveling. Encouraged I'm on the right track, I forge on.

Grace had made a separate folder for "visuals." In there I find an overwhelming number of images: details from the Bosch; those gruesome frescoes depicting religious battles; general religious imagery; screenshots from video games; frescoes of the seven deadly sins; sections from some paintings in the Sistine Chapel—not the majestic *Creation of Adam* or other images from Genesis, but rather *Judgement Day*. (My people may have guilt, but Catholics, hoo-boy, they've got heaps of fear.) Alongside these depictions of torture you don't even want to know from are photos from the cathedral in Siena showing St. Catherine's mummified head.

I find links to numerous articles on Hieronymus Bosch, the Crusades, on violence in video games, on world-building in video games.

What am I to glean from any of this? What am I even looking for in this excavation? A message from Grace? Daunted, I keep searching. And keep not finding anything.

Out of desperation I go back to a folder labeled "hr." I'd skipped over it, figuring it was the Human Resources paperwork she had to fill out for her sabbatical. Probably. But I've vowed to be thorough. Into the folder I go. It has only one Word document and an image, which I click on. Up pops David Hockney's *Portrait of an Artist (Pool with Two Figures)*. I love this painting. I love Hockney. Though what he has to do with Human Resources, I don't know.

I go back to the folder and move the cursor to the document file, which is titled "HR." When I open it, its heading reads: Hannah's Retirement.

H. R.

Duh.

Grace had been brainstorming ideas not just for her research but for my retirement. She knows how much I love Hockney, so she'd included a list of Hockney exhibits opening during her sabbatical. In 2019, this year, a bunch out West, and in 2020, two in London and one at the Morgan in New York City (wouldn't that take the taste of medieval monsters out of our mouths!). The New York City entry has a special note, the name of a hotel and a specific room to ask for.

I open the Hockney image again.

In it, a young man in pale blue pants—or maybe they're white that's reflecting light? Grace would know—a light shirt and a pink blazer stands at the edge of a swimming pool, his loafered feet planted just at the edge. He's got longish hair that he probably brushes off his face with some frequency. But his arm hangs at his side here. He's looking down into the water at a young man in white trunks, also with a full head of hair, who's swimming underwater, face down, just about to touch the side of the pool.

Or maybe not. We don't know what the swimmer's going to do—surface and whip the hair off his face, wipe the water from his eyes, acknowledge the fully-dressed figure standing over him. Or maybe he's going to touch the wall without surfacing, execute a racer's underwater flip turn, and swim back across the pool. All we see is that his arms reach in front of him, his legs look like they're mid-kick. The scene is filled with potential. The pink-jacketed man leans slightly forward. Is he waiting for the other man to surface so that he can talk to him? Or have they already talked, and the swimmer has submerged to avoid the conversation?

Grace would have better language to describe the reflections, the contrast between the lush colors and curves of the background and the harsh, bright, straight lines of the pool's edge that frame the swimmer and isolate him from the young man standing looking down at him. She could explain how Hockney captured the complexity of water, how it looks in sunlight versus the darker depths in the shadow of the side of the pool. How it is the only motion in the painting, its ripples indicated by the mosaic Hockney created, white outlines filled in with shades of blue.

The brown tiles just below the ledge of the pool stop your eyes, make you return to the swimmer. The swimmer's half-outstretched arms lead us back to the standing figure. These two men are frozen in this moment, and the artist is saying something about their relationship.

I'm jolted by a flash, swift and sudden, that this is how we are now, Grace and me. As if Grace is underwater, and I'm fully clothed, looking down at her, the border of the pool a line of demarcation between us, impassable. We're now in these positions forever. I'll stand at the edge looking down forever. She'll never surface. Nothing will change.

Unless I'm the one underwater, refusing to surface, to accept the reality of where I am.

I move from the desk and collapse in the armchair, exhausted. Grace has hardly spoken to me since I found the picture of her and Kit. It's like I've banished her from my imagination.

Can I blame her? I mean really, hasn't a part of me been looking for incriminating evidence, something linking back to Kit? Did I want to catch her in the act, so to speak? Find something that would confirm her betrayal, justify my anger?

Instead, I find proof of the opposite—Grace had been constructing her sabbatical around her research, of course, but also planning trips and outings to things she knew I would love. Every detour links back to me. Kit is nonexistent.

24
And So to Bed

I walk back from the Big House in a fog. Or maybe on a cloud? I can't get a handle on my mood. Am I happy? Stunned? Surprised? Relieved? All of the above? I can't tell. The only thing I'm sure of is that it's time to suspend my search. What more am I going to learn that I hadn't already known? That Grace loved me? I know that. Knew that. That she didn't love anyone else, not even Kit? Deep down I'd known that, too. Kit was her mistake, and Grace had dealt with it in her own way. She didn't involve me because it really wasn't about me, or about us.

Grace had betrayed me. My hurt after that discovery, my doubts about her love for me since the day I found that picture, are dissolving. Seeing that file on her computer, realizing that a big part of her sabbatical planning was centered around activities designed to surprise and delight me, brought me back to my senses. Her commitment to us shouldn't have come as such a shock, but I'd spun out so far with my wild imaginings that it's taking me time to get back to trusting Grace. I'm not at forgiveness, not yet.

Music helps. Music is something Grace and I did together. We curated quite a collection of playlists on our Spotify account, labeled and sorted by activity—soundtracks for dinner parties, traveling, even housecleaning. Many categories had subdivisions. Not just travel, but plane, bus and car travel. We'd hunt for just the right songs to set whatever mood we were going for. Like any creative endeavor, you'd put in everything at first, then pare it down. I'd found a new collection Grace had been compiling for our Adirondack adventure. This is clearly not finished, because it doesn't have Grace's usual polished and cohesive flow. It's all genres bumped up against each other, which is not unusual, but this is clearly in the rough draft stage because the songs don't follow thematically or rhythmically. Flor de Toloache, a female mariachi band, next to jazzy King Pleasure followed by Alabama Shakes into a quiet Kehlani, and how did Carrie Underwood get in there?

No matter. I just press Play and let the list run. On certain songs I hit the back arrows so I can listen again, waiting for the refrain or entrance of a particular instrument, like the horn in a Flor de Toloache arrangement, to set me off. I only understand a little Spanish, so I don't know what they're saying, but that enables me to respond viscerally. You'd think the music would bring back all sorts of memories, scenes of what we were doing when we first heard this song. But it's like I'm afflicted—or is it blessed?—with temporary synesthesia, and all I see are colors. As I listen to Coleman Hawkins' "Love Song from *Apache*" I close my eyes, enveloped in the deepest blue, that strip of color as the evening sky turns from blue to black. Maybe I get the ocean also. I'm a little embarrassed to find myself doing this. I mean, I'm seventy, not seventeen. But so what. No one else can hear it. Or see me dancing. My grief, my indulgence.

I put on headphones to encase myself in the sounds, close my eyes, and float on that deep, dark water as the actual sky turns dark.

Today I've chosen a less fraught and more familiar list—classic jazz: Bud Powell, Lester Young, Art Pepper—as I wait for delivery of the second of two pieces of furniture. After I'd moved my desk to face the window, I thought it was time to do more to make the Little House my own. At my age, I should have my own bed. A real bed. A nice bed. I'd headed back to the Danish modern store downtown and spent an inordinate amount of time staring at bed frames, finally narrowing my choice between two. But I'd deliberated so long that I could no longer tell the difference between them. Did I like the straighter lines, or the curved? Had Grace and I gone through these deliberations? Why don't I just move our old bed over to the Little House? No, the point is to start fresh, make my own space. Walking around the store to clear my head, I stopped in front of a cherry wood coffee table. Its clean lines and beautiful grain called to me, way more than the headboards. I felt bad having taken up so much of the salesperson's time, and I did need a coffee table, probably more than a bedroom set, so I bought it.

I'd gone right from there to a mattress chain store and ordered a mattress, box spring, and frame. Mission accomplished. And I'd kept it simple. Did I imagine it, or did Grace pat me on the back as I signed the credit card receipt and set up delivery?

So now here I am, sitting on the couch, admiring my stunning coffee table. Not even the stack of unopened boxes I'd shoved against the wall prevent my enjoyment of this sight. Two toots of a horn sound, and I'm on my feet to open the door for the mattress guys.

They're really sweet, probably in their twenties, one thin, the other burly. They insist not only on carrying everything into the bedroom but also setting up the frame for me. The burly one says he wouldn't let his grandmother do it by herself.

I think this is supposed to make me feel good rather than old.

While they're working at that, Nicole shows up. She'd seen the truck and was curious. "And I made more of these." She holds up a plate of those fabulous cookies and tries to hide her double take when she sees the unopened boxes, but she doesn't scold or offer to help me unpack or hock me about needing to unpack. Or to do anything, really.

How long will I be able to coast on my widowhood? The guys being so nice setting up the bedframe, Nicole bringing me cookies and letting me sit in my mess. I'd better enjoy it while it lasts.

"You didn't have to do this," I say, indicating the cookies.

"And you didn't have to listen to me go on about my problems."

After the guys leave I make tea for us to go with our cookies. And now I've got a surface to put everything on. Just like in a real home, I think, as I set everything on my new coffee table.

"This is gorgeous," Nicole says. "Shouldn't we have coasters?"

Okay, so almost like a real home. Thinking of the three (at least) sets of coasters I've left at the Big House, I grab extra napkins to put under our cups.

I don't feel compelled to talk, and surprise myself by saying, "This *is* a nice table, isn't it. Maybe I'll go back and look for a dining room set." Knowing full well I won't. But I do keep talking. I tell Nicole about the original plans for the Little House. Our plans. This may be the first time I've talked to another person about Grace since she died. And once I've started, I keep going. I tell Nicole how we met. "It was a little like you and Cristina," I say, and tell her about Diane setting us up. I tell her about Grace being willing to expand her job search out of California, taking into consideration my diminishing but still present fear of earthquakes. "Though of course at that point I'd have stayed in L.A. if that's what Grace wanted."

"And did she want to?"

"I think she would have, if Hollander hadn't recruited her."

"Wow. Kind of like what Grace did with Cristina."

I wonder how Cristina broke the news to Nicole. Was she as subtle as Grace had been?

It had been November, a few days before Thanksgiving, and we'd driven down to La Jolla to meet up with friends of Grace's who taught at UCSD. Grace and I had gotten up early to walk on the beach. I'm studying the patterns washed-up seaweed makes on the hard, wet sand. "Very Japanese, don't you think?" Even after all these years in Southern California I'm astounded and delighted that we can be on the beach wearing only jeans and a light sweater this time of year. My earthquake fears recede with the tide. I point my camera at brown pelicans floating on the water. I take a few shots of waves hitting the sand.

"What do you think of Ithaca?" Grace asks.

I'm focusing on the water, the foam, the sand. "It's been a while since I read *The Odyssey*."

"I meant the town in New York state."

"I don't know. Brrrr?" I put my camera to my eye to take a picture of the foam and seaweed. I'm still only half paying attention. "Why do I need to think of Ithaca?"

"I'm being recruited."

"I thought Cornell was precisely the kind of school you didn't want to teach at. Huge, grad students as TAs."

"This isn't Cornell. Or Ithaca College. And it isn't actually in Ithaca, but that's probably where we'd want to live."

I name some other schools in the area.

"None of those. Hollander College."

"Never heard of it."

"Because it's only existed for about ten years."

"That's a nice ego boost for you. But don't you want a real school? You know, with a reputation and some, I don't know, status?"

"It's a pretty impressive school, actually."

Grace gives me a brief history of the college, including why it appeals to her, the main reason being that they're giving her the opportunity to shape a program. She was so fluid in her scholarship and her interests that she baffled many academics who couldn't see the connection between games, AI, computer art, social change, philosophy. Especially twenty-five years ago. They missed the point: Grace herself was the connection. She brings it all together; her curiosity is boundless. Clearly Hollander recognized this.

"You're considering it, aren't you."

"Maybe. I mean, I'd get to put my ideas and theories into action. Really make an impact."

No maybe. The longer she talked, the more details she added, the more I knew that she'd already made up her mind. They'd just have to offer her the job, which sounded like it was all but a done deal.

And now today I'm sitting in the Little House with Nicole, but I can hear the waves, the gulls. I'm transported to that moment when my life changed from perpetual summer to four seasons (despite the joke that Ithaca only has three: fall, winter, and construction.) Just as she knew Hollander was the place for her, was her future, in that moment I had realized that Grace was my future, and I would be with her wherever.

"The things we do for love, right?" I say, bringing myself back to the present. "Schlep across the whole country. Except because of Grace, I had my job."

"Maybe that would have made the difference," Nicole sighs.

Do I try to prod her to talk about her relationship? Offer advice? Change the subject? "You booked your flight?" I ask.

Nicole nods.

"Are you flying through Philly or Detroit?" Ithaca, in addition to being ten square miles surrounded by reality, is also centrally isolated. Most destinations require at least one change of planes.

"Detroit."

"I like that route better." I tell her how when I was young, you dressed up to fly. It was an adventure. We skirt the real issues and instead talk about the indignities of air travel. We veer into the tradeoffs of living in a small town versus a big city.

What I really want is to tell her to be patient—and to fight for what she wants. I want to ask her what she meant when she said this has happened before with Cristina. Instead, all I say is, "Maybe some time apart will be good for you."

Neither of us is convinced.

Now I'm about to climb into my freshly made big-girl bed for the night. The dishwasher hums in the other room. I've foolishly brought a book, forgetting I don't have a nightstand to put the book on, much less a lamp to read by. I walk across the room and turn off the overhead light. Back in bed, I've got my phone, and raise it to text someone. But who? And what do I want to say? That I've made more progress? I'm sleeping in a real bed? I talked about Grace today? Used her name and everything.

Who's going to care about that?

I drop the phone on the bed next to me and lie back, hoping for the best. I'm supposed to be settling into the Little House, making it mine. I will unpack for real tomorrow. I'll be methodical: Start on the boxes in one corner and work my way around the room till everything's in its proper place. No stopping till it's all put away.

I close my eyes. In the restless dark before I fall into what passes for sleep, I see an image of myself standing by one of the moving boxes out of which I've just gathered a stack of papers and folders. But instead of taking them into what will be my office, I hold them up in front of me, like an offering, and then I simply give them a little lift and let go. The papers don't crash to the floor. They've been released. They float out across the room, out the door to the back porch. Up over the pond. Out of sight.

I know then I'm not going to unpack a single box.

25

Blooper Reel

The sun wakes me. Which means I actually slept. This is practically getting to be a habit.

I lie in my comfortable new bed and ponder my situation. I prefer that verb, *ponder,* to the verb Grace might use: *wallow.*

And what is my situation, exactly? I'm still here in the Little House. Still a widow. The only thing that's changed since I went to bed is my decision not to unpack. I'm not sure what that's going to get me, but I'm convinced it's the right thing to do. Or, in this case, not do. I feel liberated.

I watch the sun play on the bare white walls. Do I need curtains? Artwork? I should probably start with the basics: What I could use are nightstands. Given my indecision shopping for bedframes, I land on an elegant solution that will solve two of my problems. Eager to see if it's as good as I think it is, I spring—okay, that's an exaggeration, no springing at my age—I drag myself out of bed and get to work.

Half an hour later I've got matching nightstands on either side of the bed, composed of unpacked moving boxes stacked on top of each other. Just the right height. I'm very proud of myself, then I worry: Is this appropriate? I mean, I'm seventy, not a grad student. Aren't I supposed to have "nice" things? Cue mantra: Fine for now.

Repeating that a few times makes me feel better, like a weight has been lifted off me. Obligation to behave a certain way, live a certain way, conform to a certain logic, as if grief has any logic to it! This is forward progression. I can decorate any way I please! Or not decorate at all! Sleep anywhere I want—on the couch, in a bed. My life, my choices. Maybe I've entered a new phase.

I'm also feeling differently about Grace. I still can't forgive her betrayal, but I'm coming to believe she did the right thing by not telling me about Kit. Grace probably hadn't confessed to me because she knew it would destroy me, destroy us. I mean, really, if she'd told me, would I have stayed with her? Could I have forgiven her? Because had she told me she'd slept with Kit, that's where the focus would have been. To relieve herself of her guilt, unburden herself by telling me, that's all there would have been between us. Her infidelity would have been the matador's suit of lights, his red cape a distraction from the deadly sword it hid. That sword being something lacking in our relationship, or in Grace herself, that had driven her to commit this act that would deliver the death blow to us.

What I've come to believe is this: she hadn't told me because she knew that we were what mattered, the life we were building was what mattered. Telling me might have eased her conscience but not repaired what she'd done. She had to resolve her issues on her own, to live with her guilt, all while living her apology to me year after year, making it right so we could have our very rich life together. And we couldn't have had the life we did if she hadn't been all in. Deep down I know that all our years together after that trip to Chicago hadn't been a lie. Learning to accept it might take time.

I've been numb to so much since Grace died—my possessions, my dress, my state of mind. Now I'm beginning to regain memory. My initial blind rage at interpreting that photograph is subsiding. At this moment, I realize, I barely notice it. It's waned to a dull throb in my gut.

And does it even matter anymore? Grace isn't here to ask. And even if she were, if it did happen, it was over twenty years ago. What matters is what Grace and I had: a big life together.

How often did I tell my students that character is action? That what a character does reveals more than what she says. Action is character. Grace was a conscientious scholar, teacher, and a most solicitous partner and spouse. She took my interests into account when planning her sabbatical. That's action.

Maybe it was just sex with Kit and didn't mean anything and that's why Grace didn't think it worth telling me about. If it's just sex, you're too close to focus, to be able to really see the other person. Easier to have sex sometimes than be in a relationship.

It's not like I'm advocating free love, whatever that means. Love isn't free. It's responsibility. I think of the women I was with before Grace, long- and short-term, or even no-term, just a night together. I hear Boy Leslie expounding on his definition of monogamy.

What does this train of thought mean? Am I approaching forgiveness?

I think about infidelity. That brings me to The Girls. How I thought they were so good together. I admire Nicole, willing to step away from the familiar to give herself a chance to figure out what she really wants to do. And for what? If Cristina weren't being so immature running after Cass like that, I'll bet Nicole would have turned down that editing gig. She'd have stayed in Ithaca to work through whatever was going on. She moved here for Cristina, like I moved for Grace. I feel an affinity to them, to her, if I'm honest. Maybe that's why I'm so invested in their outcome. They remind me so much of us when we were young. Everything so important, equally urgent—jobs, careers, love—their futures still ahead of them.

I think about Cristina and Cass and what a bone-headed mistake Cristina may be making. It's not my place to give advice, though I want to shout at Cristina: LIFE IS SHORT. DOES ANOTHER CONQUEST REALLY MATTER? WHAT ABOUT YOUR RELATIONSHIP? WHAT ABOUT NICOLE? WHAT'S REALLY IMPORTANT TO YOU?

A slight ringing in my ears, quiet after noise, makes me realize I'd actually shouted all that out loud. I'm a little out of breath and sit on the bed.

Who do I really want to yell at? Would I feel better if I'd had it out with Kit when I had the chance? To what end? I should rant at myself. How could I be so stupid to not realize what had happened, to not dig deeper into Grace's behavior on her return from Chicago—wanting to take a job in Kansas, of all places!

But after The Troubles, we were stronger than ever. That's when we started looking for houses. What had her actions shown me—that she was committing wholeheartedly to us, to our life in Ithaca.

I have an image of her poring over real estate listings, finding the one for the Big House.

It's so vivid I can almost see her again. I'd lost her for a while, could only envision the person on the gurney in the ER, and that wasn't really my Grace. Then after I found the photograph, I could only see Grace with Kit. Now I'm barraged by images: Grace beckoning me into the warm blue water in Mexico. Posing on the Accademia Bridge in Venice. Looking from a cookbook to her cutting board, adjusting proportions. Pulling a shirt from the closet. A hundred disparate images blur into one: my Grace.

I can't say I feel restored, but I do want to test this sense that I'm returning from somewhere.

I put on real clothes—nice slacks, a pressed button-down, wing-tip Oxfords, with socks even—and check the mirror. I've lost so much weight I barely recognize myself.

I don't know that this is such a good idea, but I force myself to drive into town to Gimme, a local café where I sit outside, in public, with my double espresso. Do people wonder who I am, all dressed up among the T-shirt and shorts-wearing folk? With so few memories to inform me, I wonder the same thing myself. This manly old woman—but such nice shoes!

Why am I so obsessed with memory? With the past? What's it going to get me, anyway? Will it fill me up? Return me to whoever I was before Grace died? It won't bring Grace back.

I'm pulled out of this obsessive loop by a bright red vehicle parking in front of Gimme. It's a big van with a For Sale sign on the side window. But cuter than a van. It's so cute I have to look it up on my phone. It's a Winnebago Travato. She's perfectly shipshape, with a bed, bath, and kitchen. What else do I need? I've already named her Red. I realize how much I've liked being out of touch. Not having to worry about answering the landline. I immediately have visions of packing my small suitcase, stocking Red's little fridge, plugging in my espresso machine, and hitting the road. I walk over to check her out. While I'm doing that, an enthusiastic not-young man approaches.

"Mr. Reliable!" he exclaims in a bright, friendly voice.

"Excuse me?"

"Best purchase we ever made. Mr. Reliable," he says again, patting its side. "We've driven across the country, including Alaska, and never had any problems with him. But we're getting too old to be traipsing around."

This guy looks my age. Or my age-ish, anyway.

Who am I kidding? I'm not going to go schlepping around the country in a Winnebago of any size, even if I did change her name.

And Cristina and Nicole aren't the mirror image of me and Grace. They're not my contemporaries. I'm old enough to be Nicole's not-young mother.

I sulk off to the Prius.

That'll teach me to go out in public.

Twelve minutes after returning home I'm in the kitchen dressed in shorts, T-shirt, and running shoes. Seeing that van planted a seed. Something about my flight of fancy about roaming around in the Trovato kicked off a series of thoughts that ended in a rash of resolutions as I drove home.

I do a few calf stretches, but don't have the patience for warming up. Besides, I'm going to take it really slow. Just to the end of the driveway and up the road a little. Maybe half a mile, or not even, only a quarter mile. I don't think this was exactly the kind of hitting the road I'd had in mind, but I've got too much nervous energy to just sit inside.

And I need to get into shape for my next phase, whatever that will be. Perhaps that's why I decided not to unpack. What if my move into the Little House is just a way station? What if my next move, the final one, is out of Ithaca?

It's a gorgeous morning. Birds, soft breeze, blue sky, sun. I start at a brisk walk. That feels so good I break into a slow trot. Excellent. I feel freer already. I'm not tethered to anything.

By the time I reach the mailbox at the end of the driveway I've got such a stitch in my side I can't stand up straight. I stop to catch my breath, try to breathe into the pain.

In my haste to outrun my thoughts I'd forgotten how much I hate jogging. And how out of shape I am. WTF Grace, people do this for fun? When did I last go to the gym? Is my membership even active? Grace took care of that.

While I'm trying to recover, the dog I'd seen the other day trots up the road. "Show off," I yell, then turn and limp back to the house.

Fresh from a restorative shower, I head over to the Big House. The Girls knew I'd be coming over to work in Grace's study. They don't know that I've resolved to stop working there for the time being. No more excavating Grace's files. I've got another motive this morning.

Cristina passes me on the way out for her run and tells me Nicole's in the shower. This is good news. It means I can slip in and out without having to explain why I've got Grace with me.

My two recent revelations—not unpacking, edging toward forgiveness, or at least understanding—led me to a third: My move to the Little House may only be temporary, a way station before leaving Ithaca. And to do that, I need some closure. And if I'm going to get closure, I need to find a spot to put some of Grace's ashes.

Not a spot. Not just any old spot. The perfect spot. Which is why I've brought the hern along. In case Grace wants to give me a sign.

I haven't given this too much thought. Correction: I've deliberately tried to not overthink this. I don't want her in the garden—too obvious. But there's a beautiful elm tree on the way to the pond. We'd sometimes pull our chairs there and read or have a drink. Standing under our elm tree, Grace in my arms, I ask her, "What do you think?"

She's been awfully quiet lately, or I haven't listened for her, so I look around for a sign—a glint of sun through the leaves, a breeze coming up out of nowhere. Nothing. Just that dog again, which has shown up and stands looking at me.

This is the closest it's come. It looks like a lab mix, still young, though I don't know enough about dogs to guess its age. It's a little skinny, but not too dirty, reinforcing my theory that it must belong to someone. "Hey, buddy," I say, approaching slowly.

It backs away from me.

"It's okay. Don't be afraid." I turn away from it to lean the hern against the trunk of the tree. "See. It's safe." I hold my hands out. "I just wanted to say hello."

The dog stands its ground.

"Okay. You stay there," I tell it. "I'm going to get some tools so I can dig a little hole here."

In response, the dog moves toward me, stops. Sniffs the ground, then lifts its leg and pees on a bush.

"Well, if that's the way you feel about it."

The dog follows as I walk to the garage.

It's gone when I come out with a trowel and a hand rake. But when I get back to the tree and Grace, it's waiting there. Maybe a little closer to the tree than before. Closer to Grace.

I dig the hole, trying not to read more into this than there's a neighbor's dog watching me dig a hole to bury my spouse's ashes. I'll call around later, tell them to keep an eye on him since he's been wandering up and down the road.

As I break ground, I wonder how deep should this be. Or how not deep? And how much of the cremains—that word still makes me smile— am I going to put in? And are they loose in the hern, or in a bag?

Oops. I spent so much time thinking that I've got a pretty deep little hole here. I'm not burying a body. Go get Grace.

I stand.

The dog's still watching me. Maybe it's moved a little closer? What if *he* is a sign from Grace? Maybe he'll let me pet him? If I'm careful? I turn from the tree and move toward the dog.

I'm so intent on watching it and trying not to scare it as I carefully approach that my foot catches in the hole I just dug and I go down hard.

"Grace!" I yell instinctively. Because of course, who else am I going to call? Who else do I want to help me?

"Grace!" I call out again. As if my needing her so badly could reverse everything, return me, us, to our real life, instead of it being just me here on the grass, unable to get up. Because the pain is all too real and I am alone. Grace is dead and I'm alone and that's how it will be from now on and fuck this hurts. Grace is gone. I'm alone. The fall. The shock. And now the pain. I lose it. The dam bursts. All the tears I haven't cried flood out of me.

If this were the ending of a movie starring me, the camera would travel around the outside of the Big House to find the source of a keening wail, snake over the path toward the Little House, the noise getting louder until the scene comes to rest on a figure, her back to the camera, sitting on the ground near the elm, a dog nearby, her sobs coming from a place so deep within that her body rocks back and forth to loosen and expel them. Her hands reach in front of her, palms up, grasping for something invisible to us. Invisible also to her.

The camera would retreat then, to give this woman some privacy. Pull back and up, way up, to show our land from above. The Big House, a path trodden through the grass from the side door to the garden. The neat square of the garden, the fence barely containing its now-overgrown contents, the whole patch in disarray. The paths to the pond, the Little House. The barn.

Higher up still, you'd see the surrounding houses interspersed in the dark green trees, our quiet road leading to the barely larger highway that leads to the college. Off on one side, hardly noticeable from this height, a cut in the growth along the shoulder, made when a car careened off the road, its driver incapacitated by a stroke.

CUT TO BLACK. FADE OUT.

Only this isn't a real ending. Just me grieving what had been my life, the life I don't fully remember. Me collapsed on the ground, feeling as if I'd actually plummeted down a dark abyss, reaching out to grasp something. No. Someone. Just let me touch Grace one more time.

I sit up slowly. Dust off my shorts, then wipe my hands on them. I don't think I've broken anything, but my ankle hurts. And I bruised my palms when I fell. My phone, which had been in my back pocket, went flying. I look around for it and see it's landed just out of reach. I go to stand, but pain prevents me. This really hurts. A lot.

I've been carrying all this dead weight around. Girl Leslie and Boy Leslie. And now Grace. I bear these people in my body. Every dead soul, lost love, broken heart. My grief weighs me down. I drown in air.

How does one rid herself of this? Are leeches a thing these days? Didn't I read somewhere that they're good for everything from depression to osteoarthritis? And if they're back in fashion, surely Ithaca will have at least one practitioner. There's something to research.

Coming out of this cathartic experience I've gone from crying to laughing. At myself, at the situation I'm in, that I just fell into a hole I dug. I could work this into a routine. Include the bit about leeches. Move on to therapy. If there are no accidents, why have I done this to myself, I'd ask the therapist. Why do you think, she'd respond. To which I'd respond, I'm paying for this 45-minute hour, you tell me. Shouldn't you be asking if this was a hole I wanted to crawl into and hide, or did I trip myself to get myself to stop and pay attention? But pay attention to what? What have I missed, what dark cranny of my mind have I ignored in my months-long withdrawal from life?

I can't delve into any of that right now because my ankle hurts. Really hurts. To distract myself from the pain I turn to the dog, which has moved closer to me, recognizing that any human as clumsy and inept and oblivious—I mean, come on, she stepped into a hole she'd just finished digging!—presented no threat, at least not to dogs. To her human self, perhaps. But not to this dog.

I hold out my hand, palm up. "Come on. I won't bite."

Only as it gets up do I think, Oy, but will the dog?

Too late to worry about that now. He's stretched. Excellent downward facing dog. Maybe I should try yoga? Put it on the self-care list right after leeches should I survive this canine encounter.

The dog moves slowly toward me, close enough to sniff my hand. He must approve, because he stretches out on the grass beside me.

Cristina comes upon this cozy scene as she jogs up the path toward the Big House. She stops abruptly when she sees me. Distracted by the dog, she clearly doesn't realize I'm on the ground because I've fallen. "Hey, puppy! Where'd you come from?" Cristina doesn't take her eyes off the dog, her hand outstretched, but asks, "Who does she belong to?

Oh my god, she's so cute." The dog's gone over to her, jumping in excitement. Everyone and everything is attracted to this woman.

"She's a he," I say. "And I don't know."

I try to get up again but can't. That's when Cristina realizes something's wrong. Immediately concerned, she wants to help. Hands me my phone. "Can you stand? Do you need me—" I cut her off, wanting to do it myself. Ouch. My ankle hurts like hell. Reluctantly, I have to accept her offer because I can't get up on my own. Now I'm not only a widow, I'm the injured widow. The old, injured widow. But I do find relief in knowing I won't have to try jogging again for at least the near future.

Cristina's a strong gal. She maneuvers herself under my arm and hoists me up. She's surprisingly deft. And did I mention strong? She starts to walk us toward the house when I stop to say, "We need Grace."

Cristina doesn't get it. I motion toward the hern resting against the tree. Cristina says, "How about if I get you settled first, then come back for her?"

I clearly don't look convinced.

"I promise," she says. "Let's take care of you first."

The dog, rather than run away, moves ever so slightly closer to the hern. Hmmm, I think. Then ouch. My ankle fucking hurts.

Most of my weight is on Cristina as she helps me into the house. She settles me on the couch and opens the freezer, hoping for a bag of frozen veggies to put on my ankle—even she exclaims about the barrenness of my fridge—and returns with ice wrapped in a dish towel. "How about some aspirin?" she asks.

"I'm okay," I lie. "I can get it later."

Cristina goes back outside and returns with Grace. She holds the hern up for me to tell her where to put it. "Nice table. Nicole said you'd bought furniture. Shall I put her here next to you?"

Oh man. My plan had been to have my little burying ritual and then return Grace to her study, keeping the Little House for my new life. My empty-of-Grace and, for the moment, possessions, life. Will Cristina think I'm a terrible person if I say just put it on the shelf in the hall closet?

Unwilling to risk offending my support system, I gesture in the general direction of the kitchen counter.

Cristina sets the hern at the corner of the counter, facing into the main room.

"Thanks," I say, as she arranges my phone, the TV remote, and a glass of water within my reach on the coffee table.

"One of us will come over to check on you later, but text anytime if you need anything." She leaves.

I look at the hern. Is it admonishing me?

"What?" I challenge. "I'll be fine."

To prove my point, I grab the phone to text someone—who? Jordan? To say what? I fell? What's she supposed to do with that information? I put the phone down. I think I'm going to turn on the TV, instead I fall asleep on the couch.

I wake once and look out and see the dog asleep on the back porch.

I fall asleep again and wake to Nicole's voice. I sit up and see her on the porch, talking to the dog. Petting him.

She sees me then, slides the door open. "Hi. I heard about your accident. How are you doing?" She motions to the dog to stay. "Do you mind if I give him some water?"

"Not at all."

She again tells the dog to stay and slides the door closed. He watches her cross to the kitchen and fill a dish with water. When she goes back outside and puts it down in front of him, he laps noisily and long. "Wow. You were thirsty." She picks up the bowl and brings it inside to fill again. "When did you get him?"

"I didn't. He lives up the road." I relate our brief history.

"He sure seems to like you," she says. "I'm going to make a run to the store to pick up some things for you. Taking a wild guess here, but I'll bet your fridge is empty."

"I've got soup," I say, hoping I'm right and that she doesn't check.

"I mean real food. I'll be back as soon as I can," she says. "How would you feel if I picked up dog food while I'm there?"

"Fine with me." I look at the dog, who's now sitting up and watching us. "Don't get too much—I'm sure he belongs to one of the families down the road."

After Nicole leaves, I figure I can't move but I can at least make myself useful. I pick up my phone. "Don't worry, buddy," I say to the dog. "We're going to find your people."

Or maybe not. Calls to the neighbors reveal he doesn't belong to any of them. I lie back, defeated on all fronts.

26
After the Fall

Falling is humiliating. Humbling. Not to mention, people my age shouldn't fall—a broken hip being a first step toward the downward slide to immobility and incapacity. I try to remember when I started thinking of myself in the same category as people my age. I never really had to. My students kept me young. Grace kept me young. Is this who I am now? An old lady who falls?

I try to remember the last time I'd fallen.

All I come up with is when I was maybe eight, my two girlfriends and I spent so much time in a huge red maple in my grandfather's garden that we each had our own branch. One day, climbing by myself, I plummeted from my branch and landed belly down, folded over a limb, the wind knocked out of me. I never told anyone, not even Grace, because I hadn't remembered till just now.

These days I remember further and further back, like the names of those childhood friends—Elaine and Robin—while last week is a blur. Is that when I declined the movie invitation from Sue and Annie? When did Jordan and I have dinner?

I don't know why I need to remember anything other than my daily life with Grace, and those memories still elude me. But the other stuff? I mean really—why? And if I do remember any of it, who will I talk to about it? Who am I going to talk to about...anything?

Even I'd categorize this as wallowing.

I force myself off the couch and into the bathroom to clean up a little. This is quite an accomplishment, seeing as how I can't move my leg without experiencing excruciating pain. I find a travel-size bottle of ibuprofen in my toilet kit and swallow four without water. I also find some arnica pellets and dump a bunch under my tongue. I figure it couldn't hurt. Unlike my ankle, which is killing me.

I hobble to the porch to check on the dog, who's sleeping in the same spot near the bowl Nicole had put out for him. Carefully and awkwardly, trying to protect my ankle and not scare the dog, I lower myself to the deck to sit next to him. "Hey, buddy," I say. I pet him and he lets me check his coat. I don't find any fleas, but he's got a number of burrs, which he lets me pick out. His fur is soft, and he's relatively clean, which leads me to think he hasn't been lost for too long, and also that his people must miss him. He has to belong to someone—he's in great shape and seems relatively obedient. "What's your story?" I ask. He licks my hand. When I'm done fussing with him, he stands and shakes himself out. "Okay, buddy, you seem pretty good to me. Want to come inside?" I get to my feet, no easy task, and slide open the door. "Come on in," I say. He moves toward me. "Go ahead," I motion. "I'll catch up."

He enters the house and begins a methodical exploration of the room. Sniffing the furniture first, then the perimeter, before moving to the kitchen area. Walking is too awkward and painful for me, so I flop onto the couch just as the dog heads back toward the other rooms. I wonder if he's housebroken, but I'm in too much pain to follow him around. "Ow!" I say it out loud. It doesn't make a dent in the pain, but it makes me feel better. So I say it again, louder. "Ow!"

The dog comes trotting back to me and rests its head on the couch, close to my hand. "Thanks, buddy," I say, and pet his head. His ears are really soft.

Pain is exhausting. I fall asleep again.

Nicole returns a couple of hours later with provisions for me and for the dog, who's still settled near me. "He certainly looks comfortable," she says. In addition to kibble, she also picked up food and water dishes, plus a squeak toy, which she gives him only after she tells him to sit. Which he does. Clearly he's had some training.

"Don't get too attached," I warn. "I'm not keeping him."

"You'd think his people would have put up signs," she says over the energetic squeaks.

"Well, he's not from around here. I checked with the neighbors."

"I was hoping you'd say that."

"I'm still not keeping him." I don't tell her I don't know where I'm going to live, so can't take on responsibility for another being.

Nicole doesn't let me get up while she unpacks my groceries. "You should get your foot looked at," she says. "Maybe go for an X-ray?"

"I'll see how it is tomorrow," I say, though I'm not feeling optimistic. It hurts a lot, and I'm afraid to even look to see how many colors it's turned.

Nicole insists on making me something. I know better than to fight her. She brings a plate of scrambled eggs and toast to me on the couch and sits with me while I eat. We don't really talk, just watch the dog as he plays. He loves his toy. Nicole clears and washes the dishes, then offers to help me back to the bedroom, but I insist I'm okay. I let her adjust a big towel under my leg to elevate it.

I'm such a liar, I think after she leaves. My leg is killing me. Who was I pretending to be, the big tough butch who doesn't need help twice in one day? So here I'll stay. Serves me right. I want to get into my comfortable bed but can't face the thought of dragging myself down the hall. I turn on the TV and wander aimlessly through Netflix. I land on *Grey's Anatomy*. Which of course makes me want to talk to Grace.

"How was your day?" I ask. "You won't believe what happened to me," I say. I turn it into a really funny story, describing how I searched for the perfect place for the first sprinkling of her cremains, how I fell into the hole I'd dug. "Not keeping the dog is the smart decision, isn't it?"

She doesn't respond.

I doze on and off. Netflix accommodates my immobility by starting a new episode on the heels of the last; I don't even have to touch the remote. I wake to patients being released from the hospital, new romances sparking. Sleep again. Wake to new crises. At some point I put the towel down on the floor for the dog to lie on and stuff a cushion under my foot.

I tell myself I'm crazy to even consider keeping this dog. I mean, really. How can I keep an animal? I have no intention of unpacking the boxes I've stowed around the edges of the Little House. I don't know where I'm going to be living. That's why constructing my nightstands had felt so liberating.

I can't discuss the merits of my plan with anyone because I don't have an anyone anymore. No offense, Grace. And is what I have even a plan?

Nope. Of course it isn't. I don't have a plan because I wasn't going to be the one who'd need a plan. Grace was supposed to be the one with the plan. She was going to survive me. That was the extent of my plan. You're on your own after that, I always said.

And her response to that? She'd just ignore me.

These thoughts move through my mind sometimes as dreams, or waking dreams, or conscious thoughts. And under it all is throbbing pain.

The last thing I remember thinking is that I prefer this physical pain to the other kind, the one I've been living in since Grace died.

In the morning my foot feels too big to fit on even this huge couch, so I'm surprised to see it isn't quite as swollen as it feels. The rest of me is stiff and in considerable pain. I'd be fine staying on this couch all day. But I have another mouth to feed. I hobble to the kitchen and put out some food for the dog. Then I let it outside. I leave the door open for him. As long as I'm up, might as well make a coffee. I drag myself back to the kitchen and fire up the machine. I drink leaning against the counter, leave the cup in the sink, and drag myself back to the door to call the dog.

I don't see him outside. "Here buddy!" I yell, thinking it might be a good idea to give him a proper name, even temporarily. "Hey, boy!"

No sign of him.

Okay, I think. Maybe he's finally gone home.

Rather than let myself feel sad, I make another coffee which I drink standing up as a way to let the pain wash everything else out of my head.

I get back to the couch and lie down. I close my eyes. Open them. I feel the dog's absence. Is that crazy? He hasn't been around long enough for me to miss, has he? I tell myself it's better this way. He clearly belongs to someone, and he's gone home to them. That's good. I was smart not to get attached.

I'm making my peace about the dog going back to his people. Really. I don't need anything else to care about. Certainly nothing else to lose.

"Hannah, you up?" Cristina yells from outside. "Come on, doggie!" She comes to the door, sticks her head in, and the dog practically knocks her over in his rush to his water bowl. "We went for a run! It was great!"

The dog pays no attention. Having made a mess with his water, he's now gobbling the food. He trots over to me and drips on my chest to say hello. Then he flops down on his towel by the couch. I remind myself: Don't get attached.

"Have you named him yet?" Cristina asks.

"He's not mine to name." Don't get attached. Don't get attached.

"I like 'Scout.'"

"I'm not keeping him."

"Does he know that? He's making himself right at home," she says, rubbing his head. "I'm off to shower. You need me to get you anything before I go?"

"I'm good. Thanks."

"Okay. Bye, Scout!"

As soon as she's gone I put my hand out to pet him. "Is that what you're doing? Making yourself at home?"

I look around for Grace. "Is this your idea of a joke?" Then I raise my voice, as if maybe she's somewhere else in the Little House. "What? Do you think I need company?"

I wait for an answer. The dog sits up, looks around, like he's waiting, too. Then he puts his head on my hand. He sits right next to me as if to say, Okay, I don't know what we're waiting for, but I'll do it right here with you.

So much for don't get attached.

We stay there like that for a while, but there's only so much waiting a person can do. Eventually, you have to get up to shower. Dragging myself to the bathroom takes all my strength, and I'm in so much pain that I almost can't step over the lip into the walk-in shower. That's when I'm forced to admit that I probably should get an X-ray. And, that if I'm going out in public, even if it's only to the ER, I should at least look presentable. I should at least look like I care. Put on a good front.

This makes me laugh because it reminds me of the salesman who sold me my VW Rabbit convertible way back when in L.A. Walking from the showroom to the lot to test drive it, I spotted a cream-colored Alfa Romeo Spider, gorgeous leather seats. Just like what Dustin Hoffman drove in *The Graduate*. When I stopped to admire it, the salesman leapt to open the door for me. "Here you go," he said.

"No, no. I'm not going to buy that car."

"At least sit in it."

"No, really."

"Come on."

I sensed he wasn't going to move until I got behind the wheel, so I did. Then he closed the door, stood just out of my peripheral vision, and said, "Let your fantasies roll!"

Okay. I felt silly. What am I supposed to do, make vroom-vroom noises and pretend to shift gears? "It's a beautiful car," I said, patting the leather seats before getting out. "But it's not for me."

"Are you sure?"

"Positive."

"It makes a great impression. This town is all about image. You decide the image you want to project, then accessorize around it."

Maybe if I'd listened to him about the Alfa my whole L.A. trajectory would have been different. I'd have had a more successful career. But maybe I wouldn't have met Grace.

How did I fall down that particular rabbit hole, I think, as I gingerly exit the shower and dry off. The past is too much with me these days. I bring my focus back to what I'm going to wear. Keep it simple. Black shorts, bright blue polo shirt. Chucks. Well, one Chuck—too painful to fit a shoe on my injured foot.

Showering and getting dressed knocked me out. I'll just rest on the couch for a few minutes, regain my strength, then text The Girls to see if one of them can take me to the ER.

Maybe I slept because I know I didn't just have a conversation with Grace about seeing a photograph of my students and crying because I realize I'll never see them again. Or maybe I'm crying because I realize I'll never see Grace again. I find myself sitting up, reaching for her, arms out, palms up, using the ASL gesture for "I want."

Or maybe I'm still sleeping because I see a black Tesla park in front of the Little House. There aren't many of these in Ithaca, and no one I know drives a Tesla, so this is odd. Then, odder still, Kit climbs out. The dog has gone to the door, makes a little huffing sound, not a real bark. So maybe no one's there. Maybe I'm still sleeping and merely imagining this, given all the obsessing I've been doing about Grace and her infidelity. Or maybe I'm having a lucid dream. Those are a thing, right?

I hobble onto the porch to test the reality of the situation. I feel the sun on my face. And certainly the pain in my foot. Can you feel in dreams? Hear? Because now I hear Kit's steps on the gravel. Does that happen in a dream? Maybe I'm using this dream to heal. I'll go along with it, but proceed with caution.

I move to the edge of the porch, like I'm defending my property. If this were a Western, I'd be cradling a rifle in my arms.

"I stopped at your house and the young woman said you'd moved out." Kit makes the statement sound a little like a question, but I have no intention of answering. You don't have to talk in a dream, right? The dog has leapt to Kit's side, investigating. She pets him. "What happened to your foot? That looks like it hurts."

Kit hasn't moved away from the Tesla. I certainly conjured the perfect vehicle for my lucid dream. You don't need a car in the city, but of course Kit would have the coolest. And I've dressed her well: black linen shorts, loose-fitting grey and white striped linen shirt, black Chucks. Still with an expensive haircut. "I've been calling but couldn't leave a message," Kit says. "I wanted to tell you LeeAnne and I were going to be up this way and try to set up a date to get together. I'd like you to meet her."

I look past her to see if anyone else is in the totally cool Tesla.

"She's at the hotel," Kit says, picking up on my unasked question. Or because this is a dream maybe I don't need to speak to be understood. "We came up to go to some wineries, breathe some fresh air."

So if you're so hot for me to meet LeeAnne, why isn't she with you now? And why *are* you here? If you're actually here and I'm not lucid dreaming. But you've stepped away from the fancy car and are approaching me. Is this when I'd cock the rifle I'd be holding?

Kit stands awkwardly on the step below me and gives me a tentative hug. The smell of her cologne—the same scent she always wore—rockets me back in time and almost persuades me that this is real rather than whatever kind of dream. "I wasn't sure if I should drive out here since you didn't know I was in town. And since I couldn't leave a message— you should really clear your mailbox," she has to remind me, "it seemed a shame to come all this way" (New Yorkers are so provincial—they act like 260 miles is practically a cross-country trek) "and not at least try to see you."

She just stands there and I think she wants me to invite her in, but like hell that's going to happen, even in my dream. And definitely not in my new space. I don't care that the dog seems to like her. What kind of judge of character is he, anyway? Except now I realize how much my foot hurts and Kit can't help but notice as I start to crumple. She leaps to my side, ducks her shoulder under my arm and half-carries me into the Little House, the dog trotting alongside. She lowers me onto the couch, then looks around the room. "Great space," she exclaims, before turning back to me, pointing at my foot and asking, "Um, you're going to get that looked at, right?"

Which settles the "is this a dream" question once and for all.

Though I admit it's very dreamlike to ride in a Tesla, which is where I am now, since Kit insisted on taking me to the ER. Grace would love this. That I'm with Kit, sure, but even more that I'm with Kit in a fucking

Tesla. It's like riding in an iPad, since the dashboard is completely devoid of instruments—no fuel gauge, speedometer, gear indicator, battery indicator, just a large iPad-looking screen mounted off to the right of the steering wheel. It's so clean. Makes the Prius look quaint.

Given my condition, I feel justified in not making conversation. All I do is tell Kit where to turn. I'm guiding us toward the hospital when I realize I'm not ready to visit the ER where Grace died. "Make a U-turn," I say.

Kit shoots a doubtful glance in my direction.

"It'll be faster if we go to Convenient Care," I say, not knowing whether that's a true statement. But I don't owe Kit the truth. And I'll avoid the hospital as long as possible.

"You're the navigator," she says.

We ride the rest of the way in silence.

The irony of my current situation is not lost on me. I taught writing, for crying out loud. I know my literary techniques. My wife's lover coming to my rescue. I'm also keenly aware of the visual significance of a scene. Here we sit in the waiting room of Convenient Care, me and Kit shoulder to shoulder, just like the photo of Grace and Kit. Loath to go down that road, I text The Girls and ask whoever's home to feed the dog, make sure he's safe in one house or the other.

No problem, comes an immediate reply from Nicole. Cristina's on campus, but I'll check on the pup. Glad you're able to get out, she texts.

When I respond with where I am, she shoots back a batch of emojis— sad face, surprised face, caring face, crutches, nurses, and a glass of whiskey.

"Cute," Kit says. She's been looking at my screen. "Nice that you have people you can count on nearby."

I don't know if that was a cue to talk about The Girls, how I found them, what our relationship is, but I'm not interested in sharing details of my living situation with Kit.

"I have a confession," she says.

Didn't I predict she'd want to do that? This was precisely why I didn't want to visit with her that morning in the city. Still, I think, here? Now? Way to kick a girl when she's down.

"I wasn't completely honest about the reason for my showing up. I really do want LeeAnne to meet you, but I also wanted to check on you. I wasn't sure you were okay when I ran into you that morning. Given that," she indicates my foot, "I'm still not sure."

I don't rise to the bait, don't confirm or deny anything, though I'm relieved that's all she had to confess. And I'm saved for the moment by a technician who's come to take me back to X-ray. He helps me into a wheelchair and off we go.

After the X-ray I'm deposited in an exam room. I'm relieved at not having to wait with Kit. I don't need to hear any more confessions. My phone pings with a text from Cristina: **OMG! Let me know if you need me to come get you.** That's good to know. I won't have to spend any more time with Kit than absolutely necessary.

When I filled out the intake forms, there was a spot to indicate my pain level. I just left it blank. Have you ever tried to describe pain? It isn't easy. And the pain chart hanging on the wall here is no use. Six round moon faces, going from smiling (no hurt) to frowning/crying (hurts worst). If the visuals don't help (and they don't), you have words and numbers, starting with "No Hurt (0)" progressing to "Hurts Worst (10)", allowing for the subtle difference between "Hurts Little Bit (2)" and "Hurts Little More (4)". I study the line representing the mouth of the "hurts little more" face. How does that horizontal squiggle indicate any level of pain?

I still have no clue when I hear a knock on the door.

My first thought is to respond in a sitcom singsong, "Who is it?" I can hear Grace: **Don't make jokes.**

But I don't have time for a clever response because a brusque young doctor breezes in, introduces himself, and asks, "What happened?"

"I fell." I mean, duh.

As he pokes at the foot, the young doctor asks me if I've been falling a lot lately. Which seems like a stupid question until I realize that he sees that I'm seventy, and maybe this is something they have to ask all doddering septuagenarians. "Nope," I say. "No falling at all. Except this."

Should I go into detail about wanting to find a spot for my dead wife's cremains, how I dug the hole, then fell into it because of the dog? I could use this to shape the raw material for my comedy set. Instead, I exercise restraint. "I just tripped in the garden," I say, all light and breezy between exclamations of pain.

Which he doesn't even ask me about, even when I say, "That hurts." He tells me the X-ray was clear, I haven't broken anything. "It's just a bad sprain," he says. He recommends ibuprofen or acetaminophen, ice, and tells me someone will be in soon, I should follow up with my doctor or an orthopedist.

Then he's gone and a minute later a nurse comes in with an orthopedic walking boot and a pair of crutches. She explains how the boot works as she puts it on me, then watches me maneuver on the crutches. She makes the helpful suggestion I purchase an even-up for the other foot, a contraption that fastens to my shoe and compensates for the height discrepancy caused by the boot. "Otherwise you'll throw your whole alignment off walking in the boot and have a whole new set of problems to deal with."

I thank her and make my awkward way down the hall to the exit.

I feel ninety years old.

Kit's very gallant. She brings the Tesla to the front of the building so I don't have to walk more than a few steps. As she helps me into the car and get settled, she says, "We should come up with a good story about how this happened." She puts the crutches in the back seat. "I will say, though, one of the advantages of life in a small town: That didn't take long. If this were the city, you'd still be waiting to be seen." Before she starts the space vehicle she says, "I spoke to LeeAnne while you were in there. If you're up to it, she's at Moosewood. Or I can take you home."

What the hell, right? I'm in pain and exhausted. All I've had today was coffee. "Lunch sounds good," I say. Maybe I'm supposed to be learning something from spending this time with Kit. I text Cristina to tell her to join us at the restaurant.

Kit finds a parking space right in front of the restaurant. Does everything just fall into place for this woman? She helps me out of the car once again (who says chivalry is dead?) and walks toward the entrance, but I stop her. "Isn't this Moosewood?" she asks.

"Yes. But there are steps." While I don't mind making an entrance, I'd rather it wasn't tumbling down the small number of stairs leading to the waiting area. Maybe when I've ditched the crutches or gotten used to the boot. "I need to go in this way." I lead us to a set of double doors that open to a sloping ramp that takes us into a long hallway lined on either side with shops and further down a row of tables.

"There's a restaurant down there?"

I nod.

"Right in the middle of the hall?"

Welcome to Ithaca, I think. I've gotten so used to some of the quirkier parts that I forget my first impressions. "They do great breakfast and lunch. This building used to be a high school. Now it's retail and dining on the ground floor, plus some offices and apartments upstairs. We go this way." I direct Kit down a small hall to the right, which brings us to the entrance to Moosewood's bar area.

"So this is mecca," Kit says.

"Everything you expected?"

Kit shrugs.

It's an airy and pleasant space. The general vibe is unassuming, belying the huge impact the place has had on American cuisine since it opened in the early 70s. Vegetarians from all over the country make pilgrimages to Ithaca to eat here, buy a Moosewood cookbook or merch—baseball caps, sweatshirts, T-shirts, mugs.

Kit heads to a back table in the bright main room and I follow clumsily, bumping a few chairs with my crutches and apologizing as I go. Kit stuffs the crutches into a corner while I collapse into my seat. Not a very graceful entrance or first impression to LeeAnne, who half stands to greet me. She says something very sweet and genuine about Grace that I can't take in because between the poking, prodding, boot-fitting, awkward crutch-walking, my foot definitely "hurts worst."

And, if I'm honest, I can't take it in because I keep thinking I've forgotten something, then realize that what's missing is Grace. We came here for lunch so often that I'd almost expected her to be waiting at the table with LeeAnne.

"I hope you don't mind coming here," LeeAnne says. "One of my authors said I had to eat at Moosewood, and I also have to pick up a cookbook for her."

I learn that LeeAnne's an editor at a big New York publishing house. She and Kit met through one of LeeAnne's celebrity authors, whom Kit's PR firm represented. I learn these and other details about their relationship between their perusals of the menu and discussion of the merit of one special over the other. And since I don't need to look at my menu, I can study the couple. This is the longest relationship Kit's been in, and she seems as happy as she gets with anyone. They make a handsome pair. LeeAnne is as well-dressed as Kit, but the femme version—flowing linen, big jewelry, statement-making glasses. She's left enough grey in her shoulder-length hair to say that she isn't hiding her age. She seems very warm and open. And physical. When she isn't gesturing to make a point, she's got one hand somewhere on Kit.

We order—the day's specials for Kit and LeeAnne, soup and salad with Moosewood's house dressing for me. Cristina swoops in as we're finishing with the waitperson, points to me, and says, "I'll have what she's having." Which cracks us all up because we get that she's referencing that scene in *When Harry Met Sally* where the woman at the next table in the deli delivers that line after Meg Ryan's just faked an orgasm.

She knows how to make an entrance.

I handle introductions and then don't need to worry about keeping the conversation going because Cristina asks how we all know each other, which gives Kit an excuse to reminisce about our days in L.A. She tells stories I remember—like the first time she and I met—and some I hadn't thought about in years, like the time a bunch of us went to gay day at Disneyland. She goes back even further, talks about Grace before I met her, young Grace, a different person from the respected academic she grew into.

I keep waiting to feel the sting of jealousy I used to feel around Kit, but it doesn't come. I don't think it's only because she's with LeeAnne. I find it comforting to be with someone who's known us for so long. Even if that person is Kit.

"I confess I used to be a little jealous of Grace. Kit talked so much about her," LeeAnne says.

Kit leans over and gives her a little kiss for reassurance. "No need, babe. Once Hannah here came along, I knew I didn't stand a chance." Kit pops an olive from LeeAnne's side salad into her mouth. "Besides, Grace was always the type who was looking for commitment."

"And we know you're allergic to that," LeeAnne says. She doesn't take her hand off Kit's arm as she turns to us and says, "When we first met, she made it very clear that she needed to be able to see other people."

Kit defends herself. "I was at the top of my career, traveling a lot, meeting all sorts of people. I was having too much fun to settle down."

"What changed?" Cristina wants to know, much more interested in this than in Grace's and my backstory.

Before Kit can answer, LeeAnne sits up straight, puts down her fork, needing both hands to indicate her figure, her whole being, and says, "Would you rather come home to this or settle for a bunch of meaningless fucks?"

Oh snap. I like this woman. She's clearly a match for Kit. Maybe she's the reason Kit is checking up on me. That's the kind of thing Grace would have urged me to do—look in on a friend going through a hard time.

Kit is part of a couple, but that's not what puts me at ease. I've been reminded that Grace could never have stayed with Kit. Grace was about commitment, with a capital C, if not all caps. I've already made my peace with whatever happened between her and Kit in Chicago, and this just confirms my conclusion. Grace was mine and mine alone.

As if this day weren't already full of surprises, Kit takes LeeAnne's left hand and raises it across the table to show off a broad gold wedding band. "Plus, let me point out, *was* allergic," she adds, showing off her matching band.

I reflexively move my leg to avoid the kick I know I'd get from Grace at this news. Kit—married! "When?"

"Two weeks ago," Kit says.

"We're actually on our honeymoon," LeeAnne chimes in.

"And you chose Ithaca?" Cristina doesn't keep the surprise out of her voice.

"We're on our way to Montreal," Kit says.

"And you got lost and ended up here?" I ask.

"Kit hoped to see you again," LeeAnne says. "She told me she bumped into you in the city a few weeks ago."

"And we thought we might go to Toronto," Kit says. "So this isn't really such a detour."

Given how hard she's trying to downplay this, she must really have thought I was in bad shape. Or did she come here to pay her respects to Grace? To confess? Start her marriage with a clean slate?

Cristina looks at me. "When were you in the city?"

I'm saved from answering by the waitperson. "Can I get anyone anything else?"

Kit and LeeAnne want to order dessert and coffee, but I use my injury as an excuse to leave. LeeAnne comes around to give me a big hug. "I'm so glad I got to meet you. And I'm so sorry about Grace. Please come see us next time you're in the city."

Kit walks me to the street while Cristina goes to get the car. As she hugs me goodbye she whispers in my ear. "You take care. And call me if you ever want to talk."

On the drive home, Cristina goes on and on about Kit. "I totally relate to that need to be free. It's probably good Nicole got this editing job. I'm going to be obsessed with school." No mention of Cass. Just the idea of "being free." "Maybe when I'm Kit's age I'll be ready to settle down. But not yet."

I lean my head against the window, close my eyes, and let her talk.

When we get home, Cristina helps me get set up on my couch. The dog scratches at the back door, wanting in. Cristina accommodates him on her way out. Her parting words to me are, "You gotta name that boy!" He bounds over to me and jumps up to lick my face.

I lie back, my hand on his head. I hurt, I'm beyond exhausted, yet I feel more settled than I have since Grace died. All my roiling over what might or might not have happened more than twenty-five years ago was misplaced energy. Something to distract me from grieving. Kit was never really a threat. She might have needed to be free from commitment, but that was never Grace.

Cristina claims that same need to be free. I wonder what that really means. Free to not suffer loss?

Doesn't seem like such a bad thing to me at the moment.

27

The New World

I've been in the boot for three weeks. I don't use the crutches. I bought an even-up like the nurse suggested and that makes a big difference. I'm not quick on my feet, but it makes life a lot easier. Luckily I injured my left foot, so I can drive myself places. Not that there's anywhere I particularly want to go. For a week Buddy—hey, he answered to it and now he's stuck with it. Though Cristina calls him Scout and I think Nicole calls him Little Fella and he seems fine with all of it—and I got in the car every day to drive around the area looking for "lost dog" signs posted on trees and lampposts. I had already called the SPCA, but no one seemed to be looking for him. On one trip, ascending a hill outside the hamlet of Varna, Buddy, who'd been sticking his head out the passenger side window, started making noises and looking from the scenery back to me, agitated. I pulled over to the side of the road a hundred feet past a big white house, turned off the engine. "Does this look familiar? Is this where you're from, Buddy? Do you know where we are?" But he just licked my ear and looked at me like I was supposed to make the next move. I hooked a bright blue leash to his matching collar (yes, I had outfitted this boy—what kind of lesbian do you think I am) and we got out of the car. He was good about going slow, accommodating my boot. But he didn't pull me toward the house, merely to a promising bush, intent only on finding a good place to pee. Mission accomplished, back in the car we got.

Relief flooded over me—so much for not getting attached. I had declared our search over then and there, and now I'm a dog owner. Or we all are.

He has free rein of the property and lives in both the Big and the Little House. Every morning Cristina swings by before her run to pick him up, and off they fly. Then he spends the day with me or with Nicole. He instinctively goes where he's needed most.

My friends are thrilled for me. As soon as I announced the decision to keep him, Annie came by with dog toys and told me she made an appointment for us with Sue. She wants to make a playdate for him with their dogs.

The Girls and I settle into a new routine in the weeks between my fall and Nicole's departure for L.A. From what I observe, they seem to be in a truce period. They brought dinner over the day I got the boot. And kept doing that. Either Nicole cooks or Cristina brings something in and we all eat around the coffee table or on the back porch. We exchange L.A. stories and talk about places we know in common. They tell funny stories about their cross-country adventures. One night Nicole admits she's better at driving a stick than she let on. Cristina lobs a pillow at her. "I knew it!" Instead of being angry, she bursts out laughing and goes over to hug Nicole.

When they're good together, they're really good. You know how some couples just seem to belong together? How at a party even if they're not sitting together, they still seem connected? The Girls are that couple.

I mention this to Nicole the afternoon before she's going to leave.

"Getting along has never been our problem. Cristina would be perfectly happy with her work and her students and a fuck buddy. It's like she's allergic to commitment."

Where have I heard that before. I think back to LeeAnne and Kit at Moosewood. And Cristina's infatuation with the idea of "being free."

Nicole goes on. "And that's commitment to a relationship—not to work, or friends, or her family. Or maybe it's just commitment to me. I don't know. That's what this time will help me figure out."

"Or help her figure out," I suggest. I have no doubt Nicole will find someone who can give her what Cristina can't. Or someone will find her. "Cristina's the one who's got the figuring to do."

"Maybe," Nicole says.

"Is she driving you to the airport?"

"She wants to. I think that's crazy. She's got her department retreat that day, and my flight's at 6:00 a.m., so I need to be there by 5:00."

"Maybe even a little earlier." Three flights leave our little regional airport around the same time, and sometimes the line to get through security stretches to the main entrance.

"Definitely crazy for her to take me. I said I'd drive myself, leave the car in the lot, and she can arrange with someone to drive her there to pick it up later in the day. I'm sure Cass would be only too happy." That last said with a lot of edge.

"I'll drive you," I say.

"Don't be silly. We'd need to leave at four-thirty."

"More like four. But really. I don't sleep much. Let me take you."

I can see her weakening. No messy airport goodbye.

"Okay."

That evening I fix myself something that passes for dinner so The Girls can have their last night together. Now I'm sitting on the back porch, the dog lying at my feet. Bats swoop over the pond. I should go inside soon and try to sleep since I need to get up in a few hours. But it's so nice out here. I close my eyes. I hear cicadas and crickets, an owl. Then I hear voices, angry voices, that carry in the clear night. I can't make out exact words, only the tone. The Girls are having a huge blowout. The dog picks up his head to listen, trots off to the Big House where he's needed.

I go inside. A while later I'm brushing my teeth when I hear a knock at the front door. "Coming," I yell as I limp down the hall, muttering, "Wait for me, Marshall Dillon." Louder, I announce, "Almost there!" I open the door to see Nicole and her suitcase. And the dog. "I hope it's okay..." She doesn't finish.

"Sure," I say, grabbing the suitcase.

"Since we have to leave so early, I thought..." Another incomplete sentence.

"Good idea." I take out sheets and a blanket, grab an extra pillow from my bed.

We spread the linens on the couch. When we're done, Nicole moves toward me. "I just want to say thank you for everything." She puts her arms around me. I hug her back, and can feel her weight against me, a letting go that comes with a choked sob.

I hold her more closely. "You're doing the right thing," I whisper. I can't tell her it's all going to work out. What do I know? "You're going to be okay," I say. And I do believe that.

So now here we are. Cristina's in the Big House. Nicole's asleep—or awake, I don't know—on my couch, the dog's with her, and I'm here in my bed. Then I hear the dog moving around, the porch door sliding open, then voices. Cristina has come over and The Girls are talking. Then they're not talking. Then someone's crying. Then the porch door slides open and closed. Then it's just the crickets and the cicadas buzzing outside. I doze for a bit, wake, and check my phone. I've got time for a quick shower before we leave.

As I step into the shower, I think this is something Grace would always do before we left for the airport, even if it was 4:00 a.m. She had various rationales—not only to help her wake up, but, given travel delays, who knew when she'd get to shower again. Mostly she was just so excited to get her adventure started.

As the water pounds over me I pretend that I'm doing just that. I pretend I'm getting ready for an adventure. Nicole's off on hers. Cristina is preparing for the school year, her adventure.

I tell myself that the only constant is change. We're all unsettled in our own way. Except for Grace, who's still dead. And we'll all be okay. Not that I know what that means exactly, or even how I'm defining it. It's not stasis—of that much I'm sure. Maybe that's the best we can hope for. Fine for now, I recite. Being happy isn't the only happiness.

In this time since Grace died I'd been seeking closure. I thought it would come if I just moved into the Little House, or packed up her office, or put some of her ashes into the ground. I'd keep trying different things until I got it right. I didn't know what would do it, but I had believed something would afford me the closure I sought.

I understand now that there is no closure for this loss.

Nothing like a shower to help with clarity. Those negative ions at work.

As I dress, I think about the farewell party Grace and I threw before we left L.A. Eight of us, our core group—Diane and Leslie; Steph and Alix; Camille and Heather; Grace and me. Diane looked smug at how well her matchmaking had worked out. Everyone teased Grace, the youngest of us, on her way to tenure and job security! You're going to have to support us in our old age!

They saved some teasing for me—a screenwriter with gainful employment! Will wonders never cease! Leslie pulled her glasses down her nose, looked over them at me, and in an affected accent said, "Professor."

We rehashed stories about how we'd all met, that thread transitioning to our coming out stories. And much later, to the oddest/most public/strangest places we'd had sex. We sat outside talking and laughing until the sun set and the light faded so gradually we didn't think to turn on the deck lights, our white shirts and shorts glowing like memories.

I couldn't believe we'd be leaving these women. I didn't even want to calculate how long I'd known them. Some had been my friends originally, others Grace brought to our relationship. We were as close as if we'd grown up together, and in a way we had. Would we find such good friends in Ithaca? I reassured myself it didn't matter because Grace and I had each other. She was my home.

We never did find such good friends, but our journey together helped us absorb those losses.

That farewell night in L.A., when Grace went inside to get her famous chocolate cake, Leslie had turned to me and said, "All kidding aside, Hannah, well played. You found a young one who'll take care of you when you're old."

Yeah, well. So much for how that had turned out.

We'd had our lives planned out, not down to the minute, but in a general way, a path of semesters, an academic year plus sabbatical, time broken into book chapters, journal articles, travel. Planning for the Little

House was about the future. Our future. My retirement was an uncharted path, but one that would be tied to Grace's schedule for the next few years, for as long as she was working. We projected forward: Next spring. After I retire. When we're both retired. When there'd be time.

Here's the thing: There isn't enough time. You may think there is on a lazy Sunday, schoolwork done, household chores done, sun slanting through the window on the mess of the newspaper, remains of breakfast, an extra cup of coffee. All that lulls you into a false sense of the days stretching on into weeks, months, years.

Don't believe it.

Don't trust it.

It can vanish in an instant.

What am I supposed to do with that shot of wisdom, I think, as I secure my foot into the boot. None of that matters. All I've got is now.

Nicole's already dressed when I enter the living room. Linens folded, couch cushions straightened. Her suitcase standing by the door.

"Show time," I say.

"Cristina came over to say goodbye. We didn't wake you, did we?"

"No." It's not a lie, since technically I hadn't been sleeping.

The dog hasn't moved from his spot by the couch. Nicole pets him. "He stayed next to me all night."

"He's such a good boy." To Nicole I say, "Want me to make you a coffee? You can drink it in the car."

She shakes her head. "And I can drive myself," she says. "Really."

"No. I want to do this. You've got everything?" I ask.

"All set." She kicks her suitcase into rolling position.

I open the door for her, but Buddy rushes through first, no intention of being left behind. He knocks into me in his haste and I almost topple over. I hang onto the door to steady myself.

I once had an episode of vertigo triggered by a vigorous exercise class. I'd felt a momentary buzz, like something in my head had shaken loose and then righted itself almost immediately. Only later did I have the spins. This isn't the same sensation, but that jolt from the dog has an equally powerful effect on me. I still hold onto the open door. I feel the warm air, hear the crescendo of crickets, smell the heavy scent from the butterfly bushes. But it's like I'm somewhere else as images rush over me: Driving the 10 Freeway to the 405 on a sun-bleached day, the Santa Monica Mountains to our left. Heading over the Cahuenga Pass, a faint scent of orange blossom in the night air. Our very first snow after we moved back East, such a surprise we had to go outside and stand looking up as the thick flakes drifted down on us. Walking through the park toward Central Park South at dusk as New York City lit up ahead of us. Combing the beach in Provincetown, late afternoon, weighting our pockets with beautiful smooth stones and bits of frosted beach glass. A giddy kaleidoscope of pictures, moments, sounds, not chronological or seemingly related until I realize Grace is integral to each one. This was our life. And while it hurts to have it all returned to me, I don't want to be disconnected from any of it again.

"Are you okay?" Nicole's voice comes from very far away, a different time. "Hannah?"

No. Not from a different time. From the present. Where I belong, and to which I can return, because I know I will remember everything.

"Let's go," I say. "I'm fine."

For now.

We head outside into the warm dark morning.

Acknowledgments

Each novel I've written has had its own journey. What would have been my fourth never reached the final stage—publication—and lives on an external hard drive. Which is where *Grace Period* might have landed were it not for the enthusiastic advocacy of Michele Karlsberg, who guided it to Ian Henzel and St. Sukie de la Croix at Rattling Good Yarns Press. Ian's steadfastness throughout the editing process was admirable. His belief in the author's words made me feel appreciated. I believe I owe him a whole bunch of commas. I'll use them in the next book.

My spouse Nancy K. Bereano and I have been on our own journey for 29 years, nurturing me personally and professionally. It has been the great adventure of my life.

I do not belong to a writer's group, and no one, not even my spouse, read pages as I slogged through early drafts. Emerging after years in the dark not knowing if what I'd done held together makes me eternally grateful to my first readers: Jewelle Gomez and Matthew Lieberman, for their generous notes and gentle nudges, and to Nancy, who not only gave notes but took her red pen to it.

The Hobart Festival of Women Writers in Hobart, New York, gave me several opportunities to read, whether in person or virtually, excerpts from *Grace Period*. They also published two short stories featuring Hannah in their online journal *Now*. I thank festival organizers Cheryl Clarke, Breena Clarke, Barbara Balliet, and Esther Cohen for these opportunities to share and continue Hannah's story.

I can't count the number of times I wanted to be able to talk to my back-in-the-day first readers, Pat Eliet and Clair Peterson, about this book. We were supposed to grow old together, but I'm the only one who's made it.

About the Author

Elisabeth Nonas, the author of three published novels, has written several screenplays as well as short stories, magazine articles, and essays. She coauthored with Simon LeVay the nonfiction *City of Friends: A Portrait of the Gay and Lesbian Community in America*. The author taught screenwriting and writing for emerging media at Ithaca College for twenty-five years.

Nonas's three novels focused on how lesbians form community and create family. Given that her first book appeared forty years ago when she was in her mid-30s, she clearly has different concerns now as she ages and her life continues to unfold. These were what sparked *Grace Period*.

Originally from New York City, she lives in Ithaca, NY, with her spouse, founding publisher and editor of Firebrand Books, Nancy K. Bereano.